Lilian Harry was born and brought up in Gosport, on the shores of Portsmouth Harbour on the south coast of England. Her earliest memory is of being snatched out of bed by her sister at the first ominous wail of the air-raid siren, and rushed to the Anderson shelter at the bottom of the garden. It is that memory, together with others of World War II – the search-lights criss-crossing the sky, the roar of exploding bombs, the barrage balloons floating above and the German parachute that landed in the garden – that informs her books with such vivid atmosphere. Lilian now lives in a village on the edge of Dartmoor with two ginger cats. She has a son, a daughter and two grandchildren, and is a keen walker. Visit her website at www.lilianharry.co.uk.

Corner House Girls

LILIAN HARRY

An Orion paperback

First published in Great Britain in 2000
by Orion
This paperback edition published in 2001
by Orion Books Ltd,
Orion House, 5 Upper St Martin's Lane,
London WC2H 9EA

Typeset by Deltatype Ltd, Birkenhead, Merseyside
Printed and bound in Great Britain by
Clays Ltd, St Ives plc

The Orion Publishing Group's policy is to use papers that
are natural, renewable and recyclable products and
made from wood grown in sustainable forests. The logging
and manufacturing processes are expected to conform to
the environmental regulations of the country of origin.

www.orionbooks.co.uk

Acknowledgements

My thanks are due to the London Metropolitan Archives Library, who hold the archives of J. Lyons, together with a considerable amount of material about and by Nippies

Also to Celia Fremlin, whose observation of Nippies during the war, recorded in Tom Harrison's book *Living Through The Blitz* first gave me the idea for this series

The 'Pearlies' website, where I found the history of Henry Croft

Lyons Corner House Cakes, who give regular tea-dances for Nippies and their friends

And finally to all those lively young girls who became Nippies and gained a reputation for good service, always with a smile, which has lasted through the past 75 years, and especially to those I met dancing the afternoon away at Bristol.

Chapter One

From today, nothing would ever be quite the same again. Today, 11 May 1937, was Coronation Day, and it would change the lives of the new King and Queen for ever. And also – although they didn't yet know it – the lives of cousins Phyl Jennings and Jo Mason, who had spent the night sitting beside a fat lady on the pavement alongside the Mall.

'I don't know what our Dad's going to say when I get home,' Phyl said nervously. 'I mean, I know I left a note, and your Dad said he'd have a word, too, but I've never gone against him like this before. He'll be that wild.'

'Well, there's not much he can do about it, now you've come,' Jo observed. 'I dare say he'll rant and rave a bit, but he can't actually lock you up, can he? And maybe by then he'll have come round a bit. Anyway, whatever happens, he can't take this away from you, can he?' She looked around at the crowded pavement, the flags fluttering proudly from their tall poles, the decorations. 'You'll always be able to remember seeing the new King and Queen go by in their carriage, with their crowns on and everything.'

Phyl nodded, her brown eyes sparkling. She took a deep breath and tried to push away any uncomfortable thoughts of the argument she had had with her father over whether she should come at all.

'Stay out *all night*?' Stan Jennings exclaimed. He stared at his daughter, his brows knotted like tufts of scorched grass. 'I

1

don't know about that. Ten o'clock's your time, and has been for the past two years, since you turned sixteen. Can't you go up in the morning, early?'

'Dad, we won't be able to get anywhere near the procession if we do that,' Phyl said impatiently. 'They say there's going to be thousands there. I bet there'll be people in the best spots a week beforehand. Even going the day before, we'll be lucky to get a good place.'

'Not much use in trying, then, is there?' he said maddeningly. 'You'd be better off stopping at home and listening to it on the wireless. They're going to broadcast it all over the world, you'll surely be able to catch a whisper here in Woolwich.'

'But we won't *see* anything that way. Please, Dad.' Phyl gave her father her most appealing look, tilting her head to one side and widening her brown eyes. 'Nothing's going to happen to us. We'll be with thousands of other people and they'll all be there to see the procession, same as us. We're not going to get lost or kidnapped or anything.'

'That's a pity,' remarked her brother Norman, who was standing at the scullery sink, stripped to the waist, washing off the dirt and oil that had accumulated during a day of working in the dockyard. 'I thought for a minute there was a bit of hope there.'

Phyl made a face at him and then turned back to her father. '*Please*, Dad.'

Stan Jennings sighed. He knew – and his daughter knew, too, all too well – that he scarcely ever refused her when she looked at him like that. The spitting image of her mum she was, with those dark curls and big brown eyes, and he'd never been able to deny his May anything either. It wasn't fair to mankind, he'd remarked to his brother-in-law Bill Mason over the fence that divided their homes, it wasn't fair of God to make three of them so alike – May and her twin sister Carrie, and now young Phyl. Just as well Bill's girl Jo took after her dad instead of her own mum, or none of the rest of them would have stood a chance.

All the same, a father had to set his limits, especially for a

2

girl as bright and pretty as his Phyl. And to tell the truth, he'd been feeling a bit at a loss with her just lately. She'd got too independent, that was the trouble, too set on her own way and showing him she was 'grown up', and it made him feel frightened in a funny sort of way, and all the more determined to keep her on a short leash.

'No,' he said, sounding harsher than he'd meant to because he didn't like taking that cheeky grin off her face. 'I'm sorry, Phyl, but I'm not having you gallivanting round London all on your own all night. No, I *know* you said Jo'd be with you—' he held up a work-roughened hand to still her protest '—but as far as I'm concerned, that's the same as you being on your own. Worse. There's no knowing what a couple of giddy young girls'll get up to up there. You can stop here and listen to it on the wireless like the rest of us.'

'We'd be able to come back and tell you all about it,' Phyl wheedled, her hand on his arm. 'I bet Mum'd like that, and Auntie Carrie. They'll want to know about the Queen's frock and the carriages and all the other kings and queens what've come to see it. And I don't suppose we'll ever get another chance, not till we're too old to care, anyway.'

'I said *no*.' His tone told her this ought to be the end of it, but Phyl couldn't let it rest. She tilted her head again.

'You know how you've always told us about the time you saw Queen Victoria when she was really, really old. Well, I want to be able to tell my kids I saw King George going to his coronation. You wouldn't want me to have to tell them my dad wouldn't let me go, would you? You wouldn't want your own grandchildren thinking you were too mean—'

'If they've got any sense,' he said, bringing his hand flat down on the table, 'they'll think that their grandad had a bit of sense, not letting his daughter go sleeping all night in the open in London. You don't know what could happen to you up there, my girl, and I'm not going to tell you. Now, just take no for an answer for once. I don't want to hear another word about it, d'you hear?'

Phyl opened her mouth to protest again, but the look on her father's face told her that she was in danger of going too

3

far. Stan Jennings was a steady enough man on the whole, but he did have a temper and he believed in strict discipline. As in many households, there was a thin cane hanging behind the kitchen door and both Phyl's brothers had felt its sting on more than one occasion. Stan had never struck Phyl, and she didn't think he was likely to start now, but just to incur his anger would be frightening enough.

She thought of this as she sat on the pavement with Jo. There was no doubt that leaving a note behind to say she'd flouted his orders and gone to London anyway was going to result in real trouble. But, as Jo had said, there wasn't really anything he could do, apart from be angry with her when she got home. And maybe her mother and Auntie Carrie and Jo's father – who had agreed to his own daughter coming to watch the procession – would be able to talk him round before Phyl even had to put her head round the door.

'Don't *worry* about it,' Jo said, seeing her pensive look. 'He's not really mean, your dad – he just doesn't think his little girl's grown up yet, that's all. He'll be all right when he sees you come home, safe and sound.'

'Not grown up!' Phyl exclaimed. 'I'll give him not grown up! I'm eighteen, after all – old enough to go out to work, old enough to get married—'

'Not without his say-so.'

'I could if I lived in Scotland. Not that I'd want to, not yet, anyway. I want to have a bit of fun before I get tied down.' Phyl stared restlessly across the Mall. 'I tell you what, Jo, I'd like to get a job somewhere away from home. Be independent. I'm fed up with having to be in at ten of an evening and stop home on Sunday mornings to help cook the dinner. And I'm sick and tired of that awful factory job!'

'Well, I can't see your dad letting you leave home, not if he won't even let you spend one night away to watch the Coronation,' Jo said.

'Well, I wouldn't exactly be sleeping on the pavements, would I?' Phyl grinned. 'Anyway, let's forget it now, Jo. I've come to enjoy myself, and I'm blowed if I'm going to let anything else spoil it.'

'That's right, girl,' said the fat woman sitting close by on a heap of cushions and a raincoat. 'That's what it's all about. A bit of enjoyment. That's what we all needs, when all's said and done, and that's just what we're going to 'ave. 'Ere – 'ave a Marmite sandwich. And I got a flask of tea to keep the chill off – you can 'ave a sup of that, too.'

Phyl accepted a Marmite sandwich, and Jo produced a fruit cake her mother had given her and shared that around. Darkness was drawing in, but the Mall was lit with gaslamps and fancy lanterns, and quite a lot of people had hurricane lamps or torches. Everyone else was spreading blankets on the ground and getting out food, too, offering it about. It began to seem like a huge party, and Phyl forgot her father's wrath and began to enjoy herself.

Dawn came with grey skies, and rain fell like tears on the crowds camped on the pavements.

'Tears of 'appiness, that's what they are,' declared the fat woman as she drank coffee from another battered Thermos flask and ate increasingly soggy Marmite sandwiches for breakfast. 'Tears of 'appiness.' She thought for a moment, then added darkly, 'Not like the tears we mighter cried for the Prince of Wales, when he told us all he was going to put that American hussy before his own country. Nor like what we mighter found ourselves crying if he *hadn't* done it, and bin crowned King after all.'

Today, any tears shed would be of excitement, to welcome the new King, George the Sixth, who had been pushed on to the throne whether he liked it or not. And for his Queen, Elizabeth, the lovely young woman with the cornflower eyes, and the two Princesses – Elizabeth, who would herself one day be Queen, and little Margaret Rose.

As Phyl had prophesied, there was already a large crowd gathering beside the route, and if they hadn't arrived the previous evening they would never have managed to find a space by the edge of the pavement. Jo had brought a blanket and a couple of cushions, and Phyl's brother Norman, who

5

had been let into the secret, had produced an old ground-sheet, left over from the days when he'd been a Boy Scout. They huddled underneath it, giggling. A drop of rain never hurt anyone, Phyl said stoutly, they weren't made of sugar, and they'd got the rest of their lives to stay dry.

'I wish we lived in London,' Jo said, gazing around. 'Properly, I mean, not out where we are. It's all so exciting – there's always something going on. Just imagine what it must be like to go out never knowing if you might see the King or Queen go past in a carriage or a big car.'

'Or film stars,' Phyl agreed. 'Or actors and actresses from the big shows. We could go to see the shows, too, any time. It'd be smashing.'

They sat for a while talking about what they'd do if they lived in the middle of London. Go to Hyde Park every day. Go for boat-rides on the Serpentine. Go to the Zoo. Stand outside the stage doors of the big theatres – this was Phyl – and get famous autographs. Go to the big sports stadiums and watch all the best athletes – this was Jo. There seemed to be no end to the fun two girls could have in London.

'It's getting jobs that's the problem,' Phyl said despondently. 'And all I've ever done is that awful riveting and soldering in the factory. There's not many factories in the middle of London, and I don't really know what else I could do. I suppose I could go to night-school to learn typing and shorthand, but it'd take such a long time – I want to go *now*.'

'There's plenty of greengrocers' shops,' said Jo, who worked in one with her mother, 'but the wages wouldn't be enough to live on up here. Anyway, I bet there's no jobs going. You know what it's been like these past few years, with the Depression and all. We're stuck where we are, Phyl, that's the truth of it.'

They had tried to sleep, but what with the chilly rain and the discomfort of the pavement, even with cushions and blankets, and the strangeness of trying to sleep amongst thousands of strangers, neither of them did much more than doze. As Jo had predicted, the food they had brought gave them something to do, and the fruit cake, shared with the fat

6

woman in exchange for some jam sandwiches – so she did have something besides Marmite, Phyl thought – was soon gone. But at last it was morning, and the fat woman was saying that the clouds were shedding tears of happiness – she liked poetry, she'd told the girls at some point during the night, read a lot of it she did, in magazines – and then London itself was waking up and the crowd's excitement growing as the hour approached for the procession to begin.

'I've never seen anything so gorgeous,' Phyl breathed when it was all over at last. They stood together in the crowd, gazing up at the balcony of Buckingham Palace. 'Look at that, Jo, Queen Elizabeth in that beautiful frock, King George in all that ermine – and real crowns on their heads. Remember when we went to the Tower to see the Crown Jewels? We never thought we'd actually see them on their heads, did we, Jo? We never thought we'd see them driving in that gorgeous carriage down the Mall to Buckingham Palace itself. And then standing on the balcony, waving to everyone. Waving to *us*.'

'It's smashing,' her cousin agreed. 'Mind you, old Queen Mary looks a bit strait-laced, but, then, she always does. Thinks it's a bit beneath her to smile at the peasants, I reckon! This new Queen's different, she looks as if she likes a bit of fun. And he's nice-looking, too, got a kind sort of face. They say he's ever so shy – seems funny for a king to be shy, doesn't it?'

She stopped speaking to cheer with the crowd, and waved her hand vigorously as the Royal Family beamed down from their high position on the front of the Palace. The two Princesses, Elizabeth and Margaret Rose, wearing their own coronets, smiled shyly and around them the courtiers, dressed for the fine occasion it was, stood watchful and attentive. Then, to the disappointed sighs of the people, they all turned and disappeared inside, and everyone knew that the show was over.

Phyl turned to Jo and rolled her bright, dark brown eyes.

'I'll tell you what, if I was run over by a bus at this very minute, I'd die happy, straight I would.'

'Well, I wouldn't,' Jo retorted tartly. 'Think what it'd be like for me, having to scrape you up off the road and take you home to Auntie May in a paper bag. She'd have my guts for garters, and that's nothing to what your dad'd do. Anyway, haven't you got a date with Dave Willett on Saturday night? You wouldn't want to miss that.'

Phyl made a face. 'Oh, him! Well, I suppose going to the flicks with him *is* better than being run over by a number seven bus – but only just!' She sighed and gazed up again at the balcony of the Palace. 'Well, I suppose that's it. They're not going to come out again, are they? They must be tired out after a day like that – I bet they're in there now, taking off their shoes and flopping down on the settee and getting a servant to bring them a cup of tea.'

Jo grinned at the thought and caught her cousin's arm as the crowds swirled about them. 'Talking of tea, let's go and get a cup ourselves, and a bite to eat. I'm just about starving after all that standing about and cheering, and we've got nothing left of all that cake and stuff. My tummy thinks my throat's been cut. Where shall we go, eh? Somewhere a bit flash, to make a real day of it?'

'Let's go to the Corner House at Charing Cross,' Phyl suggested. 'They'll be busy but it's a smashing place and the food's always good. And they play music, too – there was a gipsy band when I went with our Norman once, when we come up for that football match.'

The two girls cast a last long look at the balcony and then turned to push their way through the mass of people surging along the Mall. Over a million people had come to London on this May day to see the coronation procession of King George the Sixth and Queen Elizabeth. Even the back streets were decorated, banners and rows of coloured flags strung between the houses, and every official building sported a Union Jack – most of them the right way up – and a festoon of coloured bunting. Everyone was in good humour, even though many, like Jo and Phyl, had been there for over twenty-four hours now, and all around them the girls could hear the excited chatter of people whose patience had been rewarded, and who had at last seen their new King and Queen in all their triumph.

'He's a nice, quiet sort of chap. *He* won't let us down, like the Prince of Wales did.' . . . 'Ain't she a smasher? I never *seen* such blue eyes.' . . . 'She looked right at me, she did, and smiled. At *me*!' . . . 'And what about the little Princesses, then, eh? That Elizabeth looks a little queen already, but I bet you young Margaret Rose is going to break a few hearts before she's done . . .'

'Come on,' Jo said, thrusting a way through the crowd. 'We'll nip through this way, it's a bit quieter.'

'It's all right for you,' Phyl panted, struggling to keep up with her. 'You're so tall you can see over everyone. All I can see is people's chests.'

'Well, stick close and you'll be all right.' Jo's bright chestnut head shone like a beacon as she forged through the people, all of whom were intent on getting somewhere – either to Buckingham Palace, even though it was too late to see Their Majesties, or into the park or towards one of the Underground stations. She looked back every minute or two to make sure that Phyl was still behind her, but the crowd was in good humour and parted to let them through. At last, without much idea of how they'd got there, they found themselves under Admiralty Arch and then, breathless, opposite Charing Cross station and the white façade of one of Lyons' Corner Houses.

'Blimey,' Phyl said, 'look at the queue! We'll never get a seat.'

'Yes, we will. They can serve hundreds at a time. And it'll be the same wherever we try, so we might as well join a good queue as a bad 'un.' Jo strode swiftly across the road, still so thronged with people that no traffic had a chance of getting through, and took up position at the end of the long string of people waiting to get into the restaurant. Like every other building in London, it was decorated for the occasion, with streamers fluttering from the windows and a huge Union Jack draped across its front.

The procession had been a long one, with representatives from all parts of the British Empire, as well as from other countries, each in either a grand carriage or a smart limousine. There had been platoons and regiments from all the Armed Forces, accompanied by their own bands, immaculately turned out, some marching on foot, others riding splendid shire horses that were not only dressed in gleaming bridles and harness but looked as if they'd had a going-over themselves with Cherry Blossom boot polish. It was a spectacle such as had not been seen in London for years, and it seemed to betoken an end to the hard times of the Depression and the lean years and a beginning of hope. For a few hours, the British and their Empire could shake off the shame of King Edward's abdication, could forget the bad news – the tragedy of the Spanish Civil War, the crash only a week before of the great airship *Hindenburg*, the muttering threat of Hitler's Nazis – and rejoice. For a few hours, they could sweep themselves back into the peace of the early years of the century, and feel themselves great again.

As Jo had predicted, the queue moved steadily, but it was still an hour before the two girls were inside the great restaurant. Once through the big plate-glass doors, they were faced with a choice of going downstairs to the Brasserie or upstairs to the more formal dining hall, but the quickest movement was in the cheerful, brightly lit ground-floor restaurant, and they nodded at the smiling 'seater' who guided them swiftly through the big room to a vacant table.

'Isn't it smashing?' Phyl whispered as they took their seats. 'I mean, it's like a palace itself, isn't it? All this lovely carpet and those gorgeous lights, and the pictures on the walls. I feel as if I've just been crowned myself!'

'*I'll* crown you if you don't pick up that menu and decide what you're going to have to eat,' Jo retorted. 'And so will all those people still waiting to get in. Come on, Phyl, stop chattering and make up your mind. The waitress will be here any minute and she won't want to hang about.'

'She's not a waitress, she's a Nippy.' Phyl did as she was told and they gazed at the printed menu together. 'That's what they're called, Nippies, because they nip about so quick. They're smart, too, aren't they, in that black frock with the white apron, and that little white cap? And I like all those little buttons down the front of the frock, they really set it off.'

'You might not like 'em so much if you had to do them up every day,' a voice said, and they looked up, startled, to see one of the Nippies standing beside them, her face round and smiling under her white cap, her notebook held ready to write down their orders. 'And woe betide you if you're caught with one of them loose – or not sewn on with the proper red cotton – or off altogether.'

'Well, you don't look too hard done by,' Phyl said, grinning back. 'I wouldn't mind working in a place like this, I can tell you. It'd beat slaving away in a factory morning till night.'

The girl raised her eyebrows. 'Don't run away with the idea it's easy. I tell you, we work pretty hard. But – yeah, I reckon you're right, it's better than a factory any day.' She lifted her notebook and pencil. 'Decided what you want? The poached eggs on toast are good, and come quick. We're trying to serve as many people as possible today.'

'Sounds all right to me,' Jo said decisively. 'What about you, Phyl? And a big pot of tea, we're shrivelled up.'

'And a plate of cakes,' Phyl stipulated. 'My brother'd kill me if I went home and told him I'd been to a Corner House and not had any cakes.'

'Poached eggs on toast twice, a big pot and a plate of assorted,' the girl said. 'Be here in a jiffy.' And she whisked away, threading her way swiftly between the tables to the serving door.

Phyl watched her go. 'She's nice, isn't she? I bet they're all nice here. Not like that crowd down at the factory, spiteful cows. I tell you, Jo, if I thought I could get a job in a place like this I'd ask for me cards straight away, I would. I mean, it doesn't matter how hard you have to work, it must be better in a place like this, with music playing and everyone cheerful, than stuck at a bench doing riveting.'

11

'I reckon it must.' Jo looked thoughtfully around the big restaurant. Although there must have been over a hundred people sitting at the tables, the sound of voices was little more than a murmur and the silver notes of the gipsy band drifted like perfume through the air. The lights glowed above their heads and the walls were richly decorated with pictures and heavy, draped curtains. The Nippies walked briskly back and forth, holding large round silver trays in front of them and sometimes even over their heads, laden with fresh food or piled with used crockery. In one corner a girl was changing a stained tablecloth, so swiftly and neatly that the surface of the table wasn't exposed for a second, and two Nippies stood by the cashier's desk, writing out bills. Everything was done quickly and efficiently and everyone was smiling.

'It's better than working in a shop, too,' Jo said. 'Specially a greengrocer's.' She looked ruefully at her hands, always stained by vegetables and soil no matter how hard she scrubbed them. 'Tell you what, Phyl – when that girl comes back, why don't we ask her about it? See what the chances are?'

Phyl stared at her, round-eyed. 'You mean – try and get a job here? *Us?*'

'Well, why not? I bet we could do it just as good as any of these other girls.' Jo watched the hurrying waitresses. 'It wouldn't do any harm to ask, anyway.'

Phyl ducked her head a little and drew in her mouth. 'I don't know. I'm not sure I could carry one of those trays without dropping everything. I mean, suppose I spilt soup all down a customer's neck – I'd die!'

'Well, at least you'd die in a nice place,' Jo remarked. 'Look, it's not going to kill us to ask, is it? You were the one who said you'd like to work here. And we were both talking about what it'd be like to be right in London.'

'Yes, but I never really thought—' Phyl broke off as their own Nippy arrived, bearing a tray on which rested a large teapot, water and milk jugs, sugar and cups and saucers. Quickly and neatly, she removed them from the tray and set them on the table.

12

'Oh, thanks, I've been dying for that.'

'Poached eggs'll be along in a mo,' the girl said, and was gone before they could say anything else. Jo raised her eyebrows at her cousin.

'Well, will you be mum, or shall I?' Without waiting for an answer, she lifted the pot and began to pour out the tea. 'What d'you say, Phyl? Shall we ask her? See what it's really like to work here?'

Phyl gazed at her, brown eyes sparkling. Her rosy face lit up as her dimpling smile broke out, and she giggled with sudden excitement, nodding so vigorously that a curl the colour of dark chocolate escaped from her hairband and fell across her forehead. She pushed it back impatiently and took a sip of tea.

'Yes. Yes, let's. Let's find out what you have to do and how you apply and everything. Just think of it, Jo – you and me, working in the middle of London. What a lark, eh!' Her eyes brightened further as a fresh thought struck her. 'Here – we might even get some of the actors and actresses coming to our tables – people like Flanagan and Allen, and the Crazy Gang, and Joan Fontaine. And—'

Jo put down her cup, laughing. 'All right, don't get carried away. We all know you're mad about the theatre. You'd be here to work, remember, not go out on the town. Anyway, we haven't even decided if we'll apply yet. They might not want girls at the moment, and if they do they might not want us.'

'Well, we'll find out. Like you said, it can't do any harm to ask. Look, here comes our Nippy now.' They watched as the girl made her way towards their table, her tray now set with two plates of poached eggs on toast and a dish of cakes. She smiled and began to set the food out in front of them.

'That looks smashing,' Phyl said, and then looked up into the girl's face. 'Look, d'you mind if we ask you something?'

'Ask away, only don't take too long, will you? We're run off our feet today.'

'I know. It's just – well, we've been wondering how'd you get to be a Nippy? What's it like working at a Corner House? And – and, well, d'you think *we* might stand a chance?' The

13

words tumbled from Phyl's lips, leaving her slightly breathless. Her cheeks were pink.

The Nippy raised her eyebrows and laughed. 'Well, *that* ain't a quick question! It's a whole load of questions. Look, I'll tell you as quick as I can. Like I said, it's hard work but we have a lot of laughs and Lyons is a good company to work for – they look after you. The pay's not a fortune, but you get tips and presents and sometimes the customers even ask girls out. You've got to be eighteen to be a Nippy, but if you're younger than that they'll take you in the kitchens, or you can be a Trippy – serve hors d'oeuvres and cakes on trolleys. You apply to Head Office and they'll give you an interview and then some training. And you might have to live in digs, if your home's too far away – but they make sure you've got a good place. And there's a smashing sports and leisure club out at Sudbury, we have dances and all sorts of fun there.'

'What about—?' Phyl began, but the girl shook her head and picked up her tray.

'Sorry, can't stop any longer. I told you, we're up to our ears today. Tell you what, I'll write the address down on your bill and if you're interested, all you got to do is write and ask, see?' With a quick smile, she was gone, clearing a table which had just been vacated and setting it with fresh cutlery, and in a moment she had disappeared to take another order.

Jo and Phyl looked at each other. Although the daughters of twin sisters, they were quite different. Phyl, like her mother May, was small and quick like a wren, with a bubbling sense of humour and a sense of mischief that came from pure merriment. Jo was tall and lean like her father Bill, with long arms and legs, a wide forehead with clear grey eyes, a mouth she considered too large and a mane of chestnut hair. Although a month younger than her cousin, she was usually taken for the elder, mainly because of her height. Always a tomboy, she still preferred swimming and netball to the dancing Phyl loved, and the thought of finding a sweetheart hadn't even entered her head.

'Well, what d'you think?' she asked now. 'I like the sound of that sports club. I wonder what they play.'

'She said they have dances, too. I bet there's no end of fun. Let's do it, Jo. Let's write and ask, at least, and find out all about it.' Phyl picked up her knife and fork and attacked her poached egg. 'I tell you what, I bet you get good dinners here, too. They're bound to feed the staff, and that adds a bit on to your pay when you think about it.'

Suddenly remembering how hungry they were, the two girls ate quickly, relishing the golden-yolked eggs and thick, buttered toast. Drinking cup after cup of tea, they turned their attention to the plate of cakes – a delicious assortment of jam tarts, macaroons, eclairs and fruit cake. There was barely a crumb left when they finished at last, and the teapot had been almost squeezed dry.

'That was smashing,' Phyl said, leaning back. 'I can hardly move! Imagine eating like that every day, Jo.'

'I don't suppose the staff do,' Jo said. 'Lyons may be a good company to work for, but they're not going to pamper their workers. They'll get their money's worth out of you, mark my words. Still, I must say everyone looks cheerful enough, even if they are run off their feet.' She glanced around. 'I suppose we'd better think about going. There's still a queue outside, and it's going to take us hours to get home in the crush. I reckon we'd better walk the first part and then get a bus.'

'OK.' Phyl caught sight of their Nippy and waved. 'We're off now. We really enjoyed that.'

'I'll give you your bill.' The girl produced the scrap of paper from her pocket. True to her word, she had scribbled an address on the back. 'Good luck. Maybe I'll see you here some time – and then you can see how you like doing up all these little buttons,' she added with a grin. 'And trying to keep this white cap tidy.'

'I shan't mind,' Phyl declared as they walked out into the Strand. 'I shan't mind a scrap. It'll be better than putting on a factory overall and tying a scarf round my head, *any* day of the week!'

Chapter Two

The excitement of the procession, seeing the new King and Queen on the balcony of Buckingham Palace and then the idea of becoming Nippies and actually working in London had driven all Phyl's fears clean out of her mind. But the nearer she and Jo got to the street where they lived, the more they came back, and by the time she turned the last corner she was shaking with nerves.

'Look, he's not going to kill you,' Jo said, taking her cousin's arm. 'And there's nothing he can do about it now anyway – you've been to London and come back safe and sound. You've proved you can do it, and that's going to be a real help when you tell them about being a Nippy.'

'I don't think I'll be *able* to tell them that,' Phyl said gloomily. 'He'll hit the roof. Oh, Jo, suppose he chucks me out? He could, you know.'

'Don't be daft! Your dad'd never chuck you out. You're the apple of his eye, you know that.' They were in sight of their front doors now. 'Look, if it gets too bad you can come in to us, you know that. But I don't reckon you've got a thing to worry about.'

Phyl gave her a last despairing look and lifted the knocker on the front door. This was one of the things that irritated her about living at home – that she wouldn't get her own key until she was twenty-one. If I lived in digs in London, she thought, I'd have my own key and come and go as I pleased, so why shouldn't I be able to do the same at home?

The spurt of rebelliousness gave her the courage to square her shoulders and stand up straight as the door opened. She half expected it to be her father himself, even though he hardly ever answered the door, but instead it was her younger brother Ronnie.

'Our Phyl! Coo, you aren't half in trouble. Our Dad's been going mad about that note you left.'

'Thanks for the welcome.' Phyl followed him inside and hung up her jacket in the narrow passage. 'Is he in?'

'No, gone over the allotment.' Stan and Bill shared an allotment a few streets away, where they grew vegetables. 'Mum said it'd be better if he wasn't here when you came back and he said, yes, it was, because if he was here he might do something he'd be sorry for.'

'He never!' Phyl's heart sank. It didn't sound as if anyone had been able to talk her father round. There's nothing he can do, she reminded herself. I've been to London and seen the procession and he can't do anything to make that any different. And he can't lock me up in my bedroom – this is the 1930s, not Victorian times.

Ronnie went upstairs to the bedroom he shared with Norman, and Phyl went through to the back room and found her mother there, turning one of Stan's collars on a work shirt. May looked up, frowning, but Phyl wasn't sure whether it was the tricky sewing that made her frown or Phyl herself.

She paused, and they looked at each other. Phyl felt the tears come to her eyes.

'I'm sorry, Mum. I know I shouldn't have done it – but I really did want to see the procession. And Jo could only go if I went, too. And I'm not a little kid any more,' she burst out, her voice rising. 'I'm eighteen. I ought to be able to decide for myself—'

'You know you're three years off being able to do that,' her mother pointed out, but to Phyl's relief she didn't sound really angry. 'No, you didn't ought to have done it, but you did, and you're back safe, so that's just about it, really, isn't it? But I'm not sure your dad's going to see it that way.'

Phyl sat down beside her. 'Is he very cross?'

'He's not over the moon. It's not just what you did, it's the way you did it. Sneaking off like that, leaving a note—'

'What else was I supposed to do?'

'You were supposed to stay at home, that's what!' She hesitated, then said, 'Look, Phyl, I know what it feels like to want to do something so bad and not be allowed to. There was a time once when I wanted to do something, even more than you wanted to see the Coronation, and my dad said no. It caused no end of rows and arguments and in the end, d'you know what I did? I just went and did it anyway – just like you did – and once it was done there wasn't nothing he could do about it. Sometimes, I know, you just feel you've got to do it, no matter what happens.'

Phyl was fascinated. 'What was it, Mum? What was it you wanted to do?'

May Jennings didn't speak for a moment. She seemed to be looking into her own mind, asking herself whether to go on with this story which she had never told any of her children. Finally, she sighed a little, as if she had come to a decision, and took her daughter's hand.

'I wanted to marry your dad. My dad was against it, you see – he thought we were both too young, and I ought to look a bit higher than a dockyard worker. But we were real sweethearts and had been for years, and we didn't want no one else, neither of us. And we didn't want to wait any longer.'

'But – you mean you were under twenty-one? You had to get his permission?'

'Well, no, I was of age – just. But in them days a father expected to be asked anyway, specially if you were still living at home. Not that it would have made any difference how old I was. He didn't want me marrying Stan Jennings, and that was that. And in the end, he told me straight, if you go on seeing that chap, you leave this house, and if you marry him you needn't expect to come back in again. So I knew there was only one thing to do.'

'You eloped!' Phyl exclaimed. 'Oh, Mum, that's really romantic.'

'I don't know about that. It didn't seem all that romantic to me. Specially when I had to leave my mum and our Carrie and not know if I'd be able to come home to see them again. I didn't like doing it, Phyl, I can tell you. I loved my dad. I didn't want to cross him. But the way I saw it, he didn't leave me no choice.'

'So what happened?'

'Well, I packed a bag and slipped out, leaving him a note, and I went to stay with a friend of mine up Stepney. And I wrote to your dad and told him where I was and he saw the vicar and we got married three weeks later. It wasn't the wedding I'd thought I'd have, but I didn't care about that then. I just wanted to be married and everything to be right.'

'And so it was,' Phyl breathed, her eyes shining. 'Grandad came round all right, didn't he?' She could remember him clearly even though he had died ten years earlier – a big, whiskery man with a gruff voice and twinkling eyes. He had always seemed to get on well enough with her father.

'He came round in the end. But it took a long time. It wasn't till you were born, really, though we used to go round and see the family long before that. He was always a bit cool till you arrived on the scene – he really took to you, said you reminded him of me when I did as I was told!'

'*Mum.*' Phyl laughed. Then she grew sober again. 'But d'you think it'll help Dad to understand what I did? I mean, going to see the Coronation isn't exactly like eloping, is it?'

'I wish you'd stop calling it that. You make it sound as if he leant a ladder up against my bedroom window. No, I don't think it will help him understand – but it might make him realise you've got to be allowed a bit of freedom. *My* dad could have lost me for ever, you see, and your dad won't want to risk that happening with you. That's why he gets so cross – he's frightened of it happening all over again. If you want your dad to understand you, Phyl, you've got to try and understand him a bit, too.'

Phyl was silent. She stared down at the collar her mother was working on. It had never occurred to her that her father was someone who needed understanding. He'd been there all her life, ruling the household, having the final say – and it had never struck her that inside he, too, might feel uncertain, or even scared. She felt ashamed.

'I'll tell him I'm sorry,' she said. 'I never meant to worry anyone – that's why I left that note. But I really did want to go, and there'll never be another chance.'

'I know.' The collar was finished and May held it up and examined it critically. 'I'll tell you what, I bet His Majesty don't have to have *his* collars turned! And now you can tell me all about it, Phyl. What was the Queen wearing, and is she really as pretty as they say, and what about the two little princesses? It was a long day for them – and what about all the other kings and queens? Were they all wearing crowns? It must have been lovely.' She sounded wistful. 'It was a shame we couldn't all go, really. I'd love to have seen it, too.'

'A Lyons Corner House?' Carrie Mason said doubtfully. 'But they're all in the middle of London.'

'Well, I know that, Mum,' Jo said with a grin. 'I've just come home from one, haven't I?'

'I mean, how would you be able to get there every morning? And home again at night? It's over two hours' journey. You'd never stick it.'

'Your mother's right,' Bill Mason said. He took his pipe from his mouth and frowned into it, then reached up to the mantelpiece for his tobacco pouch. 'You'd never stand all that travelling on buses, day in, day out.'

'I wouldn't have to, Dad.' Jo paused. 'I could live in digs.'

'*Digs?*' Carrie dropped her knitting and stared at her daughter. 'You mean you'd have to leave home? Live with strangers? Oh, Jo, I don't know about that—'

'Crikey, Ma, don't put her off,' Freddy said, looking up from his copy of *Wizard*. 'If our Jo goes to live in London I can have that cupboard for my books.'

'Thanks for nothing,' Jo said smartly. 'I shan't be moving out altogether. I'll still be coming home regular. You don't get rid of me that easy.'

'Will we be able to get free meals, then?' Freddy asked,

getting up to stand in front of the mirror to brush back hair as thick and tawny as his sister's. 'I mean, you ought to be able to slip a couple of platefuls to family when we come to see you.'

'I'll be more likely to slip someone else's leftovers down your neck,' Jo told him. 'You needn't think you can come showing me up. They have people there to throw out anyone causing trouble.'

'Don't be daft, Jo,' her father said. 'You know very well your brother wouldn't cause any trouble. Anyway, we haven't said you can go yet. It wants a bit of thinking about first.'

'I've thought about it all the way home, Dad. Phyl and me didn't talk about anything else – well, except for the Coronation, of course. Did I tell you about the Queen's frock? She looked so lovely in it, you wouldn't believe. Blue, it was, to match her eyes, and she had this beautiful sash across the front with stars pinned to it. I wish I'd been in the Abbey to see her have her crown put on. And the King, he looked ever so handsome in his ermine and all—'

'Never mind all that,' Bill broke in. 'I'm not sure I'd have let you go if I'd known you were going to come back with a lot of high falutin ideas about living in London and working in posh restaurants. And when I said think about it, I didn't mean you and young Phyl on top of a bus. I meant me and your mother having a proper talk about it all, as you well know. Discussing the ins and outs of it, as we do with everything else that happens in this family.'

Jo pouted. 'Dad, I'm grown up—'

'You won't turn eighteen till next month,' he stated unarguably. 'And your cousin's only just had her birthday. And until you're twenty-one, you're under my jurisdiction.' He paused and his face softened. 'Look, girl, you know I don't want to spoil your ideas, but I can't let you just jump into new things without looking at all sides of it first. It's my responsibility. Now, you help your mother make us all a cup of cocoa and some toast or summat and tell us a bit more about it, and then we'll have a talk and see what we think.

How's that?' He reached out and touched her chin. 'You know we only got your best interests at heart, don't you?'

Jo sighed and gave him a rueful smile. 'Yes. I suppose so, Dad. It's just – well, we were so excited. It'd be a lovely job, and the girl told us they're a good company to work for. And you know I don't really like the greengrocer's shop – and Phyl really hates working at the factory.'

'So Phyl's just as keen, is she?' her mother asked.

'Yes! That's the other good thing – we'd be together. We could share digs, too. It's not as if I'd be going on my own.' She looked from one to the other, her face once more alight. 'Honestly, I'd really like to try. After all,' she added cunningly, 'just because I apply doesn't mean they'll take me on.'

Bill Mason burst into laughter and ruffled his daughter's hair. 'All right, you young monkey, you've made your point. Me and your mother will talk about it tonight. But that doesn't mean we're going to say yes,' he added warningly as a wide grin began to spread across Jo's face. 'It means we'll *talk* about it, that's all. We might just as easy say no as yes, and that'll be the end of it, see?'

Freddy and Jo glanced at each other with some sympathy. It came hard, when you were growing up and wanting a bit of freedom, to be treated like kids still. But that was the way it was until you were twenty-one and got the key of the door, like it said in the song.

Unless you got a job that meant you had to live away from home . . .

Phyl knew she would have to work hard to get back into her father's good books before she even dared broach the idea of going to work in London.

'I'm really sorry if you were worried, Dad,' she said when he came in, giving her a hard look from under his brows. 'I did leave a note so you knew where I'd gone.'

'It wasn't so much we were worried,' he said heavily, going to the kitchen sink to wash his hands. 'It's more that you deliberately went against my wishes. You knew I'd put my foot down over going to see this Coronation procession, but you went just the same. That's out-and-out disobedience.'

'I know.' It wasn't the moment to point out that she was grown up, or that she'd been with Jo, or any of the other arguments she might have used. 'I just wanted to go so bad. Haven't you ever wanted anything so bad that you'd have done anything in the world to get it, Dad?'

Her father gave her a sharp look, but Phyl's face was a picture of innocence. He glanced towards his wife, but May's head was bent over her sewing. He grunted and went to dry his hands on the towel on the back of the door. To tell the truth, he'd been feeling bad about the way he'd laid down the law over this Coronation business. As Carrie had said when they'd found Phyl's note, it wasn't as if she and Jo weren't good girls and couldn't be trusted. They'd been brought up right and wouldn't do anything their parents would have disapproved of. And you had to let them off the leash sometimes, for something special.

'Well, maybe I have and maybe I haven't. That doesn't alter the fact that you deliberately went—'

'Dad, I'm *sorry*.' She went to him and laid her face against his sleeve. 'I've said I'm sorry. I can't do any more than that, can I? And we're back safe and sound, nothing happened to us – and we did have a lovely time. I'd just like to tell you all about it now. Wouldn't you like to hear about it, Dad? About the processions – the Army and the Navy? Oh, and the Royal Marine Bands, they were really smashing, you'd have enjoyed it, you really would. Next time there's a big procession on in London, you'll have to come, too, you and Mum, all of us. And you can come and have tea in the Lyons Corner House afterwards like me and Jo did, and I could serve you . . .' She stopped, her hand at her mouth, and looked up at her father from beneath lowered lids. He stared at her.

'Lyons Corner House? *Serve* us? What's all this, then? What's going on now that I haven't heard nothing about?'

'Oh, lor,' Phyl said comically. 'I didn't mean to say that. Now I *have* let the cat out of the bag.'

23

Her mother laid down her work and Norman, deep in his *Health and Strength* magazine, looked up from his corner.

'You never said nothing to me about this,' May said.

'I know. I didn't mean to till Dad was, well, in a better mood with me. Now I've gone and mucked it all up before I had a chance to tell you proper.' Phyl looked rueful. 'Trust me and my daft tongue. Jo'll have my guts for garters.'

'Is Jo in this, too? This Nippy scheme?'

Phyl hesitated, then gave a sigh and sat down at the table. 'I suppose I'd better tell you. What it was, we went and had our tea in the Corner House at Charing Cross. It's ever so nice there and we both thought what it'd be like to work there – I mean, you know I just hate the factory and Jo's not all that keen on the shop. It'd be lovely, working in a nice place like that, meeting lots of different people. So we asked the girl that served us and she told us a bit about it and how to apply. And – well, we thought we would, that's all. If – if you'll let us.'

'Oh,' Stan Jennings said with heavy sarcasm, 'so you did think of consulting us about it, then?'

'Well, of course we did! We can't go off and live in London without you saying so, can we? I mean, we don't want—'

'*Live* in London?' her father broke in. 'Who said anything about *living* in London? And what other little surprises have you got up your sleeve for us, our Phyl? Come on – you might as well let us have the whole story now.'

'There isn't any more. Honestly. We just want to apply for jobs as Nippies. It's too far to travel every day but we could get nice digs somewhere near – the girl we spoke to told us Lyons go and see all the places girls live, and make sure they're all right – and we'd be home at weekends. You'd hardly notice the difference.'

'I would,' Norman said. 'I'd notice the peace and quiet. Let her go, Dad. It's what I've been dreaming of all my life.'

Phyl glowered at him and Stan gave his son an exasperated look.

'You keep out of this. This is something your mother and me will have to talk about. It's not something to be decided in a hurry. The best thing you can do,' he said to Phyl, 'is help

24

your mother get a bit of supper ready and then get yourself off to bed. We've done enough talking tonight. Now, go and make that cocoa, and then you and your brothers can get yourselves off to bed and leave us in peace, all right?'

Norman laid down his magazine. 'Oh, Dad, it's only just ten o'clock—'

'Never mind that. It'll be nearer half-past by the time we've had our supper. And it won't do you any harm to be in bed before eleven for once. *I* know what time you came home last night, don't think I don't, and you've got to be up early in the morning. You were late once last week, and you know the foreman won't stand for it. There's plenty of other young men ready and waiting to step into your shoes if you lose your job. Jobs aren't easy to come by these days, as well you know. You're lucky to have one at all.'

Norman shrugged and gave his sister a comical look. He and Ronnie worked together in the docks, unloading cargo ships, and started their day of heavy labour early in the mornings. Norman enjoyed it – he liked the feeling of using his muscles, and spent two evenings a week at the local health club, weightlifting and body-building. He had begun to talk of posing for photographs, showing off his muscles as the models did in *Health and Strength*. You could even get paid for it, he said, and paid well.

However, not even the possession of a powerful body and rippling muscles could persuade his father that Norman Jennings was capable of running his own life before he was twenty-one. When that day came, at the end of October, he would be given a front-door key and, with it, tacit permission to come and go as he pleased and make his own decisions. Until then, he was as much under his father's rule as his sister Phyl and sixteen-year-old Ronnie.

Phyl made the cocoa in big white cups and brought it in with a plate piled high with slabs of cheese on toast. The family pulled chairs up to the square table and sat round it, eating and talking about the Coronation. Putting aside her own plans, Phyl told them more about the procession, about the decorated streets and the sound of the Abbey bells, and about the huge crowds. She closed her eyes, picturing again the smiling faces of the newly crowned monarch and his wife, and hearing the cheers . . . and then started and opened her eyes, blinking in bewilderment as her brother shook her arm and the rest of the family roared with laughter.

'You were almost asleep then,' May told her, touching her shoulder. 'Time you were in bed, my girl. You're worn out!'

'And no wonder, after a night spent sitting on a pavement and all day standing in the crowd,' Stan said. 'Go on, Phyl, get yourself off to bed. Take your cocoa with you and get a good night's sleep. You've got to get up and go to work in the morning, don't forget.'

Phyl shook her head and levered herself to her feet. 'Don't I know it!' she said wryly. 'And they'll want blood at that factory tomorrow, after giving us the day off today. Honestly, Dad, it's no wonder I'd rather work in a nice clean, smart Corner House. Wouldn't *you*?'

'Bed,' he said firmly, and Phyl rolled her eyes at him and left.

She undressed thoughtfully, wondering what was going to happen. Her dad seemed to have got over his annoyance at her disobedience, but that didn't mean he'd forgotten it, or that he'd look any more kindly on the idea of her going to live in London and being a Nippy. All the same, he wouldn't stop her going just out of spite. He might lay down the law to his family, but he was a fair man and he and May had always taken the view that their three children should be allowed to do more or less as they liked – *within reason*. That was always their proviso – that it had to be *within reason*.

Surely being a Nippy in a Lyons Corner House would be considered *within reason*.

The conversations in the two houses went on over the next few days, so similar that they could have been written down for them.

'I thought you liked working in the shop with me,' Carrie Mason said a little plaintively as she buttered toast for supper the next evening. 'It's a nice job and we see plenty of people

26

we know, have a nice chat. Why d'you want to go off to London and work with a lot of strangers?'

'I won't be with strangers. I'll be with Phyl.'

'The rest will be strangers. And you won't get much chance to stand about nattering with your cousin. You won't see any more of her than you do at home.'

Jo looked stubborn. 'All the same, I'd like to have a go. Just find out what it's all about. I mean, even if I apply, it doesn't mean I'll actually get a job – they might not want me. And London's not a foreign country, Mum – we live in London, don't we?'

'We live in Woolwich. Not in the middle of London,' her mother said. 'And you get all sorts of people up there. Not our sort either, most of them. Pass your father the bloater paste.'

'Oh, *Mum*,' Jo said, exasperated. She turned to her father, who had been sitting quietly at his end of the table, listening. 'Dad, you think it's a good idea, don't you? You'd let me go?'

Bill Mason cleared his throat and took a drink of cocoa from his large cup. 'I'd want to know a bit more about it first. Where you'd be living, for a start – it's all very well talking about digs and saying the company would make sure they were all right, but I'd want to be sure you'd be with decent people, and I know your mother would say the same. And I'd want to know what hours you'd be working and what about getting home at night – these places stay open late, you know. It's not down tools and go home at six o'clock like it is up the shop. And we'd need to have a few understandings about what you do in your spare time – I don't like the idea of you and young Phyl out on the town half the night with no one to know what you're up to and what time you're coming in.'

'Well, we couldn't be working late *and* be out on the town,' Jo said. 'Don't you trust me, Dad? Don't you think I know the difference between right and wrong, without having you and Mum to tell me all the time?'

Her father pursed his lips and gave a small shrug. 'Of course we trust you, girl. But it's not the same, living at home and living away. There's all sorts of temptations for young girls up there, and your mother's right, there's a lot of queer folk about.'

'Well, I reckon I can tell the difference between queer folk and ordinary ones,' Jo said obstinately. 'Look, Dad, it's not just a job, it's a *career*. You can get on in Lyons. The girl that served us, she told us you can work your way up to supervisor. That's a good job, with good money, too. I'd never get any further, working in a greengrocer's shop.'

Bill stared at her. 'A *career*? What's a girl like you want with a career? You'll be finding yourself a chap soon and wanting to get wed – what good will a career be to you then, eh? Tell me that.'

Jo flushed. 'You don't know that, Dad. You don't know that I'll ever get married. Not everyone does – look at Auntie Nellie.'

'That's different. Your Auntie Nellie was engaged back in 1914 and if her young man hadn't been killed on the Somme she'd have been married with her own kids. There was plenty of young women like her, never had a second chance nor wanted it, but that don't mean it's going to happen to you.'

'It might,' Jo said, 'if there's another war.'

'Jo!' her mother exclaimed, as horrified as if Jo had suddenly begun to swear, and Bill flushed a darker red than his daughter and slammed his palm flat on the table.

'We'll have none of that sort of talk in this house! You know there's not going to be a war. Mr Baldwin would never allow it. Nor will Mr Chamberlain, when he's Prime Minister. They know what it was like last time.'

'People are saying this Hitler's out to cause trouble,' Jo said. 'Look what's happening in Spain. People are being killed by bombs there, and our men are going out to fight. Why shouldn't it happen again?' She stopped and took a breath. 'Anyway, that's got nothing to do with me wanting to be a Nippy. Look, I shan't be signing my life away. It won't stop me getting married, if I want to. It could be a help – look at the things I'd learn there. How to serve meals, a bit of cooking—'

'I can teach you to cook,' Carrie said quickly. 'And you're

not going to have such a big family they'll all be sitting at separate tables.' She sighed. 'It's getting late, too late to talk about it any more tonight. But if you're really set on it – well, I dare say there's no harm in finding out a bit more about it. I'll have a talk to May, see what she and Stan think about it. They were going to have a bit of a chat about it tonight, I know. But I'll miss having you with me in the shop if you do go, I can't say I won't.'

Jo smiled ruefully and reached over to pat her mother's hand. 'I know, Mum, and I'll miss you, too. Honest. But – well, when we were there yesterday afternoon, it seemed a really good idea. And I'd feel awful if Phyl was allowed to go and I wasn't.'

Her mother gave her a glance of half exasperation, half amusement. 'And I wouldn't mind betting Phyl's saying exactly the same to your Auntie May and Uncle Stan.' She sighed. 'I thought you'd come home with your head full of kings and queens yesterday, not waitresses serving in cafés.'

'It just shows,' Bill said, finishing his cocoa, 'you can never tell which way a young girl or a cat will jump. I think I'll have another slice of toast, Carrie, if you don't mind. All this argifying's made me hungry.'

'I'll make some more.' Carrie got up and went out to the kitchen to turn on the grill. 'Our Freddy'll be in soon anyway, he's been to the pictures with that new girl of his. Now go on, Jo – Eric and Alice have been in bed for hours and that's where you ought to be, too.'

Jo knew better than to argue. She kissed her father and mother goodnight and had a wash at the kitchen sink before climbing the narrow staircase to the bedroom she shared with her younger sister. Alice was fast asleep in the top bunk, her small body smothered in knitted toy animals, her favourite rag doll Betty clutched in her arms. Jo stood looking at her for a moment or two and smoothed back the fair hair.

I'd miss you, she thought with a sudden pang. I'd miss Eric too, and our Freddy – all the family. Maybe Mum and Dad are right and it's not such a good idea after all. But it seemed so exciting when we were actually there – and I wouldn't say so to Mum, but I really am fed up with the greengrocer's shop. Fed up with seeing the same old women every day, with nothing to talk about but their bunions or their married daughter's new baby. And Phyl's fed up with the factory, too. We're young – we want to see a bit of life before we settle down.

She brushed her wavy, chestnut hair, then rolled it up at the neck and tried to imagine what it would be like wearing it like that, with a white cap perched on top. Nice, she decided. Smart. The black uniform would suit her, too, with her colouring, just as it would suit Phyl's dark curls. She looked at her hands, grimed with dirt from the vegetables no matter how hard she scrubbed them, and grimaced. She'd never get through an interview with grubby hands, that was for certain!

Well, it'll all probably come to nothing, she thought, turning out the gas lamp and getting into bed. Mum and Dad will never let me go, and I don't suppose Auntie May and Uncle Stan will let Phyl either. And maybe when we find out a bit more about it, we won't even want to.

All the same, as she drifted into sleep her dreams were not of a grand procession headed by Guardsmen on gleaming black horses, or of a king and queen in a glittering golden coach. Instead, they were of a restaurant with white marble colonnades and pillars, and huge pictures painted on the walls; of soft gipsy music playing in the background, and the cheerful murmur of people enjoying good food while smiling, friendly girls bustled to and fro with silver trays.

It was as near as she was ever likely to get to being in a palace, she thought sleepily, and she'd be happy enough with that.

'I don't know what to say, Stan, I don't really,' May said as she and her husband sat by themselves in the back room. 'She's proper set on it, you know, this Nippy business. I never seen her so keen. And it's a decent job, working with decent people, and it'll give her a good grounding for when she gets married. But – I don't know. Living away from home, up there in London . . . I know she'd be with Jo, and

Jo's a steady enough girl, but you just never know, do you? You don't know what *influences* there'd be on them. They're only young girls, when all's said and done.'

'Well, if I had my way she'd stop at home.' Stan filled his pipe with Players tobacco. 'She's got a decent job as it is. And I tell you what, I don't hold with all this talk of careers. What's a young girl like our Phyl want with a career? Bill told me that's what young Jo was calling it. A *job* ought to be good enough for a girl, something to keep her till she gets married, never mind a lot of nonsense about *careers.*'

'She really doesn't like it at the factory, though.'

'Doesn't *like* it? Who does like their job? You don't go to work to enjoy yourself, you go to earn your living. Anyway, I reckon she's got the wrong idea about this Corner House business, if she thinks she's going to enjoy it. They'll want their pennyworth out of those girls, you can't tell me they won't. Give her a fortnight and she'll be begging to come home and have her old job back.'

'Well, if you're right about that,' May said, narrowing her eyes to thread a needle, 'we might as well let her have a go. Get it out of her system.'

Stan stared at her. 'You mean, say *yes?*'

May shrugged. 'Why not? She probably won't get taken on anyway, but it'd stop all this begging and pleading and staring at you with her eyes. And if she did get a job and couldn't stick it, you'd have proved your point, wouldn't you?'

Stan pushed out his lips and stuck his pipe in his mouth. He puffed for a few moments before answering. 'I dunno, May. It's a bit like giving in.'

'There's nothing to be gained by being obstinate,' she said quietly. 'Look what it did to my dad.'

Stan gave her a sharp look. 'Did you tell our Phyl about that?'

'Yes, I did, as a matter of fact. But it wasn't so she could talk you round over this Nippy idea. It was before I knew about that. I wanted her to understand why you were so upset at the way she'd behaved, and why you didn't want her going to London in the first place. I wanted to help her see your point of view.'

'Hmm.' He puffed again. 'Cuts both ways, though, don't it?'

'Yes.' May's head was bent over her sewing, but she looked up and met his eyes. 'Yes, I think it does, Stan. No good comes of people being obstinate, that's what I think it's shown me. And our Phyl – well, like Norman and Jo, she's getting to the age where she wants a bit of independence. We've never held it back from them before, have we? I'll tell you what I think, Stan. I think we've got to the point where we've got to let 'em off the leash a bit. We've done our best bringing them up, but now they've got to learn to be grown up and they won't do that if we keep treating them as kids. And if we've made any sort of a job of it, they'll remember their upbringing. They won't go far wrong.'

'I hope you're right,' he said, and frowned into the empty fireplace. 'Well, all right, let her apply, then. Perhaps, like you say, nothing'll come of it. I dare say they get any amount of girls applying for them jobs.'

May smiled. 'I think that's the right decision, Stan. Mind you, I don't want her leaving home any more than you do – but, there, girls always have, haven't they, in the days when they all used to go into service? My mum and auntie left home at fourteen, and so did a lot of others. And I don't reckon our Phyl will have as hard a time of it as they did.' She bit off her cotton. 'She's coming in now. You tell her. She'll be so pleased, she'll probably make the cocoa without being asked!'

To Phyl's delight, Bill and Carrie had also agreed to Jo applying to become a Nippy. Fired once again with excitement, the two girls wrote off immediately and a week later met on their front doorsteps, each waving a letter. They had been invited to attend for interviews at Orchard House in Oxford Street in two weeks' time, and the letters also contained information about the job and about such things as accommodation and uniform.

'Orchard House, where's that?' Phyl asked, scanning the

letter again. 'Oh, I see, at Selfridges. That's one of the biggest shops in London. Coo-*er*.'

'It'll be a day out even if we don't get taken on,' Jo said. 'Here, will you be able to get the time off, Phyl? I mean, you can't exactly tell 'em you're going after a new job, can you?'

'No, but I can have a very nasty headache,' Phyl said with a grin. 'I know I shouldn't do it, but I never have before and some of the girls do it all the time. What about you? I suppose Mrs Tanner knows all about it anyway.'

'Mum told her straight away.' Jo looked ruefully at her hands. 'I'll have to do something about these. You can't work in a greengrocer's shop and keep your hands all soft and white. I'll have to try some of that hand cream when I go to bed.'

'Put lots on and wear gloves,' Phyl advised her. 'You've got a couple of weeks anyway. And get your mum to weigh out the potatoes and root veg.'

'That's going to be like rubbing salt into the wound. She still don't really want me to go, Phyl. And I don't know what our dad thinks I'm going to get up to – thinks I'll be going to nightclubs or something. *Me!* I don't even go to dances round here, let alone posh ones up West.'

'Well, I'm looking forward to a bit of fun,' Phyl said decisively. 'You know that girl we met told us about the sports club at Sudbury? Well, I've found out a bit more about it. They have dances there every week, and any Lyons' employee can go. That means hundreds – they must be really big affairs. And there's swimming and hockey and tennis and all sorts of other things. You'll like that.'

'Swimming!' Jo's eyes sparkled. 'Yes, that'll be smashing. I wonder if they've got a netball team as well.' Netball was the only game she'd played at school, where they'd put up a couple of poles and marked out a pitch on the playground, and it was there that her height had given her an advantage. As star shooter, she'd scored almost all the goals that had allowed her team to win. 'Mind, I'll have a go at anything like that.'

'Well, you make sure you've got nice clean hands and

fingernails on the day,' Phyl said. 'I reckon they're sure to take you on then – being so tall, you'll be able to carry your tray over everyone else's head! I'm not so sure about me,' she added a little ruefully. 'I've been thinking about it, and I think they might say I'm too short.'

'Oh, no. I don't want to go without you.' Jo looked appraisingly at her cousin. 'Tell 'em you're still growing. Girls do go on growing till they're twenty sometimes.'

'Well, it'll be a miracle if I do – I've been five foot nothing on stilts for three years now! Still, they're not to know that, are they?' Phyl's eyes gleamed. 'And I could wear high heels! I'm really looking forward to this, Jo. The two of us together, working at a Corner House – it's going to be gorgeous, you see if it isn't!'

Chapter Three

In the maze of narrow streets that ran around the back of St Paul's Cathedral lived another girl who disliked her job.

Maggie Pratt worked in a laundry. With a dozen or so other girls, she laboured all day in the steamy, bare-bricked rooms, sloshing sheets and towels and pillowcases about in great bubbling cauldrons of soapy water, dragging them out with wooden tongs and forcing them through huge mangles, then draping them over great racks to dry before folding them into the big presses. Sometimes she worked on smaller items – men's shirts and ladies dresses – which needed more individual attention, or starched white collars by the hundred. Whatever she did, it seemed that there was no end to it; a huge, eternal mound of dirty washing came in through the door and no matter how hard or how long you worked, you could never make it any smaller.

Maggie, however, had no ideas about leaving her exhausting and thankless work to find something else. She knew she had been lucky to get a job at all. There were plenty of people outside in the streets who had no work, and had to scrape a living as best they could – doing an odd hour here or there rolling barrels in a pub, going up West to hold doors open for the wealthy in the hope of getting an odd penny tossed their way, sweeping the road in front of a shop – anything so that they could buy a bit of bread and maybe a tag-end of cheese to take home for the family. Ragged, shoeless kids scavenged the street-markets, fighting over scraps of cabbage or a few potatoes, running errands for the stallholders in exchange for a bunch of carrots, and stealing the odd apple whenever nobody was looking.

Maggie knew the kind of places they lived in. The slum streets were only yards from her own house – broken roads, with stinking potholes, muddy in all but the hottest weather, littered with debris and filth. The houses were down at heel, their cracked windows stuffed with cardboard or bits of sacking, their doors peeling and hanging from rusty hinges. Inside, they were dark and crowded. Hardly any of them had gas lighting, unless a lucky break had helped them pay the bill, and none had electricity. They used stumps of candles and boiled water over the fire, when they could find the kindling, and any hot food that they had came from the soup kitchen along the street or, in good times, the fish and chip shop.

Compared with these, the Pratt family was well off. Sam Pratt worked in Covent Garden and brought home a steady wage, as well as fruit and vegetables from the stalls. It had been hard when the family was young but now that they were mostly grown up and out at work, each bringing home a wage to give to Ivy Pratt, things were much easier. All the same, everyone was well aware that it wouldn't take much to plunge them all into the kind of poverty they saw around them every day, and no one complained because their work was hard or boring or dirty. They all knew that work was life, or at least the difference between living with food in your belly or at starvation level.

Maggie kept going through the days by thinking of getting home at night. Fridays were the highlight of the week, when the women got paid, and even though they had to work Saturdays as well, most of them managed to find the energy for a drink or two down at the local pub. There, just for a few hours, they could laugh and sing with their friends and forget the troubles and the tedium of the week.

Not all troubles could be forgotten, though.

'I wouldn't mind so much if old man Parvin didn't have such favourites,' Maggie told her mother, helping her wash up after tea one day. 'I mean, that Vi Jenkins, she can't put a foot wrong, but if he sees me do so much as draw breath he's down on me like a ton of bricks. Like today, I got me backache, you know how I do on the first day, and I just straightened up for a minute and put me hand on it to give it a bit of a rub, and he shouts at me from the other end of the hall. "Get on with it, Maggie Pratt, you're not here on your holidays ..." And at that very minute, that Vi strolled in smirking, all the time in the world, and I know for a *fact* she'd been having a fag in the lavvies. But did he say anything? Not a word!'

'There's always unfairness at work,' Ivy Pratt said. She plunged her big arms into the hot water and fished out the piece of soda used to soften it, replacing it in a small dish inscribed A PRESENT FROM SOUTHEND which lay on the scullery window-sill. 'It don't matter where you are, some-one'll always have favourites.'

'I know. I just wish it could be me sometimes!' Maggie grinned wryly and picked up another plate to dry. 'It wouldn't be so bad if she wasn't such a cat! And she's got it in for me, too. I wouldn't put it past her to try and get me the sack.'

'Well, don't you get into no arguments with her, then,' her mother said warningly. 'There ain't that many jobs about these days that a girl can pick and choose. Times is hard, even with you and our Jim out at work. We still got the twins and your gran to feed and clothe, so we depends on the bit you brings in.' She tipped up the chipped enamel washing-up bowl and let the the water run down the sink.

'I know.' Maggie hung up the damp tea-towel. Stretching past her mother, she peered into the scrap of broken mirror that hung above the sink and pushed back her yellow hair. Her blue eyes were tired, her skin dulled by long hours in the steam and she thought she looked older than she should at twenty. I'll be an old hag by the time I'm thirty, she thought, a fat old hag.

Vi Jenkins had been a thorn in Maggie's side ever since they'd been at school together. Vi lived a few streets away and thought she was a cut above Maggie, whose father worked in Covent Garden. Albert Jenkins had a job on the railway, and Vi was an only child, so there had always been enough money to buy her pretty frocks and warm winter coats, and she never wore hand-me-downs like Maggie and her family did.

'I saw your Evie wearing that frock Christmas before last,' she'd say sneeringly in the school playground. 'It looked old then – where'd she get it from, the Sally Army jumble sale?'

'At least it suited her,' Maggie would retort, 'not like that primped-up thing you're wearing that looks as if it was made for a frog. Talk about a dying duck in a thunderstorm!'

Their altercations had invariably ended in a fight, with the two girls rolling on the ground, scratching and clawing and pulling each other's hair, until an exasperated teacher separated them and sent them both in to the headmistress to have their hands slapped with a ruler.

So far, they hadn't come to blows at the laundry, but it was only a matter of time, Maggie thought gloomily as she hurried to work next morning. The way that Vi was strutting about, nose in the air as if she owned the place, Maggie wasn't going to be able to answer for her actions much longer.

The overseer was by the entrance, his arm crooked to see his watch, as Maggie arrived, panting. 'You're late, Maggie Pratt.'

'I know. My gran was poorly in the night.'

'That's not the laundry's concern. You're still supposed to be here on time.'

'I had to wash out all her sheets and things, and then I overslept—'

He seized on her words. 'You overslept! So you did have time to go back to bed.'

'Yes, but I'd only had—'

'That's enough excuses,' he said sharply. 'You had time to go back to bed, so there was nothing to stop you getting up and getting to work at the proper time. That'll be an hour's pay docked at the end of the week.'

Maggie stared at him. 'But it was only a minute—'

'You know the rules. Anything under an hour, and you lose

a full hour's pay.' He smiled nastily. 'Next time, you might as well catch up on your sleep and make it fifty-nine minutes!'

Her face burning, Maggie went past him into the laundry. The other girls were already hard at work and to her disgust she saw that she was to be next to Vi Jenkins, ironing starched white collars. Of all the jobs in the laundry, this was the one Maggie hated most. They had to be done perfectly, requiring constant attention, yet the tedium of ironing an endless stream of collars was enough to drive a girl stark, staring mad.

'That's your iron,' Vi said, pointing to a flat-iron heating on the gas. Maggie picked it up and licked her finger, touching it to the sole to test the heat. There was no answering sizzle and she sighed with annoyance.

'It's the one you've been using. It's gone cold.'

'Well, so what? You weren't here to use it. I was early.' Vi's voice was smug. She picked up another collar and ran the iron over the white, glossy surface. 'I've done half a day's work already.'

'Sucking up to old Parvin, I suppose,' Maggie said caustically, testing the iron again. It still wasn't hot enough and as she stood there, waiting, the overseer bore down upon her again.

'Just start work whenever it suits you, Miss Pratt! It doesn't matter to the rest of the girls, I'm sure, that you wander in late and then need a rest to get over the strain before you bother to lift a finger. They'll do your work for you if you ask, I wouldn't wonder – wouldn't you, girls?'

The other women glanced his way and grinned half-heartedly. Mr Parvin liked his jokes to be appreciated. Vi Jenkins giggled sycophantically and Maggie glowered.

'The iron's not hot enough.'

'Not hot enough?' Mr Parvin picked it up and tested it himself. There was an obliging sizzle and Maggie thought with disgust that even the flat-irons sucked up to him. Biting her lip, she took it from his hand and picked up a collar.

'*I* was going to do that one,' Vi said, reaching across.

'Be careful,' Maggie said. 'You'll have the whole pile over. Take them from that side – oh, bloody *hell*.'

The pile of collars on her side of the table tottered and fell as Vi poked at them. Muttering under her breath, Maggie bent to retrieve them, and by the time she had piled them all up again the flat-iron was once again cold. She felt the tears come to her eyes.

'Still not working, Miss Pratt?' He was back again, like an infuriating wasp. 'And what's the excuse this time? Granny sick again, is she?'

Maggie turned a furious look on him. 'Vi knocked the collars over. I've only just picked them all up and now the iron's gone cold again—'

'What a little tale-teller you are,' he sneered. 'Always someone else's fault, isn't it – never your own. Well, let me tell you this, Maggie Pratt, for every job in this laundry there's a dozen girls at the door waiting for it, and glad to have the work, too. *They* won't come in late and then idle the hours away, they'll have more sense than that. Now, d'you want one of them to have your job? You've only got to give the word.'

'No,' Maggie muttered, seething with anger and misery.

'Well, then, I suggest you put your back into it a bit more.' He glanced at the iron. 'I should think that's hot enough now, wouldn't you? Why not have a try at ironing a few shirt-collars – just to while away the time, eh?'

He walked on and Maggie started work, angrily aware of Vi Jenkins sniggering. For a while they worked in silence and then Vi gave a muttered exclamation and Maggie glanced at her to see the other girl staring in annoyance at a collar spoiled by brown scorch-marks.

'That's your fault!' Vi said. 'If you hadn't been causing a disturbance all morning, what with coming in late and knocking stuff over and getting Mr Parvin all upset, I wouldn't never have done that. I've a good mind to put it on your pile.'

She reached over and dropped the collar on the pile in front of Maggie. Maggie gave a cry and knocked her hand away. Once again, the collars slipped to the floor and this time Vi's pile went, too.

'Oh, you *bitch*!'

Vi flew at Maggie, her hand raised to strike. Maggie, who had been about to dive for the collars, staggered and caught the other girl's wrist. With another shriek, Vi twisted her hand away and reached again for Maggie's face, her fingers extended this time in claws. Maggie gave her a forceful push, and Vi went down amongst the collars, grabbing at Maggie's leg as she went.

Now both girls were on the floor and all Maggie's good intentions flew out of the window as she reverted to the child of the playground. Within seconds, they were rolling together on the floor, clawing and screeching. Maggie screamed as Vi's nails scraped down her cheek, and when she found a handful of hair tangled around her fingers she yanked hard. Violet's howl of agony sounded throughout the laundry. Even above the rattle and thump of the machinery. The next moment, Maggie felt a hard hand at her collar, and found herself pulled away, just as the teacher had pulled her away years ago. She was dragged upright and thrust towards the group of women who had gathered around them. One caught her and held her as she staggered.

'What the *hell* do you think you're doing?' Mr Parvin's eyes were bulbous with rage. He glared at Maggie and then turned towards Vi, who was still lying on the floor. 'Miss Jenkins – are you all right? You're not hurt, I hope?'

'A bit.' Vi, who had been sobbing with rage, now turned her weeping to a more pitiful note. 'My head – she's pulled out half my hair. And I think she's scratched me. And she bit my arm.'

'I never! I wouldn't want to be poisoned!'

Mr Parvin gave Maggie a withering look, then turned back to Vi. Gently, he helped her to her feet and smoothed back her hair. Maggie, watching, felt a sudden bitter knowledge. They've been carrying on, she thought, you can see it. No wonder he's always on her side.

'That's a nasty scratch, Miss Jenkins. You'll need to get that attended to. You can have half an hour off to go to the chemist's, and you'd better have a cup of tea as well. In fact, it

41

might be as well if you took the rest of the day off. You've had a nasty shock. You're sure you're not badly hurt?'

'I don't think so.' Vi, leaning against him, simpered and gave Maggie a sly look from under her lashes. 'I think I'll be all right. And I won't have the day off. I'd rather get back to work. We're all behind as it is.' She glanced pointedly at the collars scattered on the floor.

'What an example,' Mr Parvin said fondly, and turned to the others. His tone changed. 'Well, there's no need for you lot to stand there gawping, The show's over – get back to work. We'll all have to put a bit more effort in to catch up today, so I want to hear no chattering, understand?'

'What about me?' Maggie demanded. She put her hand to her cheek and looked at the blood on her palm. 'I reckon I've got a nasty scratch, too – can I go to the chemist and have a cup of tea while I'm at it?'

Mr Parvin eyed her coldly. 'You can do whatever you like, Miss Pratt. Your time's your own now. Go to the chemist by all means – but collect your cards on the way out, and don't bother to come back. There'll be another girl standing in your place by this afternoon, and let's hope she's a bit more willing to put her back into it than you were!'

'It's not just losing me job that riles me,' Maggie said to her mother later. 'It's the way he makes out I never did it proper. I did, Mum. I worked as hard as any girl there, and a blooming sight harder than that slimy, stuck-up Vi Jenkins. Well, you can see what the situation is there. His fancy piece, she is. Just because she's got a pretty face and don't mind letting herself be pawed by an old man!'

'*You've* got a pretty face, our Mags,' Ivy said. 'Pretty as a picture, you are, with that yellow hair and nice blue eyes. That's what men like, or so I always found when I was a girl.'

Maggie grinned. Ivy Pratt had been the queen of the alley before she married. Her hair was going grey now and her ample figure, so like Maggie's, had begun to overflow, but her cheerful, optimistic personality was still there. And Maggie took after her, although the laundry had dimmed her sparkle just lately.

'I tell you what,' Ivy said, 'I reckon this'll turn out to be a blessing in disguise. That job wasn't never right for you. Now you got a chance to look around and find summat that suits you better.'

'Mum! Last night, you were saying—'

'Never mind what I said last night. Things is different now. You got your pay, Maggie, and we got a little bit put by, your dad and me. You don't have to rush into the first job that comes along. You think about what you'd *like* to do. When you was little, you always used to say you wouldn't mind working in a shop or a tearoom.'

'No, I wouldn't,' Maggie said thoughtfully. 'It'd be nice, working where I could see different people and sort of *do* things for them. Bring them nice food or help them choose things they want to buy. All right, Mum, I'll do that. I'll look in the papers tonight and see what's going.'

As Maggie Pratt opened that night's copy of the *Evening Standard* to look at the jobs page, Shirley Wood, two miles away in Islington, was doing the same thing.

Shirley hadn't lost her job, but she knew she was just about to. Since leaving school at fourteen, she had worked for the local newsagent, arriving at five-thirty a.m. to mark up the newspapers for delivery, standing behind the counter all morning to serve sweets and tobacco as well as papers, then after a short break in the afternoon coming back to go through the whole procedure again with the evening issues. It was a twelve-hour day, but Shirley didn't know anyone who didn't work a twelve-hour day – if they had a job at all – so she thought nothing of it.

Now, however, everything had changed.

For months now, the shop's takings had been going down. People couldn't afford newspapers any more, let alone pay to have them delivered. Sales of cigarettes and sweets, too, had been dropping and Shirley's employer, Mr Hollins, remarked sourly that more were stolen than paid for. He put up a notice forbidding children from coming in on their own, but the urchins simply tagged on to adults who were actually buying, and then thumbed their noses at him as they scurried out, their pockets bulging with chocolate bars.

One morning, about two months ago, Shirley had come in to find him sitting behind the counter, the morning papers still bundled up on the floor. His head was in his hands and he looked the picture of utter dejection.

'Is everything all right?' she asked timidly. Mr Hollins's temper had been uncertain just lately and he didn't always take kindly to personal questions. But she couldn't just ignore his misery.

He lifted his face and she saw to her horror that he was crying

'Mr Hollins! Whatever's happened? Is Mrs Hollins ill again?' The newsagent's wife had been bedridden for the past year, suffering from what people – whispering behind their hands – called a 'growth'.

'Mrs Hollins is always ill,' he said in a heavy tone. His voice sounded rough and difficult, as if something had gone wrong with his throat. 'There ain't nothing different there. It's this.' He thrust a sheet of paper across the counter at her. 'Look at this.'

Doubtfully, not liking to read his private letters even when given permission to do so, Shirley took the sheet of paper. Her eyes widened.

'They're putting up your rent. Why? Is it – is it a lot?'

'A lot!' he echoed with a hollow laugh. 'I'll say it's a lot. Only double what it is now, that's all, only *double*. How am I going to find that, eh? You tell me how I'm going to find it.' He stared at Shirley and she stared back, seeing the hopelessness in his eyes and unable to answer. 'I haven't even paid the *last* three months, and the bleeder knows it, he *knows* I can't stump up twice as much. I tell you what, Shirl, it's an excuse, that's what it is, an excuse to get rid of me. As if it's *my* fault nobody's got no money to spend.'

'Oh, Mr Hollins. That's awful.' Shirley looked down at the

letter again and then back into his despairing face. 'What will you do?'

'What will I do? *Gawd* knows.' He covered his face with his hands again and tears dripped between his fingers. He gave a great, rasping shudder. 'What do all the other poor bleeders do who've been chucked out of their jobs and their homes the past few years? Live on the streets, I suppose, live in some stinking basement, me and the missus, and her at death's door, too. That's all there is now for poor bleeders like us, what nobody cares about.'

Shirley felt the tears welling in her own eyes. *I* care, she wanted to say, but she knew that her words would only be greeted with bitterness, and why not? What could *she* do to help people like poor Mr and Mrs Hollins, who had worked hard all their lives and were now to be thrown on the scrap heap?

Wordlessly, she picked up the scissors and cut the string binding one of the bundles of newspapers. While there was work to be done, she thought, it had better go on, and it wouldn't take long to mark up these few papers. The bundles had been steadily diminishing during the past months as orders had dropped, and there were only two paper-boys working at the shop now, where once there had been a dozen.

Even so, those two boys would expect to find their papers ready for them, and the customers would expect them to be in their letter-boxes at the usual time. Nothing would be gained by losing these last few orders.

During the next few weeks, things went from bad to worse. Even the Coronation with its special reports didn't buck the sales of newspapers up for more than a few days, and the jubilation was cut short when, on the very next day, Shirley came in to find the doctor coming out, grim-faced, with his black bag in his hand.

This time she knew it must be Mrs Hollins. She looked at the doctor and he stopped and spoke to her. 'Do you work here?'

Shirley nodded. One look at his face answered the question she dared not ask. Everyone knew that Mrs Hollins had been near death for weeks, that the 'growth' had taken over her whole body, that she was just wasting away in the bedroom above the shop. She hadn't bothered with the doctor. If they'd been wealthy people, Mr Hollins had said once, they could have afforded visits and medicines and such, but with what she had they couldn't have done anything anyway, so what was the point?

'You'd better do what you can,' the doctor said briefly. 'He ought to have called me, you know. She didn't have to go through all that without help. Well . . . I've other patients to see. There's a neighbour in there now, but I dare say he'll need extra help in the shop for a while.' He strode away down the street and Shirley hurried through the shop doorway.

Mr Hollins wasn't in the shop. He was in the back room, where he did his paperwork and ate his meals all at the same square dining-table. He sat there in his shirtsleeves, his face grey, his eyes empty.

'Extra help!' he said bitterly. 'How does he think I'm going to pay for that, eh? You tell me that. And saying my poor Muriel didn't need to have suffered like that, as if it was *my* fault, as if I *wanted* her to suffer. Who would have paid his bills, eh? And how often would he have come if he hadn't got paid? You tell me that.'

'I'll look after the shop,' Shirley said. The neighbour, whom she recognised as 'Aunty' Sarah, the local midwife, came downstairs and into the room. 'You don't need to worry about anything, Mr Hollins. I'll see to it all.'

'Don't need to *worry*!' he echoed. 'With my poor Muriel on her deathbed and the business gone to rack and ruin and no money to pay the rent . . . No need to *worry*.'

Sarah put her hand on his shoulder. 'Now then, Perce. Your Muriel's at peace now. I've laid her out and she looks lovely, you can go and sit with her for a bit. I'll put the kettle on for a cup of tea. And young Shirley can take care of the shop, you know that, and the vicar'll be round soon to talk about the funeral. All you got to do is think what hymns you'd like, some of your Muriel's favourites, eh? There's nothing else that matters today.'

It wasn't true. As she went back to the shop and began to undo the bundles of papers and mark them up, Shirley knew that it wasn't true. Death had visited the little house, but life would go on, and life for Mr Hollins was harder even than death.

He must have come to the same conclusion, for when everyone had gone home that evening and he was left alone with his wife's body, he went down to the little kitchen, opened the door of the gas oven and, turning the gas on but not lighting it, lay on the floor and rested his head just inside.

'A proper change, that's what you need,' Annie Wood said when all the fuss was over and Mr and Mrs Hollins properly buried, side by side in the same grave. It had been doubtful for a while whether that would be done, Mr Hollins being a suicide and therefore not only a criminal but a sinner before God, but at his inquest the coroner gave a verdict of 'Suicide while the balance of the mind was disturbed', and the vicar agreed that he could have the church service. The Hollinses had been regular attenders at church until Muriel Hollins had become ill, and even when she was bedridden the vicar would call to pray with her or give her Holy Communion. It would have been a shame, everyone agreed, if they couldn't be together in death as they had been in life.

It had been hardest of all for Shirley. She had been the one to find Mr Hollins next morning, and had called the grim-faced doctor who had advised her to shut the shop and put a notice on the door. 'No rent collectors are going to hound him where he's gone,' he said dourly, and Shirley did as he told her and eventually went home, white-faced and sick. Her mother made her tea and her brother Jack sat down beside her, his arms around her neck, silently sympathetic even though he couldn't really understand what had happened. It wasn't until after the inquest and the funerals that Shirley began to recover and talk about looking for another job.

'A proper change,' her mother repeated. 'Something out of this place. It's got too many memories for you and there's too many old gossips chewing the fat all the time. You wants to go somewhere where there's a bit of life, with young people. Look in the paper tonight.'

The paper came now from a different newsagent. Shirley picked it up from the mat and unfolded it. Shop work, a job in a laundry, pulling pints in the local pub ... there weren't many jobs about, but she thought she could apply to the shop, even though it was quite a way from home and would mean a long journey each day. Then another advertisement caught her eye.

'Here, Mum, they're asking for girls to train as Nippies up at the Corner House.'

'Nippies?' her mother said. 'That's those waitresses, isn't it, the ones that run about as if they'd got a flea up their backsides?'

Shirley giggled. 'That's right. Well, they're looking for new ones. You've got to be eighteen, it says here, and of good appearance, pleasant personality and willing to work hard.'

'Well, you're all of those.' Annie Wood looked at her daughter affectionately. It was the first time Shirley had laughed for a fortnight. 'You send in a letter,' she advised her. 'I reckon you'd be a dead cert for a job as a Nippy. And you'd see a bit of life too, more than you do round here.'

Shirley looked doubtful. 'But what about you? And our Jack? I mean, working just up the street I've been able to get home quick, and help round the house a bit. If I was in London, I might not be able to do that so much.'

'Don't talk daft. Me and Jack can manage all right, can't we, lovey?' Annie reached out to stroke her son's round head and he turned and grinned at her, screwing up his small, slanting eyes.

Jack was only a year younger than Shirley but although he could talk and understand quite a lot, he was more like a child of five or six than a young man of eighteen. He was what they called a Mongol and had slanting eyes and a round face with a button nose and smiling mouth. He didn't go out much but stayed at home with Annie, helping her with the housework and cooking. He couldn't read but he liked music and could play the old mouth-organ their older brother Donald had

48

given him; he could get more out of it than Donald had ever been able to. You only had to hum a tune for him to pick it up and play it back to you, straight off.

'And you wouldn't have to leave no earlier than you do now, that's for certain,' Annie went on, still looking at the advertisement.

'No, I wouldn't.' Shirley looked thoughtfully at the advertisement and then made up her mind. 'All right, Mum. I'll do it. I'll write in today. You know, I reckon it could be quite good – being a Nippy.'

Chapter Four

The interviews were to be held at two o'clock sharp, and it seemed only appropriate that the two girls should have lunch in a Corner House first. The Oxford Street House was the nearest and they went into the Trafalgar Room, surrounded by pictures of Nelson and his ship the *Victory* in battle with Napoleon.

'Victory,' Phyl said in a slightly trembling voice. 'That's what it's going to be for us today. Ooh, Jo—' she gave her cousin a grimace '—I'm feeling scared all of a sudden. Suppose they take one look at us and say no?'

'They won't,' Jo said without much conviction. 'They'll ask a lot of questions first – and *then* say no. Don't let's think about it, Phyl. Let's think about what we're going to have to eat instead.'

'I can't eat a thing.' Phyl turned as a girl in a black dress with a double row of buttons down the front appeared beside them. 'I'll just have a cup of tea. I'll be sick if I eat anything else.'

The girl looked concerned. 'Are you feeling ill? Can I get you some water or anything?'

'It's all right,' Jo assured her. 'It's just that we're going for job interviews this afternoon and we're feeling a bit nervous. You ought to eat something,' she said to her cousin. 'You don't want your tummy rumbling right in the middle of your interview.'

Phyl groaned and the girl looked sympathetic. 'Why not try

50

a bit of toast? That always makes me feel better if I'm a bit queasy, specially if it's nerves. What sort of jobs are you going for?'

Jo gave her a half-embarrassed smile. 'Well, as a matter of fact we've applied to be Nippies, like you. We're going to Orchard House.'

'You're not! Well, if that ain't a turn-up for the book!' The waitress laughed. 'Look, you don't need to worry about a thing. They're nice as pie. They'll just ask you a few questions and watch you walk about a bit, that sort of thing, and they'll sort of assess you, and that'll be it. There's nothing to be scared of.'

'We're only scared they won't pass us,' Jo said. 'What do you mean, assess us?'

'Well, they look to see what sort of person you are – whether you'll be best at waiting or cooking, or serving behind the counter, that sort of thing. Sometimes they even pick a girl out as someone who'll make a supervisor one day. They can tell from the first interview.'

'But we want to be Nippies,' Phyl said. 'We don't want to serve at a counter, or cook.'

'Well, I expect that's what you'll be, then,' the Nippy said cheerfully. 'But they can tell, so don't you worry about it. And they won't be nasty to you.'

She took their orders – toast for Phyl, fish and chips for Jo and a big pot of tea – and went off. The girls looked at each other.

'Well?' Jo said. 'Does that make you feel better?'

Phyl groaned and shook her head. 'It makes me feel worse! I didn't know I was going to be assessed. And suppose they tell me I've got to work in the kitchen? I'll never meet any actors or actresses there!'

'I don't suppose we'll meet any anyway.' Jo spread her hands out, palms down, and stared at them. She had been assiduous in scrubbing them every evening and rubbing in lots of hand cream. 'It's these I'm worried about. What d'you think, Phyl, do they look any better?'

Her cousin examined them. 'Yes, they look a lot better.

51

And you've managed to grow your fingernails a bit too, and get all the dirt out. How d'you do that?'

Jo grinned. 'I've taken over washing our Freddy's socks! He gives me a pair every night. And I've done some of the other washing for Mum as well, specially Freddy and Dad's overalls with the washboard. It takes half an hour and my hands look like corrugated paper at the end of it, but it works a treat.'

'Well, I haven't managed to grow at all,' Phyl said. 'Dad fetched a bucket of dung from the street where the baker's horse had been standing, and suggested I could stand in it for half an hour every night! He said it works with roses, so why not with me? Not that he's ever had any roses to try it out on, not in our back yard. The most we can manage to grow is a bucket of spuds.' She leant her chin on her hand and gazed around the restaurant. 'Well, I suppose there's nothing we can do about it now. D'you think we'll ever really work in a place like this, Jo? I reckon I'll break my heart if I have to go back to that factory.'

'Of course we will,' Jo said stoutly. 'They'll snap us up. Now, here comes our lunch. Are you sure you won't have anything else, Phyl? A couple of pieces of toast isn't much to get you through the afternoon.'

'No. I couldn't eat a thing,' Phyl said, looking at the plates the Nippy set before them. 'A few of your chips, perhaps. And just that little bit off the end of your fish. But nothing else. I just couldn't.'

Jo gave the waitress a wry look. 'You'd better bring another plateful. Once she starts, she won't know how to stop – and I don't want *my* tummy rumbling all through the interview!'

Orchard House was, amongst other things, the Tea-shops Training Centre, where Nippies, Sallys, counterhands and others received their training before actually appearing in the restaurants. As Phyl and Jo found their way uncertainly to the room where they had been told to report, they passed a number of other girls, already in uniform, going to their next training session.

'That'll be us in a few weeks' time,' Jo whispered, but Phyl was more interested in the girls who weren't in any uniform and were making for the same room.

'All these must be coming for interviews, too,' she muttered. 'How many d'you think they take on?'

Jo shrugged. 'Enough to make it worthwhile doing the training sessions, I suppose. It'll be like being back at school! Who do you reckon does the teaching?'

'They have demonstrators,' another girl said, overhearing them. 'My sister's been a Nippy for two years. She's told me all about the interview and everything. It'll be a piece of cake for me.'

'Get her!' Jo whispered, and Phyl giggled. 'It's hardly worthwhile us coming if that's the sort of girl they're looking for.'

There were about thirty girls in the room now, all aged around eighteen to twenty and all looking equally nervous. Nippies in uniform came forward, smiling, to show them to the chairs set around the walls and they sat down, fidgeting and looking around them. Jo and Phyl found seats opposite the door, and a buxom girl with a mass of wavy yellow hair came and sat beside Jo.

'Hullo. My name's Maggie Pratt.' She had very round, blue eyes, like a doll, and a wide smile. 'What a lark, eh? What's your name?'

'Jo Mason. And this is my cousin, Phyl Jennings. We're from Woolwich.'

'Woolwich, eh? I'm from round St Paul's. Here, what d'you suppose they're going to ask us? I never done no waitressing before.'

'Nor have we. I suppose they'll want references, though. And I don't think it matters if we haven't got any experience – they'll train us. That girl over there, with the black hair, says they have demonstrators to teach us.'

'We've got to get through the interview first,' Phyl put in. Another girl, very slim with cloudy dark hair and blue eyes fringed with long black lashes, had sat down on her other

53

side. 'This is Shirley Wood – she says she knows someone who tried twice and they wouldn't take her.'

'Coo-er. I don't suppose there's much chance for me, then.' Maggie chuckled and settled herself more comfortably in her chair. 'Never mind, it's an afternoon out and I've heard they gives us tea before we go. I'm going to stuff myself with all the cakes I can get – it might be my only chance!'

Phyl had eaten quite a large lunch after all, and was feeling much better, her natural perkiness restored. She looked about her, as bright-eyed as a wren, wondering which of the girls would be chosen and if they would be pleasant to work with. Shirley, sitting next to her, seemed a nice girl, if a bit on the quiet side, and that plump Maggie sounded as if she'd be fun, even if she was a bit greedy. Phyl grinned to herself, wondering if the customers would get all they'd ordered or if half of it would have been sampled on the way from the kitchen!

'They're starting to call us in,' Jo said suddenly. 'That girl that spoke to us on the way in's gone already. Look, Phyl, let's arrange to meet at the main door if we don't come back in here, shall we? It'd be daft not to know where we're both going to be.'

'Didn't that fat girl say there'd be tea?' Phyl asked. 'We'll see each other there.'

'That's only if you're picked. Suppose one of us isn't? Suppose neither of us is? By the main door, all right?' Jo was sounding nervous now, her voice a little higher than usual. 'Listen – they've just called in someone whose name starts with H. That means it won't be long before it's our turn.'

Phyl opened her mouth to reply, but before she could speak she heard her own name called. 'Phyllis Jennings?'

She started and looked at Jo frantically, but Jo pushed her to her feet and muttered, 'Go on, Phyl. Good luck.' And she found herself walking across the room, feeling as if all eyes were upon her.

The woman who had called her name was tall and slender in her uniform. She smiled at Phyl and led her along the passage to a panelled door. Inside, Phyl found herself facing two women and a youngish man sitting behind a long, glossy table. She sat down in the chair indicated and folded her hands across the handbag on her lap, hoping that her nervousness didn't show.

'Miss Jennings?' The older woman, who had dark hair, fashionably done in marcel waves, looked at her appraisingly. 'Let me just introduce your interviewers. I'm Miss Rumsby, this is my colleague Miss Turgoose, and this is Mr Young. Now, there's nothing to feel nervous about. We're just going to have a little chat to find out if you'd be suitable as a Nippy. As you know, we do take great care in choosing our Nippies because to our customers they're one of the most important features of a Corner House. They're the ones who speak to them, smile at them, take their orders and bring them their food. It's essential that the Nippies give a good impression, so that the customers will want to come back, again and again.' She frowned a little. 'You are eighteen, aren't you?'

'Yes, madam,' Phyl said. 'I was eighteen at the beginning of May.'

'And you've been working in a factory.'

'Yes, riveting and soldering. I've been there for nearly four years, ever since I left school.'

'And have you enjoyed your work?'

'Not much,' Phyl said frankly. 'That's why I've applied to be a Nippy.'

'Yes, I see. But you've stayed in the one job?'

'There aren't that many jobs about, madam. I was lucky to get it, I know that. But I'd like something better.'

'Better in what way? Better pay, do you mean? Or better conditions?'

Phyl frowned, thinking about it. 'Well, both really. I mean, that's what anyone would want. But mainly I think I want something better to *do*. Something more interesting – something where I can meet people and do something nice for them. People like being served good food,' she continued earnestly. 'It makes them feel better – happier. I think that's a good thing to be able to do. And the Corner Houses are lovely,' she finished ingenuously. 'Why, working in one of them would be better than working in Buckingham Palace!'

The man behind the table laughed. He was a few years younger than her father, she thought, with dark hair and blue eyes. 'Didn't you know that Nippies often do work at places like Buckingham Palace? We do the catering for the garden parties there. It isn't all Corner House work, you know.'

Phyl stared at him. 'No. I didn't know that. But you wouldn't want no one like me working at Buckingham Palace. I mean, you'd want your best girls for that.'

'And what makes you think that you couldn't be one of our best girls?' He smiled at her, then said, 'Take off your shoes and your hat, Miss Jennings.'

Phyl gaped again. 'My – my hat? My *shoes*?'

'That's right.' He smiled at her surprise. 'It's all right, we won't ask you to do any more than that. And now walk down to the other end of the room and back, would you? No, not as if you were running to catch a bus – as if you were going to a customer.'

Phyl closed her eyes for a moment. Without her hat and shoes, she felt vulnerable and exposed, and she was acutely conscious of her lack of height. The high-heeled shoes, bought specially, had been a waste of money – they were going to see now just how small she was. Well, she would just have to *imagine* herself tall, that's all! She squared her shoulders, imagined herself in a restaurant full of hungry customers and set out for the far end of the room.

It felt like miles, and it was worse coming back, knowing that the eyes of the three behind the table were upon her. Well, if she was going to fail, she thought, she might as well fail with a bit of style. She walked straight up to the table, smiled and said, 'Good afternoon, madam, good afternoon, sir. What would you like me to get for you?'

This time, although they looked a bit surprised, they all laughed, and Miss Turgoose, who had brought her from the other room, said, 'Very nicely done, Miss Jennings. Now you can put your hat and shoes back on and sit down again while we ask you a few more questions.'

The rest of the interview was more like the friendly chat they had promised. They called her Phyllis, and Phyl found herself telling them about her home and family, about Dad in the docks and Mum who stayed at home to look after them all, and her brothers Norman and Ronnie. She told them about Jo, too, and the fact that their mothers were twins. 'But we're not a bit alike,' she added. 'I'm like Mum and Auntie Carrie but Jo's tall like her dad.'

'Yes . . .' The lady with the marcel wave looked thoughtful. 'Now, Phyllis, I'll be quite honest with you. Apart from your height, you seem to be exactly the kind of girl we're looking for to carry on the tradition of Nippies. Bright, friendly without being too forward, and you've got a sense of humour. You'll need that with some of our customers, believe me! But, as you realise yourself, you are rather *petite*. And we do have to consider the size of our girls – partly because the work is quite heavy, carrying trays of food about all day long, and partly because we have our uniforms made to certain sizes. Just how tall are you?'

Phyl was tempted to add a couple of inches but discarded it at once. They only had to produce a tape-measure to prove her a liar, and that would be worse than being short. 'Five foot,' she said miserably, and then, remembering Jo's advice, 'but I'm still growing. I'm sure I am. And I'm really strong.'

'I'm sure you are,' the woman said kindly, 'but, you see, we don't normally take on girls under five feet two. Now, I'll tell you what we could suggest. Instead of starting as a Nippy, you could be given a job elsewhere on our staff – in the kitchen, perhaps, or as a counterhand – and then, when you've grown a bit taller, you can reapply. How would that suit you?'

Phyl gazed at them. This was just what she had dreaded – being put in the kitchen or on one of the counters. And suppose she didn't grow any more? As she'd told Jo, she hadn't put on an inch since she was fifteen, and it seemed hardly likely she'd suddenly start shooting up now. On the other hand, even being on the counter or in the kitchen would be better than working in the factory, and at least she'd be in London, near all the theatres, and with Jo.

'All right,' she said, making up her mind. 'So long as I can still be a Nippy later on – if I grow, of course. So long as I don't get forgotten.'

They smiled at her and Mr Young said, 'I don't think you need fear being forgotten, Miss Jennings. It'll take me quite a while to forget you offering to serve me just now, as it is! You come back as soon as you think you've grown, and we'll be only too pleased to make you a Nippy. And meanwhile – thank you very much for coming, and we hope you'll be very happy working for J. Lyons.'

They all stood up and the younger woman came round the table to guide her out of the room. Phyl, hardly knowing whether to be pleased or sorry, followed her and found herself in another room, where a table was laid with sandwiches and cakes.

There was nobody she knew in the room yet and she took a plate of food and sat down next to a smartly dressed girl in a black costume and small, feathery hat. The girl had sharp, greenish eyes and glossy brown hair that rippled from beneath the feathers. She gave Phyl a look, as if assessing her suitability to sit in the next chair.

'Hello,' Phyl said uncertainly, feeling smaller than ever. 'How did you get on?'

'Well, I passed, of course. I wouldn't be here otherwise. They don't give out tea and cakes to the ones who were no good.' The sharp green eyes seemed to take in every detail of Phyl's appearance. 'I wouldn't have thought you were old enough yet.'

'I'm eighteen and two months,' Phyl said with dignity. She was reluctant to tell this girl the truth, even though she'd probably find out, and was relieved to see the door open and her cousin come in. 'Jo! I'm over here. Get yourself something to eat and come and sit down.'

Jo came over, grinning broadly, her plate piled with sandwiches. 'See? I told you we'd get through okay, didn't I? What did you do, lie about your height?'

Phyl made a face. 'No, they made me take off my shoes. And I can't be a Nippy – not yet, anyway. I told them I'd grow, and they said I could have a job in the kitchen or somewhere, and then go back when I'd got another couple of inches. But I never will,' Phyl ended, gazing miserably at her cousin. 'I know I'm not going to grow any more. I'll be stuck in the flipping kitchens for ever!'

'Wouldn't take you?' Jo echoed in dismay, while the green-eyed girl made an I-knew-it sort of sound. 'Oh, Phyl, I am sorry! What are you going to do? I don't know as I want to come if you're not going to be here, too.'

'Oh, I'll take whatever they offer me. It can't be worse than the factory, and at least I'll be in London and we can still share digs. And I'll do all I can to grow! Maybe some of those sports would help – netball and that sort of thing – to make me stretch. It's the uniform mostly, you see – they don't have my size. I've only got to get a little bit bigger.'

'It's not just that,' the green-eyed girl said. 'It's strength as well. I know someone who knows a Nippy and she says it's real hard work. You're on your feet all day long and you've got to be strong.'

'Well, you've got to be strong to work in a kitchen too,' Phyl retorted, 'so I'll soon be able to show 'em.' She turned back to Jo. 'I might even try my dad's idea and stand in a bucket of muck every night! I tell you what – I'm going to be a Nippy someday, no matter *what* happens! I *am*.'

Chapter Five

As Jo and Phyl had expected, it had been decided that they would need to live in lodgings nearer to the Corner House to which they had been assigned. Sympathy had been given to the fact that they were cousins and wanted to be together, and a week before they were due to start their training the two families went to see their landlady and view the room they were to share.

'Her name's Mrs Holt,' Jo told them. 'She only takes two girls at a time. She'll give us breakfast and supper, even when we're back late.'

'Yes, well, there'd better not be too much of that,' her father said sternly. 'Getting back late, I mean. I don't want you gadding around London at all hours.'

'I meant off late shift,' Jo said with dignity. 'But we'll want to go out in our spare time, Dad. I mean, you wouldn't expect us to come to London and never go out.'

'We won't be doing anything you wouldn't like,' Phyl put in, still half-afraid that her father would change his mind and say she couldn't go after all. It had taken a good deal of coaxing and promises of good behaviour to get him to agree, and she knew he still didn't really like the idea. 'And we'll be going to the social club at Sudbury mostly. It'll be just Lyons' employees there, so it's bound to be all right.'

'Well, yes, I suppose that'll be all right,' Bill allowed. 'But don't get going to nightclubs and things. You don't know what goes on in those places, nor what sort of people you'll meet.'

The girls glanced at each other and rolled their eyes. Before anyone could say more, they turned the corner into Elmbury Street and started to look for number 17.

'This is it,' Phyl said. 'The one with the little tree.'

They all stopped on the pavement and looked at the house. It was like all the others in the street, tall and thin, with a tiny forecourt and half a dozen steps running up to the front door. At the top of the steps, as Phyl said, there was a pot with a small round-topped tree growing in it. There was a bay window to one side of the door, hung with net curtains.

'The curtains look clean enough, anyway,' Carrie Mason said. 'And the step's been whitened.'

'I don't think Lyons would let us live in a slum,' Jo said with a grin. 'Come on, let's knock and see what it looks like inside. That's what we're really interested in after all – we're not going to be living on the steps!'

Phyl ran up the steps and lifted the black knocker. The door was the colour of mahogany and looked freshly varnished. Almost as if they've poshed it up just for us, she thought with a tiny giggle.

Mrs Holt proved to be a comfortable, middle-aged woman with her grey hair in a tidy bun, wearing just the sort of flowered cross-over apron that Carrie and May wore when at home. She had a nice summer dress beneath it and, as she led them through a passage covered with shining brown linoleum, the two mothers gave each other approving nods.

'This is the living-room,' she said, showing them into a back room stuffed with furniture – a small sofa and two armchairs, covered in figured brown moquette, a square dining-table pushed against a wall, a sideboard covered with framed photographs and a mantelpiece with dark brown statuettes of half-clad Grecian maidens at either end. The wallpaper had brown flowers on it and there were two old-fashioned pictures of women seated at tables while gentlemen stood nearby, and one of a stag standing on a rock in a wild valley surrounded by mountains. A wireless stood on a shelf in one of the fireplace alcoves.

The table was set for tea, with a plate of sandwiches and another of home-made rock cakes and jam tarts. Phyl glanced at it and gave Jo a nudge which Jo knew meant 'we'll be all right here'. She folded her mouth in a tiny grin of agreement.

'I gives the girls their breakfast and supper here,' Mrs Holt said, 'and they're welcome to sit here of an evening, or whenever they're at home. Some ladies expect their girls to stay in their own rooms, but that's not my way. I think they need a bit of home comfort, and I likes their company now I'm on me own. My hubby died two years ago, see, and it's been a bit quiet since then, what with my own girls having got married.'

'It looks very nice,' Carrie said politely.

'I'll put the kettle on for a cuppa tea,' Mrs Holt said. 'And while it's coming to the boil I'll take you upstairs and show you the bedroom and facilities. We've got an indoor lavatory, so there's no need to be going outside at night, and I brings the bath in every Friday night. I need a bit of a hand with that. The kitchen's nice and warm in winter, with the range going, so it's all cosy. The stairs is this way.'

The bedroom was large and had its own bay window, looking over the street. There were two beds, each covered with a patchwork quilt, two washstands, each with a large china jug and a bowl, and a wardrobe and chest of drawers. The wooden floor had a colourful home-made rug beside each bed, and the curtains had big pink flowers on them, to go with the pink-distempered walls.

Phyl and Jo looked at each other with sparkling eyes. The room was twice the size of their bedrooms at home, and as neat as a pin. They had never even been in a house with a bay window before, and here they had one in their own room! As one girl, they crossed to look down through the net curtains to the street, imagining themselves leaving each day to go to work, walking down those steps and along that road towards Marble Arch, amidst all the bustle of London yet with the stretching green acres of Hyde Park only just across the road.

'You feel all right about it now, don't you, Mum?' Jo asked later as they got on the bus to take them back home. 'You liked Mrs Holt and the room? We'll be ever so comfortable there, I'm sure we will.'

'So comfortable you'll never want to come home!' Carrie said ruefully, and then smiled. 'Yes, of course I liked Mrs Holt. She's a nice, sensible woman and she'll keep a good eye on you. And the house is clean and tidy, and that tea she gave us was lovely. If she feeds you like that, you'll have no cause to complain.'

Jo smiled with satisfaction and turned to her father. 'Dad? What did you think?'

'Well, the same as your mother. But it's up to you to see you take care of yourselves, mind. You can't expect a landlady to take the same care of you as your mother does, it's not reasonable. What you've got to do is remember the things you've been taught at home. That's what's most important.'

'I know, Dad. No nightclubs, and no late nights with strange gentlemen. We'll be so good, we'll be dull – how will that suit you?'

'There's no need to be cheeky,' her father began, but his wife put her hand on his arm and shook her head.

'She's only joking, Bill. She's just a bit excited, and no wonder. But they're good girls, both of them, you know they are. They won't forget their upbringing. We can trust our Jo and Phyl.'

Jo and Phyl, sitting together in the front seat of the bus, looked at each other and grinned with delight. They had no intention of doing anything their parents would have disapproved of, but at the same time they meant to have lots of fun in their new life. Working in a big place like a Lyons Corner House, with a lot of other young people, they were bound to. And there was the social club, too, with all the different activities that promised.

Phyl thought of the dances on Saturday nights, the amateur dramatic club, the socials and parties. Jo pictured the sports – she might be able to play tennis and hockey, and there was a

63

swimming-pool, too. She had learned to swim years ago, in a local reservoir by the river, and had once been taken to Brighton where she'd swum in the sea itself. They might even have a diving-board.

'It's going to be smashing,' Phyl said with a contented sigh. 'I just wish I was really going to be a Nippy from the start. But I will be one day, Jo. I'm set on it. I'll grow if I have to tie myself to the bed every night and stretch like being on a rack. I will, straight!'

Jo laughed. 'That's what you'll be if you do that,' she said. 'Straight! You'll get there, Phyl. I know you will. And then we can work together all the time. I tell you what – we're going to have some real larks. I just know we are.'

The girls were to start on the same day, but even as they left for work they were separated – Phyl to go straight to the kitchens of the Marble Arch Corner House, Jo to the training sessions for new Nippies at Orchard House, where they had gone for their interviews. Training would take three weeks, she had been told, and then she would be assigned to a Corner House. Because it had been promised that she and Phyl could stay together, she knew from the start that she, too, would be going to Marble Arch.

The first person she saw was the green-eyed girl who had sat next to them after their interviews. She had already told them her name was Irene Bond and she was dressed just as smartly as she had been the first time Jo had seen her. I bet she's marked out for a supervisor, or even a manageress, Jo thought. She looks as though she thinks she's one already!

'We're supposed to sit at these tables during the lectures,' Irene told her in her rather sharp voice. 'Come and sit by me. Did your cousin go in the kitchens after all? I'd hate to do that – slaving all day over a hot stove and never seeing any customers. But then she's very small, isn't she?'

She made it sound as if being small was a sort of disease, or something Phyl did just to be awkward. Reluctantly, Jo sat down at the round table and then spotted two other familiar faces and waved.

'Maggie! Shirley! Come and sit with us.' She grinned as the big blonde girl and the slender dark one made their way across the room. 'You got through all right, then. I'm ever so pleased to see you. This is Irene.'

The girls nodded at each other and Maggie turned to Jo. 'Where's your sister? I was sure she'd get through the interview all right.'

'She's too short. They gave her a job in the kitchens instead and told her to grow! And she's not my sister, she's my cousin – our mums are twins.'

'Twins! Are they identical? Coo, that must be queer – never being quite sure if it's your mum or your auntie telling you off!' Maggie looked around the room, her face alight with interest. 'Here, what d'you think they're going to teach us at these here training sessions? I mean, it can't take three weeks to learn how to carry a tray, surely!'

'There's lots more than that to learn,' Irene said loftily. 'There's taking orders and working out the bill and – and learning how to walk, and—'

Maggie hooted with laughter. 'Well, that gives us a good start – we all know how to walk, don't we? Mind, I don't know about working out the bill – I was never much of a one for arithmetic. I can add up all right, but when it came to multiplying and long division I was a real dummy. And as for fractions – well!'

'You won't need to do long division and fractions,' Jo said. 'It'll just be adding up. You'll be all right.'

'It's talking to the customers I'm scared about,' Shirley said. She had a soft, pleasant voice, with less of a London accent than the other girls. 'I mean, taking orders is one thing, but suppose they start actually *talking* to you – asking questions and that. My friend who tried to be a Nippy said she knew someone who told her lots of the girls got dates with customers. I don't know what I'd say if someone asked me for a date!'

'Oh, I shouldn't think you need worry about that,' Irene said. 'I expect they go for the really pretty girls.'

There was a short silence. Jo glanced at Shirley, afraid that she might see tears in the other girl's eyes, but Shirley was nodding in agreement, as though she herself didn't think she was pretty. Maggie, however, had other ideas.

'I think that's a mean thing to say,' she said hotly. 'Shirley's as pretty as any girl in this room, with that lovely dark hair and those big eyes. She's a lot prettier than some people I could mention!'

Irene flushed and opened her mouth to say something, but she was interrupted by a rapping sound and they all turned too see their lecturer standing at a lectern on a dais at the end of the room, holding a gavel. She was a tall woman wearing a soft brown dress with lace trimmings and tiny pearl buttons, and her face was calm and smiling. Within a few minutes, she had explained to them what the training sessions would involve – as well as lectures on the Corner Houses themselves and how they operated, they would be told how to take orders, how to load and carry their trays and how to set the tables, put the food before their customers and, if disaster befell, how to change a tablecloth without ever revealing the surface of the table.

'I've seen someone do that,' Jo whispered as they broke for coffee. 'It was like magic – but I don't believe I'll ever be able to manage it.'

'What's wrong with the surface of the tables anyway?' Maggie asked. 'They're not made of tin, are they? Or all stained and battered? Sounds a bit daft to me.'

'Well, you'd better not say so,' Irene retorted sharply. 'Just because we've got on the training course don't mean they'll necessarily take us on, you know – we've still got to pass the exams at the end. And even then, they're sure to want the ones who've got a bit of class about them – they're not interested in girls who've never seen a properly laid table before.'

Maggie took in a deep breath, as if she were about to explode, and Jo glanced at Shirley and sighed. She hoped the other two girls wouldn't spend the whole three weeks bickering. What looked like being fun could quickly become

66

tiresome if their companions were going to be at each other's throats all the time.

Shirley said gravely, 'I dare say we'll get lots of practice at changing tablecloths, and setting the tables and everything. And they'll probably show us pictures of knives and forks and all the rest of it, so that we'll recognise them when we see them again. Why, by the time we've finished the training, you won't be able to tell the difference between us and Princess Elizabeth and Margaret Rose!'

Irene coloured again and looked at Shirley suspiciously, but Shirley's face was completely serious. Without giving the other girl a chance to reply, she went on peaceably, 'Anyway, if they want us to be good at it, they're bound to take lots of trouble to teach us. And the exams are ages away, so let's just enjoy ourselves while we're here and learn as much as we can.'

'That's right,' Jo said. 'Even if we don't pass, it'll help us get jobs in other restaurants if we've had Lyons training.' All the same, she was determined to pass the exams so that she would be able to work at Marble Arch with Phyl. The idea of being a Nippy, born so casually on that May day of the Coronation, had by now really caught her imagination, and she thought she would break her heart if she didn't achieve her ambition.

The coffee-break was over and they went back to their tables to settle down for the next lecture. This afternoon, they would start practical work, being introduced to all the components of a table at a Lyons Corner House – sugar bowls, cruets, bottles of sauce – and shown what all the different kinds of cutlery were for. I'll never remember it all, thought Jo who was accustomed to just one knife, fork and spoon which were used for everything. I never realised there was so much in it.

All the same, she was looking forward to learning as much as she could. Already she knew that working as a Nippy would be infinitely more interesting and exciting than weighing potatoes in a greengrocer's shop.

*

While Jo was trying to master the complications of table settings and cutlery, Phyl was donning a white overall and cap in the big, noisy kitchen of the Marble Arch Maison Lyons. It was a completely different world from the palatial surroundings of the restaurants, with their glittering lights, their carpeted floors and glamorous décor. Here, all was functional with clean, hard surfaces and a tiled floor, and instead of the sound of music played by a small orchestra or gipsy band all you could hear was the clattering of pans, the rattle of crockery and the constant tap-tap of busy feet.

'You're a bit small, aren't you?' observed the woman whose assistant Phyl was to be. Phyl said nothing, thinking that if anyone else said anything about her size she'd prove to them that she could still swing a pretty powerful punch, learned from Norman when he'd taken up boxing . . . 'Still, as long as you're quick and can do as you're told we shall get along all right . . . My name's Mrs Martin and I'm in charge of the grill. We do the cooking as it's ordered, so it's all fresh – no soggy toast or rubber bacon – but there's a few short cuts we can use so the customer doesn't have to wait too long. That's what you've got to remember all the time, see – we might never catch a glimpse of 'em, but there's customers upstairs in the restaurants, all wanting a bite to eat and wanting it up to scratch, and it's our job to give 'em what they wants.' She pushed out her lips and blew through them. 'It might be those Nippies what gets all the credit, but they wouldn't be able to serve the food if we hadn't cooked it first, and it's up to us how good it is so, you see, *we're* the important ones at a Corner House!'

'It's a Nippy I want to be,' Phyl said. 'I'm going to apply again as soon as I've grown a bit.'

'Well, we'll see about that,' Mrs Martin said. 'You might not want to when you've worked in the kitchen for a bit. There's a lot worse things you can do than learn to cook, my girl, and it'll stand you in good stead when you gets married.'

She took Phyl on a tour of the kitchen, showing her the different counters where meat, fish and vegetables were prepared and the ovens and hobs where the cooking was done. When all was ready, the food was collected by the Nippies from a long counter where they loaded their trays, and then it was taken for the prices to be checked before being carried out to the waiting customer. It all happened swiftly and efficiently, the cooks and serving girls ladling main courses and puddings on to plates, and the Nippies passing in a never-ending procession, in through one door, out through the other, so that there were no collisions, and then back again for the next order.

'You can start with toast,' Mrs Martin said, leading Phyl back to the grill. 'Try and make sure you cut the bread all the same thickness, and don't let the loaf go crooked or you'll end up with slices like door-wedges, thick one end and thin the other. Then you grill it all on one side only, see? Make sure you've always got a good pile ready.'

'Only one side?' Phyl tried to remember the toast she and Jo had eaten when they had high tea on the day of the coronation. 'But I thought—'

'I told you, we got a few short cuts. When you gets an order, like cheese on toast, or poached eggs, all you got to do is grill the *second* side, see? That way, it don't take no time at all and it's nice and hot for the customer. We always got a few eggs on the go, and Etty here's busy grating cheese and putting the bacon on the grill ready, so all the ordinary things can be delivered within a few minutes. You can't get no quicker than that.'

'No, I see.' Phyl's heart sank at the thought of doing nothing all day but slice bread and make toast, but the cheese-grating girl, Etty, gave her a timid smile and said, 'It ain't so bad really. Mostly, we're on the go so much the time flies by. It's a bit hard on the legs at first, mind, unless you're used to standing all day.'

Phyl picked up her breadknife and a loaf of bread, baked in the Corner House's own kitchen. She looked at it doubtfully, but before she could begin to slice Mrs Martin was beside her again.

'No, don't hold it like that, against your chest – it's not hygenic. Hold it this way and just let the knife go through it gently – you're not cutting down trees. Don't worry if the first few are a bit crooked – we'll use them for breadcrumbs. You'll soon get the hang of it with a bit of practice.' She watched as Phyl sawed earnestly at the bread and then nodded and moved off to talk to someone else.

Phyl gave Etty a rueful look. 'I never expected cutting bread to be something I had to learn! I can see there's more to this job than I thought. I suppose there's a knack to grating cheese as well!'

Etty glanced at her hands. 'I suppose there is. I used to grate my fingers as much as the cheese till I got used to it.' She was even smaller than Phyl, without Phyl's sturdiness, and rather plain, with sallow skin and brown hair under her cap. Her eyes were brown, too, and her smile diffident, as if she thought she might get into trouble if she let her mouth widen too much. She looks scared of her own shadow, Phyl thought, and felt half scornful, half pitying. Still, she was someone to talk to and she must know more about Corner Houses than Phyl did.

'Have you worked here long?' she asked, sawing away at the bread. 'Did you apply to be a Nippy or did you want to be in the kitchens? I wanted to be a Nippy, but they said I'm too short.'

'Oh, I'd never dare try to be a Nippy!' Etty said, as if she had been advised to apply for the position of Queen. 'I couldn't do what they do – speaking to the customers and that! And I'd be bound to drop something.'

'I don't know,' Phyl said, watching the small fingers working neatly and efficiently at the cheese-grater. 'You don't look clumsy.'

'I'm not. I'd just be too scared. I'd be afraid of forgetting things.' Etty pushed the huge bowl of grated cheese to one side and began to lay out strips of bacon. Her movements were swift and economical. Someone called out behind her, the words spoken so quickly that Phyl didn't have time to register them, but Etty obviously did because she immediately thrust a tray of bacon and some sliced potatoes under the hot grill, and looked around for toast.

70

'Oh, crumbs, I forgot to put any underneath!' Phyl had been concentrating so much on getting her slices even that she'd forgotten they were to be toasted. Scarlet with confusion, she shoved several pieces of bread under the grill, and Etty gave her a look and pulled out the tray. Dismayed, Phyl saw that she'd plonked her bread down right on top of the bacon and potatoes.

'That's your side, there,' Etty said, picking the bread off. 'We'll be late with that order now. Never mind, they know you're new so we won't get into trouble this time.'

'Are they very strict?' Phyl asked nervously. 'What happens if you get into trouble – do they take off your pay or something?'

'Well, not much, actually,' Etty admitted, taking a warm plate from an overhead rack. 'I mean, they're strict and keep us on our toes, but they're fair as well. It's only if you really slack that they get annoyed – they won't stand for slacking.'

'Well, I'm not going to slack,' Phyl said with determination. 'I'm going to really impress them, so they can see what a good Nippy I'd make and put me upstairs as soon as possible.' She looked again at Etty. Small and plain she might be, but she was neat and quick with her movements, and she had a nice smile when she forgot to be timid. 'And I reckon you could do it, too. Let's make a pact, shall we? We'll both try to be Nippies, and not only that we'll be the *best* Nippies. What d'you say?'

Etty stared at her. Her pale face flushed, touched with soft, rosy colour, and her pale eyes brightened. Why, she could look quite pretty if she wanted to, Phyl thought in astonishment, and felt ashamed of her initial scorn.

'D'you really think I could?' Etty asked in a whisper. 'D'you really think I could be a Nippy and work in the restaurant and serve real customers? D'you really think so?'

'Of course I do—' Phyl began, and then jumped guiltily as a sharp voice sounded behind them and Etty turned hurriedly back to her work, her face now flushed scarlet.

'Nippies! You two won't last long enough to be Nippies, nor even to go on working in my kitchen if you don't stop

71

nattering and get on with your work. Phyllis, that loaf looks more like my front doorstep than a slice of bread and, Etty, there's a customer outside dying of starvation waiting for his breakfast. Come on now! You can talk while you have your dinner.'

'Sorry, Mrs Martin,' Etty said, all her timidity returning, and Phyl, feeling almost as abashed, muttered her own apology and started on a new loaf. All the same, she thought, concentrating on straight edges, I *will* do it, you see if I don't, and I'll take young Etty with me. I'm blowed if I'm going to spend *my* life slicing bread and grating cheese.

Chapter Six

The shift over, the girls went back to the dressing room and took off their uniforms. Phyl hung hers in the cupboard next to Etty's and leaned her head against the inside of the door for a moment.

'I'd never have thought I could be so tired,' she declared. 'I mean, all I've done all day is slice bread and shove it under the grill, and I feel like I've been up Everest and back. My legs are going to be as stiff as tree trunks in the morning.'

'I felt like that when I started,' Etty nodded. 'I've got used to it now, but I'm still thankful to sit down when I gets back home.' She slipped into a cotton frock and a pair of worn shoes, and picked up a shabby handbag, trying not to look at the summer skirt and white blouse Phyl's mother had made her.

Phyl glanced at her curiously. Etty had looked better dressed in her uniform, she thought. That frock looked as if it had been washed a hundred times, its printed pattern faded into a soft blur, and the collar was starting to fray. And the heels of her shoes were breaking down. She felt surprised that Lyons allowed a girl to come to work looking so poor.

'Where d'you live?' she asked. 'With your family, or in digs? We could walk along together if it's the same way.'

'Oh, it's not,' Etty said hastily. 'And I don't walk, I go on the bus.' She gave Phyl a tremulous smile and half turned towards the door. 'I'll miss it if I don't hurry up. I'll see you tomorrow.'

'All right,' Phyl answered, puzzled. 'See you tomorrow.' She followed Etty out of the door, wondering why the other girl had been in such a hurry and why she hadn't wanted Phyl to go with her and, more than that, why she'd been so definite that their ways led in different directions. *I never told her where Jo and me were staying,* Phyl thought, *I'm sure I never mentioned it. So how could she know it wasn't the same way?*

The puzzle didn't occupy her for long, however. She was too eager to get back to Elmbury Street, and to Jo, to worry about the pale little girl who'd stood beside her all day grating cheese, with barely a word to say for herself.

'Honestly, it's like working with a mouse,' she told Jo later as they shared a cup of tea in their new bedroom. She giggled. 'I must say, they gave her the right job – grating cheese! I mean, she seems nice enough but she just doesn't have anything much to say for herself, and if you make a joke she looks as if she's frightened to laugh. I can't make her out.'

'Well, never mind.' Jo curled her long legs up underneath her on the patchwork counterpane. 'You'll have plenty of time to find out. Not that you'll be in the kitchen for long,' she added, seeing Phyl's crestfallen face. 'We'll make you grow if we have to hire a special machine to do it! But it's not too bad, is it? It's better than the factory?'

'Oh, yes. Well, it will be when I get used to the standing.' Phyl bent forward and rubbed her calves, groaning. 'Honestly, Jo, if our Dad knew how tired I was going to get he'd never have worried for a single minute about me going out on the town! I haven't even got the energy to walk downstairs for supper.'

'You will have, once you've drunk that cup of tea. I must say, Mrs Holt's really turned up trumps, having that tray ready for us, with biscuits and cake and all.' Jo reached out for another shortbread finger. 'They did us well at the training, mind. We had coffee in the morning and a smashing lunch and then tea and cakes in the afternoon, but I still feel as if I could eat a horse. I'll be as fat as Maggie Pratt if I go on like this.'

'Was she there? Tell me all about it, Jo.' Phyl sat up,

cradling her cup between her hands, her face alight with eager wistfulness. 'Oh, I *wish* we could be training together – but I'll get there, Jo, I swear I will. So tell me what you did. Tell me everything.'

Jo settled back against her pillow and smiled. 'Oh, Phyl, it was smashing. So *interesting*. I mean, you'd never think there was so much to learn about carrying a tray – loading it up to start with, putting everything on in the right order so that when you set the things on the table they're in the right place, walking at just the right pace, not going slow but not hurrying either – and then taking everything off and putting it on the table without spilling things or jogging the customer or reaching across in front of them. And making sure the teapot's in front of the right person – the woman if there's just one, or the oldest woman if there's more, unless she's really old – I reckon we could spend the whole three weeks just learning all the ins and outs of that, never mind anything else!'

'So what else is there to learn? How about setting the tables?'

'Oh, yes, there's that, of course. What cutlery goes where, and how to fold napkins and fill up the cruets – that's a job we have to do every time we go off shift, ready for the next girl. And we have to look after the cutlery, too, make sure it's all polished and shining and there's no bits of egg stuck in the forks – not that there ever is, Miss Frobisher says, or heads would roll in the kitchens!'

'They would too,' Phyl said. 'The Master Chef at Marble Arch is a real tartar, so Etty told me, and Mrs Martin wouldn't stand for any sloppiness.'

'None of them would. It's standards, standards, standards all the time. And that's why Lyons have got their reputation,' Jo said earnestly. 'It starts right at the bottom and works its way right through to the top. Or the other way around. Whatever job you've got, it's got to be done the best possible way and then there's no cause for complaint.'

Phyl was silent for a minute or two. Jo was right, she thought. Even the bread had to be sliced and toasted exactly right, the cheese grated to a mouth-watering fineness, the eggs cooked to a perfection of golden yolk, and the bacon grilled to a subtle blend of crisp juiciness . . . Even the most tedious of jobs wasn't so bad when you worked to get each part to a standard. All the same, she still didn't want to spend her life in the kitchens. She wanted to be out there with Jo, 'nipping' back and forth, serving the customers and enjoying the company of a constant flow of human beings.

'Tell you what, Jo,' she said, 'why don't you teach me? Every night when we come back, you show me what you've been doing. If I practise, when I apply again I'll be able to show them just what a good Nippy I'll be!'

Jo gave her a comical look. 'You mean I've got to go through it all over again? I thought you were exhausted!' Then she grinned and uncurled herself from the bed. 'Okay, then. We'll start now. We'll go downstairs and borrow one of Mrs Holt's trays and I'll show you how to load it up and you can serve me, just as if I was a customer! And then I reckon we'll forget about going out on the town, just for tonight, eh? I reckon I'm going to be ready for bed.'

Gradually, the girls got used to their new way of life and, although they still came home tired each evening, they agreed that the move from their previous jobs had been a good one. Passing her new knowledge on to Phyl gave Jo a chance to practise what she had learned and made them feel they were sharing their new experiences, and the evenings were filled with gossip about new friends.

'That Maggie's a real star turn,' Jo said. 'I knew she would be. Mind, they're going to have to watch the cake-stands, or she'll never stop eating! Miss Frobisher said today she'll have the cost docked from her wages if she can't stop, and Maggie told her in that case she'd have to start paying to work there! But she knows she's not allowed to eat on duty.'

'Maybe it'll help her lose weight,' Phyl said. 'What about the girl with the dark hair? I liked her.'

'Shirley Wood, you mean. Oh, yes, she's all right. Quiet, but not sly like some quiet ones are. And sometimes she's really funny, only you'd never think so to look at her face – keeps it straight as a poker. The one I'm not so keen on is Irene – Irene Bond, you know, all dressed up like a dog's dinner and thinks she's Lady Muck. She's all smiles and smarm when Miss Frobisher or any of the other demonstrators are around, but behind their backs she's a spiteful little cat. But she does the work all right, and as long as she treats the customers properly I suppose she'll pass. She doesn't mean to be a Nippy for long, though – aiming for higher things, I reckon she is.'

'I'm going to apply as soon as I can,' Phyl said. 'If only I could grow a bit! D'you reckon doing sports and things would help, Jo? Maybe if we started going to the club at Sudbury I could build myself up a bit.'

'It's good food that'll build you up,' Mrs Holt said, coming into the room with a tray. She began to set plates of steaming steak-and-kidney pudding on the table, with a dish of vegetables. 'And what happened to my Nippy tonight, then? I've got used to having a slave.'

'Sorry,' Phyl said, scrambling out of the chair where she had sunk almost as soon as the girls had arrived home. 'I just felt so tired, once I'd sat down I couldn't move. We were on our feet all day long, Etty and me. I reckon I must have grilled about a thousand cheese on toasts. She looked even more tired than me when we left.'

'Have you found out where she lives yet?' Jo enquired as they sat down at the table. 'Or is she still the mystery girl?'

Phyl frowned and speared a piece of succulent kidney with her fork. 'Mmm. That's *gorgeous* . . . No, she hasn't let on a word. Funny little scrap, she is. I thought I'd have got to know her a bit better by now, but it's almost as if she was scared to let anyone know anything about her. Or thinks she's not worth knowing. But that's daft – everyone's worth knowing.'

'Not Irene Bond,' Jo said darkly, and soaked a piece of light suet crust in the thick, meaty gravy. 'Mind you, I bet she'd soon worm it out of Etty – she's as nosy as a cat, as well as spiteful. Likes to know everything, she does, just in case she can find out something to store up against you!'

Mrs Holt came back into the room and sat down to eat her own supper. 'I heard that, young Josephine, and I won't have you talking about cats in that way. My Tibby's as gentle a creature as anyone could wish, as well you know. Never been spiteful in her life and as for being nosy, that time she got shut in your cupboard was nobody's fault but your own. I don't know what this Irene's done to upset you, but I think you ought to find some other animal to compare her with.'

Jo grinned and winked at Phyl. 'You're dead right, Mrs Holt. What about a snake? Is that nasty enough for you? Or a spider? Or a crocodile, or a—'

'I don't think you ought to be talking about people in that way at all,' Mrs Holt said firmly. 'It doesn't sound nice. Just because you don't hit it off with this girl—'

'*Nobody* does, Mrs Holt! You ought to see the airs she gives herself. Thinks the rest of us are common as muck, and doesn't trouble to hide it. Honestly—'

'Well, to my mind we were put on this earth to learn to get on with each other,' the landlady said, 'otherwise Heaven's not going to be half such a nice place as they say. And I think it's time you two stopped calling me Mrs Holt. Auntie, that's what all my girls have called me. Auntie Holt. It's friendlier.'

Jo and Phyl looked at each other. 'Auntie Holt,' Phyl said, tasting the sound of the words. 'It's nice. I'd like that.'

'But wouldn't you rather wait till you know we're going to stay?' Jo asked. 'I mean, I might not pass the exam and Phyl might not grow. We might get fed up and go back home – or move on somewhere else.'

'Not pass the exam!' Mrs Holt said scornfully. 'Of course you'll pass the exam. And as for Phyl growing – well, we'll make her taller if we have to play tug of war with her every night from now till Christmas! You'll be Nippies all right, the pair of you – you mark my words.'

Phyl, however, did not grow. And the worst of it was that Etty did. Nobody noticed it at first, until one day in September when Phyl was standing beside her in the dressing room and realised suddenly that she was having to look up slightly to meet the other girl's eyes.

'Here! Have you got new shoes on?' She glanced down and saw with further dismay that Etty was actually standing in her stockinged feet. 'You – you're *taller*! You're *growing*!'

'I know,' Etty admitted shamefacedly. 'I'm sorry – I didn't realise it myself till I put on my winter skirt. I don't know why it's happened.'

'Well, obviously because you haven't stopped yet,' Phyl said in exasperation. 'There's no need to talk as if you've committed some sort of crime. But you're taller than me now – I used to be able to look down on you.'

'I think it must be the food here. I really thought I'd stopped. I was always small at – at home,' she said, stumbling over the words and flushing. 'They—Nobody thought I'd get much bigger.'

Phyl looked at her curiously, but she was too concerned with Etty's sudden growth spurt to follow up her words. 'How tall d'you reckon you're going to get? Are your parents tall?'

To her surprise, Etty flushed an even deeper red and snatched her coat from the hanger. The autumn days had cooled suddenly and there had even been a frost over the past two mornings. Most of the girls had started to wear thicker jackets or coats, but Etty was still in her flimsy summer macintosh. She pulled it around herself and did up the buttons with shaking fingers.

'I'll have to go. My bus—' She turned away, but Phyl laid her hand on the sleeve of the macintosh. Etty's arm still felt painfully thin inside it, despite her growth, and Phyl felt a sudden concern for her.

'Look, you don't have to rush off, surely. Why don't we go and have a cup of tea in the canteen? You won't be in trouble if you don't go straight home, will you?'

Etty hesitated, clearly in an agony of indecision. Phyl could see that she wanted to come, yet something held her back, some fear at which Phyl couldn't guess. What on earth was wrong with staying for a cup of tea? she wondered. Etty was eighteen, she wasn't a baby – surely she had some say over how she spent her free time.

'It's not that,' Etty said uncertainly. 'It's just, well, I always do go straight back – straight home, I mean.'

'Will your mum worry about you? Let's make it tomorrow, then. You tell her you'll be back a bit later and we'll have a good old chinwag. We're so busy all day, we never get time.'

Etty looked even more uncomfortable. 'No – she won't worry. I mean, I haven't – I just never do. Nobody's ever asked me before—'

'Well, I'm asking you now,' Phyl said cheerfully. 'And I'll tell you what – I'll ask you to supper over at our place one evening, if you'd like to come. I'm sure Mrs Holt wouldn't mind. She likes us to call her Auntie, me and Jo.' She smiled. 'Come on! Your mum and dad won't mind, will they? And then you can tell me the secret of how to grow!'

Etty gave an uncertain smile. She glanced at the door, obviously still desperate to get away, and this time Phyl let her go, though not without reminding her of the invitation.

'You tell 'em you'll be a bit late tomorrow, and I'll ask Mrs Holt if you can come over to supper one evening. Perhaps you could even stop the night, if it's too far for you to go back.'

'Yes – no – I'll have to see – I *must* go now . . .' Like a frightened rabbit, Etty scuttled out of the door, leaving Phyl frowning thoughtfully after her.

She still didn't know where the other girl lived, she thought, nor anything else about her. All she knew was that something about being invited out had scared Etty – and it didn't make sense.

There's something wrong there, she thought. And I'm not being nosy, but I mean to find out what it is. That girl needs friends, and she could do a lot worse than start with Jo and me.

Etty found a seat on the crowded bus and sat looking out of the window, scarcely seeing the familiar landmarks it was passing. Her thoughts were a tangle of delight and fear and indecision, and she almost missed her stop. The bus was just about to pull away from the stop outside the tall building with its big front door and many windows when she realised where she was and leapt up, pushing her way frantically to the back.

'Come on, love, wake up,' the conductor said, giving her a friendly push. 'I shouted twice, you know.'

'I'm sorry – I was thinking about something else . . .' She half jumped, half fell to the pavement and stood catching her breath as the big red bus pulled away. A few other girls had got off with her and they pushed past, eager to get indoors, giving Etty no more than a brief hello as they passed. She knew them all, but she couldn't call any of them real friends.

Now Phyl Jennings was something different. She was the sort who would be a real friend – if she liked you enough. In the past few weeks, as they had worked side by side at the grill, Etty had begun to dare to hope that Phyl actually did like her. And now she'd actually suggested taking Etty back to her digs, to have supper and meet her cousin! It seemed almost too good to be true.

Still half-lost in her dream, Etty made her way up the steps of the hostel and into the bare hallway. It wasn't a bad place to live. Run by the Girls' Friendly Society, it was home to a good many girls who worked in London, far from their own homes, and although it couldn't be called exactly homely, it was comfortable enough, with a big sitting-room filled with armchairs and a sofa or two – all fairly worn and shabby – and a large dining-room where meals were served. The girls shared bedrooms, some between three or four, others with as many as six, and there were a few single rooms on the top floor, occupied by older women who had lived at the hostel for years and called their jobs 'being in business' and looked down on the younger ones.

Etty had been at the hostel for four years now. She shared a room with two other girls, Pat and Cora, who were friends and didn't take much notice of her. She lived like a mouse in the corner of the room, taking up as little space as possible, keeping her narrow bed and tiny chest of drawers unobtrusively tidy, using only a tiny part of the communal wardrobe for her meagre collection of clothes. The only ornament she had on her shelf was a seashell she had picked up years ago on her one visit to the seaside at Brighton, and she spent her time reading the romantic novels she got each week from the public library.

The hostel's communal washroom boasted a bath, claw-footed and rather rough on the bottom, surrounded by a curtain so that girls could bathe in privacy. You were allowed one bath a week, and there was a rota pinned up on the wall. Etty's turn was on Monday, the least popular evening – everyone wanted Friday or Saturday, for the weekend – but Etty didn't mind. In fact, it never occurred to her to mind. She was too accustomed to being at the end of the queue, the bottom of the heap. The merest hint of rebellion had always sent her cringing into her corner, hoping not to be seen.

Yet in the past few weeks there had stirred somewhere within Etty a tiny spark of something too indefinite yet to be recognised. A quivering of life, a tendril of curiosity that reached up towards the light. The minutest spark of a personality that had seemed to be entirely buried by years of repression.

It was Phyl who had brought this about. Phyl had come into the Corner House kitchen with the bright, breezy assumption that Etty was just as much worth knowing as anybody else. She'd looked at Etty properly, not like most people did, dismissing her with a single glance, but as if she liked her and wanted to be friends. She'd talked to her and she'd listened to what Etty had to say – little though it was – and she'd made Etty feel like a real person, rather than an insubstantial ghost who flitted past and was immediately forgotten.

And now she had asked her to supper. Phyl Jennings, as bright and perky as a wren, who could have asked anyone in the whole Corner House, had asked her, Etty Brown, to supper! She had even said that she might stay the night.

Mind, I couldn't do that, Etty thought, taking her bar of

Lifebuoy soap and her flannel to the washroom. I couldn't stay the night – I wouldn't dare. I wouldn't know how to behave, I wouldn't know what to do when I went to bed or when I got up in the morning, I wouldn't know what to do if I wanted to spend a penny in the middle of the night . . . But to go to *supper*. In a real house, with small rooms and only a few people living there, to a meal cooked for just four in a proper kitchen, with everyone helping wash up afterwards . . . She, Etty Brown, who had never done such a thing in her life, not that she could remember, who had never sat in an ordinary back room or looked out at an ordinary back yard . . . That was excitement enough.

Still in a dream, Etty went down to the big, noisy dining room for the hostel supper. With the other girls and women she queued for a plate of meat pie and vegetables, ate them in her accustomed place at the end of the long table, queued again to wash her plate in a large bowl of scummy water, softened with a lump of soda, queued for stewed plums and thin custard and then queued for a fourth time to wash her bowl. In a dream, she drank a glass of water and then went into the communal sitting room to read her book while the other girls knitted, played Ludo or listened to the wireless.

For once, however, she could not concentrate on the dark and dashing hero, or on the slender, fair-haired heroine with her elfin features and soft, tremulous sighs. Their glamorous surroundings failed, for once, to awaken her heart. Instead, she dreamed of an ordinary house, in an ordinary street, and a plain, home-cooked supper with girls who treated her like a person. Like a friend.

'I tell you,' Phyl said forcefully, 'she's a good two inches taller than me now. She's growing – she admits it herself. I mean, she must be – it's not likely I'm shrinking, is it? Or maybe I am,' she added dolefully. 'Maybe that's what it is, I'm getting smaller and smaller. One day I'll disappear altogether.'

'No such luck,' Jo said bracingly. 'We won't get rid of you as easy as that, our Phyl. Look, I don't know why you're making such a song and dance about it. If she can grow, so can you. She's eighteen, isn't she? 'Same as us?'

'She's a month older than me. Oh, it isn't *fair!*' Phyl exclaimed. 'Etty doesn't even want to be a Nippy, not really – or she didn't, before I put the idea into her head. And here she is, growing like a weed, while I haven't budged an inch. Not an *inch*.'

'Are you sure? I thought you looked a bit taller yesterday—'

'I had my heels on then. Of course I looked taller. Oh, what am I going to do?' Phyl gazed at her cousin despairingly. 'I *know* I'd be good at the job. I've learnt all the things you've shown me, I've practised here – I could be a Nippy tomorrow. And all I need is two extra inches. Two inches! It's not a lot, is it? It's not as if I was a *dwarf*, for goodness' sake!'

Jo looked at her. Comical in her despair, Phyl was playing it for laughs, but inside Jo knew she was really disappointed. And even now, envious though Phyl might be of Etty's sudden spurt, she wasn't really jealous. She didn't begrudge Etty her good luck – she just wanted to share it.

'Is Etty going to apply?'

Phyl shrugged. 'I don't know. I think she wants to now, but I think she's too scared to do it on her own. If we could apply together – but we can't, and that's all there is to it. She'll probably funk it and stay in the kitchen.'

'Well,' Mrs Holt said, coming in with a pot of tea, 'maybe that's what's best for her after all. If she's as shy as you say, she might not be happy out in front anyway.'

Phyl nodded thoughtfully. 'I suppose so. I just get the feeling that she's a different person inside. As if she's been pushed down all her life and doesn't even know what she's like herself. She looks like a little mouse, but when she smiles she looks quite different. Really pretty. I'd just like to find out what she's really like.'

'You be careful,' Mrs Holt warned. 'It don't do no good, meddling in other people's lives. Stir up a whole hornets' nest, you can, poking your nose in where it's not wanted.'

Jo laughed. 'Coo, that sounds nasty! You'd better listen to what Auntie says, Phyl, you don't want hornets up your nose.

84

Worse 'n bees, they are. Anyway, you bring her home here to supper one night and we'll see what we think. You might be in for a surprise – she might not be such a little mouse when she gets away from the Corner House.'

'All right, I will,' Phyl said. 'And when we've finished this cup of tea you can show me again how to set the table for a full dinner. I still haven't quite got the hang of all those different knives and forks. To tell you the truth, I don't see the point of them all. One lot's good enough for everything, without being all fancy with funny shapes and different sizes and all that.'

'Well, don't you ever let Miss Frobisher hear you say that,' her cousin cautioned her. 'Nippies are supposed to act as if they've been brought up proper. If she thinks you don't take the job seriously you'll be out on your ear and back making cheese on toast before you can say fish-knives!'

'Oh, I shan't say a word,' Phyl declared. 'I've told you, Jo, I'm going to be the best Nippy they've ever had – if only I can *grow*!'

Chapter Seven

Jo flew out of the front door, her long legs sprinting as if she were in one of the races at the Sudbury Lyons Club sports day. Phyl was already turning the corner ahead of her, and as Jo caught up she turned and grinned.

'You'll meet yourself coming back one of these days. What happened this time?'

'Strap come off me petticoat, and then I couldn't find a needle, and when I did I couldn't thread it! More haste, less speed, as Mum always says. Anyway, it's all right now.'

They walked swiftly through the autumn morning towards Marble Arch. In Hyde Park the great trees were clothed in a glory of bronze and gold, swathed in drifting scarves of chiffon mist, and the railings gleamed wet with dew. Autumn crocuses and tiny mauve and white cyclamen carpeted the ground beneath them, and the cherry trees which had been a froth of pink and white on that May day when the girls had come to London to see the Coronation were now the colour of burgundy. The sun shone through a milky haze and there was a smell of fresh, wet earth.

Jo took a deep breath, and smiled with pleasure. 'I don't care what anyone says, Phyl, London's a good place to be. I'm glad we decided to come and work here. All we need now is for you to be a Nippy, too, and it'll be perfect.'

'I'm going to go and see the board today,' Phyl told her as they came within sight of Marble Arch. 'I made up my mind during the night. I've made Etty apply and we'll go together.

They've got to take me this time, Jo! Mrs Martin will recommend me, I know.'

Jo looked at her doubtfully. 'What are you going to do – tell 'em you've grown?'

'I *have*. I'm sure I have. I measured myself last night. I'm sure I wasn't as high as that mark on the bathroom door last time I looked. And if I do my hair up a bit higher . . . It's only an *inch*, Jo. They can't let an inch make all that difference, surely.'

Jo looked at her and then grinned. She didn't have the heart to wipe that hopeful expression from her cousin's face, and she didn't think the interview board would have either. Phyl was a good worker, she was smart and pretty and crackling with personality – she was everything they wanted in a Nippy. She was right – she had to be right. They couldn't let a mere inch make so much difference.

'Course they can't!' she said heartily, and gave Phyl a slap on the shoulder as they hurried through the side door of the Corner House. 'You go and tell 'em, Phyl. You show 'em just what they'll be missing. You'll be a Nippy soon, sure as eggs are eggs.'

She went into the dressing room to leave her bag. The other girls were already there, taking off their coats and hats, but no one was changing into uniform yet – their first tasks, of laying clean tablecloths and setting out plates, cutlery and cruets, could all be done in their ordinary clothes. Then there were the menus to be stood like little booklets on each table and a final polish given to knives, forks and spoons. Napkins were folded and put in each place and the chairs placed at exactly the right angle to the tables, just far enough out to be easy to pull back yet not so far that they became a hindrance.

As the girls worked the floor superintendents watched, pointing out a speck on a knife here, a mark on a tablecloth there. Each of these errors would be remarked upon later, as the Nippies were given their daily instructions, and although the girl responsible wouldn't be named everyone tried to avoid being the cause of criticism. It didn't matter that the other Nippies didn't know who you were – the supervisors would, because every girl had her own set of tables, or 'station', and too many black marks would soon bring real reproof.

At last everything was ready and they all trooped back to the dressing room. Jo had been surprised to find that these weren't actually in the Corner House itself, but in another building, connected by an underground passage. It was dank, dark and rather chilly in the passage, despite the gaslamps, and each girl was provided with a cape to wear over her uniform.

In the dressing room, she changed out of her street clothes and into the uniform that was her pride and joy. It had cost one pound seven shillings to buy, but she hadn't had to pay outright; like everyone else, she had two shillings deducted from her wages each week to pay for it, and she also had to replace her cap every fortnight and get her white apron and collars washed every week at the nearby Chinese laundry. It didn't leave a lot out of her seventeen shillings and sixpence to pay for her keep at Mrs Holt's and send a bit back to her mother, but if she was lucky with her tips she usually found herself with almost as much again for spending money. Next year, her pay would go up – girls who had been there for a couple of years or more were getting over a pound now, some as much as twenty-five shillings – and she would be able to afford a few nice clothes and save a bit more for Christmas presents for the family.

'Oh, blast!' a voice near her exclaimed in exasperation. 'I've got a button loose. Anyone got a needle and thread?'

Jo looked round to see Maggie Pratt staring in dismay at one of the white buttons that made a double row down the front of her dress. The third one down was hanging by a thread and would obviously be off within five minutes.

Shirley Wood came to her rescue. 'Here you are – a needle already threaded with red cotton. I keep it ready all the time.' She produced a small 'housewife', a rolled cotton holdall with various sewing implements fitted into the little pockets. 'I suppose you caught it on a tray yesterday.'

'I did,' Maggie admitted, sewing rapidly. 'I felt it go. I meant to see to it then – but we were so busy—'

'You ought to check your uniform every evening, then you wouldn't have this panic,' Irene Bond told her. 'I always make sure all my buttons are on and there's no ladders in my stockings or anything like that. A stitch in time saves nine, that's what my mum always says.'

'All mums say that,' Maggie muttered. She wound her red cotton three times round the button, pushed the needle through the fabric and fastened it with three small stitches before snipping it off with Shirley's scissors. 'Thanks, Shirl. You're a pal.' Swiftly, she peeled off her skirt and jumper and struggled into her uniform. 'Coo, I reckon this frock's shrunk in the wash, it's getting proper tight.'

'Don't be daft,' Irene said scornfully. 'You know they don't shrink. You're getting fatter, that's what it is. Too many cream cakes in the canteen.' She smoothed her own dress down over her hips, turning this way and that to see as much as she could in the mirror. 'I reckon it looks real smart when it's worn properly by someone with a nice figure.'

She slipped her feet into her black shoes and walked off down the room. Maggie, now pushing her yellow hair under her cap, stared after her and curled her lip.

'Thinks a lot of herself, that one. Well, there's another thing *my* mum always says – pride goes before a fall. I reckon she could do well to remember that. Come on, then, let's get on with it. I'm starving for me dinner!'

Jo and Shirley looked at each other and grinned. Irene was undoubtedly right. Maggie was getting even fatter, but it wasn't that she was really greedy, just that she always seemed to be hungry. Worms, Irene had said cattily when Maggie had pointed this out, and when Maggie had said that she worked hard and needed her grub, Irene had told her that she only needed so much because she had all that extra weight to carry around. 'If you lost a bit of fat you wouldn't need to eat so much. You just need to go hungry for a few days and use it up – it would soon fall off.'

'Thanks very much,' Maggie retorted. 'I don't think I want

bits falling off, and I'm sure I don't want to look like a beanpole, like some people I could mention.'

Irene smiled her supercilious smile. 'You can never be too rich or too thin. The Duchess of Windsor said that.'

'Mrs Simpson, you mean. I don't care what they call her, she'll never be a proper duchess to me. And I'll tell you this for nothing. I wouldn't want to be like *her* – no better than she should be, that's what *my* mum says, and I agree.'

They reached the canteen and queued up for their lunch. It was only a quarter past eleven but they were all ready for the plates of cottage pie and peas that were ladled out to them, and sat down to eat, careful not to mark their uniforms. Pudding was plum and apple crumble and custard, and then they all had a cup of tea, made their final adjustments to their appearance and lined up for inspection, ready to go on duty when the restaurants opened at midday.

The floor superintendents came along the lines, giving each girl a swift but thorough check to make sure hands and nails were clean, hair tidily tucked under the pleated white caps, aprons smartly pressed and buttons correctly sewn on with red cotton. Mr Carter, the older superintendent, also carried a torch which he shone at every girl's hemline to make sure she was wearing a petticoat at the correct length. Any tiny snag in the black stockings was pointed out, and one girl sent back to give her shoes another polish.

'Thank you, ladies,' he said at last, coming to the end of the line. 'All very smart and nice. Now, today's menus have two different dishes – Adam and Eve on a Raft, and Airship on a Cloud. You all know what they are, but I'll just run through the ingredients again so that you can explain them to your customers. Don't forget that cottage pie is made with minced beef and shepherd's pie with lamb. There are plenty of good fresh plums in the kitchens, so encourage them to have the plum and apple pie or crumble that you've just had for your own lunches. Otherwise, everything is as usual and I know I can rely on you to give your usual excellent service. Now, it's almost time to open so off you go to your stations, and good luck.'

The girls made for the dressing room and gathered up their capes to hurry through the passage to the Corner House. People were already queuing outside, and the Nippies walked smartly to their positions and waited as the big glass doors were opened and the customers began to pour in, some of them hesitating before being quickly put at their ease by the 'seaters' who showed them to a table, others making at once for their favourite place – or their favourite Nippy.

Jo, standing behind one of her three tables, gave a little shiver of excitement. This was the moment she loved best – when the restaurant looked clean and tidy, every table gleaming and perfectly laid, and the whole day lay before her. Who knew what might happen, whom she might wait on, what she might receive in tips or presents? If only Phyl were here, too, she thought, it would be perfect.

She didn't have time to dwell upon her cousin's worries, though. Her first customer was already being seated at a table, and she gave him a warm, bright smile and waited while he picked up the menu and studied it.

'Good morning, sir,' she said cheerfully. 'What would you like today? We've got Adam and Eve on a Raft, and Airship on a Cloud for specials. And the plum and apple crumble is really good for afters – I've just had some myself, and I know!'

Phyl and Etty waited nervously for their interviews. Because they already worked for Lyons, they hadn't needed to apply in the usual way and neither of them had been really sure until this morning whether to go through with it. They could easily say they'd rather go on working in the kitchens, and that would be that. But Phyl had been determined that Etty should apply, and Etty had refused point blank to go without her, so here they both were, every bit as nervous as the girls who had never set foot in a Corner House except to have a cup of tea and a poached egg.

'They call us in alphabetical order,' Phyl said. 'So you'll go before me.'

'By myself? I can't!' Etty stared at her in sudden panic.

'Phyl, I can't do it – I'm going to tell them I can't do it. I shouldn't ever have let you persuade me. I'll never be able to be a Nippy and talk to people, and all that. I'm best off in the kitchens.' She was on her feet, ready to run from the room. Phyl reached out and caught her sleeve, dragging her back to her seat.

'Don't be daft. Of course you can do it. We're both going to do it together. But we've got to have our interviews on our own, see? Look, there's nothing to be scared of. It's just like a friendly chat, that's all. They're ever so nice – really.' She heard her voice tremble and expected Etty to ask if that was so, why was she so scared herself? But at that moment they heard Etty's name called and it was too late to run away. Etty gave her one last despairing glance and walked over to the door.

She looks like a Christian going in to face the lions, Phyl thought, watching her. If only she wouldn't look so scared! I'm sure she'd be a good Nippy if she could only get over being so frightened. She's clever really, only no one's ever told her. I wonder why. I wonder what her mum and dad are like, that they've let her grow up into such a rabbit . . .

Thinking about Etty took her mind off her own worries. Phyl was perfectly well aware that she hadn't really grown at all, or if she had it certainly wasn't by the requisite two inches. But although she could put up with working in the kitchens for a while, as long as she knew she'd be able to move on eventually, she also knew that slicing bread and grating cheese would drive her mad if she had to do it much longer without any hope. Nor did she want to progress to any other position in the kitchen, even the more responsible roles of assistant cook or ordering food. I want to be out there looking after people, she thought. I want the bustle and the change and the fun – even if it is hard work. I know I can do it!

She didn't see Etty again before she was called in for her own interview. Entering the room, she found herself in front of the same panel – Miss Rumsby with her fashionable dark marcel waves, Miss Turgoose and the blue-eyed Mr Young.

They glanced up as she came in and then frowned slightly, as if trying to remember where they had seen her before.

'Miss Jennings,' the older woman said, looking down at the papers before her. 'Oh, yes, of course – we saw you a few months ago, didn't we? You were just a little too short and we offered you work in the kitchen.' Her brow creased. 'Why have you come to see us today? Are you unhappy with your work? Don't you like being with Lyons?'

'Yes, I do,' Phyl said. 'But you said to come back when I'd grown a bit, and then perhaps I could be a Nippy after all.' She stopped and swallowed, then blurted out, 'I *have* grown, I'm sure I have! I've been measuring myself every night. And I've been learning all about being a Nippy from my cousin Jo – she's been working here, too, and she's going to get two extra tables on her station next week. She's told me all about setting tables and carrying trays and everything, and I've been practising adding up bills as well. I really *do* want to be a Nippy,' she finished, gazing at them appealingly. 'I don't think I can *bear* to go on slicing bread much longer.'

She fell silent, scarlet with embarrassment, conscious that she had probably said far too much. Wait till you're asked questions, she'd been advised, and then answer quickly and politely. You didn't have to blab it all out at once like a silly kid. Well, that was it – she may as well turn round and go straight home. She stared at her feet, wishing the ground would open up beneath her.

'Well,' Mr Young said at last, his voice very kind, 'I think you've made that quite clear – don't you, Miss Rumsby? Miss Turgoose?'

Phyl glanced up. The two ladies nodded but they didn't look amused, as Mr Young did. They looked rather stern. Her heart sank further.

'Now, tell me,' Mr Young went on, 'you've been working in the kitchen with a young lady called Etty, haven't you? Etty Brown.'

'Yes, sir.'

'And Etty's applied to become a Nippy, too. We've

interviewed her this morning. She talked quite a lot about you, Phyllis.'

Phyl stared at him. 'About *me*? But – why?'

'She wanted us to know how good you'd been to her. She said nobody else had taken any interest in her, but you'd persuaded her to apply to become a Nippy. She obviously thinks very highly of you.'

Phyl coloured again and muttered, 'I've just been friendly to her, that's all.'

'Just been friendly,' he repeated. 'And friendliness is one of the qualities we look for most when appointing Nippies. I seem to remember, Phyllis, that when you were here before you offered to wait on me.' He smiled. 'I told you I wouldn't forget, didn't I? Now, we agreed then that you were just the sort of girl we were looking for, and that if you managed to grow that extra two inches there would be no question of you not being taken on. Tell me again – do you really think you've managed it? Have you grown two more inches?'

Phyl looked at him. She met the steady blue eyes. She wanted to say, yes, she had, she'd grown at least two inches, maybe even a bit more. But she knew she couldn't do it. Lyons might want Nippies, but they didn't want liars.

'I've grown about an inch,' she said miserably. 'At least, I think I have. I've really *tried*,' she added with a burst of desperation. 'I've done exercises and sports at the Club, *and* been swimming, and I've hung from the gym bars for hours. And I *know* I'm strong enough. I can put all Mrs Holt's crockery on a tray and carry it right down the garden path and back as many times as I've had hot dinners. I've tried as hard as I can, honestly!'

Mr Young laughed, but his laughter was sympathetic. He turned to the two ladies and Phyl's heart sank. They were still frowning and looking doubtful. They're not going to let me, she thought disconsolately, I know they're not going to let me.

'What do you say?' Mr Young asked easily. 'Shall we stretch a point in this case? Even though—' he cast Phyl a small, mischievous smile '—we can't stretch our would-be Nippy here?'

Miss Turgoose looked down her nose. 'The rules were made for a purpose, Mr Young. A certain height is desirable for a Nippy. She has to walk between tables seated with diners, carrying a heavy tray. If she should catch the edge of the tray—'

'Oh, I wouldn't!' Phyl cried, unable to restrain herself. 'I mean – I've practised and practised and I've never caught a tray on *anything*. I – I'm sorry,' she mumbled, recollecting her determination to remain silent until spoken to, and feeling her colour rise as they all turned towards her again.

Mr Young was looking rather red in the face, too, and his mouth was twitching. 'It is only an inch,' he said mildly. 'And Phyllis does seem very keen.'

'Keenness isn't everything,' Miss Rumsby pointed out. 'The height rule is for a *minimum* height. Really, we prefer our gels to be taller than that. And once a rule is broken, the floodwaters break through. We'll have all kinds of gels applying.'

'I'd never tell anyone how tall I am,' Phyl said meekly, and at this Mr Young laughed outright.

'Come on, ladies, rules are made to be broken, you know, and this is a case where I really do think we can use our own judgement. Tell me honestly, if Phyllis were three inches taller, would you have the slightest hesitation in appointing her as a Nippy?' He watched with satisfaction as the two heads reluctantly shook from side to side. 'Then I suggest we stop quibbling over a mere inch and welcome this enterprising young lady to our happy band.' He turned back to Phyl and gave her a terrifying mock frown. 'I ought to give you a good talking to,' he said. 'I ought to tell you off for wasting our time, coming here when you knew really that you hadn't grown. But I'm not going to. In this case, we're going to make an exception. We'll tell the dressmaking department that you're to have a uniform made specially for you, and you can start training as a Nippy just as soon as it's ready.' He stood up and leaned over the table, holding out his right hand. 'Welcome again to Lyons, Phyllis, and I'm sure you'll make a very good Nippy. I shall watch out for you specially. I think you could go far.'

Phyl barely understood his words. She stared at his hand, then gazed back into his eyes. They were warm and kind, and still dancing with amusement. She felt the colour rush into her face and grabbed his hand, feeling as if she'd like to smother it with kisses rather than merely shake it. Her voice trembled as she thanked him.

'You mean I really am going to be a Nippy? Oh, *thank* you, sir! *Thank* you, Miss Rumsby – thank you, Miss Turgoose. I won't let you down, I promise. I'll be the best Nippy you ever had. Oh, thank you, *thank* you!'

After that, there didn't seem to be much more to say. They'd told her at the first interview all she needed to know, and although Phyl remembered later that they had talked for a little longer, she hadn't the first idea what they'd said. She danced from the room feeling as if she were floating, and when she came into the room where refreshments were served she saw Etty straight away and made a bee line for her.

'I got through! They've taken me – they're going to have a uniform made in my size, specially. And you got through, too! You see, I told you you would! Oh, Etty, isn't it smashing? We're going to be Nippies together, us two and Jo and the others I told you about – Shirley and Maggie. You'll like them, I know you will. Oh, we're going to have such a smashing time.' She stopped and then said, 'Look, you've got to come back for supper tonight and tell Jo and Auntie Holt. You can, can't you? You told them at home you'd be late? Or are you going to stop the night, like I said the other day?'

Etty, whose pale face was pink with colour from her own success, looked about to say yes, then appeared to shrink inside herself. She half nodded, shook her head, looked frightened and confused.

'What's the matter?' Phyl asked. 'What is it? You can come, can't you? You've just got to – I want to tell the others about it all, and it won't be the same if you're not there, too.'

'Yes,' Etty said. 'Yes, I'll come to supper, Phyl. I'd like to. But I won't stay the night. I can't do that.' She got up quickly from her chair. 'I'll go and get you a cup of tea and a cake. You stop there.' A glimmer of a smile brightened her eyes and Phyl caught another glimpse of the pretty girl that Etty could be when she forgot to be afraid. 'If I'm going to be a Nippy, I'd better start practising as soon as I can. There's a lot to learn.'

She walked away and Phyl watched her thoughtfully. Already Etty held herself with more confidence, walking as if she had a purpose and wasn't afraid to be seen. I'm glad the interviewers saw it, too, she thought. It'll do Etty all the good in the world to know she can do something that other people enjoy.

All the same, there was still a mystery about her and Phyl was determined to discover her secret.

Chapter Eight

Phyl and Etty started work in the restaurant in the middle of December. Talk about throwing them in at the deep end, Phyl said with a grin. London was full of people doing their Christmas shopping and the Corner House was full of shoppers coming in festooned with heavy bags, their faces tired and their feet aching. They all wanted a cup of tea first and foremost, followed by something hot and tasty to revive their flagging energy.

Jo was thrilled to have Phyl working with her at last. She made sure there were places for both Phyl and Etty at the table where they all sat for dinner and for their breaks, and introduced them to the others. They remembered each other from the first interview, and Maggie and Shirley both smiled a welcome, making room between them for Etty while Phyl sat next to Jo. Irene Bond looked suspicious.

'I thought you were too short.'

'I've grown,' Phyl said, looking her in the eye. 'And so's Etty. More than me, actually.'

'I didn't know they were taking on kitchen girls now,' Irene said sniffily, changing tack. She gave Etty a scathing look. 'D'you really think you'll be able to manage?'

'She's done her training,' Phyl said quickly, before Etty could speak – or more likely, she thought, burst into tears. 'Passed all the exams, just the same as you did.'

Irene looked as if she doubted it, but since there wasn't any other way to become a Nippy she couldn't say much more.

She looked at Etty narrowly, taking in the dark eyes and the straight brown hair, pulled tightly back from her thin features.

'You look a bit foreign. Where d'you come from, then?'

Phyl cast Etty an anxious glance, knowing that the other girl hated to be asked questions about her home and family. She saw the colour begin to rise in Etty's sallow cheeks and butted in again.

'You mind your own beeswax, Irene Bond. Etty's as English as you and me and where she comes from is her own affair. You just leave her alone.'

Irene raised her eyebrows. 'What are you then, her keeper? You haven't let her answer a single question for herself yet. Not that I care tuppence one way or the other.' She got up, flicking her hand carelessly and caught the edge of Phyl's cup so that it fell over, spilling a stream of brown tea over the new white apron. 'Oh dear, look what I've done. I'm *ever* so sorry.'

Phyl leapt to her feet. 'You little *cat*—'

'I *said* I was sorry. It was an accident, see?' Irene brushed her away like a wasp. 'Anyway, we got to get back to work now. You'll have to get a clean apron,' she said, eyeing Phyl maliciously. 'That'll go down well, on your first day.'

She stalked away and Phyl stared after her furiously. Jo was already mopping at the stain, but she knew she would have to do as Irene had said and ask for a clean apron. She bit her lip, fighting back the angry tears. What a start to her new career as a Nippy.

'I'll get even with her,' she muttered to Jo. 'You see if I don't.'

'You'd be better to forget it,' her cousin advised her. 'It don't do any good to get involved in arguments with her sort. Specially as you're new.'

'But it isn't fair,' Phyl stormed. 'And it's not just that, it's the way she spoke to Etty. Plain downright nasty.'

'I know. But that's just the way she is. We don't take no notice. You go and get a new apron, Phyl, and I'll cover your station for you. Lucky they only give new girls a couple of tables to start with.' She grinned. 'They know everyone drops something the first day.'

But I didn't drop it, Phyl thought, seething with resentment as she hurried to fetch a clean apron and still get back to work on time. She did it deliberately. And I don't care what Jo says, I'm *not* going to let her get away with it!

Nothing, it seemed, could diminish the energy of the Nippies. No matter how many times they went back and forth with laden trays, no matter how aching their own legs when they finished their shifts, they always had energy to enjoy themselves in the evenings or at weekends. They took to going out together as a group – Phyl and Jo, Maggie and Shirley, Irene – who might look down on the rest of them but wasn't too proud to go to the cinema or a dance in their company – and now Etty.

They went to see all the latest films, from *Lost Horizon* with Ronald Colman as the traveller who finds Shangri-La, to Walt Disney's cartoon of *Snow White and the Seven Dwarfs*. For weeks, the dressing room echoed to choruses of 'Hi-ho, hi-ho, it's off to work we go' while Maggie and Phyl sighed together over Greta Garbo in *Camille* and Jo was enthralled by Sonja Henie's skating in *Thin Ice*. I could do that, she thought, if I only had a pair of skates and the Serpentine froze over.

Exciting though this new life was, however, it was impossible to forget that there were still troubles in other parts of the world. The war in the Far East, with Japan's ruthless bombing of Shanghai and invasion of China, might seem far away, but closer to home, in Germany, Adolf Hitler was becoming even more powerful. He had almost single-handedly, it seemed, hauled his country out of the recession that had swept over the whole world, and his people loved him for it – but when Jo watched the Pathe Pictorial news at the cinema and saw him address the vast Nuremberg Rally, she felt again that stirring of unease. He doesn't look sane, she thought, ranting and waving his arms like that. He looks frightening . . .

She dared not mention her fears at home. Her father was still adamant that there would be no war, and she knew that he had suffered too much when he had served at the Somme in the Great War of 1914–18 to let himself think about it all happening again. It was a fear that many people dared not face. The horrors of which they seldom spoke were still there inside them, a nightmare that was best buried and ignored. You couldn't think about it happening again, you just didn't dare.

'Of course there's not going to be a war,' Irene Bond said impatiently. 'We're friends with Hitler, aren't we? Why, the Duke of Windsor himself went to stay with him and review his troops in October – we saw the pictures. You don't think he'd do that if Hitler was our enemy, do you?'

Jo didn't think the Duke of Windsor was necessarily a friend after all that had happened, but she didn't say so. She'd noticed Etty almost shrinking in her seat while they'd been watching the pictures of what was happening in the rest of the world, as if it affected her personally. She'd been in tears when they saw shots of refugees trailing miserably away from their homes, carrying no more than a few pathetic possessions, and Jo didn't want to upset her further by suggesting it might happen here.

China, Japan, Spain – the world didn't seem any more peaceful than it had been twenty years ago. Why should the rest of Europe be immune? she thought apprehensively. Why shouldn't one man who had come so swiftly to power want more?

Phyl too had noticed Etty's reactions.

'You know,' she said to Jo as they got ready for bed one evening just before Christmas, 'that Etty had a rough time before she came to Lyons. That's why she looks so scared sometimes, I reckon. And I'm not sure it's all behind her now either – otherwise why should she be so cagey about her family? She's been here twice to supper now and never said a word about any of that, only that she lives in a GFS hostel, and it was like getting blood out of a stone to get her to admit that. But a hostel's nothing to be ashamed of, and she must have a proper home somewhere.'

'I'm surprised she hasn't told you,' Jo observed. 'She

follows you about like a puppy-dog. I'd have thought if she was going to tell anyone, it'd be you.'

'I know.' Phyl was darning her stockings. She had followed Shirley's example and kept mending things always ready at work, but there were always ladders or holes to be repaired at home. Determined to justify the expense caused by having to have a uniform made specially for her, she took great care to appear for work every day bandbox-smart, and had never yet been pulled up for the tiniest thing. 'I've tried to find out without asking her straight out, but she's like a clam. It's as if she's ashamed.'

'Well, maybe she is. I mean, she don't look as if she's ever been looked after properly till she came here. Maybe she lives in the slums.'

'Lyons wouldn't ever take a girl from the slums!' Phyl said, shocked. 'You know they want girls who've got some idea how to go about things. Some of those slum kids don't even go to school regular, they can't read or write or anything. Etty's not like that.'

'No, she's not,' Jo agreed thoughtfully. 'All the same, there's something funny about her. Don't get me wrong, Phyl, I like her all right, but it's queer how she never lets on anything about herself. I mean, we hear all about other people's families – so what's she got to hide?'

It was true that most of the girls chatted freely about their homes and families. Maggie, for instance, talked constantly about her brothers and sisters. Nobody was ever quite sure how many there were but when Jo and Phyl counted up they made it at least five, possibly six. There was a married sister, Evie, who had two small children, an older brother called Jim, and two or three younger ones, too. They had at least two cats and who knew how many rabbits, and the youngest brother had several white mice. They had all got out one day and caused mayhem, with the cats chasing the mice, the family chasing the cats and Maggie's sister Evie standing on a chair and screaming at them all, her baby in her arms.

'Her grandma lives with them, too,' Phyl said, finishing her darning. 'Cantankerous old biddy, Maggie says, as likely to give you a swipe with her brolly as look at you. A bloke tried to snatch her bag off her one day when she was down the shops and she hit him over the head and nearly poked his eye out. He ran so fast he nearly disappeared in a cloud of smoke, and they never saw him down that way again.'

'Go on,' Jo said sleepily. She was already in bed, reading. Jo read a lot but her favourite book had always been *Little Women*, mainly because there was a girl in it with the same name as her, a girl with long legs and tomboyish ways who had spirit and wanted to do something more than get married and stay at home with children. As it happened, later books showed her doing just that, but somehow she did it in a different way from her sisters and Jo still liked to model herself upon her American namesake. 'How d'you find all that out, Phyl?'

'We were just talking,' Phyl said vaguely. It wasn't at all unusual for her to find out someone's life story within a few minutes of meeting them. People responded to her interest somehow and opened up with all kinds of information. That was what made it all the more frustrating that Etty kept herself so close.

Even when she'd come to supper, she hadn't opened up. If anything, she'd seemed even more nervous – almost over-awed by the house, uncertain what to do with her coat, afraid to ask where the lavatory was. It was as if, as Jo remarked to Phyl, she'd never been in an ordinary house before.

'You'd think it was Buckingham Palace,' she said. 'That's what makes me wonder if she comes from the slums. I know she doesn't seem like it in other ways – I mean, she's polite, she knows how to behave – but I've never seen anyone so scared of being asked to tea with her mates before.'

'Well, she'll tell us in her own good time,' Phyl said, folding her blouse and laying it on her chair. She got into bed. 'Have you finished reading, Jo? I want to turn out the gas.'

'Mmm. I don't like this chapter so much anyway.' Jo laid the book down on the floor beside the bed. 'It's all about Amy – selfish little prig. How is it a nice woman like Marmee can have four children all so different, and all nice except for one?'

Phyl chuckled. 'Don't ask me.' She turned out the light and snuggled down under her blankets. 'Ask Maggie. If all she says about her grandma's true, it's a wonder she produced any nice kids at all, but Maggie's a smasher for all she's so fat, and her mum's just the same. She came into the Corner House one day and I served her. You'd think they were sisters.' She lay quietly for a while, then said thoughtfully, 'I wonder what Etty's mum's like. I wonder if she'll ever tell us.'

Jo didn't answer. She was already fast asleep.

The Corner Houses were open every day except for Christmas Day, and Christmas dinners of turkey or roast beef or pork were served, with all the usual Christmas trimmings and followed by Christmas pudding and mince pies. The Nippies were kept busy dashing to and fro with laden trays, but the hard work was eased by the cheerfulness and Christmas spirit of the customers. The restaurants were decorated with coloured paper chains, balloons and baubles and everyone was dressed in their best. The orchestra played Christmas carols and songs, and every place was laid with crackers. The customers pulled them and put on the paper hats and read silly jokes to one another, and the place was full of laughter.

'The only snag is, we'll all be too worn out to enjoy Christmas when we finally get to it,' Maggie commented, passing Phyl with a tray piled high with plates of turkey, roast potatoes and vegetables. 'D'you know, I don't think I'm going to be able to face Christmas pudding? All I'm going to want is a nice boiled egg and me feet up.'

'I'll believe that when it happens,' Jo grinned, overhearing. 'Be quick coming off shift, Phyl, we don't want to miss the bus home. I'm really looking forward to seeing our Alice's face when she sees that dolly I've got her. She's always wanted one with a real china face.'

Phyl nodded, but for her the Christmas jollity was spoilt by Irene Bond's attitude. Irene and Phyl had never hit it off, since that first morning when Phyl had sprung to Etty's defence, and Irene had knocked her cup over. Any other girl would have forgotten it in a couple of days, Phyl thought, but not Irene. She was like a sly, spiteful child, never missing a chance to nudge Phyl's elbow as she carried a laden tray, or bump against her as they stood in the queue down in the kitchen.

'Oh, sorry, didn't see you down there,' she would say, smirking, while Phyl felt her colour rise at the reference to her height. 'Sure you can see over the counter?' And, in an aside to one of the other girls, but making sure that Phyl could hear her stage whisper, 'I'm really surprised at Lyons, you know, taking on dwarfs.'

Phyl whipped round, furious. 'I'm *not* a dwarf! That's a horrible thing to say.'

Irene stared at her innocently. 'Did I say anything about you, Phyl Jennings? I was just talking to my friend here about someone she knows at Cadby Hall. Anyway, you know what they say about eavesdroppers. Listeners never hear good about themselves.' She sniggered. 'You might have short legs, but you've got long enough ears – like a donkey's, they are!'

Phyl, scarlet-faced, took a deep breath, but Jo hastily stepped between them. 'All right, Phyl, calm down. She's not worth bothering with.' She gave Irene a withering glance. 'Leave her alone. We all know what you're up to. *I* saw you sneak that cake off Phyl's tray yesterday afternoon.'

'*I never!*'

'You did. You were trying to get her into trouble, same as when you put a dirty knife on her table. Well, let me tell you, if you're not careful you'll find you're the one in trouble. Mr Carter's started to notice and he's not a fool. You'll be sniggering on the other side of your spiteful little face one of these days.'

Irene sniffed and turned away disdainfully, but there was a spot of angry red on her cheek and her mouth was a thin, angry line. Jo watched her walk away to her station and then turned back to Phyl.

'Don't let her rile you. I told you, she's not worth it.'

'I know. I don't take any notice, most of the time. It was just when she said that about dwarfs. It's when she starts on Etty I get really cross, though. Honestly, Jo, I don't know why we let her go around with us, to the pictures and that.'

'Nor do I, really. It's just that we started going out together and it's just sort of gone on.' Jo came to the head of the queue and picked up her loaded tray. 'Well, here we go again. See you later, Phyl.'

Since then Phyl had tried hard to take no notice of Irene's jibes. But as she hurried to and fro on Christmas Eve, thinking partly about her customers and partly about how nice it would be to finish and go home, she found the other girl even more irritating than usual. The Christmas spirit seemed to have passed Irene by, as far as Phyl was concerned.

'Your customer's looking really fed up,' she hissed, passing Phyl by the kitchen doors. 'If you ask me, he's sick of waiting.'

'He hasn't waited any longer than anyone else,' Phyl retorted. 'And he's not fed up, he's worried about his wife. He told me she's in hospital.'

'Mr Carter won't like you standing about gossiping with the customers,' Irene said, changing tack. 'Not when we're this busy.'

'Oh, shut up.' Phyl brushed past her and Irene gave a squeal.

'*Now* look what you've made me do! I've spilt this glass of milk. That's *your* fault, Phyl Jennings.'

Phyl glanced at the tray, now swimming in milk. Irene would have to go back, unload everything, get a clean tray and a fresh glass of milk, none of which would go unnoticed by the floor manager. She sighed.

'You did it yourself, Irene. I hardly touched you. Anyway, I've got a customer to serve—' She walked briskly away, pinning a bright smile on her face to hide her exasperation, and served the customer who was anxious about his wife.

The next time she came back to the kitchen, with a fresh

order, Mr Carter was waiting for her. Irene was beside him, looking smug and self-righteous.

'I understand there's been a spot of bother, Phyllis. Irene here says you deliberately pushed her arm and caused her to spill a glass of milk.'

'I didn't, Mr Carter. Irene was telling me one of my customers was getting impatient. I told her he wasn't and as I passed her I touched her arm, but it wasn't enough to upset anything, honestly.'

'Is that the customer at Table Seven?'

'Yes, sir. He told me he was worried about his wife because she's in hospital. I served him as quickly as I could, but I couldn't rush away when I could see he needed someone to talk to.'

'No.' Mr Carter looked at her thoughtfully, then turned to Irene. 'It seems as if the mishap was no more than an accident, Irene. Perhaps you're a little too ready to cast blame, don't you think? Now, get back to your work, both of you. This is the busiest day of the year and we really can't have our staff wasting time squabbling.'

'Little sneak,' Irene hissed as they made their way back to the kitchen. 'You only said that because you know *his* wife's in hospital, too.'

'Oh, for heaven's *sake*!' Phyl turned her back. Jo was right, she thought. Irene Bond just wasn't worth bothering with. And there was far too much to do to bother about her now. It was Christmas, and everyone was out to enjoy themselves. I'll enjoy myself, too, Phyl thought, and Lady Muck can like it or lump it!

Irene had evidently decided to lump it, at least for the time being. She said no more but cast black looks at Phyl as they finished their shift, first carrying out all their normal jobs of counting the cutlery and filling the salt and pepper pots for the girls coming on for the rest of the day. Their trays must be cleaned with whitening and polished with a damp cloth, and their uniforms hung carefully in the cupboards with fresh caps and aprons ready for their next shift. For some of the girls, this would be on Boxing Day, with only one day off for

Christmas itself, but Jo and Phyl were lucky and had two days off.

'That Irene!' Phyl exclaimed as they scrambled aboard their bus and sank into seats, sighing with relief to get the weight off their feet at last. 'She's a real spiteful little cat. I'll be thankful not to have to look at her nasty face for a couple of days.' She grinned suddenly and hugged herself. 'Oh, Jo, isn't it smashing to be going home for Christmas?'

Jo agreed. 'We wouldn't have been able to if we hadn't got the extra day. We couldn't have got back in time. Mind, I don't think Auntie Holt would have been upset to have us there. She was a bit disappointed not to be cooking a turkey, you know.'

'She'll be glad of the rest,' Phyl said. 'And she won't be on her own – she's going in next door for her Christmas dinner and spending Boxing Day with her friend in Summer Street. She doesn't depend on us for company.' She gazed out of the window at the soft, greenish light cast by the gaslamps and added thoughtfully, 'The one I feel sorry for is Etty. I wish we'd asked her back with us.'

'We couldn't have done that! She's got her own family to go to.'

'Has she?' Phyl turned and looked into Jo's face. Her brown eyes were troubled. 'I'm not sure she has. Someone said something the other day that made me wonder. Suppose she hasn't got anyone to go to. Suppose she's only got that hostel after all.'

'She must have somewhere else,' Jo said uncertainly. 'She must have *some* family. I mean, *we* don't live at home either, we stay with Auntie Holt, but we still go back to our families for Christmas.'

'Yes, but that's just it. Etty doesn't. Honestly, I don't think she's got a family to go back to. That's why she didn't mind working on Boxing Day – I wouldn't mind betting she put in for it specially. I reckon she'd rather be at the Corner House than in her own room, and that's the long and the short of it, Jo.'

*

108

At home, everything was in full swing for a merry Christmas. As usual, the two families were joining together and there was much coming and going between the two houses. Bill and Stan told each other they'd have to make a connecting door between the two passages to save losing all the heat, but since they told each other this every Christmas, not to mention Easter, August Bank Holiday and almost every birthday, nobody took much notice. It was never going to happen.

Alice was first to the door when Jo came in. She rushed across the room, her face bright pink with excitement, a stream of half-finished paper chains trailing from her fist. Her curly blonde hair looked as if it hadn't been brushed for a fortnight and there was a smear of icing sugar across her cheek.

'Jo! Jo! It's *Christmas*!'

'Go on,' Jo said, laughing. She dropped her suitcase and picked up her sister to hug her. 'Crikey, haven't you grown? I can hardly lift you any more.'

'Well, I'll be eight in January,' Alice explained. 'It's my birthday on the tenth. You won't forget, will you?'

'I don't suppose I'll get the chance. But let's get Christmas over first, shall we?' Jo set her back on the floor.

Alice pulled a face. 'I don't want Christmas to be over. I want it to last for ever and ever.'

'Then you'll never be eight.' Jo went through the back room to the kitchen, where her mother was busy cutting pastry rounds for mince pies. 'Hello, Mum.'

Carrie Mason dropped the cup she was using to cut the rounds and beamed all over her floury face. 'Jo! I never heard you come in. Oh, it *is* good to see you.' She held out her arms and gave her daughter a hug. 'How are you? You're looking tired.'

'I'm fine, Mum. I'm as fit as a fiddle. I've just finished a day's work, that's why I look tired. You wouldn't believe how busy we've been this past week – we must have served thousands of Christmas dinners, thousands.'

'There she goes,' Freddy said, coming in through the back door. 'Exaggerating as usual.'

'I'm not. Just think, if the restaurant can seat a thousand diners and we serve only one dinner an hour, that's a thousand, and we do lots more than that – two an hour, easy, and more if it's just a snack, so that's—'

'Tell her to stop, Ma,' Freddy begged. 'Not home five minutes and she's got us doing sums already. Well, you'll be able to wait on your whole family tomorrow and show us just how good you are.'

Jo groaned and Carrie shook her head. 'She'll do no such thing. She'll have a rest, that's what she'll do, take the weight off her legs and be waited on for a change. She didn't come all this way home for a busman's holiday.'

'No, and I didn't come to be the lady of the manor neither,' Jo said. 'I came for a proper family Christmas, with everyone mucking in like we always do. And I'll start this minute by making a cup of tea. Move over, our Freddy – let's get at the kettle.'

When Bill Mason came in from work an hour later the mince pies were just out of the oven, rich and golden and smelling like heaven, and there was a fresh pot of tea just made. The kitchen and scullery were clean and tidy and a fire was burning in the grate of the back room. His family were all there, hair brushed and faces clean of flour, icing sugar and the grime of travel, and the table was set for tea.

'Well!' he said, stopping in the doorway. 'If that ain't a sight for sore eyes. Who's coming, then, the King and Queen?'

'Daddy!' Alice squealed, uncurling herself from the rag rug in front of the fire and throwing herself at her father. 'It's Christmas! *Christmas!*'

'Is that what it is? Well, I did hear a rumour.' He was standing awkwardly, Jo thought, one hand behind him as if trying to conceal something. She smiled to herself and pretended not to notice, but Alice had no such inhibitions.

'What's the matter, Daddy? What have you got behind your back? Is it a Christmas present – is it *my* Christmas present?'

'Alice!' her mother said sharply. 'Don't be so silly. You

know it's Father Christmas brings Christmas presents. Let your father get through the door and leave him alone.'

'Willy Crewe says that's not true, about Father Christmas,' Alice said, reluctantly relinquishing her hold on her father's legs but still trying to peep round him. 'He says it's your mum and dad give you the presents.'

'Then he's got no right to say any such thing,' Carrie said. 'And I've told you before, you're not to play with Willy Crewe. I don't like him, and his big brother's already been down the police station three times, to my knowledge. I don't want you getting into bad company.'

'I'm not.' No amount of telling Alice that children should be seen and not heard, that she shouldn't speak until she was spoken to or answer back, or a hundred other things meant to keep her under control ever stopped her from speaking her mind. 'He's not bad company, he's good company. He makes me laugh and he thinks of interesting things to do. And Daddy *has* got something behind his back, I can tell he has.'

'Well, whatever it is, it's got nothing to do with you. Now, let him go out to the scullery and have his wash and we can sit down to tea before these mince pies go cold. I made enough for us to have one each tonight, but that's all – the rest are for Christmas.'

'It's Christmas now,' Alice muttered, one eye on her mother and the other on her father as he sidled through the room. 'It's Christmas Eve, so it must be Christmas – *ow*! Jo, you're pinching me. Mum, our Jo's *pinching* me.'

'No, I'm not,' Jo said, fastening her fingers round one of Alice's arms and drawing her sister towards her. 'I just want you to stand here by me and tell me about school. Was there a party for Christmas? Did you make paper chains?'

Alice nodded. 'I made all these,' she said, nodding at the chains that streamed across the ceiling from corner to corner. They were made of newspaper, scribbled over with coloured wax crayon, cut into strips, then glued into interlinking circles. 'And we had a currant bun each on the last day, and Miss let us play games all afternoon. We played Ring a Ring o' Roses and Farmer Wants a Wife.'

Outside, in the scullery, they could hear their father moving things about. It sounded like boxes and pots and pans. Alice stared at Jo with round eyes and made half a move towards the door, but Jo tightened her grip on the small arm. There was a distinct sound of scuffling and a muttered expostulation.

'What's he *doing* out there?' Alice demanded. 'What's he *got*? There was something, I know there was.'

'Listen, I'm just going next door to see Phyl,' Jo said, trying to keep a straight face. 'Why don't you come with me? She'll tell you all about what she said to the customer who had three helpings of Christmas pudding, and what happened when someone sent back his plate of roast beef and said it was underdone. And by the time we get back, Dad will have had his wash and we can all have a game of rummy before you go to bed.'

'I've got to go to bed early,' Alice said. 'I've got to go early in case Father Christmas comes round this way first. Mum said.'

'I thought you didn't believe in Father Christmas any more,' Freddy began, and bit off his words as Jo glowered at him. 'Actually, I think that's a good idea,' he went on hastily. 'Why not go now? I thought I heard bells jingling when I was on my way home, as a matter of fact.'

'Leave her alone, Freddy,' Jo said, getting to her feet. 'Come on, Ally, you haven't seen Phyl yet and she was saying on the way home how much she wanted to see you again.'

'I always thought there was something funny about that girl,' Freddy remarked, and ducked, grinning, as Jo took a swing at him. The two sisters made their way to the door, Alice still casting wistful glances towards the scullery. They were almost out when there was a crash of falling saucepans and a yell of pure despair.

'Out!' Jo said firmly, and pushed Alice through the door. '*Out.*'

The mysterious crashes weren't explained until Christmas

morning, when Alice woke to find a small, marmalade kitten climbing on to her bed.

'*Jo!*'

The scream woke everyone in the house and sent the kitten scuttering for safety. Jo, in the lower bunk, stretched out an arm just in time, inadvertently, to catch it as it tumbled to the floor. She cradled it in her hands, soothing its panic and marvelling at the delicate markings of deep orange, striped with paler gold and cream, like a miniature blond tiger, and then got out of bed and grinned at her sister.

Alice was puce with excitement.

'Did you see it, Jo? Where is it, where did it go? Oh, catch it, catch it, it's a kitten, it's *my* kitten that I've always wanted. Will Crewe's wrong, there *is* a Father Christmas – *nobody* else knew how much I wanted a kitten.'

The whole street had known how much Alice wanted a kitten, but Jo didn't remind her, neither did she mention their father's strange behaviour the evening before, or the crashes from the scullery as the kitten escaped from the lunch-box it had travelled home in. After Alice had gone to bed, the tiny creature had been brought out from the shoebox Carrie had left ready for it and allowed to run around the living-room. It had used the earth-tray put in one corner, making them all laugh with its vigorous and determined efforts to cover up what it had done, and it had snuggled up on Freddy's lap and gone to sleep, purring like a little engine.

'Here he is,' Jo said, handing the kitten up to the top bunk. 'Handle him gently, now, he's very tiny. He's only six weeks old and he left his mum yesterday so he needs lots of cuddles, but he'll need a lot of sleep as well. What are you going to call him?'

'I don't know. Oh, isn't he *sweet*? Look at his blue eyes.' Alice cuddled the kitten against her and it looked up into her face and poked out a minute pink tongue to lick her face. 'Oh, did you see that? He kissed me! He really did, he kissed me. He knows he's mine. Oh, you darling, you lovely, lovely darling.'

Well, my china doll's not going to get much of a look-in, Jo thought wryly, but she was touched to see how tender Alice was with the little cat, and she put out one finger to stroke his head. The kitten reached up a pawful of needle claws and caught her fingertip, and she yelped and withdrew her hand quickly. Alice giggled.

'He's mine. He knows he's mine. He's protecting me.'

'He'll need protection himself if he doesn't watch those claws,' Jo observed, and rubbed his ears with some caution. 'Blue eyes mean he's still very young – they won't stay that colour. They'll probably go orange, or green.'

'He's beautiful whatever colour his eyes are.' Alice cradled the kitten against her, and he turned in her arms and planted his front paws against her chest, his purrs growing. 'See, he loves me already!'

The rest of the family were at the door now, peering in to see how Alice liked her present, and Freddy said, 'Why not call him Ginger?'

'Oh everyone calls ginger cats Ginger.' Alice gazed down, her face soft. 'I know, I'll call him Robertson.'

'*Robertson?* What sort of name's that for a cat, for goodness' sake?'

'It's marmalade and he's a marmalade cat,' Alice explained with dignity. 'And he can be Robbie for short, can't you, my sweetheart? But on special days like Christmas and birthdays, he'll be Robertson.'

Robertson was the centre of attention all over Christmas. Nobody else had a present to compete with him. He was passed around from hand to hand, happily exploring each new lap, curling up in a furry orange ball when he felt tired and refusing to wake. He used his earth-tray right in the middle of Christmas dinner, stinking the place out so that it had to be emptied at once, and Alice spent the afternoon stuffing an old pillowcase with bits of rag to make him his own cushion. He was given a few pieces of chicken for his own dinner, cut into tiny pieces, and he tucked into them as if he'd been eating chicken all his life, and then drank a whole saucerful of milk.

'Look at that big fat tummy,' Alice said to him, picking him up tenderly in case he burst. 'Just look at it. You're full right up, aren't you? Now you'd better have a nice sleep on your very own bed.' And she laid him on the new cushion, on the top bunk.

He did as she told him, before waking at midnight to start careering around the room, using the faint glimmer of moonlight to see his way as he leapt from the bunk to the chest of drawers and then the top of the wardrobe. Finding himself higher than he liked, he clung there, mewing pathetically until Jo, who had just got off to sleep, staggered from her bed and rescued him.

'You'd have been better off calling him Macbeth,' she said after the fourth time.

'Why? Why Macbeth?'

'Because he murdered sleep.' Jo sank back into bed. 'Honestly, Ally, I thought I might get a bit of rest at home.'

'It's not my fault,' Alice said with a giggle. 'It's Father Christmas's.'

'Well, next time Willy Crewe tells you something, believe him. It might save us all a lot of trouble.' In truth, she envied Alice. The cat they had had before, a big, grumpy tabby called Smudge because that's what he had looked like as a kitten, had been over-teased by Freddy and had grown up with an uncertain temper and inclined to be free with his claws. Bill had been the only one who could do anything with him, and none of the family had been particularly sorry when he went into the garden one day and died under a blackcurrant bush. Since then, Alice had never stopped begging for a kitten, and it looked as if this one was going to be a real charmer.

After that, Robertson settled down, falling asleep in the crook of Alice's arm so that she dared not move for fear of disturbing him, and when they woke in the morning she was stiff for at least a quarter of an hour.

The two days of Christmas passed in a flash. Both front doors were kept unlocked and people went to and fro all day, playing cards or Ludo, or getting out pencils and paper for a game of Consequences, making sandwiches and jellies and pots of tea, and all gathering in the Masons' front room in the evenings for sing-songs round the piano. May and Carrie, in red frocks, with their dark curly hair showing identical touches of grey, sang a duet and Freddy, Norman and Ronnie played a comb and paper band. Alice pretended to be Shirley Temple until Eric pretended to be sick, and Jo and Phyl did a short act about Nippies, with Phyl as the customer. Their quickfire repartee brought the house down and they sank back in their chairs, aching with laughter.

'Oh, that was a gorgeous Christmas,' Jo said as they went back to Marble Arch on the bus the day after Boxing Day. 'All the family together – that's what Christmas is meant to be. I hope all the other girls had just as nice a time as we did, Phyl.'

'So do I,' Phyl said, snuggling down into the red woollen scarf her mother had knitted her. 'So do I.'

Maggie Pratt's Christmas was a noisy, sprawling affair, with Evie's baby crawling on the floor and the toddler staggering cheerfully about with no nappy on and his little china po always handy because he was being 'trained'. Her brother Jim spent much of his time tinkering pleasurably with the old Francis Barnett motorbike his dad had got for him for Christmas from a mate at work, and the younger boys built strange and wobbly structures with their Meccano. Like the Mason and Jennings families, they all came together in the evenings for a sing-song, more raucous but full of good humour, just as Maggie Pratt's mum was full of good port, and they slept late next morning and got up with headaches. Maggie only just made it to work on time.

Shirley Wood had a quieter holiday, but only because her family was smaller. Her mother's asthma and bronchitis were always worse in the winter so Shirley did most of the cooking. She had already made and iced the cake, roughing up the surface to make it look like snow and putting on top a little green paper tree made with laborious care by Jack, his round face screwed up in concentration. He had made paper chains, too, and they were festooned around the living-room. The

Christmas pudding had been ready for weeks, and everyone searched their portion for the silver threepenny bits. Years ago, Annie had put in only one but there had been such a fuss between Shirley and Donald when they were small that now she put in enough for everyone to have one, and did her best to make sure they were in the right portions.

'I've got a new card trick to show you after tea,' Donald announced. Donald was two years older than Shirley. He had done an apprenticeship in the docks but now he wanted to join the Army and see the world. Alf Wood wasn't keen on this and they were still arguing about it, but Shirley thought Donald would win in the end. He'd be twenty-one soon, after all, and nobody would be able to tell him what to do, so their father might as well give in now.

After the card trick Jack entertained them with his mouth-organ and they listened to the wireless and played simple games that Jack could understand. Snakes and Ladders was his favourite, until he found himself sliding down too many snakes and started to get fretful, and then Shirley suggested reading them a story, and they all settled down by the fire while she got out a new book. It was called *The Hobbit*, and she'd thought Jack would enjoy the story about dwarves and dragons and buried treasure. To her surprise, they all did, and from then on Jack talked of nothing but hobbits who lived in homes in hills, like rabbits only with furniture, while Donald said that the man who'd written all that about battles and armies knew what he was talking about.

Irene spent Christmas with her parents and eight-year-old brother Bobbie.

Henry Bond was scarcely less distant at Christmas than at any other time of the year, and her mother, who never hugged or kissed, showered her children as usual with expensive gifts. Irene, who had been an only child until she was ten years old, assessed every present given to herself and Bobbie for price so that she could work out who had been most favoured. She watched jealously as he unwrapped a wristwatch – she hadn't been given a watch until she was sixteen. They ate a dinner which was exquisitely cooked but not very ample from a table that was properly laid in a chilly dining room, with a glass of cider each – except for Bobbie, who had orange squash – and then returned to the parlour to read books and, in the evening, play a few decorous pencil and paper games. Henry Bond wound up the gramophone and put on a few records – 'Poet and Peasant', 'White Horse Inn', 'The Thieving Magpie' – and then they all went to bed. Nobody slept late next morning and nobody had a hangover, and when asked what kind of a Christmas they'd had, they replied that it had been 'quiet' and managed to make it sound like a virtue.

Etty stayed in the hostel on Christmas Day. Most of the girls had gone home and the hostel felt big and draughty. Pat and Cora gave her a small box of chocolates between them before going off on Christmas Eve, and she gave them two white handkerchiefs each, with their initials embroidered in one corner. She went to church in the morning, for the company, and enjoyed the singing, but felt lonelier than ever afterwards when everyone stood about wishing each other a Merry Christmas, and then went off to their own dinners. They all seemed to be wearing new gloves, she noticed. Did everyone get new gloves for Christmas? Etty had never had a pair in her life – or, at least, not since she was seven – that she hadn't knitted herself.

She made her way back to the hostel. The others who had stayed were mostly the older 'businesswomen', who had their own rooms at the top of the house and didn't mix much with the younger girls. One of the cooks was on duty, a tired-looking woman whose husband was out of work and who needed the extra money, but she was an indifferent cook and the chicken – a tough old hen that ought to have been boiled – was dry and hard, and the sprouts cooked to a mush. The small group sat together at one table, but the older women took little notice of Etty, sitting mute in her chair. They had treated themselves to a glass of sherry up on the top floor before dinner, but Etty hadn't been invited. Perhaps they hadn't even realised she was there.

Afterwards, she went into the sitting-room, where a small

and inadequate fire had been lit, and read one of her library books. As well as the public library, Etty belonged to two subscription libraries and she had taken out the thickest books she could find. She knew there would be many empty hours to fill before she could go back to work again on Boxing Day.

For her, it was a slow and dreary day, passing all too slowly. For others, however, it seemed to go like a flash. And then, despite Alice's wishes, Christmas was over. The bustle of preparing for the New Year was upon them. Nineteen thirty-eight was about to begin.

Chapter Nine

As 1938 opened, more and more people began to wonder what was happening in Germany and the rest of Europe. Adolf Hitler was like a comet, shooting up into the sky, taking power wherever he wished, and the war in Spain was still being bitterly fought. Shirley Wood said her brother Donald had threatened to go and fight in Spain if he wasn't allowed to join the Army at home, and her mother was nearly out of her mind with worry. 'Dad says he's being really selfish, when he knows Mum's not strong, but Don says if there's a war he'll be conscripted anyway, so he might as well join up now.'

'There's not going to be a war,' Irene Bond said scornfully. They were in the canteen having lunch before starting work. 'My dad's in the Civil Service and he knows. Mr Chamberlain's all for peace, and this Hitler's done a lot of good for Germany.'

'Not for the Jews, he hasn't,' Etty said, and they all turned to stare at her. She so seldom spoke up that it was as if the table had suddenly joined in the conversation. 'He's making them all go and live in certain parts of the cities and they have to wear yellow stars to show who they are. They're not even allowed on the same buses as other people. I think it's awful.'

There was a short silence. Then Irene said dismissively, 'Well, I expect they'd rather it was that way. They've always kept to themselves, the Jews have.'

'Well, I don't like it either,' Jo said. She finished her steak and kidney pie and laid her knife and fork on the empty plate.

'And I think there *could* be a war. People are talking about bombs. They say thousands of people could be killed. It'd be much, much worse than the Great War.'

'It's not going to happen,' Irene insisted. 'Mr Chamberlain won't let it. My dad says so, and he *knows*.'

Henry Bond wasn't alone in his view, but the authorities seemed more pessimistic. London and other big cities had been discussing for some time the measures that would have to be taken to protect their citizens if war should come. They had already carried out exercises – blacking out the streets by turning off all the gaslamps, pretending that gas and water mains had been broken, houses set on fire, people hurt and killed. While most people were fast asleep in bed, fire engines, ambulances and first-aid workers worked as if a bomb had actually fallen and casualties were taken to hospitals where extra staff behaved as if they really had been brought in with horrible injuries – burns, wounds, arms and legs torn off.

There was even talk of gas masks being issued to everyone.

'Gas masks!' Maggie Pratt said. 'Oh, that's horrible. They make you look like a monster – I couldn't wear one of those, I just couldn't.'

'I suppose you'd rather get gassed than spoil your beauty.' Irene said caustically. 'You wouldn't look so beautiful then, I can tell you. My uncle was gassed in 1916 and he's never got over it. He said it was the worst thing that could happen to anyone. He was lucky not to have died. Not that there's any point in all this fuss anyway,' she added. 'It's all a waste of money, there isn't going to be a war—'

'Because your dad's in the Civil Service and he *knows*,' everyone chorused, and Irene flushed bright red and closed her mouth tightly.

Mostly, however, the girls didn't discuss war. There were too many other interesting things happening. Many of the Nippies were finding themselves sweethearts, either from their fellow Lyons employees or from the customers they served. Maggie Pratt had surprised everyone by being immensely popular, despite her fatness. It was her yellow hair, Phyl said, or – according to Jo – her big blue eyes, but

Irene, of course, had another view. She said it was because of the way Maggie threw herself at the men.

'So long as it's wearing trousers, it'll do for her. She's got no self-respect, that one.'

'I have a lot of fun, though,' Maggie said with a wink, and swayed her rounded hips as she made her way through the restaurant to her station. One of the tables had just been occupied by three young men in smart overcoats, their hair waved and shining with Brylcreem. They shrugged off their coats to reveal Fair Isle pullovers under their jackets, and smiled at Maggie as she approached. One in particular had nice eyes, she thought, darker than her own, like little bits of sky when the sun was just going down.

Startled by this poetic thought, she hesitated, and the blue-eyed young man said, 'Hullo, Nippy. You're looking gorgeous today.' His hair was a deep copper colour and very wavy.

'Thanks,' Maggie said, recovering herself. 'I might say the same about you.'

The boys rolled their eyes. 'Hear that, Tommy? She fancies you already.'

'Go on,' he said. 'I bet you talk to all the boys like that.' He grinned at her. He had a nice, curling mouth and white teeth, and Maggie's heart skipped a little.

'That depends,' she said. 'I'm a bit choosy myself. And what are you thinking of choosing yourselves today?'

They laughed and he gave her a twinkling smile. 'That's a dangerous question! Shall I have a look at the menu while I think about it? What's Adam and Eve on a Raft?'

'You don't want to know,' one of the others said. 'It's rude.'

'It's sausage and eggs on toast,' Maggie said. 'There's nothing rude about it.'

'Depends how the eggs and sausage are laid out,' the boy retorted. He looked nice, too, with black hair and brown eyes like a spaniel's, but Maggie thought he wasn't quite as attractive as Tommy. 'Anyway, what do you suppose Adam and Eve *would* get up to on a raft?'

'It's not meant—' Maggie began, but their laughter

drowned her words and Tommy gave his friend a look of mock reproof.

'Shut up, Mike. Can't you see this Nippy's a nice respectable girl? She wouldn't even understand what's in your grubby little mind.'

'Maybe she'll come out with me tonight, then,' Mike suggested, 'and I'll give her a few lessons.'

'Chance would be a fine thing!' Maggie retorted. 'And I could teach you a lesson or two you wouldn't forget in a hurry. Now, what are you going to have? I've got other customers to serve, too, you know.'

The boys laughed again and consulted their menus. With a good deal of banter they chose their meals and Maggie went back to the kitchen and ordered three poached eggs twice.

'This isn't what we asked for,' Mike said, staring at their plates when she brought them to the table.

Maggie opened her eyes wide. 'Isn't it? I made sure that's what you said. Well, what a shame. I'd offer to take them back, only we're so busy in the kitchens just now, I don't know how long you'd have to wait . . . I'm *ever* so sorry.'

They gave her a dark look, which she returned with bland innocence, and then they burst out laughing. 'You're just getting back at us! You're paying us out for the things we said.'

Maggie's innocent stare never faltered. 'I don't know how you can say that. I never even understood the things you said. I'm a respectable girl, remember?'

'You're a cheeky baggage,' Mike said, and they picked up their knives and forks and began to eat their poached eggs.

After that, they came in every Saturday, made straight for Maggie's table and ordered a fantastic concoction of dishes – and Maggie brought them poached eggs on toast. Mr Carter heard them once and stared in astonishment as Maggie brought the tray. He drew her into a corner.

'That wasn't what those customers ordered. I heard them. They wanted all our most expensive dishes, and you've brought them poached eggs! Why?'

'Because that's what they really wanted,' Maggie said,

grinning. 'They always do it. It's a sort of game. They'd die of fright if I brought them what they ordered.'

He gave her a dubious look. 'Well, if you're sure. We don't want any complaints.'

'Don't worry,' Maggie said, balancing her tray on her hip. 'I know how to deal with them. They're just out for a bit of fun, that's all.'

On the third Saturday Tommy asked her to go out with him when her shift was over. 'I'd like to take you to the pictures. There's a good flick on at the Odeon – it's called *The Lady Vanishes*. It's a thriller.'

'I know. I've heard about it.' She didn't say she'd also seen it. 'Thanks, I'd like to come.'

'Smashing,' Mike said, overhearing. 'Who are you going to sit next to, me or Charlie?' Charlie was the third member of the group, a quiet young man with straight brown hair and hazel eyes. He joined in the banter as well, but never to quite the extent that Tommy and Mike did. He looked at Maggie now and blushed a little.

'Here, I didn't know it was going to be a group outing,' Maggie said, and Tommy shook his head and gave his pals a glare.

'It's not. They're not coming within a million miles of us. This is just you and me, Nippy.' He paused. 'Here – I can't go on calling you Nippy. What's your real name?'

'Maggie. Maggie Pratt.'

'Maggie,' he said. 'Maggie and Tommy. Sounds nice, doesn't it?'

Maggie went back to the kitchen, pink with excitement. It wasn't the first date she'd had with a customer, but Tommy was far and away the best-looking one she'd landed yet, and she'd liked the way he repeated her name. The other boys were nice, too, and she wouldn't have minded going out with any of them, but Tommy was the one who'd attracted her. Tommy and Maggie, she thought, and gave herself a little shake of delight. It *did* sound nice.

'What have you been up to?' Phyl asked, seeing her bright eyes. 'Getting off with someone?'

Maggie turned even pinker, but before she could reply Irene pushed past with a tray and remarked acidly, 'I suppose you realise that while you've been flirting with the customers the rest of us have been getting on with our work. It's not even as if that lot are good customers – all they ever have is poached eggs. Can't you persuade them to have something a bit more expensive, push the commission up a bit?'

Maggie turned her back and winked at Phyl. 'They always order posh dishes, but I only ever let 'em have poached eggs, that's what it is,' she whispered, and Phyl giggled. She had herself sometimes given customers the wrong order, to pay them out for complaining or being rude, but she knew from Maggie's tone that this was a game which all the players understood. 'Have you got a date, then?' she asked, making out her own order and popping it into her pigeon-hole.

Maggie nodded. 'Pictures tonight. *The Lady Vanishes* at the Odeon.'

Phyl stared at her. 'But we went to see that on Wednesday.'

'Won't matter if I miss a bit of the story here and there, then, will it?' Maggie flashed her a broad wink and went to the counter to collect the order for another of her tables. This time it was for the most expensive dish on the menu, and she gave Irene a triumphant glance as they passed in the restaurant.

'Hey, Maggie!' Mike's voice, in a stage whisper, seemed to carry more than if he'd shouted. Maggie turned and went over to their table again, frowning.

'You're not supposed to call us by our names. We're Nippies.'

'But I don't want a Nippy. I want you.' He opened his spaniel eyes very wide. 'Listen, why don't you bring a couple of your mates along tonight and we can all go to the flicks together? How about that? I bet there's a few haven't got dates tonight. It'd be fun.' He gazed at her persuasively. 'Go on, Maggie, say yes. Otherwise Charlie and me's going to be all on our ownsome.'

'Stop it, you're making me cry,' Maggie said. She glanced at Tommy. She'd been looking forward to a night out with him, but it was true there was safety in numbers. Her mum had always said that. 'I'll ask a couple,' she said, making up her mind. 'Anyone you particularly fancy?'

'You mean we can choose? You won't just bring us poached eggs?' Mike grinned wickedly. 'Well, if I had my choice it'd be that little dark one – she looks as if she likes a bit of a laugh.'

'That's Phyl,' Maggie said. 'She's a nice girl, mind, respectable. She wouldn't want any funny business.'

'As if I would!' Mike said innocently, and gave Charlie a nudge. 'What about you, mate? Which one d'you want to take out?'

Charlie looked embarrassed. 'Oh, I dunno. I don't mind. I mean, I don't suppose any of them'd want to go out with me – I'll just go home and have an early night—'

The other two hooted and Maggie said quickly, 'I'll find you a nice girl, don't you worry. Look, I've got to go – there's another of my tables wants serving. I'll see you later, right? Outside the staff entrance.'

She noticed that they didn't need to ask where the staff entrance was. So this wasn't the first time they'd asked Nippies out. Well, it didn't matter – it wasn't the first time she'd been out with a customer either. Or Phyl, come to that. Even quiet, demure Shirley had had a date or two. In fact, the only ones who hadn't were Jo and Etty.

Time they did, she decided.

The three girls hurried through their changing and then jostled in front of the mirror, putting on fresh lipstick and Pond's face powder. Jo had refused to go, saying she didn't see the point of sitting through the same picture twice, however good it had been, but Phyl had agreed with alacrity. That left either Etty or Irene or one of the other Nippies, and Maggie certainly wasn't going to ask Irene. She'd been doubtful about Etty too, wondering if she would dare open her mouth the whole evening, but in the end decided that this might suit the quiet Charlie.

'Me?' Etty said, staring at Maggie as if she'd been told to

126

jump off Tower Bridge wearing a fireman's uniform. 'But I've never been out with a boy before.'

'Well, now's a good time to start,' Maggie said briskly. 'Look, they seem like decent boys even if they are a bit cheeky – not that the one you'll be with is cheeky', she added hastily as Etty's eyes widened in dismay, 'and it's only their fun anyway. I don't think we'll have any trouble with them. Bit of hand-holding in the back row, couple of kisses on the way home – that's all they'll expect, the first time anyway.'

Etty looked as if she thought even that would be too much for her to cope with, but Phyl said, 'Maggie's right, Et. There's got to be a first time, and me and Mags will be there, too. It'll be easier after this, you see if it's not.'

'But I don't – I never thought – well, boys just aren't interested in me. He'll be disappointed. I mean, I'm not pretty or anything, like you two—'

Maggie hooted with laughter. 'And me the size of a house! At least you've got a neat little figure, Et, and you'd be as pretty as the next girl if you took a bit of trouble. Listen, me and Phyl will do you up a bit before we go, all right? Put on a bit of lipstick and powder and tie your hair up a bit better. Anyway, it's only one evening. You're not being asked to sign your life away.'

Etty had agreed at last, and now Phyl and Maggie were carrying out their promise to smarten her up. The girls often went out straight from work, to save the journey home and back into town, and their home clothes needed only a string of beads or a brooch to be ready for the evening. Nobody had much money for glamour anyway, and the boys they were going out with would have been embarrassed if they had looked too stylish.

'There,' Maggie said, drawing a bold Cupid's bow on Etty's mouth and stepping back to admire her handiwork. 'Doesn't that look a bit of all right, Phyl? You wouldn't know it was our Etty, would you?'

Phyl looked at her doubtfully. 'You don't think it's a bit much? I mean, she's only got a small face – you've made her look like a rabbit chewing a carrot. No offence to you, Etty,' she added quickly. 'It's just that I think Maggie's gone a bit too far.' She took a scrap of cotton wool and scrubbed at Etty's mouth. 'There, that looks a bit better.'

'Yes, maybe.' Maggie found a comb and started on the other girl's hair. 'How d'you want this done, Etty, loose or in a French pleat?'

Etty's mouth was now smaller, though still with a pretty shape. She stared in the mirror as Maggie swept her hair back from her face and twirled it behind her head. 'Oh – I'm not sure. It makes my eyes look so big . . .'

'Yes, it does, doesn't it?' Phyl said. 'You know, you've got really lovely eyes, Etty. They're a sort of amber colour when you look at them properly. I tell you what, if you darkened your lashes a bit—'

'With mascara?' Etty asked, horrified. 'Oh, I couldn't!'

'Yes, you could. Lots of girls do. Or look, if you don't want to do that, just smear a bit of Vaseline on them to make them shiny.' Phyl would never have dared go home and let her father see her wearing mascara, but here in London it was different. 'There. You look smashing. Charlie'll think he's the luckiest bloke in London to be going out with you.'

'No, he won't,' Maggie said, stretching her mouth wide to draw her own Cupid's bow. 'Tommy's going to think that. But Charlie and Mike can be second and third luckiest.' She smacked her lips together and then curled them up to make sure she hadn't got lipstick on her teeth. 'There! That's me ready. Right, girls – let's go and paint the town red, shall we?'

Irene, shrugging into her own coat, gave them a scornful glance.

'Anyone'd think you were going out with someone really special. You've just been picked up, that's the truth of it. Well, I hope you don't find you've bitten off more than you can chew, that's all.'

'Oh, I don't think we're going to be biting anything off,' Maggie said solemnly. 'Not on our first date, anyway.' She turned to the others and winked. 'Come on, you two. This is going to be fun!'

Maggie was right. The three young men were good

company and put themselves out to give the girls a good time. They gave them tea first in the cinema's own teashop (with Maggie and Phyl dying to make comparisons with the Corner House, but restraining themselves for the sake of good manners). Then they got seats upstairs in the next to back row – 'almost as good as the back,' Maggie giggled in Phyl's ear – handing each girl a small box of chocolates as they sat down.

During tea, they'd all got to know each other a bit better. The boys all worked at a gentlemen's outfitter's shop in Oxford Street. That was why they were so well dressed, because they had to look smart for the shop and could buy their clothes at staff discount. It was all right, Mike said. Not very exciting, but you had to be thankful for a job at all these days.

At the pictures, Etty sat almost frozen with nerves beside Charlie. So far, they had barely spoken to each other, letting the banter and backchat of the other four sweep them along. She wondered if he would try to hold her hand when the lights went down. Glancing sideways at Phyl, who was sitting next to her, she noticed that Phyl's hand was resting innocently on her knee as if its owner hadn't even considered the possibility. Etty relaxed a little. Perhaps boys didn't try to hold your hand first time out, and, anyway, Charlie wasn't likely to want to hold hers – she was only here for company. It wasn't as if he'd chosen her. He'd have had Jo beside him if Jo hadn't turned the idea down.

The cinema was almost full now and the lights dimmed, leaving only those which were playing on the heavy curtains. Etty watched, fascinated by the way they drifted across the velvet drapes and changed colour. The whole effect was so rich and sumptuous, so unlike anything she had ever known in her own life, like being in a palace. The cinema was ornately decorated, too, like a theatre with golden cherubs on the ceiling and murals on the walls. Etty could have stared at it all for hours.

However, it was now dark and the curtains had parted to let them see the advertisements. Etty watched pictures of smiling couples emerging from jewellers' shops or choosing furniture. To her, they were as different a world as the cherubs and velvet curtains, but she knew that girls like Phyl and Maggie saw them as part of their own future. Getting engaged, married, setting up home . . . It'll never happen to me, Etty thought. I wouldn't even know how to start.

Pathe Pictorial came on, with a short film about a candle factory, and then news of the latest events in Europe. Hitler had declared himself Supreme Commander of the German armed forces and had taken over control of foreign policy. He had thrown out some of the generals and established a new government, with old friends like Goering and Hess and von Ribbentrop as his advisers. There was talk of him sending his army into Austria, to take over the country of his birth.

Etty was thankful when the news film ended and the B film came on. It was a cowboy film, and she quite liked them – it was nice to see the wide open spaces. She watched as Hopalong Cassidy cantered on his white horse across the prairies and through rocky canyons, and wondered how they ever found their way about out there.

Halfway through the film she noticed that Mike's hand was holding Phyl's. She glanced nervously at Charlie, but he appeared to be engrossed in the story. Surreptitiously, Etty moved her own hand so that it was out of his reach, and clutched both her hands together in her lap.

The cowboy picture ended and the lights came up again to give people the chance to buy ice cream from the girls who stood at the front of the cinema or at the doors leading to the stairs. Tommy and Mike got up and Charlie glanced at Etty and asked her in a mumble if she wanted an ice. She shook her head in panic, as if he'd offered her a spider, and he subsided, staring at the curtains which had been drawn across the screen again. They sat in silence while Phyl and Maggie scraped at their little cardboard tubs and chattered like magpies beside them. Etty was unable to think of a single word to say. He'll never ask me out again, she thought miserably, and didn't know whether she would be glad or sorry.

During the big picture, she observed that Tommy and Mike had each got an arm round the shoulders of the girl beside them. Phyl and Maggie didn't seem to mind. They sat gazing at the screen, as if so mesmerised by the film they'd already seen once that they hadn't really noticed the arms, but they'd also moved slightly, to make it more comfortable, and Maggie was definitely snuggling up. Etty felt her face burn with embarrassment, but Charlie hadn't seemed to see what was happening, and he hadn't even glanced at her hand. Obviously, he just wasn't interested in her, and although she was relieved she also felt obscurely dispirited. Still, it was no more than she'd expected, and at least she'd always be able to say a chap had taken her to the pictures once.

The film ended and they all stood for the National Anthem. Afterwards, they stood on the pavement, hesitating about what to do next. Tommy and Mike said that they'd see the girls home, and Charlie glanced interrogatively at Etty. She shook her head quickly. She could catch a bus at the corner, she said, and the stop was right opposite where she lived. There was no mistaking the look of relief on his face.

Etty sat on the top of the bus, alone amongst the couples who were occupying the rest of the seats. Phyl and Maggie were being escorted home now – Maggie to the house where she lived with her sprawling family, Phyl to her digs where Jo would be waiting. Without doubt, the boys would put their arms round the girls' waists as they walked along, and probably want to kiss them goodnight at their doors. Phyl might not allow it – she was the sort of girl who wouldn't on the first time out – but Maggie might. Maggie was the kind of girl who liked being kissed and didn't see any reason to say no.

Etty got off the bus and went into the hostel just before the door was locked for the night. The bedroom she shared with Pat and Cora was empty. They were both out at a dance and had a key for getting in late. She washed in the cold bathroom and got into bed and lay there, thinking about the velvet curtains and the cherubs and Charlie sitting beside her.

I never even said thank you for a lovely evening, she

realised with a sudden rush of guilt. I hardly said anything at all the whole time. And he hardly said anything to me.

Customers weren't the only ones to offer opportunities for evenings out. There were plenty of young men working at Lyons, and plenty of chances to meet them. The best opportunities were at the Sports and Leisure Club at Sudbury, and the girls were encouraged to join. Lyons wanted their employees to be one big happy family, playing as well working together, and there were activities to suit everyone. They arranged cheap train fares, too, so that everyone could get there easily.

Jo went for the sports. She joined the hockey club and was soon playing in team matches against the other Corner Houses. She also played netball, where her height gave her an advantage, and looked forward to summer when she would be able to swim. She thought she might even go to Hammersmith and learn to row.

'There's an amateur dramatic club, too,' she said to Phyl. 'Why don't you go along?'

'D'you think I'd be good enough?'

'You, good enough? Haven't you been acting ever since you could walk? Weren't you in the Sunshine Kiddies, doing concerts in the church hall? Course you'd be good enough, Phyl. Don't be daft.'

'I don't know. It's a bit different from the Sunshine Kiddies.'

'It's a bit different from the London Palladium, too,' Jo retorted. 'It's just an amateur club. You're not being asked to act with Clark Gable. What's the matter with you? You've never been shy of putting yourself forward before.'

'I'm not really.' Phyl grinned at her. 'Matter of fact, I've been thinking about it myself. You never know, I could end up with my name in lights after all.'

'Fairy lights, maybe,' Jo scoffed. 'But honestly, Phyl, I do think you ought to try. You're a smashing little actress.'

Phyl followed her advice and got herself into the amateur dramatics. They put on plays and revues, and she was given a small part in one of Noël Coward's plays. She did well and was promised a bigger part next time.

'I suppose you're dreaming of your name in lights now,' Jo teased her. '"*Phyllis Jennings, in* Bitter Sweet *by Noël Coward.*" I shall expect free seats, you know.'

'Don't be daft,' Phyl said, brushing her hair. 'I haven't got a chance. Anyway, I'm not sure I want to.' She paused, gazing at her reflection. 'It does sound a bit of all right, though, doesn't it? Or d'you think I ought to change my name to something more interesting? I mean, Jennings is pretty ordinary, isn't it?'

Jo started to laugh, and Phyl turned round and threw a pillow at her. 'All right! I know it'll never happen. But it doesn't hurt to dream a bit!'

As well as the sports and drama, there were Saturday night dances and the big staff balls at Seymour House. There were staff awards, too, handed out at the Olympia Hotel, where the kitchen and catering departments demonstrated their skills. The Nippies gazed in awe at the exhibits – cold dishes, elaborately arranged and decorated with aspic and colourful salads, and a magnificent sugar model of Westminster Abbey, correct to the last detail, which won first prize and a gold medal.

'It's no wonder Lyons does the catering for Buckingam Palace parties,' Jo said. 'It's a work of art, that is.'

Phyl and Maggie had been out again with Mike and Tommy, but Etty had refused to go, and although Charlie still came to the Corner House he was absent from the excursions to the cinema. Etty blushed when she saw him and turned her face away and once, when Maggie's tables were all full and the boys came to one of hers, she begged Phyl to serve them instead.

'I can't do that. You know we have to stick to our own stations.'

'I'll say I've got a headache. I'll say I feel sick. Please, Phyl.'

'You're being daft,' Phyl said, looking at her curiously. 'You know them all, they're not going to bite you.'

'They'll order all sorts of things and I shan't know what to do. Maggie always takes them poached eggs, whatever they ask for – but suppose they mean it this time? They might report me.'

'Oh, for heaven's sake! Of course they won't report you. They're friends, Etty. Don't be so wet.'

Etty gave up and went to her table, shaking. Mike and Tommy looked at her kindly and said hello, just as if she were a normal person. She spoke to them as if she'd never seen them before, as if they were customers who had come into the Corner House for the first time in their lives and had to be made welcome.

'Good afternoon, gentlemen. What can I bring you?'

Mike grinned. 'Hear that, you two? She called us gentlemen. Old Charlie must have behaved himself better than us that night at the flicks.'

Etty blushed and Charlie looked determinedly away. Tommy gave Mike a nudge with his elbow.

'Shut up, you're embarrassing the lady. We'd like three poached eggs, twice,' he said to Etty. 'And a pot of tea for three. And you're looking very nice this afternoon, if you don't mind my saying so.'

Etty flushed to the roots of her hair. 'Oh. No. No, I don't mind. I mean, thank you. Th-three poached eggs twice?' She could hardly believe they hadn't teased her and pulled her leg like they did with Maggie. She escaped quickly before they could change their minds and ask for lobster or something equally exotic that she was sure they didn't mean.

Charlie had said nothing, hadn't even glanced at her. She felt miserable and then shrugged. What could she expect after the way she'd treated him?

'If they ask for a date,' Maggie whispered in the kitchen, 'tell 'em we're busy tonight but we might make it next week.'

'They won't ask me. Don't you want to go out with them any more?'

'Oh, yes, but me and Phyl are getting a bit fed up with them just coming in here on a Saturday afternoon and asking us out as if they know we've got nothing else to do. Don't want 'em thinking we're on the shelf. It's time they realised

134

there's a queue. Anyway, it's the dance tonight and that good-looking masher from the Brasserie in Oxford Street Corner House has asked me if I'll go with him.' She hurried off to collect her orders.

The boys didn't ask her directly to go out with them that evening. Instead, Tommy enquired casually whether she knew if Maggie and Phyl were doing anything. Etty stammered something about the dance and saw them lift their eyebrows. She escaped again, thankful that her tables were all full and she had too much to do to stand about talking. When she went back to clear the plates and ask if they wanted anything else, she found a note pressed into her hand.

It'll be for one of the others, she thought, preparing to put it into either Maggie's or Phyl's pigeon-hole. But when she glanced at it to see which name was written on the outside, she saw with astonishment that it was her own.

Stunned, she unfolded it and read the brief inscription. It was from Charlie, and he wanted her to meet him at the staff entrance at the end of her shift. *We could go to the pictures again*, he had written. *You didn't say you were going to the dance, so I hope you'll say yes. Charlie.*

I can't, she thought in panic. I can't go out with him all on our own. I shan't know what to say, and there won't be anyone else there. And what if he wants to hold my hand this time, or put his arm round me? He might even try to kiss me. I *can't*.

The trouble was, she didn't know how to say no.

Chapter Ten

Phyl wasn't the only one to be curious about Etty. Irene Bond, at first surprised to see the pale, quiet girl who had recently been promoted from the kitchens, had quickly become curious and determined to find out all about her.

Irene liked to know all about everyone. Her curiosity didn't stem from a natural interest in her fellows, as Phyl's did, but from a furtive desire to know things that might be useful to her. She liked the powerful feeling of knowing secrets.

She buttonholed Etty one day. 'How are you getting on? D'you think you'll enjoy being a Nippy?'

Etty blushed. She was getting used to serving, and although she wasn't as lively as some of the girls, she had her own brand of shy friendliness that seemed to go down well with a certain kind of customer. She was quick and neat in her movements, too, and eager to please, which was the main quality that Lyons looked for in their staff.

'I hope so. It's much nicer than being in the kitchens.'

'I bet it is,' Irene said. 'Look, let's sit together when we have our lunch tomorrow. I can give you a few tips about how to go on.'

Etty was dazed by this attention. She had already realised that Irene wasn't the most popular of the girls, but thought that it was because Irene's superciliousness was genuine class, and that the others were in awe of her. To be asked to sit next to her seemed like an accolade.

Phyl was surprised, too, when her protégée took a chair on

136

the other side of the table next day. Lady Muck won't like that, she thought, preparing to defend her chick, but to her further astonishment Irene gave Etty a friendly smile and passed her the salt without being asked. Well, there was a turn-up for the book.

'So how d'you like being a Nippy?' Irene enquired, in the pleasantest tone anyone had ever heard her use. 'It must be quite a change after being a slavey in the kitchens.'

'It wasn't all that bad in the kitchens,' Etty said, a shade defensively. 'Mrs Martin was good to work for – strict, you know, but fair. To tell you the truth . . .' She hesitated, feeling disloyal to the others, but Irene's nod encouraged her to go on. 'Well, to tell you the truth, sometimes I wish I was back there. It's not that I don't like being a Nippy – I do. Only I'm not always very good at it.' She gazed into Irene's interested eyes and whispered, 'Sometimes I can't remember what the customers ordered.'

'Oh, I know,' Irene said sympathetically. 'Not that I've ever forgotten anything myself, but I can see how easy it'd be. If only we were allowed to write things down . . .' She had a suspicion that Etty couldn't write, but she must have been wrong because Etty sighed and nodded.

'It'd be such a help. I get in a panic, you see. Why, only yesterday a man asked for coffee and a dash, and you know what I took him? Sausage and mash!' Her eyes were enormous in her small face. 'I thought I was going to die, honest I did. Luckily he was a gent and saw the funny side, and he even said he'd eat it, so long as I brought him his coffee as well – but it could've been awful, he could've kicked up a real fuss. I didn't know whether I was on me head or me heels all through the rest of the shift.'

'I'll tell you what you can do,' Irene said, shifting her chair a little closer. 'Take a bit of paper and a stub of pencil in your pocket and just scribble down the initials of what the customers order. S for sausage, M for mash, that sort of thing. No one'll notice you doing that, and it'll be just enough to jog your memory.'

'I suppose I could do that,' Etty said thoughtfully. 'Yes, I will! Thanks ever so much, Irene. That'll be a real help.'

They continued their meal and after a few moments Irene spoke again. 'Where do you live?'

Etty coloured. 'Oh. I live in – in a sort of girls' boarding house. A hostel.'

Irene saw nothing odd in that. Plenty of girls from out of London lived in digs or hostels. 'I meant, where's your home? Your real home? You don't sound as if you come from the country.'

'I don't. I mean, I've always lived in London.' Etty glanced around with some desperation. 'D'you want some more gravy?'

'No, thanks.' Irene studied her thoughtfully. Obviously, Etty was embarrassed about something, something to do with her home. This could be worth pursuing, but it would have to be done carefully. 'You've got a boy, haven't you? One of those chaps who comes to Maggie's table.'

'Oh, no, he's not really my boy.' Etty's blush deepened. 'I mean, it's just that there's three of them and they wanted three of us, and Jo didn't want to go so Phyl asked me—' She stopped, uncomfortably aware that Irene herself could have been invited, but hadn't. 'I don't think he really likes me all that much,' she finished, and remembered the note he'd passed her. She'd worried all the rest of that shift about how to avoid him but eventually, with a sense of doom, she'd come out of the staff entrance to find him waiting, and they'd walked off together without a word. And that was how it had been for the whole evening. A silent tea together, nearly three hours in the cinema spent watching the films so intently they might have been going to be tested on them, and then a brief goodnight as he saw her on to her bus. I've spoilt it all, she'd thought miserably as she'd jolted through the dark streets towards the hostel. He'll hate me now, he'll never want to see me again.

He had, though. They'd been out together three times since, twice with the others and once on their own, and still they'd found no way of breaking the ice. The continued

138

silence had become almost comfortable. Etty thought now that if either of them did speak, it would be as if a tree had come suddenly to life. But did all that mean he was her chap, she was his girl? She didn't see how it could.

Irene felt a tug of impatience. This girl was really hard work. She had no idea of conversation. It was as if she'd spent her life in a bubble, seeing other people but unable to join in with them. Once Irene had found out what she wanted to know, she would drop her.

Serving lunches an hour or so later, Etty scribbled down the initials of the dishes that had been ordered, as Irene had suggested. She went backwards and forwards between the restaurant and the kitchens, feeling more confident every minute. Until the moment when she glanced at her notes and saw the letter C.

C. What did it stand for? Carrots? Cucumber? Cauliflower? Her mind went blank and then whirled in panic. She couldn't go back to the customer and ask. What would happen if she took back the wrong dish? He hadn't looked the patient sort, like the sausage-and-mash man, he looked more like a complainer. Tears came to her eyes and she put up a shaking hand.

'What's the matter, kid?' Her mentor was at her side. Thankfully, Etty turned, blinking rapidly, and her voice wobbled as she explained.

'I don't know what he wants.' She showed the scrap of paper with its scribbled notes. 'It could be anything – anything beginning with C. What am I going to do? It's the second time I've made a mistake.' She bit her lip. 'Oh, I knew I shouldn't ever have applied to be a Nippy, they'll send me back to the kitchens straight away. Or sack me altogether.' The tears were threatening to spill over. 'I don't know what I'll do if I lose this job, I don't know *what* I'll do!'

'Now, stop getting in such a tizzy.' Irene studied the notes. 'Let's think what it could be. What do these other letters mean?'

Etty peered over her shoulder. 'I don't know. LC – oh, that's lamb chops. And P must be potatoes – no, BP is boiled potatoes and P is peas. But I don't know what C—' Her voice began to rise again.

'Carrots,' Irene said decisively. 'It must be. They wouldn't want two green veg, would they, and it wouldn't be cucumber. You take carrots, Etty, and it'll be all right, you'll see.'

'Carrots,' Etty repeated, and her face cleared. 'Yes, that's right, it was carrots. Oh, Irene, thank you, *thank* you.' She shot off to the collection counter, determined to give her customer the best meal she could to make up for her stupidity.

After work, Irene took her out for tea. They went to an ordinary teashop, where they weren't likely to be seen by any other Nippies, and had toasted teacakes and a plate of assorted fancies. Irene insisted on paying.

'Oh, no. I must pay for myself.'

'Who says so? It was my idea so it's my treat.' Irene got out her purse and pushed Etty's hand away. 'Tell you what, we'll pay turn and turn about – your turn next time.'

'Next time?' The thought of tea with Irene becoming a regular event hadn't occurred to Etty. She felt her face grow pink again. In fact, she felt pink all over – pink and happy and excited. I've got another friend, she thought incredulously. Phyl and Jo, and now Irene. And all through being a Nippy.

Tea with Irene did become regular, just as did going home with Phyl and Jo. True, Irene never suggested taking Etty back to her own family, but Etty didn't mind. It was enough to go into a teashop with her and be waited on for a change. She found herself growing to trust Irene, and telling her things she hadn't yet even told Phyl.

'Where did you live before you went to the hostel?' Irene asked one afternoon.

The question took Etty by surprise. Her face closed up. 'Oh, you wouldn't know it.'

'Why wouldn't I? I know London pretty well, as it happens. Come on, Etty, you can tell me. I'm your friend, aren't I?'

Etty looked at her. Irene was a cut or two above the other

Nippies. She wore smart clothes and had her hair done by a hairdresser. She kept herself slightly apart from the other girls, yet she had picked Etty out of all the other Nippies to sit beside her at lunch. She'd helped her out of a hole over the carrots, and they regularly had tea together. Of course she was a friend.

'You won't like me any more once you know,' she said uncertainly. 'You won't want to know me any more.'

'Don't be daft,' Irene said. 'Why on earth shouldn't I?' Her curiosity was almost unbearable. She leaned forward. 'Come on, Etty. Tell me all about it.'

Etty hestitated. She badly wanted a special friend, someone to talk to and share secrets with, but she had been hurt before by thoughtless or even cruel remarks, and was afraid to risk it again. She'd been trying to pluck up courage to talk to Phyl, who was friendly and had taken her back to have tea at Mrs Holt's, but Phyl had Jo for her special friend, and plenty of others besides. Etty didn't think Phyl would want to share secrets, however kind she might be.

Irene didn't seem to have any special friend. She behaved as if she were somehow better than the other girls and she hadn't gone out of her way to be particularly friendly with any of them. Etty was flattered by her attention. The idea of being singled out by someone like Irene, so smart and refined, to become her special friend, was heady.

'Well,' she said, taking her courage in both hands, 'you know I live in a hostel?'

'Yes, you told me that,' Irene said carelessly. 'There's nothing wrong in that. Quite a few of the Nippies do. I suppose your proper home's out in the country somewhere?'

Etty shook her head and licked her lips. It wasn't too late to draw back. She could tell a fib, say yes, and make up some kind of story . . . Irene's green eyes were fixed on her, like lights burning into her mind, and she knew she couldn't do it. She'd never been able to fib and get away with it, and she wouldn't be able to now.

'I haven't got a real home,' she said in a whisper. 'I mean, the hostel's where I live – all the time. I – I haven't got anywhere else.'

Irene stared at her. 'But what about your mum and dad? Where do they live?'

'I haven't got a mum and dad,' Etty whispered. 'I haven't got anyone.'

There was a short silence. Etty stared at the tablecloth, waiting for Irene to get up and leave. I wish I hadn't done it, she thought miserably, I wish I hadn't told her. She wasn't the right one after all. She doesn't want to be my friend. She just wants to *know* . . .

'You mean you're an orphan?' Irene hadn't got up and walked out. She leaned across the table again and Etty glanced up and met her eyes and mistook their burning avidity for compassion. 'Come on. Tell me. Tell me where you grew up and what happened to your mum and dad. Look, it's all right, I won't spread it around. Tell me all about it . . .'

In March, Hitler returned in glory to Vienna, cheered through the streets in a procession led by forty army tanks. Wearing the brown uniform of a storm trooper, he stood in his open car, his arm held out stiffly in the Nazi salute, and all along the route were banners and flags bearing the swastika. He declared himself the Führer of a nation of over seventy million people.

In Spain, General Franco declared the civil war over. Democracy did not work for his country, he said; it had done great damage.

All this was shown at the cinema on Pathe Pictorial but, apart from Jo, the Nippies were more interested in the 'big pictures' they had gone to see – *Jezebel*, with Bette Davis and Henry Fonda, *Robin Hood* with swashbuckling heart-throb Errol Flynn, Spencer Tracy and the pint-sized boy actor Mickey Rooney in *Boys' Town*.

Tommy and Mike wanted to see Humphrey Bogart and James Cagney in *Angels With Dirty Faces*. It was a gangster film, but Phyl and Maggie went anyway. You had to let them have what they wanted sometimes. In fact, Maggie was letting Tommy have pretty well anything he wanted these days, though she wasn't sure about Phyl and Mike. As for Etty and Charlie, no one could understand their relationship. Whenever they went out with the others, neither of them seemed to speak a word, and it didn't seem likely they said much more when they were on their own.

'Old Charlie's always been a quiet sort of a bloke,' Tommy said as he and Maggie found a secluded spot amidst some bushes in Hyde Park. 'I suppose that's why Etty suits him.'

'You'd think he'd want someone with a bit of conversation,' Maggie argued. 'I mean, after that first time I thought he'd never bother again, and Etty was petrified when he asked her out on her own. But they keep on meeting all the same. It's as if neither of them knows how to break it off.'

'Well, maybe they don't want to. All you have to do is not turn up if you don't want to go on with it.' Tommy pulled her down on the grass. 'Don't let's worry about them, anyway. Have I told you lately you're a smasher, Mags?'

'Go on,' she said, pleased. 'You know I'm too fat.'

'Not for me. I like an armful.' He demonstrated it by wrapping his arms around her. 'I love every pound of you, you know that?'

'You're just saying it.'

'Want me to prove it?'

Maggie pushed him away. 'No, I don't! Stop it, Tommy, you're like an octopus. Don't you ever think about anything else?'

'Not much,' he admitted cheerfully. 'Why should I, when thinking about you's the best thing I know? How about giving me some more to think about?'

'I said no.' But her voice was nicely judged to be not quite convincing enough, and he grinned and started to unbutton her blouse, kissing her at the same time.

Maggie slapped his hand away. 'Tommy, I'm warning you . . .'

'Go on,' he murmured into her ear. 'What are you warning me? What dreadful punishment are you promising me? I hope it's the same one as last time!' He slid his hands inside her blouse and tickled her.

Maggie collapsed against him, giggling. 'Tommy, you're awful. What am I going to do with you?'

'I just told you,' he said, getting her bra unfastened and burying his face in the pillow of her warm, soft breasts. 'The same as last time, I hope.'

Phyl's and Mike's relationship was much more decorous, although it wasn't for want of trying on Mike's part. They went for walks in the park or on Hampstead Heath and held hands, and when they were in a suitably sheltered spot Mike would put his arms around Phyl and kiss her. She kissed him back, but she never allowed more than three or four kisses, and then she firmly pulled away and took his hand to walk on. She knew that Mike would have liked more kissing and, no doubt, a good deal else besides, but although she liked him and enjoyed being with him she was never tempted to go any further herself.

'Let's sit down for a while,' Mike would suggest, indicating a hidden dell or a small clearing amongst the trees, and Phyl would agree but remain sitting firmly upright while he lay on his back and looked up at her. He stroked her arm and tugged it gently, but she simply smiled and looked at him as if he were a mildly naughty small boy.

'Come on, Mike. I said I'd be home for supper.'

'What did you do that for?' he grumbled, getting reluctantly to his feet. 'I thought we'd spend the evening together. I said we'd meet Tommy and go to the flicks.'

'Well, you can still go to the pictures with Tommy, but Maggie and me are going to the Club. There's a dance on.'

'You'll be dancing with other blokes,' he said jealously.

'That's right. And I won't be letting them do any more than I let you, so there's not a thing for you to worry about. Not that you've got any right to worry,' she added thoughtfully. 'You're not my sweetheart, Mike. We're just friends.'

'What do you mean, just friends? You let me kiss you.'

'I like you kissing me. And it's good practice.' She laughed at the look on his face. 'Come on, Mike. We're not engaged, nor ever likely to be. It's just a bit of fun, you know that.' She gave him a challenging look. 'I bet you go out with other girls.'

He blushed. 'Only as friends. There's no one serious.'

'No,' she said. 'And we're not serious either. Come on, if we go now we can have an ice cream before we get the bus back. I fancy a strawberry cornet – what about you?'

Jo wasn't interested in dancing, or in going out with boys. She was still modelling herself on her namesake in *Little Women*. Like Phyl, she would have enjoyed having a nice chap just as a friend – a boy like Laurie, for instance – but unlike Phyl, she didn't want any kissing or 'soppy stuff'. Anyway, what boy would want to go out with a girl like her, as tall as him or perhaps even taller? Boys liked small girls like Phyl or even Etty, or cheerful, cuddly ones like Maggie.

Irene didn't seem to attract many young men either. She was friendly enough when she waited on them in the restaurant, but she didn't respond to their banter. She was cool, calm and efficient, and sometimes she was taken for a supervisor, or one of the more experienced Nippies who knew all the Corner Houses and moved about to cover for girls who were off sick.

Irene enjoyed these mistakes. She had set her sights on rising in the Lyons' hierarchy and didn't intend to remain a Nippy for a minute longer than she could help.

'My mum says I'm too good to be a waitress,' she said in the staff dining-room. 'She wouldn't have let me apply anywhere else but Lyons, but she says you can always get on in a good firm, if you want a career.'

'I don't see the point of "getting on",' Phyl said. 'We'll all be getting married in a few years anyway. Our sort of people don't bother about *careers* and all that.'

'Speak for yourself,' Irene said haughtily. 'Anyway, what do you mean by "our" sort of people? My dad's in the Civil Service.'

'I know, and you've got an inside bathroom and a front

garden with grass,' Phyl said, sounding bored. 'Well, if all that just means you've got to have a career instead of a proper home and family, I'd rather manage with a tin bath hanging on the wall and an outside lavatory, thank you very much. I bet we have more fun down our way than you do.'

She was surprised when Irene turned up at the Saturday dance a week or two later, and even more surprised to find that she was a good dancer. She was asked to dance by one of the men from the Coventry Street Corner House, who didn't know her, and once it was seen how good she was a lot of the older men, men in their late twenties or even thirties, asked her as well. She was never off the floor, Phyl remarked a little jealously to Maggie.

Etty only came dancing once, spending almost the whole evening sitting on a chair near the door looking as if she wanted to escape. The other girls took pity on her and danced with her themselves, but they knew she wouldn't come again. Irene didn't bother. She was too busy enjoying the unaccustomed attention herself, and she seemed to have dropped Etty now. She no longer saved a seat beside her at lunch, and there were no more excursions to the teashop.

Etty hid her hurt feelings. She wished she had never confided in her but, then, she'd known all along that Irene wouldn't want to befriend her once she knew the truth. Just for once, she'd hoped it might not be true but, just as she'd expected, Irene had cooled off rapidly, paying the bill for their tea and saying goodbye on the pavement outside, then hardly speaking to her next day. Etty, still hoping that she had at last found a friend, had made to sit down next to her at lunch, but Irene had walked pointedly round to the other end of the table and not even glanced at her during the meal.

I'll know better next time, Etty thought miserably. I won't tell *anyone* any more – not even Phyl. Nobody wants to know a girl like me. She withdrew into herself and became quieter than ever.

The two big dance crazes then were the Big Apple, a strange ritual composed of jerky hand gestures, and the Lambeth Walk. Everyone had been to see the musical show,

Me And My Gal, with Lupino Lane doing his new song-and-dance routine and making them all join in with the chorus – 'I want you all to shout Oi! as loudly as you can, all right? First the ladies – no, I can hardly hear you – try again – that's better. Now the gentlemen – and now all together – Oi!' – and at some point in the evening's dancing it was inevitable that they would all line up, parading in a big circle round the room, jerking their thumbs over their shoulders and shouting '*Oi!* ' as the master had trained them to do.

Jo came to the dances sometimes, for something to do, but she was more interested in the sports. She had shone in both the hockey and netball teams and as the weather improved she began to enter the swimming races. Some of these were held at Sudbury and some in the Serpentine in Hyde Park. There were meetings every Tuesday afternoon and evening, with races for men and women. Jo's swimming improved rapidly and by June she was starting to win races and even the diving competitions. Her lanky gawkiness was transformed to streamlined grace in the water, and her swimming costume showed off her slender figure.

'That girl in the red bathers is a bit of all right,' Phyl heard a voice say close behind her as she sat watching one Sunday afternoon. She resisted the impulse to turn and look, but pricked up her ears.

'Too skinny,' another voice disagreed. 'I like something a bit more cuddly myself – like that little dark one in front.'

And they say listeners never hear good of themselves! Phyl thought with a tiny giggle. The first boy spoke again.

'Well, I've seen them going about together. Why not see if we can click with them?'

Phyl kept her eyes determinedly on Jo, who was now back on the high diving board. She spread her arms wide, stood poised on tiptoe for a brief moment, then seemed almost to float out into mid-air, drifting down like a swallow and bringing her arms together at the last moment, to enter the water with scarcely a splash.

'Say what you like, she's a smashing diver,' her admirer

said, and Phyl turned at last, unable to restrain her curiosity any longer.

'Actually, she's my cousin.'

The boys gazed at her. For a moment, she wasn't sure which was which, then she realised that one was looking at her with more interest than the other. So that must be the one who liked cuddly girls!

Phyl returned his interest. He wasn't bad-looking at all, she decided, with soft auburn hair and bright blue eyes amongst a sea of freckles. He was taller than she was – but few people weren't! – and he wasn't thin, but he wasn't fat either. She grinned at him and his fair skin coloured.

'Were you listening?' he demanded challengingly.

'Course I was. You shouldn't talk so loud if you don't want people to hear you.' Phyl looked at the other boy. He looked about nineteen or twenty, with dark, rather curly brown hair and hazel eyes. Nothing special, she thought, just ordinary but nice enough. He'd do for Jo to practise on – it was time she had a chap.

'If you want an intro, I'll take you over when the diving's finished,' she offered, and he blushed almost as pink as his friend.

'I don't want to push in—'

'Well, you're not going to meet many girls, then, are you? You've got to put yourself forward a bit. Anyway, Jo hasn't got a steady boy, not just at the moment.' She wasn't going to admit that Jo hadn't yet had a steady boy at all – or even an unsteady one, come to that. 'Come over with me and I'll tell her you're interested in diving.' She glanced at the red-haired boy and added offhandedly, 'You can come, too, if you like.'

Jo had one more dive to do. They watched as she drifted gracefully down and slid into the water, surfacing halfway along the pool to swim easily to the shallow end. She climbed out, pulled off her rubber bathing-cap to shake out her chestnut hair, and walked away towards the changing-rooms.

'Still think she's a bit of all right?' Phyl asked slyly, and grinned as the brown-haired boy flushed again.

'I didn't mean anything by it—'

'Yes, you did. You meant she looks nice and you fancy her.' Phyl laughed and shook his arm. 'Well, she *is* nice! And I should know – our mums are twins and we've lived next door to each other all our lives. We're Nippies at Marble Arch.' She tilted her head at the two boys. 'And if I'm going to introduce you, you'd better tell me your names.'

'I'm Nick Laurence,' the brown-haired boy said. 'And this idiot here's Sandy Smith. He's got a proper name but nobody ever uses it, I can't even remember what it is.'

'Yes, you can,' Sandy retorted, but he didn't say what it was and Phyl guessed that he probably didn't like it much. She stood up, brushing the back of her skirt in case it had got dusty on the bench.

'Well, come on, then. I said I'd meet Jo by the tea-bar. She's always thirsty after swimming. And we've got to go soon, so if you're going to make your mark you'd better make it quickly.'

As it happened, Sandy seemed to make his mark more quickly with Phyl than Nick did with Jo, who received his introduction and compliments rather coolly. They stood for a while talking a little awkwardly, then went inside for a cup of tea. It was always a treat for the girls to be waited on, and they sat back in their chairs, sipping their tea and nibbling at buttered scones. But although Phyl and Sandy were soon laughing together, Nick didn't seem to be making much headway with Jo.

'What was the matter with Nick?' she asked as they walked to the station. 'Didn't you like him? I thought he looked okay.'

'Yes, he's all right,' Jo said indifferently, and Phyl gave her cousin a sharp glance.

'Come on, Jo, spit it out. There's something you didn't like about him, isn't there? What was it? He seemed a decent boy to me.'

'Oh, I expect he is.' Jo paused, then said in a rush, 'Well, if you must know, it's his name!'

'His *name*?' Phyl stopped and stared at her. 'What on

earth's the matter with his name? What's the matter with Nick?'

'Not that name. His other name. His surname.' Jo looked at her as if she ought to understand. 'It's *Laurence*.'

'Laurence? Well, I know it is. Nick Laurence. I still can't see anything wrong with it, though. It sounds quite nice . . . Oh-h-h . . .' She widened her eyes. 'It's the name of that boy in the book, isn't it? *Little Women*. He's called Laurie. But what can it matter? I thought he was one of your favourite characters.'

'He is.' Jo scuffed her toe on the pavement. 'All right, Phyl, you can laugh all you like. But when I saw him and heard his name – Phyl, he even *looks* like Laurie in the book – well, I know it's daft but I just thought I didn't want to have anything to do with him. I mean, you know what happened to Laurie, don't you?'

'No.' Phyl had never read any of the sequels to *Little Women*. 'I can't say I do? What did happen to him? Something awful?'

Jo laughed a little despite herself. 'Well, I suppose he didn't think so, but I did! He married *Amy*. That silly little stuck-up, conceited, selfish brat! And I *know* it sounds silly, but I just thought – well, Jo and Laurie – I don't stand a chance really, do I?'

Phyl shook her head slowly, then took her cousin's arm.

'You're right. It does sound silly. It sounds plain crazy, if you want to know the truth. And I'll tell you something else, Jo Mason, it *proves* that it's time you had a proper boyfriend and got all these crackpot ideas out of that head of yours! You know what? You're just looking for excuses. You're just so scared of boys, you'll find any excuse not to go out with one!'

'Phyl, I'm not!' Jo exclaimed, hurt and indignant.

'Well, then, prove it to me. Now listen, did Nick Laurence ask to see you again?'

'Not exactly,' Jo muttered. 'He just said he'd be at the Club next Sunday afternoon and he'd look out for me at the swimming-pool.'

'So he's willing to give you another chance, and if you ask

me it's more than you deserve,' Phyl said with some force. 'And you're going to be there, aren't you?'

'I don't know. I thought I might go home next week—'

'You're going swimming,' Phyl said firmly. 'And you're going to be nice to Nick Laurence – it's not *his* fault he's saddled with a name that reminds you of some bloke in a book! – and if he asks you out, which he will if I have to break his arm to make him, you're going to say yes. Is that clear?'

Jo glanced at her and grinned a little shamefacedly, her cheeks colouring. She does like him, Phyl thought jubilantly. She was miserable because she thought she'd messed it up.

'Was I really rude to him?' Jo asked a little meekly.

'Not *really* rude. But you weren't very encouraging either. Now, we've got a week to give you some lessons. Oh—' She stopped, remembering. 'Except for Tuesday, that is.'

'Why not? What are you doing Tuesday?'

Phyl gave her cousin a wicked look. 'Going out with Sandy Smith, of course. He's taking me to the pub for a drink!'

In May, they all went to the Nippies' Day Out – a sports day and games day when, as well as the ordinary races and competitions, there were all kinds of more bizarre events that anyone could enter. The girls pored over the programme, planning which they would try.

'Slow cycling,' Maggie said. 'That sounds all right. I can't even get over a railway arch without puffing. What are you going to do, Phyl?'

'Fireman's Uniform, that sounds fun. Here, Etty, what about going in the three-legged race with me? We're nearly the same size. It's no good me going in with our Jo – talk about the long and the short of it.'

Etty looked doubtful, but Phyl ignored that – Etty always did look doubtful, but she wasn't a bad sport, she would usually join in. Jo decided to enter the Ladies' Tug of War, which was definitely not serious, and Irene announced that she would go in for the hurdles.

'Can you do hurdles?' Phyl asked. 'It's not very easy. You have to sort of bend your leg sideways.'

Irene gave her a contemptuous glance and, to their astonishment, went on to win with ease. Clearly, she had done hurdle races before and knew exactly how to bend her leg sideways.

'Well, she could have said so,' Phyl said indignantly. 'Making me look a fool.' She went off to line up for the Fireman's Uniform race, quivering with vexation.

'What on earth do they have to do?' Maggie asked, staring at the line of competitors and the piles of firemen's uniforms piled a short distance away.

'They've got to run to the uniforms, put them on and then run a hundred yards to the winning post,' Jo told her. 'And the uniforms have got to be on properly, no buttons done up wrong or anything.'

Soon all the spectators were doubled up with laughter as the competitors struggled frantically with the thick, unco-operative material and the unfamiliar buttonholes. I'd rather a Nippy's uniform any day, Phyl thought, breaking a nail on one of the shiny buttons. Fastened in at last, she rammed a helmet on her head and galloped towards the winning-post, arriving neck and neck with Shirley Wood.

'Equal first,' they reported, returning to the group dishevelled and hot. 'Phew, I wouldn't like to be in one of those uniforms all day, specially when you've got to fight fires in them. I mean, it's like being in a bearskin.'

'Be cooler in a bare skin,' Maggie said slyly, and they all laughed as she went off to take part in the slow cycle race.

That wasn't as easy as it seemed either. The whole point was to come last, and this meant cycling as slowly as possible. If you stopped, got off or fell, you were disqualified, and the girls held on to each other and sobbed with mirth to see plump Maggie struggling to keep her balance, the front wheel of her bicycle wavering wildly this way and that. Inevitably, she fell sideways and had to put her foot to the ground, far short of the winning post. A small, athletic-looking girl from the Strand Corner House won, cycling very slowly past the winning post long after all her rivals had given up in disarray.

'That was a real good day,' Maggie said as they made their

way home on the train. 'I reckon Phyl and Etty were the best, though, in that three-legged race. I never saw anything so funny.'

'What do you mean, funny? We won, didn't we? Not like you on that bike – now, that *was* funny. Anyway, Jo's our star – she won proper races, and long jump and everything.'

'And, of course, you've forgotten that I won the hurdles,' Irene said from her corner, her voice as acid as usual. 'I wouldn't expect you to remember that.'

'Well, you didn't give us much chance to forget either,' Phyl told her. 'Anyway, you could have said you'd done it before.'

Irene shrugged, as if to question why she should bother to tell them any such thing. 'My mum always says you shouldn't boast.'

'Does she? Well, that's one thing your mum says that you've never troubled to take any notice of before!'

Irene took a deep, angry breath and Shirley intervened quickly. 'It doesn't matter, does it? We've all had a good day out, and that's what it's meant to be. I tell you what, I think we're jolly lucky to work for a firm like Lyons. There's not many companies do so much for their staff.' She glanced around the carriage at the sunburnt faces. 'It's a sight better than working in a factory, I know that much.'

'You're right,' Phyl said, thinking of the years spent riveting and soldering. 'Or working in a greengrocer's, weighing out carrots, eh, Jo?'

They looked at each other, thinking of the jobs they'd had in the past – working in steamy laundries, standing for hours behind shop counters, treadling away at sewing machines. Being a Nippy was better than any of those.

Yet none of them wanted to go on being a Nippy for ever. For each girl, there was another dream, always present in her mind, always there for her to reach out for. Being a Nippy was just a start.

Japan continued to bomb China, killing thousands of people, and the war in Spain still wasn't over, despite Franco's

153

declaration. In England, more and more people were beginning to worry about Adolf Hitler, and Bill Mason had admitted at last that he dreaded another war.

'I couldn't ever face it before,' he said to his wife, 'but I know it looks bad. Oh, Carrie, when I think what it was like last time – bits of boys no older than our Freddy, sent over the top, just walking into machine-gun fire like they were going to the shops, knowing that if they stopped or even hesitated their own officers would shoot them . . . It don't bear thinking of. They can't let it happen again, surely.'

'You've always said they wouldn't,' Carrie reminded him staunchly. 'You've always believed in Mr Chamberlain. What's the matter, Bill, have you stopped believing in him? Don't you trust our own people any more?'

'I don't know, Carrie. This Hitler – he's different. He's got so much power, and he's come up from nothing. Who knows what a man like that'll do? We might have to fight him, to save our own country.'

Carrie was silent. She didn't want to think Bill was right. She didn't want to think of her own son going off to war as Bill had gone twenty years ago, as so many other young men had gone who had never returned. But Bill was right about Hitler. He was different. He was evil. What could you do against evil?

'They're talking about bombing,' she said. 'They say if there is a war, the Germans would start bombing us straight away. There'd be thousands killed in the first week, like in China. Nowhere would be safe, Bill.'

'The countryside'd be safe. Places like London wouldn't.'

They looked at each other, thinking of Jo and Phyl working in the centre of London. Even here, at Woolwich, it wouldn't be safe. Nowhere would be.

'Those girls ought to be got away, out into the country.'

'They'd never go,' Carrie said. 'You know how much they're enjoying those jobs they've got, and that social club and everything. They wouldn't want to chuck all that up.'

'Never mind what they'd want. They're still under twenty-one—'

'And living away from home,' Carrie said with a sigh. 'We might as well have given them the key of the door when they first went to stay with Mrs Holt, Bill. Not that she don't look after them well, I won't say that, but she's not their mother when all's said and done and they're free to come and go as they like. They're not going to throw it all up and move out to the country just because *we* say so. Anyway, what would they do out there? What sort of jobs could they find, out in all those fields?'

Others were thinking about war as well. Shirley's brother Donald had got his Army papers and was off to start training. He was convinced he would be fighting within a year, and struck fear into his mother's heart when he talked about bayonet practice and rifle-shooting. Shirley took him to task, scolding him with unaccustomed severity for his thoughtlessness, and he looked contrite but pointed out that if war did come, everyone was going to have to face it.

'Well, we'll wait till then,' Shirley said. 'There's no point in worrying Mum before you have to.'

Norman Jennings and Freddy Mason thought about joining up, too, but decided to wait until things seemed more definite. No point in tying yourself down if there's no need, Norman said. That Mr Chamberlain was still trying to get Hitler to see sense and realise he couldn't take over all of Europe, and there couldn't be anything much duller than being in an army when there were no battles to fight.

On the whole, people decided, there wasn't anything they could do about it anyway, and there wasn't much point in worrying. But as spring crept into summer, nobody could ignore the increasing talk of air raids and trenches and gas masks.

'I tell you what,' Maggie said, 'I reckon we'd better enjoy life while we can. If a quarter of what they say is true, none of us might be here in two years' time, and I'm not going to miss any fun I don't have to.'

She went out into the restaurant, flashing her bright smile at the customers with more verve than ever. It did them good to see a happy face, she said, and it was part of what they came to Corner Houses for. Not just for the food, good though it was, or the reasonable prices or comfortable surroundings – they came for the Nippies and their cheery smiles and friendly manner. It made them feel cosseted and cared for, and everyone needed to feel that once in a while.

'And you get lots of presents, as well as being asked out for a bit of extra cosseting,' Irene said with a touch of cynicism as she came back with a sixpenny tip. 'I suppose you call it working after hours.'

'I don't know what you mean by that—' Maggie began dangerously.

'I don't mean anything. It's up to you what you do in your spare time. I'm sure I don't care.'

'Then keep your long nose out of it and your nasty mind to yourself,' Maggie retorted. 'You'd get asked out a few times yourself if you didn't behave like Lady Muck.'

'I do my job, and I do it properly.'

'Properly! You act as if a smile will cost extra on the bill. We're supposed to make customers feel at ease, not frighten them to death.'

'Nobody's ever complained—'

'Only because they're too flipping scared,' Maggie said, and marched out to the restaurant again, her bright smile once more in place. Her customers, a tired-looking elderly couple with a pair of heavy bags apiece, looked at her with relief and she chatted to them, bringing a chuckle to their lips, as she helped them choose a hot snack. When she cleared the table afterwards she found they had left a penny under the plate.

'*They* won't get so much attention next time,' Irene said.

Maggie looked at her coldly. 'That's all you know. I've served them lots of times and they always leave a penny. I wish they wouldn't, because I don't reckon they can afford even that. But d'you know what? It means more to me than a big box of chocolates or a half a crown from some well-heeled gent with wandering hands and a leer on his face who wants to take me out for a posh dinner. Because I know I've made their day a bit better for them, see?'

'And don't you make the rich gent's day better, too?' Irene asked with a sneer.

'No, I don't! I like a bit of fun, I don't deny it, but I'm not a tart, Irene Bond, and you'd better not forget it.' Maggie pushed past her, her face red with anger, and Phyl gave Irene an irritated glance.

'You ought to stop getting at her. What's she ever done to you?'

Irene shrugged. 'Oh, we just don't hit it off. I've never liked her sort. She's common. That's what my mum was most afraid of when I said I was coming to work here, that I'd have to mix with common girls. I told her it wouldn't be for long, and I don't mind the rest of you, but that Maggie's just a slut.'

'She's no such thing. And we're not common, none of us is.'

'D'you have a bathroom in your house?' Irene asked. 'Or an inside toilet? Your dad's a labourer, isn't he? In the dockyard? And so's your cousin's dad. And Shirley's isn't much more. My dad—'

'*Your* dad's in the Civil Service – *we* know. Well, if having a decent, hard-working man for a father and a bath on a nail in the back yard makes us common, I'm glad of it. I wouldn't want to be anything else. At least we're not snobs!'

Phyl turned away, as angry as Maggie, and went to present a bill at one of her tables. After that none of the girls spoke much to Irene and when she came to join them in the dining-room there was no space at their table. She gave them a searing look and walked off to join some older Nippies at another table.

'Let's go home on Sunday, instead of to the Club,' Phyl said to Jo. 'I want to see Mum and Dad, and even our Norman and Ron. I want to be *common* for a while!'

Chapter Eleven

The shadow of war grew heavier, blacker. It was quite common now to see policemen and wardens with gas masks, carrying out exercises. Their grotesque apearance brought home, more than anything else could have done, the horror of what might be looming ahead.

'What will they do about little children and babies?' Phyl asked as they sat round the table having their lunch. 'They can't wear awful things like that.'

'They'll have special ones,' Irene said. She'd been allowed back into the fold after a few weeks, not because anyone liked her or even felt sorry for her but because it seemed silly and childish to squabble while such momentous worries lurked so close. 'They're more like boxes, you can put the baby right inside. And there'll be little ones for small children, sort of fancy shapes. My dad told me.'

Nobody added the words *and he's a civil servant*. They sat round the table, thinking of tiny babies pushed into rubber boxes, frightened and crying.

'There's Jews coming out of Germany,' Etty said suddenly. 'Hitler says they've all got to have special identity cards and they can only go to certain places. If they're found anywhere else, they'll be put in prison. There's a girl in the – the place where I live, she's got a cousin in Berlin. They haven't heard from her for a month.'

Maggie looked at her kindly. 'Why don't you say "hostel",

Etty? We all know you live there, it isn't anything to be ashamed of.'

Etty blushed and bit her lip. 'Don't know,' she muttered. 'I thought you wouldn't be interested.'

'Of course we're interested,' Phyl cried. 'We're your friends.' She deliberately didn't look at Irene. 'Look, you've been to the digs where Jo and me live, you've been to the pictures with us all. You know all about us and we still don't know anything about you. Tell us where you come from. Where do your mum and dad live, how many brothers and sisters have you got? We'd *like* to know.'

Etty lifted her head and looked at them. They gazed back, all but Irene eager and interested. They nodded encouragingly.

'Come on, Et,' Maggie coaxed. 'Tell us your life history. It's got to be better than talking about war!'

To their astonishment, Etty's eyes filled with tears. Her face scarlet, she jumped to her feet and stared wildly around at them. Then, with a muffled sob, she turned and ran straight out of the room.

There was a brief, shocked silence.

'Oh, flipping heck,' Phyl said in dismay. 'What have we said?'

'Too much, by the seem of it,' Maggie answered. 'Hadn't someone better go after her, see she's all right?'

'I will.' Shirley stood up and walked quickly out of the room. People at other tables, who had looked up in surprise and concern when Etty fled, seemed to think that she would now be looked after, and returned to their meals and chatter. The four remaining Nippies looked at each other again, still uncertain.

'We seem to have put our foot in it proper,' Phyl said at last, looking at Maggie.

Maggie nodded glumly. 'I wouldn't have upset her like that for the world. But she's such a mystery. I mean, we know all sorts about each other but we still know sweet Fanny Adams about Etty. What's so awful about her life that she won't talk

159

about it? Her dad in prison, or something? I mean, it can't be *that* bad or they'd never have taken her on as a Nippy.'

'Oh, no?' Irene said, speaking for the first time since she'd told them about the gas masks. 'I wouldn't be too sure about that, if I were you.'

The others looked at her. She sat looking down at her lap, an odd little half-smile playing about her lips. Maggie felt a sudden powerful urge to shake her, preferably by the throat.

'You know something, don't you? You know about Etty?'

'Do I?' Irene said with pretended innocence.

'Yes, you do,' Jo said slowly. 'That's why you're always getting at her. That and the fact that you're a spiteful cow. Well, come on, then. Tell us.'

'How do you know she'd want me to tell you? She'd have told you herself if she wanted you to know.'

'Well, I know as sure as God made little chickens that she didn't tell *you*,' Jo retorted. 'You found out, somehow or other, and you've been holding it over her ever since. So come on, out with it. It's not fair on Etty that you know and we don't.'

'Yes,' Maggie said. 'Spill the beans.'

Irene looked up. They had shifted their chairs closer and were sitting in a ring, watching her with unfriendly faces. She opened her mouth to refuse, thought better of it, shrugged and said offhandedly, 'Well, you asked for it. Don't blame me if you wish you hadn't asked, when you know what that whey-faced little creature really is. You might understand then why I don't want anything to do with her. And, just for your information, she *did* tell me – so there!'

'Stop beating about the bush and spit it out, for God's sake,' Maggie ordered tersely.

Irene tried to look as if it couldn't matter less, but her small, sharp eyes were avid and her thin mouth twitched in spiteful triumph. 'All right, then. She can't tell you about her mum and dad because she hasn't got one. She hasn't got anyone, that's why she lives in that hostel. She's never lived in a proper house in her life. She grew up in an orphanage. She's an orphan, and before that she was illegitimate. A by-blow. A *bastard*. Even her mother didn't know who her father was. She was born in a pub down the East End, and if you can't guess what her mother was, *I'm* not going to tell you!' She paused for breath, then added venomously, 'And that's not all. You know what her name is, don't you?'

'Well, of course we know what her name is, you twerp,' Maggie said impatiently. 'It's Etty. Etty Brown.'

Irene snorted. 'Etty! That's only what it is for short. Her name's really Esther. *Esther*.' She glared around the table, as if she had just proved something.

'Well, what if it is?' Phyl enquired. 'Esther's a pretty name. She ought to use it all the time, not shorten it.'

'*Esther*,' Irene said again. 'It's a Jewish name, isn't it? It's the sort of name Jews give their children. It means her mum was a Jew. A *Jew*. That's why she gets so upset about all these Jew stories we keep hearing. *Her mum was a Jew* – and that means *she's* one as well!'

She got up, staring round at the shocked faces with a bitter triumph, then turned on her heel and stalked out of the room.

There was a stunned silence. The girls looked at each other. Phyl's dark eyes were seething, her face scarlet, and Jo was tight-lipped. Maggie was flushed, her blue eyes sparking. She looked as if she'd been plugged into something electric.

'Well, I don't care *what* her mum and dad were,' she burst out. 'Etty might be a bit of a mouse but she's a decent sort of kid, and if what old Po-face says is true she's had a rough time. And what if she *is* half-Jewish? Isn't it people like that, *persecuted* people, what all this trouble's about? That Irene's no better than Hitler herself. You know what?' She looked around the table. 'I'm going to take young Etty – Esther – back to our place for tea this very afternoon, give her a bit of family life.'

'Phyl and me've taken her back to our digs a few times,' Jo said, feeling that this was some sort of criticism.

'Yeah, I know, and she likes going back with you, she told me. But that ain't *family* life, is it, with just you two and your landlady? I bet she's never been in a house with a real family before. I bet she's never even seen a baby in its cot, or a kid

161

sitting on its po, or helped wash up the tea-things or anything like that. I bet she's never had a bath in the kitchen, with everyone taking turns—'

'Well, I don't know as that's much loss,' Phyl said. 'I can tell you, having a proper bathroom with a geyser's a heck of a lot better than dragging the tin bath in every Friday night and having to empty it with a tin can.' She saw Maggie's indignant expression and changed her tone of voice. 'Oh, I'm sorry, Mag. You're being kind and I'm just picking holes. You take Etty home with you. It sounds as if she'll have a real beano at your place.'

Maggie looked at her suspiciously, but just then the bell rang for the end of lunchtime and they all got up hastily and went out to collect their capes ready to go through the underground passage to the Corner House. Irene and Etty were already there, each standing by her locker and avoiding the other's eyes. Etty looked as if she'd been crying.

Phyl marched straight up to Irene.

'You know what you are? A nasty little cat, that's what. You think you're better than anyone else and the truth is you're the lowest of the low. You're a Hitlerite and a fascist and I wouldn't be surprised if you were a *spy*. Nobody here likes you, Irene Bond, did you know that? And why should they? *You* don't like any of us, and you don't even take the trouble to *try!*'

Irene turned first white and then red. Her eyes narrowed and she tightened her jaw, then raised one hand and slapped Phyl hard across the face.

'Ow! You *bitch!*'

Phyl's reaction was swift and automatic. She returned Irene's slap, at which the other girl lunged forward and grabbed a handful of Phyl's hair. Phyl squealed with pain and clutched at Irene's arm, and in a second both girls were staggering across the floor, screaming insults at each other. The other girls stood horrified for a moment, then Jo leapt into the fray and tore them apart, holding them away from each other with her long arms. Maggie and Shirley sprang to help, each catching a flailing fist and pinning it behind the owner's back.

'Stop it!' Jo shouted. '*Stop* it, both of you. You'll have Mr Carter in here. I don't know *what* he'd say if he found you brawling like that – he'd give you both the *sack*.'

'Oh, he wouldn't sack little Phyllis,' Irene sneered. 'She's his favourite, didn't you know that? Even though she's only knee-high to a grasshopper!'

'That's *enough*.' Jo shook her angrily. 'You'd better get your cape on and go through to work, Irene. Come on, Phyl, we don't want to be late. And no more fighting, for goodness' sake, you'll have us all in trouble.'

Phyl gave Irene a last scathing glance and turned away. She was shaking and almost in tears. For the rest of the day, she was subdued, and she and Irene pointedly ignored each other whenever they met. Later, as she and Jo left the building after work and walked to their bus stop, she was silent, but as soon as they were aboard she burst out.

'We're just like those people in Germany, Jo! Fighting over Jews. If that Irene had her way, poor little Etty would wear a yellow star and have to sit at a different table. It's awful.'

'I know.' Her cousin's voice was sober. 'But people like Mr Chamberlain and the others ought to be able to find another way to make things better, Phyl. Fighting and wars – they don't solve anything. They only make things worse – much, much worse.'

Etty had watched the fight with wide eyes. Her face was white and she looked as if she was about to faint. Maggie, letting go of Irene's arm, went over to her and put her arm round the thin shoulders.

'Don't you worry about that, kid. People like that Irene need taking down a peg or two now and then. Here.' She handed Etty a powder compact. 'Put a dab of that on your nose and then pop it back into my pigeon-hole. And don't look so tragic. Nothing awful's happened, and I want you to come back home to tea with me after work.'

Etty paused in the act of powdering her nose and stared in astonishment. 'Me? You want me to come to tea with you?'

'Yes, what's so surprising about that? There's always room at our table for another one. It won't be nothing posh, mind. Not like what you're used to!' Maggie gave a quick glance round. 'Here, put that compact away quick – the supervisor's looking this way and they'll be opening the doors any minute and letting in the ravening hordes.'

'But I'm not sure—' Etty began.

'Well, *I* am. You need a proper friend, not a snake in the grass like that Irene. I suppose she wormed it out of you all those times she took you out to tea. Oh, yes, we all heard about that – how Lady Bountiful treated poor little Etty to a slap-up tea and how you poured out all your troubles. Well, I'm not going to say nothing about that, not if you don't want me to, but I'm telling you, you're coming home to tea with me and it won't be slap-up, it'll be pot-luck and you'll have to take us as you find us. We're common, you see.' She grinned. 'Common as muck, that's us! We don't look down on *anyone*. There ain't no one lower down than us to look at!'

She gave Etty a huge wink and marched away. Etty stared after her, hardly knowing whether to laugh or cry. She felt almost dizzy with the speed of events since they had all sat down to lunch together. But she knew now that she would go with Maggie after work.

'Don't expect anything grand,' Maggie warned her as they got off the bus near the back of St Paul's. 'Our house is always in a bit of a mess – there's too many of us to keep it tidy, and Mum wouldn't have time anyway. And it's noisy, I ought to tell you that. Can't hear ourselves bellow sometimes.' She gave Etty a thoughtful look. 'You won't be scared, will you? There's nothing to be frightened of, we're all human – just!'

Etty smiled tremulously. 'How many are there?'

'Well, that's hard to say, we never know just who's going to be sitting down at the table, see. But there's our Evie, she's married and she don't really live with us but she might just as well, she's always over in the afternoon to see Mum. She's got two kiddies – Billy, he's just on two, and Queenie, she's the baby, she's nine months old and a proper little princess, never mind queen. Then there's Jim – he's a bit older than me and he's got a motorbike, he spends all his time tinkering with it, he'd take it to bed with him if he could. And there's George and Gerry – they're twins but you don't need to take no notice of them, they're just boys. And then there's Ginnie.'

'Ginnie? Is she another sister?'

'Yes. She's our baby – or she was, till Evie started to produce. She's seven and she's like a little fairy. Everybody loves our Ginnie.'

They turned the last corner and came into the street where Maggie lived. Etty gazed about her with interest. As Maggie had said, there was nothing posh about the area. It wasn't in the slums, but the houses were all in need of a lick of paint and the road was rough and hadn't been repaired for a long time.

The paving stones were marked out with chalk for games of hopscotch, and half a dozen little girls in torn frocks were leaping from one square to another, balancing precariously on one foot as they bent to pick up the stone they had thrown. A few yards further on, two boys were bowling iron hoops, and another group of children were dipping for a game. They stood in a circle as a small red-haired girl recited a rhyme, pointing to each one in turn.

'Eeny-meeny-miney-mo, Catch a nigger by the toe, If he hollers, let him go, Eeny-meeny-miney-mo.' On the last word, she jabbed her finger with extra force and that child stood back while the count began again.

Maggie laughed. 'That's not what we used to say! Our dip was "Eeny-meeny-miney-mo; Sit the baby on the po. When he's done. Wipe his bum; Tell his mother what he's done."'

Etty smiled timidly. She could remember games being played in the orphanage, but there hadn't been much dipping or counting, and few rhymes. Perhaps children in orphanages didn't get the chance to learn them, just as they didn't get the chance to learn a lot of other things.

'One, two, three
Mother caught a flea.
Put it in the teapot, made a cup of tea.
Flea jumped out,
Mother gave a shout,
In came father with his shirt hanging out.'

The children had finished their counting and began the game itself. They were playing Statues. The girl left until last began to walk very slowly along the road, while the rest crept after her, watching carefully. Suddenly, she turned and they all froze, some on only one foot. The girl stared at them and then began to point.

'You moved! You moved! I saw you, Micky Martin, you moved, and so did you, Sheila Price.' The two children named made faces and dropped out, and the game began again.

'I bet it was fun living where you did, wasn't it?' Maggie said cheerfully. 'All those other kids to play with.'

'We never seemed to get time to play,' Etty said. 'There was always too much to do.'

Maggie looked at her in surprise, but before she could speak a door opened a little further down the street and a small girl appeared, wearing a white frock, her yellow hair tied with a pink ribbon in a huge bow. She saw Maggie and flew down the pavement towards her, holding out her arms. Maggie lifted her and swung her round, laughing, and the girl squealed with delight.

'You're late! Jim thought you weren't coming but I said you would, I knew you wouldn't forget it was my birthday. Have you brought me a present? Have you? Have you brought me a cake from Lyons?'

Maggie laughed and set her on her feet. 'Of course I've brought you a present. *And* a cake. And, what's more, I've brought you a guest as well.'

'A guest? What's a guest?'

'This is,' Maggie said, dragging Etty forward by one arm.

166

'Somebody to come to tea, that's what a guest is. This is Etty, she's one of our Nippies.'

'Etty?' The little girl turned huge blue eyes on Etty and studied her. 'She looks nice.' She turned back to Maggie and whispered, 'Has she brought me a present, too?'

'No, she hasn't. She didn't know it was your birthday. Now, let's go indoors and you can open the box I've brought you and have a look at your cake.'

The houses in this street were tall and thin, with basements and short flights of steps up to the front doors. Ginnie led them up the steps and into a narrow passageway, almost blocked by old pushbikes and a toy pram. Maggie stopped and looked at it.

'Is this your birthday present? Is this what Mum and Dad gave you?'

Ginnie nodded vigorously. 'They got it at the second-hand shop on the corner. Dad said he had to give up beer for a week to afford it. Isn't it smashing? I've put all my dollies in it.'

'Well, I hope there's room for one more,' Maggie said, 'because that's what I've got you.' She produced a cardboard box which Ginnie fell upon with delight and tore asunder. The doll was small but almost new, and there were no chips in its china face. It had real hair, too, as yellow as Ginnie's own.

'Oh, *Maggie*. She's beautiful.' The small fingers stroked the china face with reverence. 'Oh, look, she shuts her eyes! I *wanted* a dolly that could shut its eyes.' She looked at the pram, then cradled the doll against her chest. 'I won't put her in straight away. I'll give her a cuddle first, so she knows I'm her new mummy.'

Etty followed Maggie and her sister along the passage and into a large, cluttered room. It was filled with people, all talking at the tops of their voices. Etty drew back, waiting for them to stop talking and stare at her, but although they all turned to see who had come in the noise grew rather than diminished.

'It's Mags! Come on, Maggie, we been waiting for you to

167

get home. Ginnie wouldn't let us light the candles on her cake till you were here.'

Maggie grinned cheerfully and thrust her way through the crowd, dragging Etty with her. A large woman, even bigger than Maggie and with the same yellow hair now turning grey, was sitting on an old, orange-striped deckchair by an iron range. She beamed at the two girls and held out her hands.

'Maggie, love. Miss yer bus, did you? And who's this, then, a friend of yours?'

'That's right, ma. Her name's Esther, only most people call her Etty, and she grew up in an orphanage. I brought her back to tea, so she can see what a family's like. Not that we're anything to write home about!' She winked and burst into laughter.

Mrs Pratt's face softened and she took hold of Etty's hand and drew her closer. 'You poor soul, you. Didn't you never have no mum or dad, then?'

Etty stared at her. It had never occurred to her that Maggie would blurt out her secret in such a blunt, matter-of-fact way – as if it were nothing to be ashamed of. But this big, yellow-haired woman, with her fat body overflowing the edges of the deckchair, didn't seem to think it was any matter for shame.

'Come and sit down here by me and tell me all about it,' Mrs Pratt said. Her voice was full and warm like her sprawling body. 'I knew a girl once grew up in the children's home down the end of our road – best friend I ever had, she was. Where was you, then? Barnardo's home, was it, or council?'

'Council,' Etty said in a whisper. 'My – my mum died when I was two.'

'Oh, that's a shame, that's a terrible shame. And what about your daddy, then, or didn't you ever know him?'

Etty shook her head mutely. Such an admission had been her greatest shame in the past; she could almost see people drawing their skirts aside. It wasn't my fault, she wanted to cry, I didn't ask to be born, and anyway my mum loved my dad, she must have . . . But the fact remained that she *had* been born out of wedlock – the 'wrong side of the blanket', whatever you liked to call it – and since she'd been only two when her mother had died she couldn't possibly say for certain that she had loved her father. Or even known who he was . . .

Ever since Etty had known the rudimentary facts surrounding her birth, she had made up stories about herself and her parents. Her father had been a lord in a grand house, her mother an innocent milkmaid. They'd been in love but he'd been forced to marry an aristocratic girl for the sake of the family home . . . Or it was her mother who had been a grand lady, destined to marry an old man when she'd fallen for the strong and handsome young woodcutter on the estate. She'd been turned away from home, and the woodcutter forced into the army and killed at war – the dates didn't quite fit this scenario but Etty was sure there would have been a feasible explanation – and Etty's mother forced to wander the streets with her small white bundle, begging for food . . .

All she really knew was that she'd been born in a pub in the East End of London and that her mother, who'd worked as a barmaid, had died when Etty was barely two years old. Of TB, Etty had been told at the Home, but you weren't encouraged to ask questions there and the Matron might have been making the whole thing up. The other staff neither knew nor cared.

Growing up in an orphanage had left huge gaps in Etty's experience, gaps she scarcely knew existed. Until she was fourteen years old, she had been accustomed to a big, rambling house with large rooms, devoid of any but basic furniture. The floors had been of linoleum, worn almost through by the passage of many feet, the walls of plain distemper. The biggest room, with long tables and benches, served for both dining-hall and schoolroom, and it was there also that you sat or played if it was too wet to go outside. The rest of the house consisted of dormitories, with plain iron bunks and straw mattresses, and staff quarters.

There was no dragging in of tin baths on Friday nights, Two large bathrooms, one for the boys and one for the girls, held a row of iron baths with geysers that spat and gurgled,

169

and you were given a time and day on which to use them. The youngest children, little more than babies, were washed by the nurses, the three to sixes by older girls, and after that you were supposed to look after yourself.

Nurses or older children inspected your face, neck and ears, and brushed your hair. Etty remembered her surprise when she looked for the first time into a mirror. She was six years old and had never seen her own reflection, other than in a darkened window – mirrors weren't considered necessary for small children, who never needed to use them. She had been even more surprised when one of the nurses had been taking her to the dentist and Etty, waiting for her in the staff quarters, had seen her wash her face with a flannel. It had never struck her until then that nurses might need to wash.

There hadn't been much difference between the orphanage and the GFS hostel in many ways, but at least you had a mirror and could come and go more or less as you pleased. Until Phyl and Jo had taken her back to Mrs Holt's house, however, Etty had never been in a house with small rooms, she had never encountered rugs on the floor and she found, to her embarrassment, that she had no idea where the lavatory might be.

And until today, coming into Maggie's home, she had never been in a house with a family – an assortment of people from small babies to an ancient grandmother, and all related to each other.

Maggie Pratt's mother saw her face and let the question pass. She reached forward and scooped up Evie's baby, who was crawling past on the floor. Queenie offered no resistance and sat on her grandmother's lap, regarding Etty with large brown eyes.

'Takes after her dad,' Ivy Pratt said fondly. 'They've all got lovely dark eyes in that family. Look at her curls, too. Our Evie can't hardly get a brush through it.'

Queenie turned to her grandmother and reached up to wind the pepper-and-salt hair around her fingers. Ivy Pratt squealed, pretending to be hurt, and thrust her fist into the round little stomach so that the baby squealed in turn and wriggled with delight.

Etty was used to babies. She'd had to take her own turn in looking after the youngest children at the Home, but she'd never known one quite like this, bold and secure in its own family, knowing it was loved. The babies in the Home had been left in playpens most of the day, where they had sat or crawled aimlessly, unsure and bereft, belonging to nobody. The older girls who had charge of them had no time to give them the cuddles and tickling that they needed, even if they had known how.

Queenie's reaction was startling to Etty. She watched as Ivy Pratt played with the baby, marvelling at the rich chuckles and beaming red face. She was fascinated by the games that Ivy knew.

'Round and round the garden,' Ivy recited, walking two fingers on the baby's grubby palm, 'like a teddy bear. One step . . . two step . . . tickly under *there*.'

Queenie looked as if she might burst with giggles. Ivy played the game two or three more times and then set her back on the floor. The baby crawled off, to be picked up and made much of by another member of the family.

'You mustn't take no notice of us,' Ivy said to Etty. 'We're all a bit up in the air today, what with it being our Ginnie's birthday and all. Half the street's come in to bring her summat and have a bit of cake. Here – we haven't even offered you a cuppa. You must be parched.'

'It's all right, Ma,' Maggie said, appearing beside them with a large white cup on a saucer with a faded pink pattern and several chips. 'Some of us thinks about it. I'll just go and get one for Gran as well, she's looking a bit down in the mouth.'

'Gran always does,' Ivy said, unperturbed. 'That's my Sam's ma,' she told Etty. 'Lived with us ever since we got married, Sam and me, and the last time she cracked a smile was on Coronation Day. That's why we all put the flags out!' She laughed, her body shaking like a jelly. 'Still, you got to live and let live. She's had a hard life. Sam's dad was killed in the Boer War at the turn of the century and she had him just seven years old and three other little'uns to bring up, and another one on the way what she lost at birth. Took in washing, she did, scrubbed ninety shirts a week *and* starched their collars, and my Sam left school and started work in the Market to help out when he was twelve years old. Did well, too – costermonger, he is now. So you got to make allowances, aincher.'

She drew Etty closer and started to point out the various members of her family. George and Gerry, the twins and as unlike each other as if they'd come from different families, were in one corner with a complicated edifice they were building of Meccano, while Billy, Evie's toddler, tried without success to join in. Evie herself was deep in conversation with two other young women, evidently cousins from the next street, and the ancient grandmother was now settled with a cup of tea. She was short and rather stout, dressed in a rusty black frock, with a shawl round her shoulders despite the warmth of the day, and her sparse white hair was drawn back into a bun. Beside her chair was a walking stick and in a nearby corner stood the famous black umbrella.

A door opened and two men came in. One was obviously Maggie's father, Sam Pratt. He was huge, with big spreading hands that almost swallowed Etty's small fingers, and a broad, smiling face. He was completely bald, his big round head as red and shiny as one of his own apples, and he had bright, twinkling brown eyes.

'So you're one of our Maggie's china plates,' he said, still holding her hand. 'Why didn't she tell us she was bringing home a nice little mother of pearl – I'd have put on me best whistle and flute!' He grinned at Etty's bemused expression and turned to his wife. 'Come on, our Ivy, how about a nice cup of Rosy Lee before I dies of thirst, or d'you want me to go down the battle cruiser and get elephant's trunk?'

Ivy shook her head at him. 'Stop it, Sam, you're frightening the girl.' She turned to Etty. 'He talks like it all the time – Cockney rhyming slang. Don't tell me you've never heard of it.'

Etty stared at her. Battle cruiser? Elephant's trunk? China

plate? It was a different language. Maggie saw her face and burst out laughing.

'Don't you take no notice. He makes half of it up as he goes along. China plate means mate, see? Friend. And battle cruiser's the boozer, and elephant's trunk means drunk. You want to go down the Market some time and listen to 'em all shouting the odds.' She watched as comprehension slowly dawned. 'Here, tell you what, I'll bring you along to see us in all our pearlies some time. That'll open up your eyes!'

'Your *pearlies*?'

'Yes. We're Pearlies – Pearly kings and queens. Well, Mum and Dad are kings and queens, and I'm a princess and the boys are princes. You ought to see us in all our get-up. You want to come in October when we all gets together for the Harvest Festival at St Martin in the Fields. A proper sight, that is.'

Etty felt as if she had wandered into a fairy-tale. From a sprawling, noisy family she had found herself transported to a world of kings and queens, princes and princesses, elephants' trunks and pearls. It was like something from the stories of the Arabian Nights that she'd heard once from one of the teachers at school – a magic land where anything could happen. She looked from Maggie to her mother and then, timidly, to Sam Pratt. He gave a sudden bellow of laughter and put an arm like a tree-trunk round her shoulders, squeezing her breathless.

'Don't know what to make of us, do you, girl? Well, you don't have to worry, we won't bite you. You just sit here quiet and try and make a bit of eighteen pence of it all. I'm off for a bit of a wash before I has me Tommy Tucker.'

He vanished and Etty heard his big feet clomping up the stairs – 'apples and pears', Maggie told her with a grin – and, still feeling rather stunned, she turned to find the other newcomer beside her. He was much younger, only two or three years older than herself, with corn-coloured hair falling over his bright blue eyes. His hands and face were streaked with oil. He grinned at his sister and looked at Etty with interest.

'Here's my Jim,' Ivy said with pride. 'My eldest, he is. Been out in the back yard messing about with that old motorbike of his. He works in a garage, mechanic he is, wouldn't go in the Market with his dad, oh, no, not him, wanted to work with engines, he did. The twins are just as bad, fiddling about with that Meccano of theirs morning, noon and night, but what can you do, eh? That's boys for you these days.'

Jim fetched himself a cup of tea and came to sit beside his mother.

'I bet you've heard all sorts of stories about me,' he said to Etty. 'They're not true. You don't want to take no notice of what my sister says, and our Mum's not much better.'

Etty smiled nervously and Ivy Pratt gave her son's arm a slap.

'Don't tease the girl, Jim. Can't you see she already thinks she's in a loony bin? She's not used to all this, grew up in a Home, she did, never had no brothers nor nothing, so you just be a bit careful, see? Anyway, what makes you think we bin talking about you? Got better things to do than that, we have.'

By now, Etty was beginning to get used to people telling each other where she had grown up. Astonishingly, none of them seemed to think there was anything out of the ordinary in it. Like the others, Jim accepted it without comment and gave her a friendly smile.

'Like to come and see my motorbike?' he invited her. 'Dad give it me for Christmas. It's not new, but I've been getting it up to scratch and it goes smashing. I'm just giving it a de-coke.'

'Jim!' his mother remonstrated. 'Of course she don't want to see your old bike.' But Etty was already on her feet, and when she hesitated, not wanting to offend her hostess, Jim grabbed her arm and pulled her through the door.

'At least it's a bit quieter out here,' he said, leading her along another passage and through a big, untidy kitchen smelling of warm scones and fish paste sandwiches. They went out into a yard, surrounded by high walls, with a door to one side through which Etty caught a glimpse of an alleyway.

'This is my scorcher.' He indicated the machine and stood back so that Etty could admire his pride and joy.

'It's smashing,' she said, looking at the skeleton of the motorbike. The petrol tank and half the engine seemed to have been removed and lay nearby on the ground. A large lump of grey, ridged metal lay beside it, with a small heap of scrapings of some kind of black deposit, like soot. 'What's the matter with it?'

'The matter?' he said, looking puzzled. 'There's nothing the matter with it.'

'But you're mending it, aren't you?'

Jim shook his head so that the fair hair fell into his eyes. 'No, I'm giving it a de-coke. See, this is the cylinder head and it gets all caked up with muck and stuff so every now and then I have to take it to bits and get it all off. Then I give it a good rub and polish and put it all back together and it goes like a bird.' He gave Etty a grin, showing nice white teeth. 'I'll take you for a ride if you like.'

'Oh.' Etty scarcely knew what to say. She'd seen plenty of motorbikes, of course, usually ridden by young men like Jim and often with a girl on the pillion, her arms clutching the driver's waist. The idea of holding Jim like that made her face burn. 'Well, I don't think there's time – I mean, I'll have to be going soon, I only came for tea and—'

Jim gave a shout of laughter. 'I didn't mean right now! It's going to take me all evening to put this little beauty together. No, I meant – well—' In fact, he hadn't meant anything at all, it had just been something to say to this funny, mouse-like little girl, but now he came to think of it, there wasn't anyone else he specially wanted to take out this weekend, and it was certainly more fun going out with a girl on the back . . . 'I meant this Saturday,' he said. 'Or Sunday – whichever you like. What do you say? We could go out in the country somewhere. Have a bit of tea. I'll come and pick you up.'

Etty gazed at him. He really meant it. He wanted to take her out on his motorbike, and he would come to pick her up. The other girls at the hostel would see her going off on a motorbike.

'You don't know where I live,' she said helplessly, and he gave her an odd look of almost gentle exasperation.

'Well, you can tell me, can't you? I haven't got to catch a bus, you know.' He caught a flash of something in her eyes and looked at her more intently. 'Don't look like that. I'm only chi-iking you. You'll have to get used to that if you're going to be coming round here with our Maggie. Listen—'

They were interrupted by Maggie herself, erupting from the kitchen door to stand, arms akimbo, her expression resigned.

'I might have known it. He drags everyone out to see his precious motorbike. Come on, the pair of you, Ginnie's going to blow out the candles on her cake, you've got to come and sing "Happy Birthday".' She tucked her arm through Etty's. 'Don't let our Jim start talking motorbikes, you'll never get away. He never thinks about nothing else.'

Etty glanced at Jim. He winked at her and bent his head to whisper in her ear.

'Sunday afternoon, all right? I'll come and pick you up at two o'clock. Don't forget to tell me where you live before you go!'

'No, I won't,' Etty replied and, as if in a daze, went indoors to watch Ginnie blow out her birthday candles and to sing 'Happy Birthday'.

Chapter Twelve

'It's time you had a chap to go around with,' Phyl said to her cousin, not for the first time. 'The rest of us have all got boys, even Etty. You're the only one without one.'

'Who says I want one?' Jo was mending her swimming costume. The diving competitions were being held on the following Sunday and she was going to try her new swallow-dive from the top board. 'I haven't got time for all that soppy stuff.'

'Go on, everyone's got time for a bit of romance,' Phyl retorted. 'It's natural. You're nineteen, lots of girls are married by the time they're nineteen.'

'Well, I'm not and don't want to be. Not for a long time, anyway. And I'm not sure I want to be out with a different chap every night of the week like some people I could mention.' Jo examined her swimsuit to see if there were any other seams coming loose.

'I'm not out with a different chap every night,' Phyl said with dignity. 'There's only Mike that I go to the pictures with, and Arthur from Coventry Street to dance with at the club, and Sandy Smith down the pub on Tuesdays—'

'And Dave Willett when you go home.'

'Oh, Dave Willett,' Phyl said dismissively. 'Anyway, we're not talking about me, we're talking about you and getting you a boyfriend—'

'I'm not talking about getting me a boyfriend. You are. You never stop talking about it, as a matter of fact.'

'Well, it worries me. I want to see you having a good time, like the rest of us. What happened to Nick Laurence? I thought he was nice, and he liked you – anyone could see that.'

'Well, he never turned up again, did he? Obviously he didn't like me that much after all.'

'He had a cold. Sandy told me.'

Jo sniffed. 'He had a good excuse. Why didn't he come the next week, then?'

'He's been on a different shift. Honestly, Jo, you ought to give him a chance. Every time I see Sandy he gives me a message for you from Nick. Why don't you let me tell him we'll all go out together next Tuesday? You'd enjoy it.'

Jo shook her head. 'I'm quite happy as I am, ta very much.' She put the costume in her drawer and sat on the bed with the latest copy of *Lyons Mail*. All the reports of the sporting activities at Sudbury were there, together with poems sent in by Lyons employees, photographs of people in the company news and competitions that could be entered. There were wedding photographs, too, usually featuring the happy couple posed beside the wedding cake that Lyons gave to all its employees, and news of babies born to women who had worked for Lyons. All this was part of the Lyons policy of treating its staff like a big, happy family so that they all worked well and contentedly together.

Phyl lay back on her bed, unable to dismiss Jo's lack of a sweetheart from her thoughts. It would have been nice if her cousin would agree to go out with Nick so that they could go out as a foursome, or maybe in a group with Maggie and Tommy and even Etty and Charlie, but it was Jo's business if she wasn't interested. Funny, when she'd been such a one for playing with the boys when she was a kid, always out in the street with a football or an old cricket bat. Since she'd grown up, however, she seemed to have lost interest. Or maybe she'd really always been more interested in playing games, not in the boys at all.

Phyl enjoyed going out with boys. Young men, she supposed they ought to be called now, since they were mostly in their early twenties, but 'chap' was the best word to use. That could mean anyone, any age. 'Masher' was another word, but it meant something a bit different, a bit more flashy, and it was old-fashioned now anyway. She thought of the 'chaps' she went out with – Mike, who was still trying to get her to go all the way with him, Arthur who was a smashing dancer but didn't have a word to say for himself and had only recently plucked up courage to kiss her, and Sandy who took her to the pub on Tuesday evenings for a port and lemon. And, as Jo had reminded her, Dave Willett at home, who'd always been sweet on her, but you couldn't really call him a *chap* – not someone you'd known all your life.

It would be nice to meet someone really special, Phyl thought. Someone well heeled, maybe with a flat in one of the posh parts of London, like Mayfair, with window-boxes filled with flowers and a balcony to sit out on of an evening. People who lived in places like that didn't have to do their own housework – they had charladies coming in, perhaps even cooks to get the meals ready for them. They lived like film stars, like Anna Neagle and Michael Wilding in their pictures. I'd like to live like that, Phyl thought.

In reality, she knew it wouldn't happen. It was far more likely that she would marry someone like Mike, or Sandy or even Dave Willett, and settle down in a house like her mum's and have kids and worries. But it was nice to dream.

Etty, too, seemed to be living in a dream these days.

She had been out twice with Jim on his motorbike. He came to the hostel on Sunday afternoons and revved up in the road outside, bringing all the girls to the windows to stare as Etty walked self-consciously out and climbed on the pillion. The first time she'd done it, she'd felt awkward and clumsy, and very nervous about putting her arms round his waist, but he'd just laughed and squeezed her arms against his sides and after that it had been easy.

They'd buzzed through the streets and out into the suburbs. Before long, it seemed, they were in open country-side, riding along country roads and lanes with trees and fields on either side. Etty clung to Jim and gazed about her in wonder. She had never been into the countryside, never been out of a street except to go into the London parks. Out here, it was like one enormous park that stretched on for ever and ever. And there was more . . .

'Cows!' she squeaked suddenly in Jim's ear, making him jump so that the bike wobbled. 'Look, in the field, there's a whole flock of them!'

'Cripes,' he exclaimed, swerving back out of the hedge, 'haven't you never seen cows before?'

'Not in fields,' she said humbly. Conversation on the bike was difficult – the wind whipped your words away almost before they were out of your mouth – but if she spoke close against his ear and he twisted his head sideways to shout back at her they could generally manage to talk a bit.

'Anyway,' he said, pulling the bike into a field gateway and stopping the engine, 'they're not flocks, they're herds.' He got off the bike and took Etty's hand to lead her over to the gate. They leant over it together, watching the big brown animals browsing in the grass.

'I know. I was just so surprised – it was the first word that came into my head.'

'Surprised? Didn't you expect to see cows out in the country?'

'I didn't think about it. I was just thinking how it all looked like a big park and then I saw them. I never realised how big they were – I've only seen them in pictures before.'

'Haven't you ever been out of London?' he asked.

'I went to Brighton once. Someone paid for us all to go on a trip and we went on the train. I suppose I might have seen them then, but I was only a kid and I don't really remember.'

'I'll take you there again one day,' he said. 'And if you like big parks I'll take you to Windsor. And Hampton Court, we could go in the maze. And we could go on the river. We can go anywhere on the bike.'

Etty stared at him. 'You really mean it? You'd take me to all those places? But – but why?'

'Why?' he repeated. 'Well, because I want to, I suppose.

It's nice having someone to take out on the bike – someone to talk to and enjoy things with.'

'But there must be masses of girls—'

He glanced up and down the lane, craned his neck to peer round the field. 'I can't see any.'

'You know what I mean,' she said, shaking his arm. 'There must be lots of girls you know who'd like to come out with you.'

'Well, what if there are? I asked you.'

'Yes, but . . .' She frowned. 'It isn't because Maggie asked you to, is it?'

'Maggie? Why on earth would she ask me to take you out?' He seemed genuinely astonished.

'Well – because she's sorry for me. That's why she's so kind to me. That's why she brought me back to your house in the first place.'

Jim stared at her. 'Well, I don't know about that. I thought it was because she liked you. You're a friend of hers, aren't you? You go to the pictures and things together?'

'Yes, but that's – that's different. There's a group of us—'

'Look,' Jim said, 'you wouldn't be part of the group if they didn't like you. You wouldn't get asked to go to the pictures, you wouldn't even be told they were going. And our Mag wouldn't ask you back home, not just because she's sorry for you. Anyway, why *should* she be sorry for you? What's the matter with you?'

Etty looked down at the grass at her feet. She felt the colour creep over her face. 'Well – you know what she told you. About me growing up in a Home. And about my mum being Jewish, and dying. And not knowing who my dad was, and—'

'Well, yes, I can see anyone'd be sorry about that,' Jim said frankly. 'It's a horrible thing to happen to a kid. But you don't have to look as if it's your fault, Etty. And I wouldn't ask you out on my bike just because of that. I mean, I'm not a ruddy saint!'

Etty laughed. Jim looked at her and she saw his expression change a little.

'Here, that's better. You look really pretty when you laugh

– did anyone ever tell you that?' He bent his head suddenly and kissed the tip of her nose. 'Do it more often.'

Etty blushed again and rubbed her nose as if to make sure it was still there. 'Well, you make me laugh and I will,' she said, astounding herself with her own retort. She couldn't believe she was doing this, laughing and holding hands and being kissed by a boy in a country lane, with cows grazing all around them. Why hadn't it ever happened with Charlie? Why had they never been able to find a word to say to one another?

They left the bike parked in the gateway and went for a walk. Motorbikes were fine for getting you where you wanted to go, Jim said, but once you were there you just wanted to enjoy it. They found a field with no cows in it and climbed over the gate to walk beside a narrow stream with golden kingcups growing along its banks. They sat under the drooping boughs of a willow and Jim picked long grasses and wound them together.

'I've never been anywhere like this,' Etty said, lying back on the grass and staring up into the branches, watching the long fronds of leaves move gently against the sky.

'Well, nor had I much, till I got the bike,' Jim admitted. 'We used to go down to Kent every summer for a month though, hop-picking. Didn't you ever do that?'

Etty shook her head. 'We never did anything like that in the Home. I wish we had.' She lifted her head and gazed around her. 'I like the country. It's nice.'

'It's nice to come to for an afternoon out,' Jim observed, 'but I don't know as I'd like to live here. I mean, there's no shops for miles, and no streetlamps, and no pictures to go to. I should think it's pretty dead, really.'

They got up and walked a bit further, and then went back to the bike. Just before he climbed on, Jim put his hands on Etty's shoulders.

'Just you forget all that stuff about people being sorry for you,' he said. 'It's rotten not having a mum or dad, but it doesn't make you a different person. And your mum being Jewish doesn't matter neither. We're not in Germany.' He looked into her eyes. 'It's been nice having you on the back of the bike, and going for a walk in the fields. I like being with you – you don't chatter all the time like most of the girls I know, and you don't think everything ought to be done just to suit you. You're nice.'

'Oh,' she said, totally at a loss. 'Oh. Um – well, you're nice, too, Jim.'

He laughed. 'Oh, I know that! Our Maggie tells me all the time.' To her surprise, he gave her another quick kiss, this time on the lips, and then swung his leg astride the motorbike. 'Come on, Etty. Let's go home and see what Mum's got for supper. It's usually jellied eels on a Sunday!'

Shirley was another of the girls who didn't have a regular boyfriend. There always seemed to be too much to do at home, what with Mum needing so much help around the house, and Jack wanting attention. Not that he was any trouble, and he did quite a bit to help, with his regular little chores like clearing out the fireplace of a morning and washing the dishes, but he was always begging for stories or songs or games of snakes and ladders, and didn't seem to understand that it couldn't be a party all the time. And because nobody had the heart to refuse him, it took up a lot of time.

'*The Hobbit*,' he said when Shirley asked what story he would like. 'The story about when he went in a big ship.'

There wasn't a story about the hobbit going in a big ship, but Shirley had expanded the original book into an everlasting saga of Bilbo's adventures and Jack listened with his loose mouth open and his slanted eyes fixed on her face as she recounted the tale. Afterwards, satisfied for the time being, he went contentedly to do the washing-up, humming to himself as he did so. Annie Wood, who was feeling poorly that day, looked up from the settee and smiled.

'You're ever so good with him, Shirley. A lot of girls your age wouldn't bother with their brother.' She meant in particular a brother like Jack, but Shirley had long since taken to thinking of him more as a baby brother, who would never grow up, and had the same patience as she would have had for a toddler.

'He's no bother,' Shirley said. 'Anyway, a lot of brothers wouldn't bother with their sister either, so that makes us quits.' She picked up the jumper she was knitting for her father's birthday. 'Where's our Donald?'

Donald had finished his Army training and was home on a weekend's leave. The Army had changed him already – he walked with a straight back and took endless care in polishing his boots and tunic buttons. Jack followed him round the house like a puppy, and his greatest pleasure was to sit whitening Donald's belt with blanco.

'Where d'you think he is?' Annie said with a wry look. 'Out with Eileen, of course.'

None of the family were all that struck on Donald's girlfriend, who was sharp-tongued and bossy, but Donald seemed to think the sun shone, as Alf Wood said, out of her backside. Before joining the Army, he took her to a dance every Saturday and to the pictures on Wednesdays, as regular as clockwork. On Sunday afternoons they went for a walk and back to tea at her house. Eileen worked on the jewellery counter in one of the big shops in Oxford Street and talked – when she remembered – in a posh, refined voice. She came into the Corner House occasionally, but ostentatiously avoided sitting at Shirley's table so that she wouldn't have to acknowledge that her boyfriend's sister was a waitress.

Joining up and being away from home hadn't cooled Donald's ardour at all. He couldn't wait to get round to Eileen's house, to make sure she was still his girl.

'You should have seen him getting ready,' Annie continued with a smile. 'Standing there as solemn as you like, ironing his shirt and pressing his trousers! I said to him, "I thought you were joining up to fight for your country, not learn laundry work," and he said without a flicker of a smile, "A clean soldier is an efficient soldier, Mum." I tell you, Shirl, I didn't know where to put my face. I'd swear he didn't even know what an iron was when he went!'

'He's gone all tidy, too,' Shirley said, frowning at her

stitches. 'When I went in their bedroom to get Jack's socks for darning, I thought I was in the wrong house. Everything that wasn't put away was folded up. I wouldn't have believed it. He'll make someone a lovely wife!'

'Well, not that Eileen, I hope. I don't want him to get too serious about her,' Annie said as Shirley started to knit. 'I don't think she'd suit our Donald. She's the kind who wants to wear the trousers. It's all very well a chap being able to take care of himself, but I wouldn't want to go round his place and find him ironing his wife's smalls.'

'I shouldn't worry. Eileen won't be satisfied with our Donald. She'll set her sights higher than a dockyard apprentice, and that's what Donald was before he joined up. She just likes being seen out with a chap in uniform.' Shirley frowned at her stitches. The jumper was her first attempt at Fair Isle knitting and the colours were getting into a tangle on the wrong side. 'Still, he'll be away again soon. I don't think Eileen Foster's the sort to want to sit at home on Saturday nights.'

'Not like you, eh?' Annie reached out and patted her daughter's hand. Her own was frail and thin, and her breath came wheezily. 'Don't think I don't appreciate what you give up for me, Shirley. You ought to be out enjoying yourself on Saturday nights, too, not sitting here with your mum.'

'I don't mind.' Out in the scullery, Jack had finished the washing-up and started to play his mouth-organ. It was wonderful how he could get any tune he liked out of that, without being able to read a note of music. He could make it throb with deep, passionate notes, or he could make it sing like a bird. 'I like being at home.'

'All the same,' Annie said, 'it's not right for a girl your age. You ought to be making the most of your youth. Why don't you go out to that Club you were telling us about? Go to one of their dances. You'd know people there, it wouldn't be like going on your own. You'd enjoy it.'

'And you'd be here all on your own.' Shirley's father always went to the pub on Saturday nights to play darts with his mates from the dockyard. 'I'd sooner stay here.'

'Well, I'd sooner you didn't,' Annie said with unusual firmness. 'And I won't be on me own, I'd have our Jack. Promise me you'll go next week.'

Shirley hesitated. To tell the truth, she'd often thought it would be nice to go to one of the dances, or maybe to the pictures with the other girls. They'd asked her often enough.

'All right,' she said. 'I'll go next week.'

Irene went to the following Saturday's dance as well. She and Shirley encountered each other in the ladies' cloakroom where Irene was busy smearing her mouth with bright red lipstick.

'What are you doing here?' Irene asked, as if a dance was the last place she would have expected to find Shirley. 'I thought you always stopped at home on Saturday nights.'

'Not always.' Shirley combed her hair in the mirror. She didn't want to talk to Irene at all, after the way she'd treated Etty, but she couldn't help seeing the other girl in the mirror and comparing their hairstyles. Her own soft, dark cloud looked very ordinary beside Irene's newly set waves, she thought. And her frock was ordinary, too, a pale blue cotton sprinkled with tiny daisies, tight-fitting over the bust and with a full skirt. She'd made it herself. Irene's dress was also blue, but it looked as if it had come from a shop, a more expensive shop than most Nippies would be able to afford, and it was made of silk with a lace collar and puffed sleeves. She had white shoes on as well. Shirley was wearing her ordinary summer sandals.

'You look quite sweet really,' Irene said with a dismissive glance. 'I dare say some of the kitchen boys will dance with you. I've already promised most of my dances to my partner.' She swept out, leaving a drift of Evening in Paris on the air, and Shirley shrugged ruefully and followed.

Irene was already dancing and Shirley's lips twitched as she saw the other girl's partner. An inch or so shorter than Irene, a bit on the tubby side with a sweaty face, and forty if he was a day! Was this the partner she'd been boasting about? Shirley hadn't seen him before so he didn't work at Marble

Arch – probably he was at one of the other Corner Houses, or perhaps he managed one of the smaller teashops. When the dance came to an end he and Irene left the floor together, his arm lingering around her waist. There was a damp patch in the middle of her back where his hand had rested.

'Would you like to dance?'

She looked round, startled. The young man standing in front of her had brown hair and eyes and a quizzical expression. He looked pleasantly ordinary – a year or two older than herself, she thought, and wearing the sort of suit Donald would have worn before he joined the Army. The band was playing a quickstep, one of the dances Shirley felt confident in doing, so she nodded and stood up.

'I haven't seen you here before,' he said as they moved off together. He danced neatly and without any ostentatious twirls, steering her past the couples who were being more adventurous. 'Where d'you work?' He had a lilting, almost sing-song kind of accent.

'Marble Arch. I'm a Nippy. I haven't been to many dances.'

'Don't you like dancing? You're good at it.'

'It isn't that.' She thought about it and realised that she did like dancing. It was nice, letting yourself go with the music. 'It's just that I usually stay at home. My mum isn't all that well, you see.'

He nodded but didn't reply. Shirley felt sorry she'd told him about her mother. He won't be interested in me now, she thought. Boys don't like girls to have problems at home. Not that Mum was a problem, or Jack, but a boy wouldn't see it that way. She sighed a little, waiting for the dance to end and for him to escort her back to her chair and then leave her.

'I know what it's like,' he said suddenly. 'My dad's an invalid and Mam has to go out to work. I generally spend Sunday doing things around the house, but Saturdays I like to go out. But not many girls understand about Sundays.'

'What's the matter with your dad?' she asked.

'Some sort of lung disease. The doctor says it's not TB, he says Dad caught it down the mines when he was young. We used to live in Wales, see, but when he got ill we come to London to see if my uncle could give him a job. That's my mam's brother, see. Only Dad couldn't even do that for long, so Mam had to do it instead.'

'The same job?' Shirley felt as if she was learning a lot in a very short time. The boy seemed to need someone to talk to, or perhaps it was just because he was Welsh.

'Yes, Uncle John's got a shop, see. Mam could serve in it just as well as Dad. And then I got a job with Lyons and my sister works for a tailor – clever with a needle she is – so it turned out fine. Except for Dad's lungs, of course.'

'My mum has chest problems, too,' Shirley said. 'Asthma and bronchitis. Some of the time she's all right, and sometimes she just can't do much but lie on the settee.'

The dance came to an end and they stood in the middle of the floor, looking at each other uncertainly. Then he took her arm and they began to walk back to the seats.

'Will you dance with me again?' he asked. 'Unless you've got someone else . . .

I mean, if you've already got a partner, I'll make myself scarce.'

'No, I haven't got a partner. I'd like to dance with you again.'

'Oh, well,' he said, 'that's all right, then.'

There was an uncertain pause. Shirley could see Irene across the floor, still with the sweaty man. There were other people there that she knew, too, other Nippies and Sallies, kitchen staff and supervisors. Everyone came to the Saturday dances.

The music started again, a waltz this time, and the boy held out his arms. Once again they moved off together, easily and in tune.

'What's your name?' he asked suddenly. 'Mine's Owen. Owen Prosser.'

'Shirley Wood,' she said. 'Do you work in one of the Corner Houses?'

He shook his head. 'No, I'm at Cadby Hall. I work in the office, ordering food. I'm an office-boy!' He laughed.

Shirley didn't believe he was just an office-boy. He might have started off as one, but by now he was more likely to be a clerk, with responsibilities. She liked the fact that he hadn't tried to make his job sound better than it was, though. He wasn't boastful.

They spend the rest of the evening together, dancing and talking. Owen brought her a drink and, later, an ice cream. Now and then, Shirley caught sight of Irene with her partner. He looked sweatier than ever as the evening progressed. Owen, on the other hand, stayed cool and when he held her his hands felt dry and pleasant.

'Can I see you home?' he asked during the last waltz. They were dancing quite closely now, and Shirley realised suddenly that she didn't want the evening to end. She felt a twinge of surprise, remembering that she'd only come to please her mother and hadn't expected to have more than one or two dances. I meant to go home early, she thought in astonishment.

'It's a long way.' Everyone went back into London on the train and then dispersed. Boys who took their girls home might not get back to their own places until the early hours.

'I don't mind. I don't like to think of you going by yourself.' The dance ended and they stood still for the National Anthem. 'Will you come to the dance again? Will you come next week?'

Shirley looked at him. There was nothing outstanding about him, she thought, no film star looks or aura of wealth. He just looked ordinary – a nice, ordinary boy with a pleasant smile and friendly eyes.

'Yes,' she said. 'I'll come again. But I don't want you to see me home. There's a bus from my station and the stop's right outside our door. We'll just go back on the train together, all right?'

Irene's partner, Herbert Lennox, had also asked if he could see her home.

'Well, I wouldn't mind,' she said with a tiny shrug. 'A girl needs an escort this time of night. It's quite a long way from the station, though.'

'How do you usually go?' he asked. 'Walk?'

'Oh, no! I'd have a taxi. I don't like walking by myself when it's late. You don't know who might be about.'

They went on the train with everyone else, choosing a carriage where there was nobody they knew, and sat squeezed close on the crowded seat. Herbert's body felt very hot and damp against Irene's, and she hoped he wasn't staining her frock with his sweat. Now that she could see him in a brighter light, he didn't look so attractive. His teeth were yellowed by nicotine and although Irene smoked herself, she didn't like such obvious signs of it. And the collar of his shirt wasn't all that clean either, as if he'd worn it a couple of days already.

Irene tried to move away a little, but found herself pressing close against a girl on the other side. The girl sighed impatiently and Irene eased back and stared at the floor.

Herbert's hand found hers and held it. It was like being wrapped in hot fish-and-chip paper. He was leaning against her, his breath steamy on her neck.

'You know what, Irene?' he muttered in her ear. He pronounced her name with a long 'e' – *Irenee*. 'You're a little smasher. I thought so the minute I laid eyes on you. A right little dolly that one is, I said to meself, a real little goer.'

'I don't know what you mean by *goer*,' she said frostily, removing her hand. 'I'll have you know I'm a respectable girl.'

'Course you are. Course you are. I never said nothing different, did I? All I meant was, you're a smashing girl. Good-looking, full of pep, *you* know. Cut above some of them others.'

'Well,' she said, slightly mollified, 'I must say I don't intend to be a Nippy any longer than I can help. I'm looking for something a bit better than that.'

'Course you are. Supervisor's job. Manageress. That's what you're cut out for, Irenee, anyone can see that. I bet they've noticed you already, I bet they've got you marked down.'

Irene thought so, too, but she wasn't going to let him think she was an easy conquest so she lifted her chin and shrugged. 'They'll have to do something about it soon, then. I've got a few other irons in the fire as well.'

'Oh, what's that, then?'

Irene hesitated. She had once gone after a job in an insurance office, but it hadn't come to anything. The idea of such a job, wearing a business suit and sitting at a desk in a warm office, was still appealing, though. She said offhandedly, 'Oh, this and that. I can type and do shorthand – I might go into business. Secretary to a managing director, that sort of thing. A proper career.'

'I bet you could do it, too,' he said admiringly. 'But what's a lovely girl like you doing, thinking about a career? You'll be getting married.'

'I might not.'

'Course you will. Some lucky bloke's going to snap you up soon as look at you.' He paused. 'Might even think about it meself.'

The train rattled to a stop at a station and there was an upheaval as various passengers got out. There was more room in the compartment now, but Herbert didn't move away. Irene looked out of the window, seeing her own reflection in the darkness. She shifted slightly so that Herbert's body wasn't pressing quite so closely.

'You're a fast worker,' she said coolly.

'I only said *might*. I wouldn't want to offend a nice girl like you by being presumptuous.' He took her hand again. 'Hope I haven't given offence, Irenee.'

She didn't answer that but asked a question of her own. 'What's your job, anyway? D'you work in one of the Corner Houses?'

'Me? No, love, I'm at HQ – Food department – I'm responsible for seeing the goods are the right quality, see, and making sure it gets to the right places. If it wasn't for me you might find yourself short of a few sausages one morning – that wouldn't do, would it?' He winked. 'Just you think, next

191

time you serve up Adam and Eve on a Raft, it might've been yours truly who sent it over.'

The train had arrived at Irene's station. She withdrew her hand again and prepared to stand up. Herbert also stood up and left the train with her, putting his hand under her elbow as they walked off the platform. There were a few taxis about and he stepped forward quickly, waving his other arm.

Irene had made up her mind. She got in quickly and pulled the door closed before Herbert could climb in beside her. She gave the driver her address in a low voice, so that her escort wouldn't hear, and then turned with a bright smile.

'Thank you, Herbert, for a lovely evening. Perhaps I'll see you at the dance again.'

He stared. 'But I thought I was going to see you to your door, Irenee. I thought we was pals.'

'And so we are,' she said. 'You're a lovely dancer, Herbert, and it was nice of you to see me back. But, like I told you, I'm a respectable girl and I want to get on in life, so ta-ta for now, and I'll remember what you said about Adam and Eve on a Raft.'

The taxi pulled away, leaving Herbert standing open-mouthed on the pavement. Irene settled back in her seat, smiling derisively.

A warehouseman, that's all he was! Fancy a warehouseman trying to get off with her, Irene Bond, on the first time they'd met. As if she'd fall for that. He must have thought she was green or something.

As Irene had told Herbert Lennox, she was looking for something a bit better than *that*.

Chapter Thirteen

Summer drew to a close. Talk of war intensified. Nobody could now doubt the threat that Hitler presented in his determination to take over yet more countries. Czechoslovakia was his latest target, and at the same time the stories of what was happening to the Jews in the countries he already dominated were becoming more and more disturbing. Thousands of them were fleeing, to Britain and to America, and it didn't seem right just to stand by and let them suffer. Somehow, Hitler ought to be stopped.

'We don't have to fight him, though,' Stan Jennings said, clinging to straws. 'There was that treaty they all signed when the Great War ended. That was supposed to stop this sort of thing happening again. All they've got to do is make him stick to that.'

'Yes, but it's that treaty that's caused all the trouble,' Bill Mason pointed out. Jo and Phyl were home for the weekend and the two families were having Sunday tea together in the Masons' house. 'It's stopped Germany from doing what it wants. That's what Hitler's making all this fuss about.'

'I'm not sure he's the sort of man who sticks to treaties anyway,' Jo said, helping herself to lettuce and tomatoes to go with her sliced ham. 'I think he's the sort of man who wants to take over everything. Honestly, I think he's a bit mad. The way he shouts at those rallies. We saw him again the other night at the pictures, he's like a lunatic.'

'They're saying Mr Chamberlain's thinking of going over

to see him soon,' her father said. 'He'll sort something out then. That's what these leaders are for – to keep things nice and steady, not to start wars. Mr Chamberlain doesn't want war – he's said so time and time again.'

'I don't want war either,' Jo said, 'but I don't think it does any good, giving in to bullies. They just get worse.'

'Let's talk about something else,' her mother said. 'It's Sunday teatime and we don't often have it all together now. I'm fed up with hearing about Hitler and wars. Look, May's brought in this lovely trifle. Who's going to have some?' She began to spoon it out into bowls.

'Yes, tell us a bit more about London,' May agreed, looking at the two girls. 'We don't seem to hear much about young men these days. How's that Mike, Phyl – you still seeing him?'

'On and off,' Phyl said with a blush. 'I've told you before, Mum, it's nothing serious.'

'Not with all the other chaps she's got dangling after her,' Jo said with a grin, passing the bowls along the table. 'Honestly, Auntie May, sometimes you can't get out of our front door for blokes, all after our Phyl. I have to make an appointment to see her myself.'

'Jo!' Phyl protested as the family laughed. 'You know that's not true. I don't have crowds of boys after me. Only Mike—'

'And Arthur, and Sandy, and that smoothie Richard Godwin, and Dave Willett and—'

'Stop it! You know very well they're all just friends. There's nothing more to it than that.' Phyl was scarlet, half laughing, half annoyed. She gave her cousin a murderous glance which Jo returned with a broad grin. They both knew that neither of them would have let out anything that was really secret.

'What about you, Jo?' Carrie asked, seeing that her niece wasn't far off being really embarrassed. 'Haven't you got any young chaps after you?'

'Come on, Mum,' Freddy said, 'you know Jo's only interested in football and cricket. Boys just come along for the game as far as she's concerned.'

Jo turned and stared at her brother. She knew he hadn't

meant the words cruelly, but she felt, quite unexpectedly, as if she had been stabbed. Heat rushed into her face and she answered sharply. 'They don't! And I don't play football and cricket now, I do hockey and netball, so that shows how much *you* know, Freddy Mason.'

'Coo-er,' he said, raising his eyebrows. 'Touchy, aren't we?'

'Leave her alone, Freddy.' Carrie was sorry she'd mentioned the subject now. She did wonder sometimes why Jo didn't seem to have any boyfriends, but there was plenty of time – the girl was only just twenty and although a lot of girls seemed to think they were on the shelf if they weren't at least engaged by then, she was glad that her own daughter and niece didn't seem to be in any rush. 'The right man'll come along for our Jo, same as he does for any other girl. She don't have to be flighty about it. There's a bit more of this trifle left if anyone wants it. Bill, if you want some more tea you'd better pass your cup along. Norman, what are you looking so down in the mouth about? Have a piece of this Victoria sponge – it's lovely and fresh, I only made it this morning, and that's my home-made raspberry jam in the middle. Freddy, you can stop picking at that ham – there's only just enough there for your father's sandwiches tomorrow.'

After tea, Freddy and Norman went out to tinker with Norman's motorbike and the rest of the family settled down to a game of cards. At eight o'clock the two girls set off to return to Mrs Holt's, to be ready to go to work next morning. They walked up the street together.

'You'd like a boyfriend really, wouldn't you, Jo?' Phyl asked.

'Oh, Phyl, not again,' Jo groaned. 'Look, I've got nothing against boys but I just don't fancy all that lovey-dovey stuff, and that seems to be all they're interested in.'

'Well, not quite all,' Phyl said with a giggle. 'I mean, Mike and me have a lot of laughs, and it's better dancing with Arthur than with another girl, and even Sandy can be quite funny. I tell you what, I'd feel better about going out so much if you had a bloke as well. I mean, it doesn't seem right, me going out two or three times a week and leaving you by yourself.'

'I'm not by myself. I go to the Club. I like the sports.'

'Yes, but you don't meet blokes there, do you? It's all girls' teams. The boys do their training separately. Anyway, even when one did show a bit of interest you just gave him the cold shoulder.'

Jo said nothing. In fact, she had begun to feel surprisingly envious of the other girls as they discussed their boyfriends and nights out. Until now, she hadn't minded seeing Phyl go off for the evening with one of her 'chaps'; she'd been quite content with her sports or a book. But perhaps she really was missing something. She thought of Nick Laurence with his dark, curly hair and bright brown eyes. If only he didn't look quite so much like that other Laurie.

'I just wish people would stop going on about it,' she said. 'You'd think there was something *peculiar* about a girl who's not interested in boys. Not everyone wants to get married.'

'No, I suppose not.' Phyl did think there was something a bit odd about it, though she didn't want to upset Jo by saying so. It was fun, having boyfriends and flirting and kissing. 'Mind, I'm not in any hurry to get married, but it's fun having a boy to go out with, and flirting and all that.'

'And having him slobber all over you?' Jo asked with a shudder. 'Honestly, Phyl, I just don't fancy it. Half of them don't even clean their teeth.'

'Well, there's plenty left in the other half. Tell you what, Jo, if you're really not interested in Nick, why don't I get Mike to bring along one of his mates next time we go out? You like the pictures, and you don't have to talk to him if you don't want to. At least it'd stop people going on at you.'

'No, it wouldn't. They'd just start going on about when were we going to get engaged.' The bus came along and they scrambled aboard. 'All right, Phyl, but tell him it's got to be someone reasonable. I don't want some weird-looking dumbo that nobody else will go out with.'

Phyl knew exactly who Jo wanted to go out with. She wasn't

at all fooled by her cousin's protestations and she determined to bring the two together. Anyone could see they were meant for each other, she thought, and Jo herself knew it although she had this daft idea about some bloke in that book she was forever reading. It's time she got her nose out of books and stopped running about on sports fields and started living a bit of real life, she told herself.

On the next Tuesday evening, she discovered she wasn't the only one thinking like that.

'I want to talk to you, Sandy,' she began the minute he came back to their table with their drinks – a pint of bitter for himself and a large lemonade for her. 'It's about our Jo and that Nick Laurence.'

'That's a coincidence,' he said. 'I was supposed to talk to *you* about them.'

Phyl stared at him, then laughed. 'Has Nick been asking you to fix up a date?'

'Sort of. He's been mooning about like a dying duck in a thunderstorm, can't seem to get her off his mind. But he's got this idea she doesn't like him. I told him, there's only one way to find out, but he says it's no good, she wouldn't come if he did ask her.'

'Well, I don't think she would,' Phyl said. 'But it's not because she doesn't like him – she does.'

'So what's the matter with her? Is there another chap?'

'*Another* chap? It's taken me all my time to get her interested in *this* one!' Phyl shook her head. 'No, I can't tell you why – it sounds too daft. But I'll tell you what, if we could just get them together once, I reckon it'd be all right. It'd be up to them then, and if Nick can't get her interested in going out with him a second time, well, that's his lookout, isn't it?'

'So what do we do? Fix up a blind date?'

'That's what I wanted to talk to you about,' Phyl said with a grin. She took a swig of her lemonade. 'And it doesn't have to be blind as far as Nick's concerned – he can come along with his eyes wide open. You just tell him to be by Hyde Park Gate at seven o'clock on Saturday evening. My Saturday-night boyfriend Mike'll be there, and I'll see that Jo comes with me. And I reckon after that it'll be all plain sailing.'

Sandy gave her a rueful look. 'Plain sailing for Jo and Nick, and plain sailing for you, too, I suppose – but what about your Saturday-night boyfriend, and your Tuesday-night one? I reckon Mike and me would both like to be in each other's shoes.'

'Well, you can't.' Phyl sipped again. 'I've told you all straight – I don't want to go serious with no one. I'm not two-timing you – you know just where you stand. I just want to have fun for a while before I settle down, that's all.'

'All right, all right, you don't have to spell it out,' Sandy said, holding up both hands. 'So why don't we do that? Forget all about your cousin's problems and concentrate on having fun, eh? How about another drink – something a bit stronger this time?'

Phyl grinned at him again. He was a nice lad and didn't expect too much, and she had a pretty good idea that he had one or two other girls on a string as well. And why not? She couldn't expect him to sit in of a Saturday night when she was off with Mike.

'I'll have another lemonade,' she said firmly, and then added with a wink, 'But you can ask the bloke to put a drop of port in this time as well.'

The girls were on early shift that week, so there was time to go back to Elmbury Street and change for the evening. Phyl and Jo had arranged to meet the boys at the entrance to Hyde Park. They could go for a walk and then have a bite to eat and a drink in one of the park's cafés.

The boys were already there when Phyl and Jo turned the corner. Jo took one look and stopped dead.

'Phyl!'

Her cousin strolled on, every movement of her body expressing total innocence.

'*Phyl!*'

'What's the matter? Been stung by something?'

'Yes – you.' Jo threw a quick glance at the waiting boys and grasped her cousin's arm. Her face was burning. 'You did this deliberately.'

'Well, it'd be a job to do it by accident. Look, Jo, anyone could see you liked the look of Nick Laurence, and if it wasn't for that stupid book you're always on about you two would have been going out together for weeks and probably planning the wedding by now ... All right, maybe you wouldn't have got that far,' she added hastily, seeing Jo's face, 'but I bet you'd be getting on all right. And what would it matter if you didn't? It's just one evening out. Nobody's asking you to sign your life away.'

Jo took a deep breath and then smiled ruefully. 'I suppose you're right. But I still think it was a mean trick to play.'

'Why?' Phyl asked innocently. 'You said I could get Mike to ask anyone he liked. All you said was he mustn't be a weird-looking dumbo, and he's not.'

'Just you wait till I get you home,' Jo threatened in a low voice as they approached the gate. 'I'll beat you with pillows and tickle you till you're *sick.*'

Phyl rolled her eyes, pretending to be frightened, and they were both laughing as they reached the waiting boys. Mike grinned at Phyl and pulled her to him for a kiss, while Nick gave Jo a nervous glance.

'Is this okay? You don't mind me coming?'

'Why should I?' Jo answered lightly. 'After all, we were supposed to be seeing each other at the Club some time, if I remember rightly.'

Nick flushed. 'I'm sorry about that. I had a cold, and then my shifts were all wrong—'

'It doesn't matter,' she said. 'It doesn't matter in the least. By the way, I didn't know you knew Mike and the others.'

'What others—?' he began and flushed a deeper scarlet than ever. 'Oh, yes, well, you know how it is ...' He took a breath and then said quickly, 'Look, Jo, I've never met Mike before in my life, nor any of "the others". I just wanted to see you again. I asked Sandy to fix it but he said if Phyl asked you along on a Tuesday you'd smell a rat and never come. So – so, well, we did it this way.' He stopped and gave her a helpless look. 'I'll go away now, if you like. I don't want to be a bother to you.'

Jo studied him. He was a nice-looking boy, she thought, with all that dark, curly hair and those hazel eyes. He had a nice smile, half shy and half merry, and an appealing way of wiggling his brows. And it really wasn't his fault that he not only had the same name as her hero, he looked just like him, too.

'No, don't do that,' she said, her own wide, friendly smile breaking out at last. She held out her hand and he took it, so that they were shaking hands as if they'd just been formally introduced. 'Don't go away. Let's go for our walk and have a bite of supper and a chat, and get to know each other. Let's see if we can be friends.'

Shirley was out dancing that night with Owen. They met most Saturdays now, when her shifts allowed it, and either danced or went to a 'social' – where there were games as well as dancing – or sometimes to the pictures. On Sundays, they stayed at home, helping their invalid parents.

Shirley saw Irene at the dances, too, but they rarely spoke much. Irene had ignored Herbert Lennox the next time they'd met but had now taken up with a floor supervisor who was better looking and took home a fatter wage packet each week. He was smart in a rather oily way, and Irene always dressed up to the nines and put on far more make-up than she would have been allowed to wear at work.

'I've got something to ask you,' Owen said in his lilting voice as they finished an energetic tango and found themselves chairs.

'What's that?' Shirley was watching Irene. She and her supervisor had been dancing almost indecently and it had been touch and go whether Irene's bosom would fall out of her frock. They went off into a corner and sat close together, his hand on her thigh.

'Look, I know what your situation is,' he said, speaking rapidly, 'and you might want to say no. Well, what I'm saying is, if that's what you want, you just say it – I don't want to exert no pressure on you, see? I won't be upset.' He smiled suddenly. 'I'll be sorry, mind, but I won't be upset, if you see what I mean.'

Shirley looked at him with more attention. He was looking very serious despite his smile and she had a sudden feeling that he was going to propose to her. Oh, no, she thought, not that, not here. I'm not ready – and this isn't the place. I'd want it to be somewhere quiet, somewhere pretty ... She gazed at him, willing him not to ask her to marry him.

'Look, what it is, I just want to ask you ... well ...' he floundered, and Shirley closed her eyes. If only there were some way to stop him ... But there was nothing she could do, she could only sit and listen.

'Look,' he said again, 'I just want to ask you – well, I know what Sundays are, they're special for you same as they are for me – but d'you think you could see your way clear – I mean, just this once, d'you think you could come over to tea at our place tomorrow? Meet my dad and mam, like, and my sister Bronwen. I've been talking about you at home, see, and they'd all like to see you. But you just say if you don't want to, mind,' he finished earnestly.

Shirley felt a wave of relief sweep over her. Sunday tea! That was all it was. Of course, Sunday tea did have a certain meaning, everyone knew that, but even if it was the first step, it was still quite a small one. As Phyl would have said, it wasn't like signing your life away.

'Yes,' she said, smiling back at him. 'Yes, I'd like to come. I'd like to meet your family. And maybe next week you'll come and meet mine.'

It had never occurred to her as she'd got ready for the dance that evening that she'd end up inviting Owen to tea next Sunday. But quite suddenly it felt right and she knew she was looking forward to it.

The fear of war seemed suddenly to recede in October, when Mr Chamberlain made his visit to Munich, returning with a piece of paper in his hand which he declared meant 'peace in our time'. There would be no war, he said, waving to cheering crowds, first at Heston Airport and then from the balcony at Buckingham Palace where he stood with the King and Queen. It had been agreed to hand over the disputed territories of Sudetenland to Hitler. This would satisfy him and now everyone could settle down to a peaceful Europe.

'I hope the Czechs are as happy about it,' Bill Mason said. He agreed with Jo that bullies went on bullying until they were stopped. In fact, the Prime Minister of Czechoslovakia had been reported as saying it was the most tragic moment of his life, but in the cause of peace he accepted the ruling.

There were celebrations everywhere. Churches held special thanksgiving services, crowds gathered to rejoice. Jo went home again, taking with her a copy of the new magazine *Picture Post*. The photograph on the cover, of two girls leaping in the air in spotted blouses, fringed leather skirts and cowboy boots, seemed to illustrate the exhilaration they all felt. It was like Christmas coming on the first of October.

The magazine was filled with interesting stories and pictures – an account of a hospital operation, with photos of the surgeon and nurses, an old man dancing the Lambeth Walk to an accordion in an ordinary street, a story about people on the pavement outside Number 10, Downing Street. There was nothing about the Munich crisis, or about impending war. There were no pictures of society people at posh parties – it was all ordinary people, doing ordinary things. It was like a breath of fresh air.

'I like this,' Bill Mason said. 'We'll get it regular, Carrie.'

But the euphoria did not last. Within a week, Hitler's troops had marched into the newly acquired territory of Sudetenland. War had been averted, but the new regime looked frighteningly military. A few weeks later the worst report yet of anti-Semitism came out of Berlin – a night of terror, when shops were smashed, synagogues set on fire and almost a hundred people killed in reprisals after the assassination of the Third Secretary of the German Reich in Paris. The assassin was a young Polish Jew, aged only seventeen, who said he had done it because he had been treated like a dog just because he was Jewish. 'The Jewish people have a

202

right to exist upon this earth,' he said. But the Nazis, it seemed, did not agree.

Etty felt sick when she heard this. She hadn't forgotten the teasing she had suffered at the Home, or the way Irene had treated her. Although she hadn't been brought up as a Jew, she felt the bond keenly, and it was as if she herself had been forced to sew a yellow star on her sleeve and been treated like a dog.

The other girls sensed her unhappiness and treated her kindly. They turned their backs when Irene came into the dressing room, and she became the outcast. Her eyes smouldered and her mouth took on a sullen droop, but she said nothing and went to sit with new friends in the canteen, or on her own in a corner.

Jo especially seemed to understand Etty's feelings.

'It isn't just countries and territories,' she said to Nick as they walked in Hyde Park one afternoon. 'It's people. It's awful, and Hitler's an awful man. I don't see how anyone can really believe there's never going to be another war.'

'We've got to try to believe it, though,' Nick said. He took her hand in his and stroked her fingers. 'We've got to keep hoping. It's no good giving way to him, that's just what he wants.'

'But we *are* giving way,' she argued. 'That "piece of paper" – it just let him go on and invade someone else. You know what I think? I think he's just laughing at Mr Chamberlain behind his back. The minute he was on that plane with his precious piece of paper, Hitler was telling his troops to pick up their guns. And he'll keep on and on doing it until he's got all of Europe under his flaming boot, and that includes us!'

'Jo, don't get so upset.' Nick stopped and put his arms around her. 'I know what you say's true – but it's no use getting ourselves all worked up before it happens. We've got to go on hoping, like I said, but get ready as well. Then we'll be able to stand up to him when the time comes.'

'And meanwhile,' she said, laying her head against his shoulder, 'people like poor Etty will be bullied and tormented

– people in those other countries, I mean – and frightened to live their normal lives. It's not right, Nick. It's *not*.'

'No,' he said heavily, 'it's not. But we'll put a stop to it, Jo. He won't be allowed to go on for ever.'

Neither of them spoke of their greatest fear – that if it came to war Nick and others like him might have to go away and fight. But Jo's arms tightened around his neck and she pressed herself close, as if to keep him with her, as if some cold shadow had reached back from the future and touched her with its chill.

Since that evening when Phyl had engineered their meeting, Jo and Nick had been meeting regularly. At first afraid that she was attracted to him mostly because of his resemblance to her dream hero, Jo had finally admitted that it was Nick himself she liked. More than liked, she thought as she lay awake at night, remembering his smile, the expression in his eyes, the way he touched her hand. And there was far more to him than his looks – it was as if he were her twin soul. She chided herself for being 'soppy' but again and again came back to the sense that he was her other half, just as Auntie Carrie was her mother's other half. There was an understanding between them that went deeper than words. He's my friend, she thought, he's the friend of my spirit.

The thought of losing him to war was a horror she could not face.

Nobody wanted to face war, and nobody wanted to talk about it. Like her friends, Jo tried to push the thoughts away and threw herself into her own life. She worked hard at the Corner House, loving the bright, colourful surroundings, the music and the cheerful faces of the customers as much as ever. In her spare time she played hockey and netball at Sudbury, and applauded Phyl in her first apearance on stage with the amateur dramatic club, though she wasn't too keen on seeing the way she and her leading man had to canoodle on stage in front of everyone. And she went to the dances and the pictures and theatre with Nick Laurence.

'Why didn't you want to go out with me?' Nick asked her one day as they wandered along the river-bank after a rowing club meeting at Hammersmith. The season was over and they'd been laying up the boats for the winter. 'Didn't you like me?'

Jo blushed. 'It wasn't that. It – well, it's too silly to say, really. You reminded me of someone in a book, that's all.'

Nick burst out laughing. 'A book! Me! Who was it, then, the villain? The wicked squire? The murderer?' He lowered his voice and made it sound hollow and sinister.

'No, he wasn't any of those,' Jo said, laughing despite her embarrassment. 'Actually, he was nice – he was my favourite character.'

Nick stared at her. 'So why didn't you want to go out with me? Did you think I wouldn't measure up?'

'I told you it was silly.' She frowned, suddenly thoughtful. 'No, it wasn't that either. It was more that – well, that *he* didn't measure up.' Her blush deepened. 'I don't think I want to say any more, Nick, it just sounds more and more stupid.'

'Oh, come on! You can't leave me in mid-air.' He studied her face, then put his arm around her shoulders and gave her a light squeeze. 'All right, Jo, don't get upset. I'm not going to make you tell me anything you don't want to. We'll forget it, shall we?'

Jo said nothing for a few moments, then she shrugged a little and shook her head, her loose chestnut hair flying about her face. 'No, I'll tell you, otherwise you'll go on wondering. But you're not to think there's anything – well, serious in it, Nick. You see, he didn't measure up because he didn't marry the right girl. The one he ought to have married.' She was scarlet by now but plunged on. 'The one that reminded me of me. The one that was called Jo.'

There was a silence. Jo avoided Nick's eyes, looking at the river, the autumn colours on the trees – anything rather than meet his glance. Eventually, staring at her shoes, she mumbled, 'I told you it was daft. Don't let's talk about it any more.'

'Well, we won't if you don't want to,' Nick said after a moment. 'But there's just one thing I'd like to say, Jo.' He put one forefinger under her chin, lifting her face so that she had to meet his eyes. 'There's nothing to stop us putting it right, is there?'

'Putting it right?' she whispered, staring at him.

'Yes. This Nick in the book—'

'Laurie.'

'Laurie? Oh, you mean his name was Laurie. Well, this Laurie, then – *he* might not have known a good thing when he saw it, but that don't mean no one else can. *I* can. Ever since I first saw you, diving off that high board in your red bathers, I knew you were the girl for me. And just because a bloke called Laurence in some old book didn't marry his Jo, it don't mean to say Nick Laurence in real life can't marry his. Does it?'

'No,' she whispered, her head spinning as she tried to take in his words. 'No, it doesn't. But, Nick—'

'But nothing,' he said, grinning. 'This is a proposal, Jo Mason, so just shut up while I do it properly.' He paused, cleared his throat, took her hand in both of his and then said, very seriously and with great tenderness, 'Jo, I love you. Will you marry me? *Will* you?'

'Nick . . .' she breathed, the blush fading from her face to leave it as pale as milk.

'You don't have to answer straight away,' he said, his voice trembling a little now. 'You can tell me when you like. Only – don't say no straight off, please, Jo. Think about it for a while, at least.'

'I don't – I don't have to think about it.' Her eyes were like stars. 'I want to marry you, Nick. I do!'

His face broke into a huge smile and he flung his arms around her, clasping her tightly. He kissed her face, her eyes, finally her lips. It was the first time he had ever done so, for Jo had kept her distance even although over the past few weeks she had allowed him, slowly, to come closer. There had been nothing until now but a goodnight peck and a little hand-holding in the darkness of the cinema. But now she let him kiss her and even found herself kissing him back. I know what Phyl was talking about now, she thought, but I don't believe it's ever been like this for her.

206

Nick stopped kissing her and pulled away a little.

'You're not just saying this because of that other Laurie, are you? You're not getting us muddled up?'

'No, I'm not.' A character in a book couldn't kiss and hold you like this, she thought, delirious with the discovery. 'Oh Nick, I love you! I do – I *love* you. Not him – *you*.'

They both laughed, seeing the sudden incongruity of a situation in which anyone could be jealous of a character in a book. Nick pulled her close and she rested her head on his shoulder. We've wasted so much time, she thought, dazed. Weeks and weeks, when we could have been close like this. But it doesn't matter now, because we've got the rest of our lives . . .

Thinking of the rest of their lives brought, even in the midst of such delight, an odd little shudder. Jo looked at the bare river-banks, so recently crowded with people watching the races – happy, laughing, cheering people – and wondered suddenly whether the boats really would be brought out again next spring. Or whether, by then, they might already be at war.

'You're worrying again,' Nick said, observing her face. 'I'm getting to know that look, Jo. You're scared we won't have a chance, aren't you?' He hugged her again and rested his lips against her cheek. 'Stop being so afraid, Jo,' he whispered. 'Stop being afraid it's all going to be taken away from us. It's not. I promise you, it's not.'

'You can't promise that,' she said shakily. 'It's not up to people like us. Oh, Nick – I'm sorry, I can't help it, it's just that I'm so happy and I just couldn't bear it if anything happened to you.'

'Nothing's going to happen,' he soothed her. 'Anyway, if there's nothing we can do about it there's no point in worrying either. Let's be happy while we've got the chance.' He lifted his head and looked down into her eyes, his own dancing with delight. 'We love each other and we're engaged – yes, we are, and I'll buy you a ring to prove it! – and it won't be long before it's Christmas. What could be better than that?'

★

To the Pearly kings and queens, October meant something special. This was the date when they celebrated the Harvest Festival at St Martin in the Fields. Pearlies from every London borough flocked to the service, and Etty stared in amazement and delight as hundreds of ordinary men and women from back streets all over the city marched down the Strand in their shimmering costumes.

'It's lovely,' she said to Maggie, who was resplendent in her own glory. 'I've never seen anything like it.' She gazed in admiration at the dress and coat her friend wore, each encrusted with tiny pearl buttons. Men and women alike wore the pearls, and she thought that if you could count all the buttons there that day it would run into millions. Children, too, were dressed in Pearly costumes, even down to babies like Queenie. That must be why they called her that, Etty thought suddenly, because she was a real little Pearly Queen.

'D'you really mean to tell me you'd never heard of us?' Maggie asked. 'I thought everyone knew about the Pearlies.'

'Well, I'd heard of you, but I didn't really know anything about you. I can remember seeing something at the pictures once, years ago – on *Pathe Pictorial*. A funeral, or something.'

'That was Henry Croft,' Jim said. He was in costume, too, looking as splendid, Etty thought, as anyone who had been in that other royal procession eighteen months ago, when King George had been crowned. 'He was the first Pearly. He started it in – oh, 1875 or thereabouts when he was just a kid. Here—' he shook Etty's arm '—I'll tell you something else about him, too. He grew up in an orphanage – just like you! He had to leave when he was thirteen, of course, and he got a job as a roadsweeper and ratcatcher in Somers Town Market.'

'So how did he get the idea of starting the Pearly kings and queens?' Etty asked, fascinated.

'Well, he didn't, not just like that,' Maggie said. 'He used to work for the costermongers down the market, see, helping keep things clean and tidy round their barrows. He worked hard and he must've bin a friendly sort of kid, and they liked him. They used to look after him, see, like they looked after each other – had a whip-round if anyone was bad, that sort of thing. I suppose that give him the idea of looking after people, and he wanted to do something to help the kids back at the orphanage.'

'I still don't see—'

'Well, hang on, I'm telling you, ain't I? The costermongers used to sew pearl buttons down the seams of their trousers and weskits, see, make 'em look a bit different from the other blokes in the market. They called them "flash boy suits". And young Henry Croft, well, he looked at these and he thought if he went one better he could make people sit up and take a bit of notice of him, see, and that way he could collect money for his own mates back at the Home, and for anyone else what needed it. So he got hundreds and hundreds of buttons and he sewed them all over his suit, not just down the seams, and then when he'd finished he come out in it for one of the local carnivals. Walked through the streets in the processions, carrying his bucket, and it just filled up with money. Well, he was only a bit of a kid, see, and people thought he deserved it. And so he did. And after that he used to wear it whenever he could, and he collected money for hospitals and blind people, deaf and dumb people – anyone who needed it. He used to get asked to raise money specially, he got so well known.'

'He must have been a smashing chap,' Etty said, feeling ashamed. Here was a boy only thirteen years old, living by himself after growing up in an orphanage just like herself – but had he whined and felt sorry for himself and tried to hide his origins? No, he'd got on with it and done something to help other people. Something that had lasted years and years – beyond his own lifetime – so that by the time he died his funeral was filmed and shown at the pictures for all to see.

'After a bit,' Jim went on, raising his voice a little so as to be heard above the sound of the bells pealing above, 'he thought he could raise even more money so he asked the coster-mongers to help, and they all made themselves pearly suits. They got the idea of calling themselves kings and queens and soon there was a pearly family in every borough in London, and there still is today, and we still raise money for people in need.'

The Pearlies had reached the church now and were thronging inside, the gleam of their suits lighting the sudden darkness. Etty, walking between Maggie and Jim, felt conspicuous in her ordinary skirt and blouse. Nobody seemed to care, however, and they looked at her and smiled, their welcome as warm and genuine as the Pratts' had been the first time Maggie took her home.

'Henry died in 1930,' Jim murmured in her ear. 'All the Pearlies went to his funeral and followed his coffin to Finchley cemetery. There's a statue of him there now, wearing his suit, all marble from Italy it is. It looks really smashing. I'll take you to see it, if you like.'

'Oh, yes, please.' Etty gazed around the church. It was filled with fruits and vegetables, the trade of the costermongers, piled high in elaborate displays. Vegetable marrows the size of which she had never seen, firm round cabbages, huge carrots and large, creamy potatoes all adorned the window-sills, the altar steps or were clustered around the lectern and even on the pulpit; there was scarcely room for the smallest tomato between them. As well as the vegetables there were flowers – huge orange and white chrysanthemums, red and yellow dahlias and Michaelmas daisies of soft mauve. Their sharp autumn scents filled the air and as the sound of the bells ceased, to be replaced by the thundering splendour of the organ, Etty felt a sense of awe and privilege at being here, at this special service, with all these people who were carrying on such a magnificent tradition.

It's time you grew up, Etty Brown, she told herself, feeling her eyes prickle as the Pearlies stood up and began to sing the first hymn to harvest time. 'We plough the fields and scatter the good seed on the land . . .' That's what they're doing in a way – scattering good seed, helping other people. And all because of a little boy who grew up in an orphanage and didn't let it spoil his life. Maybe he was even a better person because of it.

She straightened her shoulders and stood a little taller.

And, glancing up, met the eyes of the tall young man who stood beside her, sharing her hymn book. They smiled at each other and Etty felt the warmth of love spread through her body. Family love, she thought, letting her arm touch Jim's. And love for other people – like Henry Croft had felt, all those years ago.

Chapter Fourteen

Shirley's first visit to Owen's home had led to a regular exchange of Sunday teas. One week she would go to his house, the next he would come to hers. They got to know each other's families, each easily able to accept the constraints of an invalid parent.

'I'll do that for you,' Owen said, the first time he saw Shirley's mother carrying in a scuttle of coal. 'And I'll fill it up again before I go home, see? You don't want to go lifting heavy things.'

'Go on, I've got our Shirl and my hubby to help me with all that,' Annie Wood said, looking pleased all the same. Fetching in coal had been one of Donald's jobs, which had now been added to Shirley's and her father's. Jack could do some of them, too, but he was likely to get distracted while he was in the back yard by next-door's black and white tomcat or a cluster of squabbling sparrows. And he didn't really like going in the coalshed anyway because he hated spiders.

'Well, it won't hurt me to do a few jobs for you, take the burden off them, like. I could tidy up the garden for you, too.' Being a builder, Alf Woods could do anything around the house but his interests didn't extend beyond the back door. There was a patch of rough grass there and a few flower-beds, growing more weeds than flowers since Donald had gone away, and Owen regarded it and suggested they use it to grow a few vegetables.

'Vegetables?' Alf Wood said. 'We can get plenty of them down the market.'

'We might not be able to get so many if a war starts,' Owen said quietly. 'I reckon we'll all be glad of a bit of ground to grow our own food then. Wouldn't do no harm to get a bit of a start, like, now would it?'

'There's not going to be a war,' Annie Wood said, her face suddenly pinched and anxious as she thought of Donald. 'Mr Chamberlain—'

'No, I don't suppose there is,' Owen agreed, seeing her expression. 'All the same – it don't do no harm to be prepared, like.'

'Why will we need to grow vegetables if there's a war?' Shirley asked. 'We won't be eating any more then than we do now.'

'No, but we get a lot of stuff from overseas, see, and one of the ways the Germans will fight us is to stop that sort of thing getting through. Putting us under siege, like. Anyway, like we just said, I don't suppose there's going to be a war. But a few seeds put in the ground now won't do no harm. It'll be nice to look at rows of spuds and cabbages growing, instead of dandelions and stinging nettles. Mind you,' he added with a grin, 'I've heard you can eat stinging nettles, they make good soup, and you can make wine out of dandelions.'

'Well, there you are, then,' Shirley said, returning his grin. 'We don't need to plant potatoes – we're already growing our own food!'

At Owen's house, Shirley was the one to offer help. Mrs Prosser had to do all her husband's tasks as well as her own when she wasn't serving in her brother's hardware shop. Owen took a lot of the heavier jobs over, but Susan Prosser always looked tired on Sundays, the one day she didn't have to go to the shop, and Shirley soon offered to make the tea and bake cakes while she was in the house.

'I do them at home for my own mum, so it's no trouble,' she said as Susan's face lit up at the sight of a pile of fresh, warm rock cakes. 'I can easily whip up a few for you, too, while I'm here.'

'You're a good lass,' said Mrs Prosser, who had come originally from the north of England. Her father had been a miner as well and had gone to Wales in the twenties, taking his family with him. That was where she'd met Owen's father, Rhys Prosser. She smiled at Shirley and added, 'Our Bronwen's clever as clever with a needle, but she doesn't like cooking much and I don't like to make her stop in of a Sunday, not when she works such long hours at the tailor's.'

Bronwen was a year younger than Owen, small and dark with rosy cheeks and curly brown hair. After a week of treadling away at a Singer sewing machine she wanted nothing more than to get out with her friends. She was never there when Shirley arrived, but came home for tea, eager for her share of the rock cakes, before the whole family went off to the evening service at the Methodist chapel.

'You don't have to come,' Owen said apologetically, but Shirley said she'd like to. She'd been brought up to go to Sunday school and then to the little local church on the corner of the street, and she enjoyed the hearty singing of the Methodists. Afterwards, Owen took her home on the bus and they lingered for a while at the corner by the tiny churchyard, saying goodnight.

'It's nice, the way we get on with each other's families,' Owen said, as they paused in the deep shadow of the yew tree. 'It's like as if it was meant.'

Once again, Shirley had the feeling that he was about to propose to her. But she still wasn't really ready. Sunday tea every week was one thing – tea every day for the rest of your life would be quite different. She gave Owen a quick kiss and said breathlessly, 'I'll have to go, Owen. I promised I wouldn't be late tonight. Thank you ever so much for bringing me home – and – and everything. And you tell your mum that she's to eat those rock cakes herself, not give them all to you and your Bronwen, see!'

Owen said nothing for a moment. Then he put his arms round her and kissed her back, a soft, tender kiss that made her want to take back her careless words and let him say what he wanted to say.

'It's all right, Shirley,' he whispered. 'I told you before, I'm not going to press you. We'll just take it easy, see? We've got plenty of time, after all – all the time in the world.' He drew her out of the shadow and they walked along the last few hundred yards of road, hand in hand. At her front door, he kissed her again. 'Goodnight, Shirley. I'll see you next week, all right? At the dance on Saturday?'

'Yes,' she said, and smiled at him. 'And on Sunday it's your turn to come here.'

She put her finger on the doorbell and watched him walk away down the street as she waited for someone to answer. He stopped at the corner and she knew he would stand there until she went inside. She felt a gentle warmth of affection for him, a gratitude for his understanding.

All the time in the world, he'd said. All the time in the world.

Nobody else knew about Jo's and Nick's engagement until Christmas Day. They spent it together, partly at the Masons' house and partly with the Laurences. Nick borrowed his brother's motorbike to come over in the morning for Christmas dinner, and then took Jo back for tea, returning later for the last few hours of the big family party.

They'd been along to Samuel's the jewellers the week before and chosen the ring. Jo had been nervous that she might pick something Nick couldn't afford, but he'd been in earlier and told the man what his top price was, and Jo was shown a tray of rings, each embedded in soft cream velvet, that had no prices on. 'You can have whichever one you want,' Nick said, and she gazed at them, bemused, until the jeweller took pity on her and started to pick them out and slip them on to her finger.

'That's a nice one, the solitaire.' She looked at the tiny stone, admiring the colours that flashed from it as she turned it about. 'Mum's got three stones and Auntie May's got a half-hoop with five stones, but I think I like the single one best.'

'You get a better stone for the price,' the jeweller told them.

'The others aren't more than chips, but in the end it all depends what suits your finger.'

They decided on the solitaire, and Nick had put the little box into his pocket. It was there now, Jo knew, and all they needed was her father's permission for it to be taken out and slipped back on to her finger.

'Engaged!' Bill Mason said, when Nick got him alone in the front room to ask his permission. 'Well, I don't know about that ... Our Jo's only nineteen, you know, and she's never had a proper boyfriend before you. I don't know as she's ready for nothing serious.'

'Oh, *Dad*,' protested Jo, who had been hovering nearby, unable to keep away. 'Of course I'm ready. Lots of girls are engaged at nineteen.'

Bill rubbed his chin thoughtfully. In truth, he wasn't surprised – Carrie had said to him only a few days earlier that she thought there was something in the air. Jo had changed lately and it was clear it was to do with Nick Laurence. He'd been prepared for such a request, but that didn't mean he had to agree to it straight away.

'I'll have to think about it a bit,' he said. 'It's not something that can be decided all in a hurry.'

'But we've got the ring!' Jo cried. 'You can't say no, Dad – we wanted to get engaged on Christmas Day. *Please.*'

'Well, this isn't the only Christmas Day there's ever going to be,' he pointed out, trying to keep a straight face. 'There'll be another one next year. It's not all that long to wait.'

'Dad—'

Carrie came into the room and Jo turned to her, her face anguished. 'Mum – Nick and me want to get engaged at Christmas and Dad won't let us—'

'That's enough, Bill,' Carrie ordered, her mouth twitching. 'Stop teasing the poor girl. Of course you can get engaged,' she said to Jo. 'We've been expecting it. Your dad's just having you on, you know what he's like.'

'Well, he's not master in his own house, that's obvious,' Bill said, but he couldn't keep up his stern expression any longer and his wide mouth broke into a grin almost as broad as his daughter's. 'I thought it was supposed to be the father who gives his permission. Come here, girl, and give your dad a kiss. And you make sure you look after her, young man – she's one in a million, our Jo.'

'Oh, Dad,' Jo said, almost in tears. 'Oh, Mum – thank you, *thank* you. Oh, let's tell the others – let's make a proper announcement—'

Nick grabbed her as she turned to whirl from the room. 'Hang on a mo. You haven't got your ring yet. They won't believe you if you're not wearing a ring.'

Carrie gave her husband a significant look and, when he didn't respond, dragged him by the arm through the door. Jo giggled and flung her arms around her new fiancé. He pushed her away and struggled to get the little box out of his pocket.

'Sit in that chair,' he ordered, and went down on one knee. 'I'm never going to get the chance to propose to anyone again so let's make a proper job of it.' He took her hand and looked into her wide eyes, his own suddenly serious. 'Jo – Jo Mason – I love you. Will you marry me? Will you be my wife?'

He opened the box and took out the ring they had chosen together. The tiny diamond caught the light and flashed with colour as he slipped it on to her finger.

'Oh, Nick,' Jo whispered, her eyes suddenly filled with tears. 'Oh, Nick, yes. Yes, please. You know I will . . .'

Etty had never known a Christmas like it. Both Jim and Maggie had taken it for granted that she would spend it at the Pratts' home and she had immediately gone into a panic, not knowing what to do about Christmas presents, counting out her money, trying to find out how many Pratts would actually be there.

'What can I get your gran?' she asked Maggie in despair. 'I've never known anyone old before. What sort of things does she like?' She thought of the old woman, sitting in her corner like a squat black goblin, watching everything that went on with her black-button eyes, her walking stick kept handy to poke anyone whose attention she wanted to catch.

When she went shopping, she put on a rusty black coat and hat and marched off down the street like an army on the move, carrying her black umbrella instead of the stick if it was raining. She did a lot of knitting, huge shapeless black garments that seemed designed for a whale but were usually handed to Maggie's dad for work, but apart from that she seemed to have no interests.

'She likes her food,' Maggie said. 'She might not have many teeth but the ones she has got have to work hard for their living. Here, I'll tell you what, Etty, why don't you just get a tin of biscuits from the retail counter? They've got some real nice stuff there and it would do for the whole family.'

Etty thought that was a good idea. After her shift had finished, she went to the retail counter, where boxes of chocolates, tins of biscuits, cakes, fruit, flowers, wines and spirits and tobacco were all displayed in glittering array. The chocolates looked sumptuous enough to give to a film star. 'Silver Cottage' at eight shillings for a two-pound box, 'Four Seasons' at ten shillings for two pounds. But the most glamorous were the 'Lacquer Caskets' at seven shillings and sixpence for a pound, or seventeen shillings and sixpence for a two-and-a-half-pound casket which would be good enough to keep jewellery in – if you had any – after the chocolates were gone.

If I had a mum, Etty thought, I'd buy her one of those. And she felt the surge of loneliness that had sometimes threatened to swamp her completely, at Christmas or on her birthday, a loneliness at not having a mum she could buy presents for or who would think her birthday was something special. Behind her, where everyone else had a family, there was nothing but a void.

Still, this Christmas at least she did have a family. Maggie had suggested biscuits would do for all of them, but Etty counted the money she'd saved from her tips and decided she could afford a small box of chocolates as well for Maggie's mum, and one for Maggie, too, and a small bar for Ginnie's stocking.

The girl behind the counter, 'Sally the Salesgirl', in her blue uniform and big cap wrapped the gifts in glossy paper and handed them over with a smile. 'Someone's going to be pleased on Christmas morning.'

'I'm going to stay with Maggie Pratt,' Etty told her. The Sally's real name was Joan and they knew each other by sight and from meeting in the canteen or at Sudbury. 'The biscuits are for everyone and the chocolates for Maggie and her mum, but I ought to get something for Jim as well. He takes me out on his motorbike.'

'Oh, going steady, are you?' Joan asked with a wink, and Etty blushed. 'Well, a boy doesn't want chocolates, does he? What about a nice packet of cigarettes?'

Etty considered. Jim usually smoked Woodbines but she thought he would appreciate something a bit more special. Craven A, perhaps, or Players. She didn't know much about cigarettes and the display was confusing. 'Which are the best?'

'Well, these du Maurier are popular. They're French – a bit more posh. I bet he'd like them.'

Etty looked at the price and decided she could just afford them. She handed over the money, then went away with her purchases.

They finished work late on Christmas Eve and then joined the rush home. All the buses and Underground trains were crowded, but it was a cheerful crowd and there was a festive smell of whisky and cigars in the air. Etty, burdened with her Christmas presents as well as a small cardboard suitcase containing her nightdress and best blouse, struggled along behind Maggie, excited and nervous at the thought of her first real family Christmas.

At home, everyone was there. Ivy Pratt had laid on a good supper of boiled gammon, potatoes done in their jackets, carrots the colour of sunsets and dark red cabbage. Vegetables were never in short supply at the Pratt home, with Sam Pratt being a porter in the Market, and he usually managed to bring home a joint of meat as well. For Christmas he'd brought the gammon and a big rib of beef, and Ivy had made mince pies and a huge Christmas pudding full of silver threepenny bits.

The meal was noisy and jolly. Sam had brought bottles of beer, with cider for the younger boys. Maggie drank beer, but Etty preferred the cider. She sat quietly at her end of the table, sandwiched between Jim and Ginnie, who was wildly over-excited about Christmas.

'He'll be here before eleven o'clock, Jim says, so we've all got to be in bed before then,' she told Etty. 'And Mum says I can leave him a mince pie. He's going to be full up if everyone leaves him a mince pie, isn't he, but I don't reckon any of them'll be as good as our Mum's, so probably he won't bother with the others ... I'm saving this carrot for his reindeer.'

'What's he bringing you?' asked Etty, whose memories of Christmas Eve were only slightly less bleak than any of her others. They hadn't been given stockings to hang up, and only those children who had come from families at a later stage in their lives had known anything at all about the story of Father Christmas. The rest had listened in some bewilderment to their accounts of reindeer flying through the sky and an old man coming down chimneys with sacks full of presents. It was as hard to imagine as living in a small house, with a bedroom each and a father and mother who actually belonged to you.

Etty understood now that the myth was perpetuated from generation to generation and that you went along with it until the children themselves came to realise it was just a story. She wasn't sure what Ginnie would feel when her turn came – would she resent the lies that had been told to her? – but thought perhaps that the warm, happy memories of belief would overwhelm the disappointment. Or perhaps the disappointment wasn't so bad after all – perhaps when you were old enough to understand the truth you were also old enough to shrug it away.

I wish I'd known about Father Christmas when I was little, she thought. I wish I'd had him to believe in.

Ginnie, asked what he was bringing her, reached up a hand

and pulled Etty's head down to hers so that she could whisper.

'I *think* he might be bringing me a scooter.'

'That's smashing,' Etty said softly. 'You'll be able to go all over the place on that.'

Ginnie nodded, her eyes sparkling. 'I know how to ride it. Rosie next door's got one, she let me try. You just put one foot on and scoot with the other, and you can go ever so fast. I hope mine's got red wheels. Rosie's has got blue wheels but I like red better.'

Soon it was time for Ginnie to go to bed, leaving with a kiss for everyone and a stern warning that they must all be asleep by eleven. As soon as she was safely out of the way they all produced their presents for her, and had a hilarious half-hour blowing whistles, trying to do puzzles that required small ball bearings to be guided into tiny holes, and reading stories from comic annuals. The bigger presents were put into a pillow-case and the smaller ones squeezed into one of Maggie's lisle stockings, with an orange and a few nuts in the toe. The scooter was brought in and leant against the wall.

'It's lovely,' Etty said, admiring the freshly painted blue frame and footboard and the scarlet wheels. 'It's just what she wants.'

'Sam got it from a mate down the Market,' Ivy said proudly. 'He's been painting it up in our Bert's shed, down the road. She's been on about those red wheels for weeks.'

Etty slept that night with Maggie and Ginnie in the double bed they used to share with Evie. It was strange but comforting, sleeping with Maggie's warmth beside her. Infected by Ginnie's excitement, added to her own wonder at being, at last, part of a real family Christmas, she thought she wouldn't sleep at all, but it seemed no more than a moment before she was woken by Ginnie's ecstatic voice shrilling in her ear.

'He's been! He's been! My stocking's all lumpy, I can feel it. Light the gas, Maggie, quick. I want to see what he's brought me!'

'*I* want to see what time it is,' Maggie grumbled, yawning

and stretching as she sat up to do as Ginnie begged her. 'I don't seem to have been asleep five minutes.' But she knew it had to be after seven, for Ivy Pratt wouldn't have substituted the filled stocking and pillowcase for the empty ones until she'd got up herself and gone downstairs to light the range ready for cooking the joint of beef. She groped for the matches and lit the gas mantle over the bed.

The yellow light flickered and then steadied as Ginnie scrambled down to the foot of the bed to retrieve her booty. The stocking came first and every tiny gift was exclaimed over, the bar of chocolate unwrapped and shared with her sister and Etty, the orange left till later. The pillowcase revealed a pile of presents from every member of the family, including the aunties and uncles who lived down the street, and then Ginnie, her eyes like stars, said, 'I wonder if there's anything downstairs . . .'

'Shouldn't think so,' Maggie said, lying back and closing her eyes. The bed was smothered with presents and torn wrapping-paper. 'I should think that was all he had room for in his sack. Wouldn't you, Et?'

Etty was dazzled by the number of gifts Ginnie had received. It wasn't that anyone had given her anything expensive, or been over-generous – it was just that there were such a lot of people in the family and they all loved Ginnie. The other children, George and Gerald and Evie's babies, would have done just as well.

'Let's go down and have a look,' she said to Ginnie, wanting to see her face when she saw the scooter with the red wheels. 'Just in case there was anything he couldn't get up the stairs . . .'

The rest of Christmas passed like a wonderland for Etty. Ginnie's excitement had set the tone for the whole holiday. The rest of the family had their presents after breakfast and Etty's biscuits and chocolates were received with delight, even Gran giving her the smile Ivy had said she only cracked on special occasions. Etty herself was almost overwhelmed by her own little pile of gifts – chocolates for herself, a new pair of stockings, a small tub of Pond's vanishing cream, a bar of scented soap – and watched nervously as Jim unwrapped his packet of du Maurier cigarettes.

'Gosh, they're smashing,' he exclaimed. 'Real posh. Thanks, Etty. And—' his face grew suddenly pink '—I've got something for you too.'

They were sitting in a corner together and he glanced around to make sure that everyone else was occupied with their own presents. Etty felt her heart suddenly begin to beat hard. She watched as he took a small box from his pocket and handed it to her.

'I hope you like it,' he said shyly, and her fingers trembled as she opened the little box.

Inside was a small brooch in the shape of her own initial E. It looked like gold and had tiny, glittering stones spaced along it. Etty thought it was the most beautiful thing she had ever seen.

'Oh, *Jim*,' she whispered.

'Is it all right? It's not real gold, you know, I couldn't run to that. But I will one day, I'll give you proper gold. D'you like it, though? D'you really like it?'

'It's lovely,' she said, her eyes stinging. 'It's gorgeous. Oh, Jim, I've never had anything so nice. Thank you. *Thank* you.'

He took it from her and pinned it on her blouse. The look in his eyes was as serious and intent as if he were fitting a ring on her finger. It was like a promise, she thought, and she met his eyes with her own heartfelt pledge.

'This is the best Christmas I've ever had,' she said shakily, and he grinned and kissed her nose quickly, before anyone could see.

'I tell you what,' he said, 'it hasn't even started yet!'

All the girls worked on New Year's Eve. The Corner Houses were still decorated for Christmas, and the revellers came pouring in. Some were going on to dances, and there would be a great crowd soon making their way into Trafalgar Square, the traditional place for celebrating the coming of a new year. The bells of all London's churches would ring out, some muffled to mark the passing of the old year before the twelve notes of midnight would toll and the clappers be freed in clarion concert.

By eleven o'clock the restaurants were filled with those who were making the Corner Houses the main part of their evening. Coloured streamers festooned the ceilings and walls, and as the magic hour drew nearer reels of them were tossed from table to table, gradually enveloping the diners in swathes of bright orange and green and blue. Paper hats appeared and the noise of laughter almost drowned the music of the gipsy band. The diners were all ordering special dishes, and the Nippies were kept busier than ever as they dashed to and fro.

Mike, Tommy and Charlie were at their usual table and for once had something more glamorous than poached eggs, though Maggie teased them by saying that everything else was 'off'. They ordered the special New Year's Eve menu and when she brought it fell to with gusto. Tommy's eyes followed Maggie wherever she went and Mike watched Phyl wistfully. He knew that she was seeing other boys and didn't want to be 'serious', but since Jo and Nick had announced their engagement he had felt an increased longing to be the special one for her. But he was beginning to think there wasn't a chance. How could an ordinary boy like himself, an assistant in a men's outfitter's, compete with that bloke Sandy, who had a good job at Cadby Hall and was sitting at one of Phyl's tables now, with Nick Laurence and Owen Prosser?

It was almost midnight. The level of noise, which had risen until it was almost deafening, was suddenly stilled by a strange, unearthly lament. Everyone fell silent as the gipsy band ceased its music, and then, through the big kitchen doors, marched a lone figure.

He wore a swinging tartan kilt, and his arms were wrapped around the swollen plaid pouch of a bagpipe. He strode into the centre of the dining-room, where a space had been cleared, and there he stopped while his pipe sobbed for the passing of the old year. Not another sound could be heard.

Jo felt her eyes prick and looked around to see that Phyl's

eyes were also bright with tears. Maggie wasn't even bothering to wipe them from her cheeks, and Shirley, standing close to the table where Owen and the others were sitting, looked almost sad. Only Irene Bond, frozen in the act of clearing a table, looked unmoved.

The lament drew to a close. One of the supervisors struck a large gong, twelve times in solemn rhythm, and the music moved into the more familiar lilt of 'Auld Lang Syne'.

It was as if a spell had been broken. The guests leapt to their feet, reaching out for each other, for the Nippies, for anyone. Caught in the traditional cross-armed hold, they swayed to the rhythm, sang the words so many of them got slightly wrong – and didn't care if they did – and stamped their feet as they surged back and forth between the tables. As the song came to an end, they broke away and turned to each other, kissing and laughing and wishing everyone a Happy New Year.

Jo and Nick were together, their arms around each other's waists. Phyl was caught between all her boyfriends, laughing as they battled to be the one to kiss her first. Maggie and Tommy hugged, and Shirley and Owen stood hand in hand, content just to be together.

Etty and Jim were in a corner, a little distance away from the others. Etty had worn her brooch, flouting all regulations, and he touched it gently with one finger. It was as precious to them, she thought, looking up at him with her heart in her eyes, as if it had been a diamond ring, like the one Jo was wearing on her left hand.

'It's been the best Christmas and New Year's Eve I could ever have dreamed of,' she whispered, remembering the party at the Pratts' home, with everyone happy and laughing, lots of lovely food and games and a rowdy sing-song which had ended with everyone doing the conga out in the street, and all the other families in the street coming out to join in. They'd be doing the same again tonight, she thought, and visiting each other with lumps of coal and crusts of bread. It was a party wherever you looked.

'It's going to get even better,' Jim said. 'Next year's going to be *our* year, Etty. It's going to be a year to remember.'

'I'll always remember 1938,' Etty said, laying her face against his shoulder. 'I can't believe that 1939 will be even better.'

'It will,' he said, and kissed her. 'I promise it will, Etty. 1939's going to be a year we'll never forget.'

Chapter Fifteen

Nineteen thirty-nine. The year that no one was going to forget.

In Spain, Franco captured Barcelona and was at last recognised by Britain as the country's leader.

In Germany, Jews were forbidden to practise as dentists, vets or chemists. By February, they were ordered to leave the Reich at the rate of almost a thousand a week.

In Czechoslovakia, there was complete collapse, and Hitler entered Prague in triumph. All of Slovakia was now under his rule. He and Mussolini both sent congratulations to General Franco. Fascism and Naziism were gaining in strength all over Europe.

As spring laid a delicate haze of green over London's parks, the threat of war loomed blacker than ever. 'Peace in our time' sounded hollow to the ears. People started to talk again about air raids, shelters and gas masks. Britain and France signed a pact with Poland, who feared she might be next on Hitler's list, and promised to stand by her side if she had to defend herself by force.

'That's war,' Jo said when she went home to see the family. 'That's what that means. If Hitler tries to take Poland, we'll have to fight him.'

'It still might not come to that,' her father said, as if he were trying to think it was true. 'It'll make Hitler think twice, us having signed up with Poland. And it's not just us. The

Russians want to come in on our side, and there's America, too. He wouldn't be such a fool as to take on all that.'

'Don't kid yourself, Dad,' Jo said. 'You're already starting to believe it yourself – talking about *our side*. We're going to have to face it some time – we might as well start now.'

He sighed and didn't answer. He looked older these days, she thought, as if the memories of that other war had become too heavy to bear. He'd never talked about it much, but everyone knew that it had been a cruel and horrible war. It wasn't fair that people should have to go through that twice in a lifetime, she thought. It just wasn't fair.

'Well, let's enjoy ourselves while we can anyway,' she said, sorry now that she'd started the conversation. 'How about you and Mum coming to see me at the Corner House one day? We could have a walk in Kensington Gardens – all the cherry blossom will be out soon, it looks ever so pretty. And I could serve you a slap-up meal, one of Lyons's best.'

'That's not a bad idea, Bill,' Carrie said to her husband. 'We could do with a day out. Perhaps our May and Stan will come, too.'

They came the following Saturday, meeting the girls in Kensington Gardens for a picnic by the Round Pond with its statue of Peter Pan. The park was carpeted with daffodils, cherry blossom lay in drifts as pink as coconut ice over the trees. Pink and white candles were just beginning to light up the horse-chestnut trees, and beneath them glowed the smiling faces of cat's-eye pansies, with early tulips standing at attention, as stiff and proud as scarlet-capped soldiers, amidst a sea of forget-me-nots.

'It really is pretty,' Carrie said. 'You couldn't have better in the proper countryside.' She sighed. 'It seems awful to think of what's going on in other countries, doesn't it? I mean, it must be just as pretty as this in places like Czechoslovakia and Poland, but they can't enjoy it when they're all so frightened of what's going to happen next. And even here . . .' She looked around at the sweeping expanse of green, at the gay flower-beds and blossoming trees. 'I heard on the wireless the other day they're talking about digging trenches in Hyde Park for people to hide in if there's a war. Digging up all this! It don't bear thinking of.'

'There'll be proper shelters, surely,' her sister said. 'I mean, they can't expect people to get into holes in the ground, not when the weather's bad. It'll be all muddy, and—'

She was interrupted sharply as Bill Mason leapt to his feet, his face livid. 'Don't talk like that! Don't talk about trenches and mud and – and all that! I don't want to hear. I don't want to hear nothing about it.' He stared down at them all, but it was as if he saw a different, more ominous scene. His face worked painfully as he spoke, and he sounded as if he were about to cry.

'Can't we even have one day out without thinking about war and bombs and people dying? Can't we? Wasn't the last lot enough? Wasn't it bad enough then, in the trenches and the mud, seeing blokes you knew shot to bits before your eyes? It's not like what you see at the pictures, you know, in those cowboy pictures, it's not just a man falling down and holding his shoulder and dying all nice and tidy with a few last words. It's people getting torn into little bits, arms and legs and lumps of muscle and great gobs of blood, spattered all over the place, spattered all over *you*. It's hearing men scream, scream like little kiddies for their mothers. It's kill or be killed, and it turns you into a monster.' He shuddered to a halt, then drew a deep, gasping breath before starting again.

'And don't think it's just going to be a matter of getting into a shelter or a hole in the ground neither. It's going to be worse than that. They reckon there'll be hundreds of bombs falling on London the first day, millions of people killed in the first few weeks. There's one bloke says one gas-bomb, *just one*, could kill everyone between the Thames and the Serpentine. That's us here, sitting having a picnic. There's another one says even the *sound* of a bomb going off can kill people. And that everyone's going to panic and try to get away, and while they're running the Germans will just fly over in planes and machine-gun them. *That's* what we've got to look forward to, and I don't want to talk about it, I don't want to *think* about it. I just want to have a day out with my family and enjoy the sunshine and the cherry blossom and the daffodils, because to my mind it's the last time any of us are going to see any of them!'

He stopped, covering his face with trembling hands while they all stared up at him, too shocked to speak. Then Carrie got to her feet and took him shakily by the arm.

'Come on, Bill. Come on, love. Sit down again and have a nice hot cup of tea. I've got the Thermos here. We'll just sit quiet for a bit and have a bite to eat and look at the flowers, and then we'll walk through Hyde Park and have a look at the shops before we have our tea at the Corner House. Our Jo and Phyl are going to serve us themselves. And then we'll go and see that picture you want to see at the Odeon, and nobody's going to say another word about war, the last one or – or anything else. Come on now.'

Bill, trembling and white now, allowed himself to be seated again on the old check blanket Carrie had brought. He accepted a cup of tea from the Thermos flask and after a while he took an egg sandwich and bit into it. The rest of the family, shaken but doing their best to pretend that nothing had happened, started to talk at random and got a conversation going, and May produced a fine fruit cake that she'd baked last week and been keeping in a tin to be at its best today.

Jo sat close to her father. She wished that the subject of war hadn't been mentioned, but how could it be forgotten in these days? She was certain it was coming, and she knew her father believed it, too. That was why he got so upset – because he'd seen it before, and he knew what it could be like.

Just how horrible was it? she wondered. Were the things her father had said true? And if it really was that bad, how could all these leaders contemplate letting it happen again?

But she knew it wasn't that simple. The world was facing a stark and impossible choice. Either to go to war against Naziism, or to allow Hitler and Mussolini to carry on riding roughshod against the face of Europe, taking over countries at will, driving out the Jews – or anyone else who incurred their disapproval – and reigning through terror.

Czechoslovakia today. Poland tomorrow. And after that, where else?

Picnics in the park and going to the pictures seemed trivial beside what was looming ahead, but what else could you do? It wasn't for dockyard labourers or Covent Garden porters or Corner House Nippies to say how the world should be run. Well, you got your chance at elections in a way, but even then you could only vote for one man, and whoever got into power just went ahead and did what they wanted – they didn't come and ask you again.

'There's no point in worrying about it,' Maggie Pratt said. 'If it's going to happen, it's going to blooming well happen, and there's nothing we can do about it. We might as well enjoy ourselves while we can.'

A lot of people seemed to have that feeling. Nobody knew what lay ahead, so why not take what pleasure and happiness and fun they could while they had the chance? The girls went to dances and to the pictures, they went out on dates with young men, they went to the zoo or on country walks or to Brighton for the day, and tried to forget the threat that hung over their heads.

Etty and Jim spent all their spare time on his motorbike, exploring the South Downs and the Thames valley and the woods of Berkshire. Charlie had completely faded from the picture. Two or three Saturdays when Etty hadn't gone to the pictures with the rest of them seemed to have been enough to give him the message, and as far as she knew he wasn't very upset. Maggie reported that he'd found himself another girl – one who never stopped talking, according to Tommy – and they were thinking of getting engaged. Or maybe she was the one who was thinking of it, Charlie, as usual, never opening his mouth.

Maggie was still going out with Tommy, but she shook her head and laughed when anyone asked if they were serious. 'I'm not going to get serious for a long time,' she declared. 'I want a bit of fun before I settle down to a hubby and a

231

houseful of kids. Not like my mum, married and expecting her first before she was nineteen.'

Phyl wasn't keen to settle down yet either. She still saw quite a lot of Mike but she went out with other young men, too – mostly customers who came regularly to her tables and gave her presents instead of tips, but sometimes with Lyons employees, too. She was getting friendly with one of the floor supervisors, spending a lot of time with him at the Saturday evening dances at Sudbury.

Jo didn't approve. 'He's too smooth, Phyl. And you know they say he's got a reputation.'

Phyl laughed. 'A reputation for what? Having lots of girlfriends? That just means we all like him, Jo.'

'And he likes you,' Jo said darkly. 'You be careful, Phyl. I've never trusted men with yellow hair.'

Mike could have told Jo that her cousin was very careful indeed. He still hadn't managed to get her to go even half the way, let alone all of it. She wouldn't even let him undo her blouse. Kissing was all right, and he often got the feeling that she really wanted to go further, but when he tried she backed away and shook her head.

'No, Mike. I've told you before.'

'I wouldn't do anything you didn't like,' he said cunningly, but Phyl shook her head again.

'You're not going to get the chance. I don't want to end up in the family way.'

'You wouldn't. I'd make sure. I – I'm prepared, Phyl.'

'Well, you shouldn't be,' she said unreasonably. 'You shouldn't be taking it for granted. I think I'd like to go home now.'

Mike sighed. He hadn't taken anything for granted – he'd just hoped. The hope was growing fainter instead of stronger, but he didn't want to give up on Phyl. He knew she was a decent girl and decent girls 'didn't' – not till the altar was safely in sight anyway. He thought perhaps one day it would be, but not yet. Meanwhile, he liked Phyl a lot and he wanted to go on kissing her, even if she didn't let him do anything more.

The floor supervisor was called Richard Godwin. Not Dick or Ricky, he told Phyl as they danced together, but Richard. He worked in the Coventry Street Corner House so they didn't encounter each other at work, but soon after he met Phyl he joined the drama club. However, since Coventry Street was open all night their meetings could only be erratic.

'He does night shifts quite often,' Phyl said as she and Jo got ready for bed. 'It must be funny, working at night, mustn't it? Just think, while we're getting into our pyjamas they're putting on their uniforms and polishing up the cutlery. And when we get up in the morning, they'll be coming off shift.'

'I'm glad we don't have to do that.' Jo was already in bed, reading *Little Men*. I wouldn't really mind having a lot of kids if they were all boys, like Jo Bauer had, she thought. Tommy in the book was a proper little imp, and Dan was going to grow up to be a real heart-throb. She could have done without mimsy little Daisy and her goody-goody brother Demi, and it was still a disappointment to her that Laurie had married Amy. But it was a good story, and the idea of a big house in the country with a rambling, overgrown garden was something that appealed to her very much.

'I'd like to live in the country,' she said, laying the book down. 'I'd like to be a farmer's wife, with lots of animals around, and grow things. I'd like to learn to look after horses.'

'You don't mean it!' Phyl was removing red nail varnish from her fingers. Nippies weren't allowed to wear coloured varnish at work, or any make-up other than a very natural-looking lipstick, but most of them liked to dress up a bit for the dances. 'Pitch dark at night, and owls hooting and bats in your hair. Ugh – I wouldn't like it.'

'You liked going hop-picking when we were kids.'

'Hop-picking's different. Everyone's together in barns or tents, and you have a lot of fun. It wouldn't be like that if you lived there all the time. There's nothing to do.'

Jo thought there would be plenty to do, but she was aware that not many of her friends would agree. She and Nick had decided to join the cycling club and were saving up for bikes. Once they'd got them, they'd be able to spend Sundays in the country with a crowd of others who liked getting out of London. She looked forward to summer afternoons drifting along the quiet lanes, past fields and woods and streams. Nick had been to the library and borrowed a book about birds, and they were hoping to see swallows and finches and tits, maybe even a kingfisher.

They hadn't decided anything yet about getting married. It would be a long time, Nick said, before they could afford it, and meanwhile the bikes would be their luxury. They had agreed just to enjoy being engaged for a year or two.

Richard Godwin took Phyl to the theatre. They saw all the best shows in London and had supper afterwards, sometimes in one of the Corner Houses, sometimes in one of the smaller restaurants where nobody would recognise them.

'I want to keep you all to myself,' he said, holding her hand. 'If the other chaps see what a prize I've got, they'll all be after you.'

Phyl wasn't sure she liked being described as a 'prize' – as if he'd won me a in a raffle! she thought – but the look in his dark blue eyes and the way his fingers stroked her palm disarmed her. She smiled back, a little tremulously, and wondered if he would kiss her goodnight. Suppose he was like Mike and tried to do more than that? Phyl wasn't at all sure that she'd be as strong as she was with Mike. Half of her hoped he wouldn't – but the other half hoped, guiltily, that he would.

Richard didn't try anything. He took her home in a taxi and kissed her at Mrs Holt's door. His kiss fizzed through her body and her head swam. Mike's kisses were nice, but not like this – like robust old ale, she thought giddily, set against the champagne of Richard's lips. She leant against him, feeling his arms around her and his hard body against hers, and wondered if she would be able to resist him after all.

Above them, she could see the light on in the bedroom and knew Jo was still awake and would have heard the car. She fiddled nervously with her keys and whispered that she really had to go in.

'I know.' His hair gleamed like polished gold in the light from the gas lamp on the corner. He looked down at her and stroked her cheek with one finger. He had to bend his head quite a long way to kiss her again. 'When shall I see you again? Saturday?'

'I don't know.' Phyl had promised to go to the pictures with Mike on Saturday night. She thought of writing a note to his house to tell him she couldn't go, but it seemed a shabby sort of thing to do. Yet if she didn't go with Richard, would he find some other girl? Jo's remarks about his 'reputation' came back to her. She might lose her chance . . .

And what if you do? she asked herself, bracing her shoulders. If it's lost that easy, would it have been worth having anyway? And what sort of a reputation will *you* have, Phyl Jennings, if you chuck one man over just because another one comes along?

'No, I can't,' she told Richard regretfully. 'I'm already going out on Saturday.' It wouldn't do him any harm to know he wasn't the only fish in the sea, anyway. 'But thanks for asking me.'

'That's a shame,' he said, 'but I'll ask you again. I've enjoyed tonight, Phyl.'

'So have I,' she whispered, relieved that she hadn't thrown away her chance after all.

'See you at the drama club on Tuesday,' he said, and kissed her again. 'I'm going to audition for the male lead – why don't you go for the girl?' He winked. 'We could rehearse together.'

Phyl went indoors, dizzy with excitement. The play they were doing was a romantic comedy, with lots of kissing between the man and the woman. She felt a quiver of terror at the thought of kissing Richard Godwin in front of a hall full of people, but the terror was of a delicious sort and Richard's hint about rehearsing held delicious promise.

The play was to be put on in September. That gave them all the summer to rehearse . . .

'I'm thinking of joining up,' Tommy said to Maggie as they buttoned up their clothes in a secluded corner of Hyde Park.

'Oh? I hadn't noticed you were falling apart.' She grinned at him. 'Joining up what?'

'Ha, funny ha. Joining the Services, of course. The Army, as a matter of fact.'

Maggie stared at him, her fingers frozen on the top button of her blouse. 'What you want to do that for?'

'Because I might as well do it now as wait to be conscripted,' he said.

'*Conscripted?* You mean called up?'

'Yeah.' He looked at her. 'Don't kid yourself, Maggie. That Hitler's not going to go away. He's not going to stick to any promises not to try and take over Poland, nor anywhere else he takes a fancy to. We're going to have to teach him a lesson sooner or later. And that means a war.'

'You mean you think they'll call up *everyone*? Even blokes with jobs already?'

'The Army's not a labour exchange,' he said. 'If there's a war, they're not going to worry about whether you've already got a job or not. They'll just want as many soldiers as they can get.'

'I don't see why *you've* got to go, though,' she said, her voice trembling. 'Not till you have to.'

'If I go now, I can choose which regiment I apply for, I'll get a bit of say in what I do. I'll get a proper training. If I wait to be called up I'll just get sent wherever they need blokes most, and if it's anything like the last lot, they won't be bothering about training. They'll send us out there with no more idea how to fire a gun than fly in the air.'

Maggie felt sick. 'I wish you wouldn't talk like that. You sound like Jo.'

'I'm sorry, Mags, but it's the truth. There's going to be a war and we're all going to get caught up in it, and we'd best be prepared. Jo's got her head screwed on the right way. There's a lot of people got their heads in the sand, like ostriches, and they're going to get a nasty shock before long.'

Maggie had never heard Tommy talk so seriously. She sat on the grass beside him, feeling her skin pimple with cold. The warmth of the summer evening seemed to have fled.

'I think I'd rather be an ostrich. It's horrible, thinking of you going away and fighting.'

He put his arm round her. 'I know. But we're going to have to face up to it, Mags.' He hesitated. 'Look – I don't suppose it'll happen all that quickly. Even if I do apply, I won't get taken straight away. There's medicals and all sorts of things, and I'd have to work out my notice at the shop. And if they take you for the reserve you don't have to go till war's actually declared – you just do training one evening a week. That's all it'll be to start with.'

'Well, that don't sound too bad,' she said with a touch of doubt.

'And if I do ever have to go away—' he hesitated again '—it'd make it a lot easier if I knew I'd got you waiting for me, Mags.'

'What d'you mean – waiting for you?'

'You know what I mean,' he said, squeezing her against him. 'I'd want to know you were there when I came home – ready to go out with me and all that.'

'All that!' she mocked him. 'That's all you boys ever think about.' But her voice was still shaky and her eyes were filled with tears. 'Oh, Tommy, you daft ha'porth, of course I'll be ready to go out with you. But you aren't going away – not just yet. I'm not going to let you.' She grinned suddenly, the old Maggie breaking through the fear. 'I'll tell you what, I'll go over and knock old Hitler's block off meself, that's what I'll do, and that'll put an end to all this malarkey!'

Mike was going to join up, too. He told Phyl as they sat on Brighton beach one Sunday afternoon. They'd gone down by train, their swimming things rolled up in towels and a picnic in Phyl's shopping bag, and they were drying off after a swim. Mike had fetched two ice-cream cornets from the Stop Me And Buy One cart further along the beach and they were licking industriously before the ices melted.

Phyl's tongue stopped licking, just as Maggie's fingers had ceased buttoning her blouse.

'The Air Force? You're going to join the Air Force?'

'That's right. Think of it, Phyl – up there in a plane, looking down at all this.' He waved his free arm comprehensively at the blue sky, the glittering sea, the crowds of people. 'I've always wanted to be a pilot. And if it gives me a chance to get back at Hitler—'

'But you could get killed!'

Mike laughed easily. 'Not me! I've got a charmed life. I'm like a cat – always fall on my feet. Didn't I ever tell you, Phyl, my auntie reads tea-leaves and she said I'll live till I'm ninety years old and have a beautiful wife and a lot of kids. So I know I won't get killed, see?'

'You don't believe in all that,' she said unsteadily.

'I do. Tell you what, I'll take you to see her and she can tell your fortune, too.' He winked. 'Maybe you're going to live till you're ninety as well, and have a handsome husband and a lot of good-looking kids. What d'you think?'

'If I am,' Phyl retorted, 'he must be someone I haven't met yet.' She thought briefly of Richard Godwin with his corn-coloured hair, and felt her face colour. Mike saw the blush and laughed again, misunderstanding it. He reached for her hand.

'Come on, Phyl. What've you got to lose? She makes a smashing cup of tea.'

'Stop it, Mike. You're changing the subject. You're not really going to join the Air Force, are you?'

'Yes,' he said, serious now. 'We've been talking about it at work. We reckon there's going to be a war, Phyl, and we'd be better to get in as regulars before it starts. Me and Charlie—'

'Charlie? You mean he's joining up, too?'

'Yes, and Tommy. We all want to. Tom's keen on the Army, but me and Charlie want to go in the Air Force. We're going to go along to the recruitment office and see about it tomorrow.'

Ice cream trickled down on to Phyl's hand. She licked it away automatically. It didn't seem to taste the same as it had done a few minutes ago. She looked around her at the people on the beach, some running in or out of the water, some playing with large coloured beach-balls, some lying stretched out on their towels, soaking up the sun. All laughing, all apparently oblivious to the shadow that seemed suddenly to have fallen over everything. She felt oddly detached from the brightness and the noise, as if someone had suddenly enclosed her in a glass bubble. Her eyes felt hot and stinging.

'It doesn't matter what I think, then?' she asked, trying to speak with a bright offhandedness. 'I mean, you'll do it whatever I say?'

Mike looked at her. She realised that she had never seen him look like this, without his ready smile twitching at the corners of his mouth or his spaniel eyes twinkling. She felt a sudden lurch of fear.

'Of course it matters what you think,' he said. 'But I'm going to do it, Phyl. It's not just for fun, you know. That man's got to be stopped before he ruins the whole world.'

That man's got to be stopped.

Hitler was *That Man*. The newspapers carried reports of his latest doings, published cartoons showing his strutting figure, his commonplace face with its straight black hair and small moustache. You couldn't deny any more that war was looming again. Preparations were taking place all the time, just as if it had already been decided.

Trenches were dug in Hyde Park, just as Carrie had said they would be. Leaflets started to come through every door, telling people of all the arrangements that were being made for protection against bombs. Where people had room in their gardens, they would be given sheets of corrugated iron to make into Anderson shelters; where there were no gardens, shelters would be built in the streets. Gas masks would be issued and would have to be carried all the time. Children would be evacuated from some of the large cities to the countryside.

'What about cats?' Alice asked, hugging Robertson, now a

large beast with huge green eyes and paws like boxing gloves. 'Will they get evacuated?'

Her father shook his head. 'They'll have to stay at home.'

'I shan't go, then,' she said definitely.

'You'll have to,' Carrie said. 'You won't have no choice. It's for your own good, Alice. You don't want to stay here and be bombed, do you?'

Alice looked at them. 'Are you going to be bombed?'

'Well, we don't know, do we? But your father can't go, he's got his work to do, and I'll have to stay here to look after him. And Robbie will have to stay as well. You can't take a cat with you to the country.'

'Why not? He'd like it. He could catch birds and mice. He'd be useful.'

'He'd be more useful here,' Freddy said, joining in. 'There's always a lot of rats about in wartime – he'll be needed to catch them.'

Alice thought for a while. The big cat lay in her arms, as soft as a knitted toy. From the very first time they'd met on Christmas morning eighteen months ago, they had been inseparable. Robbie slept on Alice's bed at night, accompanied her downstairs in the morning, watched at the window for her to come home from school. If he was already out, he would go down the street to meet her, miaowing loudly as she turned the corner. When she'd been ill with whooping cough he'd stayed on her bed almost all the time, curled up against her.

'If Robbie can't come,' she said at last, 'I'm not going.'

'Alice, you'll have to—'

'He'd miss me,' she said, and closed her mouth as if the discussion was over.

'I'll miss her, too,' Carrie said later, when Alice and Robbie had gone to bed. 'I don't want her to go and live with strangers out in the country, maybe for months. We don't know where she'll be, nor how she'll be treated, nor nothing. I don't know how I'll bear it. And there's our Jo, too, right in the middle of London, just where all the bombs'll be.' She turned and stared at Bill. 'It's serious, Bill, isn't it? This talk of war.'

'Yes, it is, girl,' he said heavily. 'It really is.'

They sat quietly in their chairs on opposite sides of the fireplace. Carrie looked at her husband's face, seeing the new lines etching themselves sharply above the old. Bill had always had a furrowed brow, making him look older than his age, and she knew that it had been caused by his experiences in the Great War. For twenty years he had done his best to forget them, and now the spectre of another and possibly worse war was bringing them back, a nightmare that wouldn't go away.

'What happened to that piece of paper that Mr Chamberlain brought back last year?' she demanded, suddenly fierce in her anxiety. 'What about those agreements they signed? Don't they count for nothing?'

'Not in Hitler's book,' he said. 'I don't reckon agreements and signatures mean anything at all to him. He'll agree to anything and then just go his own way, and if he thinks he'll march into Poland or any other country, that's just what he'll do. There's only one thing a man like that understands, and that's a lot of soldiers fighting each other. In the end, it just comes down to whose army can win.' He paused. 'And that means we'll have to get a lot more soldiers. And sailors, and airmen, too. They'll be conscripting, just like last time.'

Carrie stared at him. 'You won't have to go, Bill, will you?' she whispered.

'I don't reckon so, girl. I don't reckon they'll take men over forty. But they'll be looking for the younger ones. Boys like our Freddy and Eric, and your May's Norman and Ron. They'll be calling them up, mark my words.'

'Oh, Bill,' she said, almost in tears. 'It don't bear thinking about.'

'No,' he said, his voice heavy, 'it don't.'

'Are you going to join up?' Phyl asked Richard Godwin.

They were in a rowing-boat on the Serpentine. Both had been on early shift and finished work at three-thirty. The June

241

afternoon was warm and Richard had taken off his jacket and rolled up his shirtsleeves. The sun lit the hairs on his arms with gold and Phyl could see the ripple of his muscles as he pushed the oars back and forth. She looked up at the sky and thought of Mike up there in an aeroplane.

'Join up?'

'The Services,' she said. 'For if there's a war.'

'Oh,' he said easily, 'let's wait until we know there's going to be one, shall we?'

'Well, lots of people think there will be.'

'But there isn't yet. A fine fool I'd look, signing my life away for nothing. I've got prospects with Lyons, Phyl. I'm not going to chuck all that up just to get a uniform on.'

'It's not just for a uniform. It's to save your country.'

'As far as I know,' he said coolly, 'my country's not been threatened. It's all these other places – Czechoslovakia, Poland – that Hitler wants to take over. I don't see the point of throwing my life away for them. Anyway, I don't know what they're making all the fuss about – he's done a good job for Germany and Austria, getting them out of the Depression. They were having to pay people twice a day before he came along, you know, the value of money was going down so fast.'

Phyl frowned. 'I know, but . . . If he's such a good man, why is everyone so scared of what he'll do next? And what about the Jews?'

'Nobody's ever liked the Jews,' Richard said, rowing easily into the shelter of a tiny inlet, overhung with shadowy rhododendrons. 'Come here, Phyl, and let me kiss you. Stop worrying about something that may never happen.'

She hesitated. 'A lot of people do think it's going to happen,' she said again. 'I know boys who are joining up now, to be ready for it.'

'Well, good luck to them. But I'm not going to be carried away by mass hysteria. That's all it is, Phyl. You wait, in a few weeks all this fuss will be over and they'll be filling in those trenches in Hyde Park, and those chaps you know'll be sweating on parade grounds and wishing they were back in

Civvy Street. Nobody with any brains is going to get caught like that. And now stop worrying and let me kiss you.'

Phyl let him kiss her. Perhaps Richard was right, she thought, perhaps it was all a storm in a teacup and things would settle down soon and go on just as before.

Mike, Charlie and Tommy would indeed be sorry that they'd rushed into joining the Services.

Something about the conversation made her feel uneasy, though. Perhaps it was Richard's easy assumption that all would be well; perhaps it was the contrast between his casual dismissal of what was happening in Europe and the fervour with which Mike and – Maggie had told her – Tommy had said that *That Man* had got to be stopped.

After a while, however, under the intoxication of Richard's champagne kisses, she forgot to worry.

Chapter Sixteen

By the following weekend, the boys had all signed up. They were sent home to await their call-up papers and came into the Corner House as usual on Saturday to tell the girls about it.

'They're looking full of themselves today,' Irene remarked sourly, seeing them come striding in, all smiles, to sit at their favourite table. 'Won the football pools, have they? D'you suppose they'll actually order something worth having?'

'Course they will,' Maggie said, pulling a couple of curls out from under her cap. 'Poached eggs on toast twice each – can't do better than that. I wouldn't like to be one of your customers, Irene, with you looking down your nose because I didn't order something smart.'

'I treat all my customers the same, whatever they order,' Irene said with dignity. 'I hope I know my job. And I wouldn't bank on you keeping yours much longer, Maggie Pratt, if you go tarting yourself up like that. You know you're supposed to keep your hair under your cap.'

'And *you* ought to keep *your* hair *on*!' Maggie sailed gaily out into the big dining-room. Thinks she's a blooming supervisor already, she thought, and gave the three young men a broad grin. 'Well? I suppose you think you're heroes already?'

'Not half,' Tommy said, with a cocky look. 'Just signing that piece of paper took a bit of nerve, I can tell you. There's no going back from that, you know. Take the King's shilling, and you're his for life.'

'Well, not for life exactly,' Mike said. 'At least, I hope not! I'm not joining the Air Force just to get shot down the first week.'

'Someone will be, though,' Charlie said seriously. 'I mean, if you go to fight someone's going to catch it. It stands to reason.'

'Shut up, Charlie. We don't want to talk about reason. We're going to be fliers – pilots. We're going to wear those leather jackets and caps they wear and learn to fly aeroplanes, and shoot the Germans down before they can drop their bombs.' He turned to Tommy. 'I wish you'd joined the RAF as well. We could have all been together. It would have been smashing.'

Tommy shook his head. 'You don't get me up there in one of those string and glue contraptions. I'd rather drive a nice solid tank.'

Maggie listened in dismay. There was a new note in the boys' voices, a note of strung-up, nervous excitement, as if they were looking forward to the fighting, actually *looking forward* to shooting – and killing. What's happening to them? she thought. They sound as if they're going to enjoy it.

They went out together as usual that evening, and Charlie came, too. He'd broken up with his girlfriend, having managed to get a word into her chatter long enough to say 'no' when she talked about getting engaged, so he was at a loose end again. He sat on the other side of Maggie, as quiet as ever, but during the interval he loosened up a little.

'I don't think I'll get taken as a pilot,' he said as they ate their ice creams. 'I haven't got the education. Mike was good at maths at school, but I wasn't. He always wanted to be an engineer really.'

'Perhaps he'll be a mechanic,' Maggie suggested.

'Well, they do say that whatever you say you want to do, they'll put you into something different,' Charlie said with a quick, shy grin. 'We'll probably end up doing some job we never even knew existed.'

He's all right, really, Maggie thought. Once you get him talking, he's quite an interesting sort of boy. He just needs someone who'll give him a chance to say something and then listen to him. She felt sorry he hadn't got a real girlfriend.

Phyl sat next to Mike, thinking more about air battles than the picture they'd come to see. She couldn't imagine what it would be like. Mike had talked about shooting German planes out of the sky. Had he thought that it might be the other way around – him being shot out of the sky? And what exactly would happen? She imagined an aeroplane, riddled with bullets from a machine-gun, falling to the ground, and she felt sick. It's crazy, she thought, the whole thing's crazy, they can't let it happen.

Pathe Pictorial was filled with pictures of what was happening in Europe. It didn't seem any more settled than it ever had. The 'piece of paper' was worthless. Hitler was taking no notice of it, and now he was gathering his own allies about him – making his 'pact of steel' with Mussolini, his 'non-aggression' agreement with Estonia and Latvia. Non-aggression was a joke, everyone said, it just meant they'd fight everyone else instead of each other. But when you looked at the power he was amassing, the joke wasn't very funny.

'Everyone who goes into the Air Force doesn't have to be a pilot, do they?' Phyl asked as she and Mike walked back to Auntie Holt's. 'I mean, they haven't actually said that's what you'll be, have they?'

'I'd better be. I've always wanted to fly an aeroplane, Phyl. This is the best chance I'll ever get.'

'But Mike, it'll be so dangerous—'

'Well, war *is* dangerous,' he said. 'Flying a plane's not going to be any worse than driving a tank or just firing a gun. It won't be all that much worse than staying at home and being bombed!'

'Mike, don't talk like that. As if it's all a game. You could get killed. I – I don't want you to get killed, Mike.' She heard the break in her voice and bit her lip, annoyed with herself.

'I'm not going to get killed. Remember what I told you about my auntie and the tea-leaves? I'm going to live till I'm ninety and have lots of kids. That means I'll still be around in two thousand and ten. You don't have to worry about me, Phyl.'

They arrived at the front door and he pulled her into the shadows and kissed her. She remembered thinking that his kisses were like old ale, strong and sturdy, and comparing them with the champagne of Richard Godwin's kisses. Perhaps old ale was the best anyway, she thought, strong and comforting. Perhaps Mike was right and he wouldn't be killed in the war.

'Oh, Mike,' she said, laying her head on his shoulder, 'I hope your auntie's right.'

Sunday was a day for the club, but Jo and Phyl decided to go home instead. With all the worry in the air, they felt drawn back to their families, wanting to find everything going on as normal. Instead, they discovered a huge pile of corrugated iron in the street and the men all helping each other build air-raid shelters in their small back gardens.

'We got to dig a big hole, see,' Freddy said, leaning on his spade as Jo stared at the destruction of her father's vegetable bed. 'Then we put one end of the iron down inside, and the other end's bent over to make a roof. Coupla steps down and a bit of a door fixed on, and bob's yer uncle.'

'You mean people are expected to stay in there for hours on end? It'll be horrible – like being in a dungeon.'

'Better'n being blown to smithereens,' he said, wielding his spade again. 'Mind out of the way, Jo, we got to finish this by teatime, then we're going to do Uncle Stan's.'

Jo went indoors, her heart cold. She found her mother and aunt drinking tea with Phyl, while Alice played with Robertson on the rag rug.

'We've had all these leaflets, see,' Carrie told her. '*Things You Should Know If War Should Come*. There's one about food, and another one about gas masks and blacking out the windows, and this one here about evacuation. They're coming through the door every day. I can hardly keep up with it all.'

'I'm not being evacuated,' Alice said from the floor. 'I've told Mum, if I can't take Robbie, I'm not going.'

'You'll do as you're told, my girl,' Carrie said, her voice sharp. 'I'll look after Robbie. He's best off here, where he knows everything.'

'You don't have to go,' Alice began argumentatively. 'Annie Bragg from up the road said it's volunt'ry. She's not going.'

'Doesn't matter what Annie Bragg says or does. If your dad and me decides you got to be evacuated, evacuated you'll be, and it won't depend on a cat. And there'll be no more back-answers, if you don't mind.'

Alice opened her mouth but saw the look on her mother's face and thought better of it. She buried her face in Robertson's orange fur, muttering. Carrie gave her an exasperated look and handed Jo another leaflet.

'Look at this one. *Your Food In Wartime*. The Government's been building up food for the past eighteen months – all the time they've been telling us there'd be peace. They've been making plans and collecting stuff, while we've been thinking it was all going to be all right. Now they say we've got to store things as well, but we mustn't *hoard* – what's the difference, I ask you? – and they're going to ration everything. We'll all have ration books and we won't be able to have anything that's not on them.' She shook her head.

'I don't see how it's going to work. Men like your dad, they've got big appetites, they need their food for their work, and there's others just working in offices don't need as much, but they'll have the same ration books. That's not going to be fair, is it? And then there's this one, all about what they call the blackout. We've all got to have new curtains, thick ones, on every window, so that no light can shine out and guide enemy planes – where are we going to get the money for all that, I ask you? And we've got to do all this *now*, before we even know if there's going to *be* a war. I mean, it won't matter so much having got more food if it don't happen, we can always use that up, but what are we going to do with yards and yards of horrible black curtain material that nobody in their sane senses would want to buy?'

Her voice rose higher and higher as she talked, the words tripping over themselves. Jo and Phyl gazed at her in consternation and May put a hand on her sister's arm.

'Carrie, Carrie. Don't get yourself all worked up, now. What does it matter, spending out a bit on black material if the war don't happen? Would you rather it was the other way round? We just got to be prepared, that's all, be prepared but hope it never happens, hope for the best.'

'That's what we do at Brownies,' Alice said. 'Like Boy Scouts and Girl Guides do. If we're saving up food, Mum, can we save up lots of chocolate Smarties? Will sweets be rationed?'

'Alice, for goodness' *sake*—'

'Pour your mum another cup of tea,' May said to Jo. 'She's upset by the air-raid shelters, and all these papers coming – we all are. It makes it seem so real. And we're getting our gas masks next week, too. And she's worried sick about the boys.'

'You mean Freddy and Norman? They're not joining up, surely?'

'Not yet. They might be counted as being in reserve occupations, see, being mechanics. I mean, we can't have all the lads going off to war and leaving things at home to get on by theirselves, can we?'

Jo handed her mother a cup of tea and Carrie sipped gratefully and gave them all a watery smile. 'I'm sorry. I never meant to make so much fuss. It just all got on top of me for a minute, and thinking about our Alice going off to strangers . . . I'm sorry.'

Phyl was looking thoughtful. 'But the women did a lot in the last war, didn't they? They took over a lot of the men's jobs. They even joined the Forces themselves – they were in the Navy and the Army.'

'You're not doing that!' May said sharply. 'It's bad enough you being in the middle of London, you're not going off in the Forces.'

'I didn't mean that. I just meant women might do jobs like being mechanics and driving buses and all that sort of thing.'

'God help us all if we're reduced to that,' Freddy remarked cheerfully, coming into the scullery to wash his hands. He poked his head round the door. 'We're now the proud owners of a brand-new air-raid shelter, Ma. Good as a spare bedroom, it is – you'll be able to take in lodgers. Come and have a look.'

The four women crowded out through the back door, Alice tagging behind with her arms full of ginger cat. They went down to the bottom of the garden and gazed at the shelter.

'We've still got to get some wood for the door, but you could put a bit of old curtain up for the time being,' Bill explained. 'Not that we're going to need it yet awhile, maybe never. It'll be nice and cool for storing perishables,' he added to his wife. 'Set jellies down there and all.'

Carrie peered in. 'I don't fancy it much. It stinks of damp.'

'That's because it's only just been dug out. The earth'll dry out with a bit of hot weather. We'll put a couple of camp beds down here and a hurricane lantern. It'll be snug enough then.'

Nobody looked as if they agreed with him, but they trooped back up the garden for another cup of tea before the men started on the next shelter. The whole street was busy. People were digging in each other's gardens to make the job easier and there was almost a party atmosphere, with jokes and banter flying from fence to fence.

'It's times like these bring people together,' May said, bringing out a plate of ginger biscuits. 'Everyone helping each other. That's what it'll be like if there's a war, and it don't matter what Hitler does, he'll never be able to change that.'

Gradually, people stopped grumbling and went out to buy their blackout material and put it up at the windows. They made blinds that could be rolled up during the day, or big frames that had to be lifted into place each evening and removed in the morning. If you had dark enough blinds you could get away with just painting the edges of the windows black to make sure not the faintest glimmer of light could escape. Skylights had to be covered or painted, too. Getting ready for war became a full-time job.

'You've got to hand it to the Government really,' Stan Jennings remarked. 'They've thought about all sides of it. They must have had people working on it for months.'

'Let's hope there's nothing they've forgotten,' Bill said soberly. 'I remember the troops in the last lot, getting issued with all left-footed boots. And rifles with the wrong ammunition. I've seen grown men cry with the uselessness of it all, and knowing they were likely to get killed next day just because some silly fool safe in an office somewhere couldn't be bothered to do his job right.'

'Well, I should think they'll have learned better by now. It's no good thinking about those days, Bill. We've got to look forward now and get this business settled. If you ask me, the best favour anyone could do the whole world would be to slip over there and bop old Hitler on the napper, put him out of the way. I don't reckon we'd have no more trouble then.'

There seemed to be an unwritten law that nations didn't do that, though. In history, you heard of kings leading their armies into battle and perhaps getting killed, like Harold fighting William the Conqueror, but that didn't happen nowadays. Battles were only a part of the war – they might be directed by generals and admirals on the spot, but the war itself would be fought from Parliament, by men who never fired a shot.

'You'd never get near enough to Hitler to assassinate him,' Bill said gloomily. 'He's safe in one of his castles.'

The Corner Houses were making arrangements for war, too. Restaurants were not to be subject to the same rationing as ordinary people, but there were bound to be some restrictions and shortages so the chefs began to try out different recipes. Their main aim, as always, was to feed people well for a low cost, and they were determined that this should be even more true in wartime.

Gas masks were issued. The girls took them out of their cardboard boxes and stared at them, shuddering. They put them on in the dressing room and looked in the mirrors, their giggles sharpened by an edge of hysteria.

'We look like monsters! Things from outer space!'

'If the Germans invade, we'll only have to put these things on and they'll run like hell!'

'I can't wear this. It smells horrible. I can't breathe.'

'You won't be able to breathe if you don't wear it,' Jo said, taking hers off and shaking out her hair. 'That mustard gas is cruel stuff, turns your lungs to acid.'

'They don't half muck up your hairdo,' Irene said disapprovingly, finding her hairbrush, but nobody bothered to answer this. What did messy hair matter when your lungs might be turned to acid?

Air-raid warnings were sounded so that everyone knew what they were like, and the Corner House had a drill. Instead of going outside, as they did for a fire-drill, everyone had to go down to the basement which was being fitted out with benches for sitting on. They crowded down the stairs, pushing and scuffling, and waited until they heard the all-clear.

'What about the customers? Will they be allowed down as well?'

'There's shelters out in the street,' Phyl said doubtfully. 'Perhaps they'll have to go to them.'

'And what about the kitchens? They'll be in the middle of cooking. They can't leave hot fat, there'll be a fire, and anyway all the food'll be spoilt . . .' There seemed to be no end to the problems.

'I'm fed up with this before it even starts,' Maggie grumbled. 'It's going to be nothing but a nuisance.'

She met Tommy later and they went for a drink in a nearby pub. It was full of people, all talking about the war preparations. Tommy bought a beer for himself and a port and lemon for Maggie, and took out a packet of Woodbines.

'I've got something to tell you,' he said, and she slowly lowered her glass and stared at him.

'What? Why are you looking like that, Tom? What's happened?'

He lit a cigarette and gave it to her before lighting one for himself. 'Don't get in a state, Mag. It's not the end of the world. It's just that I've got my papers.'

'Your papers? What papers?'

'My Service papers,' he said patiently. 'I'm in the Army, Mags. I've got to report for duty the week after next.'

'The week after *next*? But – why? The war's not starting then, is it?' She stared at him, confused. 'I haven't heard nothing—'

'I told you, Maggie, don't get in a state. Of course it isn't starting then. They're just getting ready for it, like they've been doing all these weeks – months – years for all we know. They want to get us trained.'

'Us? What d'you mean, *us*?'

'All the ones who've already signed up,' he said patiently. 'Chaps like me and Mike and Charlie.'

'Are they going, too? Mike and Charlie?'

'Dunno, but I should think so. I haven't seen them. I wanted to tell you first.'

Maggie shook her head. She still couldn't quite take it in. She drew deeply on her Woodbine and said, as if she were working out a difficult problem, 'So what you're saying is that the week after next – like, Monday or Tuesday – you're going to leave the shop and join the Army and start driving a tank.'

'Well, not straight away,' he said with a grin. 'I expect I'll have to do some training first. Square-bashing and that. And I'll have to learn to drive it.'

'And if there's a war . . .' She shook her head again. Suddenly, the hovering spectre seemed much closer, more substantial. '*Tommy*—' Her voice rose suddenly, razor-edged.

'What?' he asked gently, and put his hand over hers.

'I don't know,' she whispered. 'I – I don't think I want you to go, Tommy. I feel scared.'

'It's all right,' he said. 'There's nothing to feel scared about. You don't get rid of me that easy.'

'You can't say that. You can't know. Nobody can know. If there's a war . . .' Her eyes filled with tears and she squeezed his hand convulsively. 'People get *killed*, Tommy. *Soldiers* get killed.'

For a minute or two he didn't speak. Then he said quietly, 'I know, Mags. I know that. But we got to do it, see? We can't let that man just trample over everything. Look what he's done already. Look what he's done to the Czechs and the Jews. And if he goes into Poland and we don't stop him, after all we've said – well, what's he going to do next? How long is it before he decides England's next on his list?'

'I know. I just can't bear to think of you—' She looked up at him, her eyes swimming and magnified by the tears. 'Oh, *Tom* . . .'

Tommy put his arm around her shoulders and pulled her close. They sat together in the corner of the smoky saloon bar, feeling each other's warmth. Maggie struggled to understand what was happening. Her own feelings had taken her by surprise. Tommy was going away, he was going to be a soldier. But she'd known that for weeks. Why did it suddenly affect her like this?

'Maggie,' Tommy said suddenly, and she looked up into his face. He was looking very serious, even more serious than when he'd told her he was joining up. 'Maggie, there's something else I wanted to say. Something I want to ask you.'

'What is it?' She spoke almost dreamily. 'Look after your best suit? Go and see your mum? You know I'll do whatever I can, Tom.'

He grinned and she caught a glimpse of his old wickedness. 'You ought to find out what I'm asking you to do before you say that! Look, this isn't the way I wanted to ask you this – it was meant to be all romantic, down on one knee and all that. But, well, seeing as I'll be gone soon, how about us getting spliced, Mag? I know we can't do it before next week, but we could get the licence and everything and do it the first chance we get. I'll get leave after six weeks. We could do it then. What do you say?' He gripped both her hands and stared into her eyes. 'Say yes, Mags. Please say yes.'

Maggie gazed at him in astonishment. A proposal was the last thing she had expected. Her brain whirled.

'You want us to get *married*?'

'Yes. We would have done in the end, wouldn't we? I mean, we've been going steady for months now. We're as good as married already.' He gave her his cheeky grin, though there was a shadow in his eyes and his voice shook a little. 'I just want to make an honest woman of you, Mags, before I go away.'

'I'm an honest woman now,' she said sharply, then her voice softened. 'Oh, Tom, I never thought – I mean, I didn't know you wanted—' Her colour rose as she stumbled over her words. 'I thought we were just having a bit of fun,' she whispered at last.

'You mean that's all it was? You're not really, well, fond of me at all?'

Maggie felt a surge of guilty shame. '*No!* I don't mean that. Of course I'm fond of you.' She thought again of her reaction to his news a few moments before. 'I'm *really* fond of you,' she said shakily. 'That's why I don't want you to go. I just didn't realise – well, that you were that fond of *me*.'

'Maybe neither of us realised it,' he said, 'but we know now, don't we?' He looked at her seriously and traced the shape of her face with his fingers. His voice was husky. 'I want to know you're here waiting for me, Maggie. I want to know you're mine. My wife.'

'Yes,' she said. 'And I will be, Tom. I'll marry you as soon as you get your first leave. You won't have to go away not knowing we belong to each other.'

Chapter Seventeen

For one reason and another, it was quite a long time before Jim got around to taking Etty to see the statue of Henry Croft in Finchley cemetery.

They parked the motorbike at the gate and walked along the paths between the graves, reading some of the inscriptions. Albert Smith, aged 42, and his wife Betsy. Percy Corner, laid to rest in 1867. Susannah Sutton, died peacefully 1899. Joined in peace with her husband Henry.

Etty gave a little shiver.

'It's queer, thinking of all these dead people all around us. Imagine if you could see under the ground and look at all those bodies. Ugh! It gives me the heebiejeebies to think of it.'

'Don't think about it, then,' Jim advised her. 'Think about a lot of people fast asleep and dreaming. That's much better.'

The statue came into view. Even at a distance, it was different from any statue Etty had ever seen. It shimmered in the sunlight, like a real Pearly king, the intricate inlay of marble giving a genuine impression of the thousands of tiny buttons that Henry Croft had sewn on his suits. As they came closer, Etty could see that it was of a young man, little more than a boy, wearing a top hat, short jacket, waistcoat and trousers, all gleaming with the pearly marble. He was resting his left arm on a stone plinth.

'So this is where he is,' Etty said softly, looking at the statue. 'Lying under there, fast asleep, just like you said.'

'That's right. All the charities he'd helped gave the money

for the statue to be put up. That shows what they thought of him. He was sixty-eight when he died, and he'd come up from nothing to having this done for him.' Jim looked at the statue and Etty saw the pride in his face. 'It just shows what people can do.'

'Even people like me and Henry Croft,' Etty said. 'Jim, I wish I could do something worthwhile. Not to have a statue put up to me, of course – I couldn't ever do anything *that* good – but just something that would make people feel better somehow. You know, I've always felt so sorry for people that don't have a proper home – not just me, but people like the Jews, being thrown out of Germany, and that sort of thing. It's an awful feeling, not to belong anywhere. I wish I could do something to help people like that.'

'Well, perhaps you can,' he said as they turned away after a final glance at the statue and began to walk back towards the cemetery gates. 'I mean, some of them are here, aren't they, in London? And there'll be more coming, the way things are going on. I bet there'll be something you can do – you just have to wait till you see what it is.'

'Or maybe not wait,' Etty said thoughtfully. They reached the motorbike and Jim pulled it off its stand and swung his leg over the saddle. Etty waited until he'd kick-started it, and then climbed on behind him. 'Maybe I should go and *find* something to do.'

There was great excitement in the dressing room at the Corner House when Maggie announced that she was getting married.

'September the second? But that's only six weeks away,' Phyl exclaimed. 'How are we ever going to get ready in time?'

'What do you mean, get ready?' Maggie demanded. 'It's me that's got to get ready – the bride. I'm the one that's got to find a wedding dress and all. I don't remember saying any of you lot was invited.'

'Don't be daft,' Jo said, buttoning up her frock. 'Of course we're coming. To the church, anyway. You can't stop us doing that.'

'No, you can't. We'll bring great big bags of confetti and chuck 'em all over you and Tommy. And we'll hang boots and tins on the back of your taxi, and follow you about on your honeymoon, and—'

'You dare,' Maggie threatened. 'Just you dare. If I see one speck of confetti, just one, I'll cut off all your buttons, so there.'

'Whoo!' Phyl said, rolling her eyes. 'I'm really frightened. Seriously, Mags, have you actually fixed the date? Booked the church and the choir and everything?'

'Here, you know you'll get a cake from Lyons, don't you?' Jo broke in. 'You won't have to bother with making that.'

'I know. I've already put in for it. We reckoned the 2nd of September'd be a good date. Tom'll have finished his basic training and he'll be on leave, so we can even have a bit of a honeymoon.'

'You'll have to take an ironing-board with you, then,' Shirley observed. She had been listening quietly as she smoothed her dark hair and tucked it under her cap. The other girls stopped what they were doing and stared at her in astonishment.

'An *ironing-board*?' Maggie repeated incredulously. 'What the flipping heck do you think we're going to be doing, Shirl?'

Phyl giggled. 'You do know what honeymoons are for, I suppose?'

'I know what most honeymoons are for,' Shirley said. 'But if your Tommy's anything like our Donald was when he came back from basic training, he'll have changed into a tidiness maniac. He'll want creases like knife-edges in his trousers, you'll have to fold all your clothes in a pile, and *in order*, before you go to bed, and you'll probably have to serve breakfast by numbers. That's what basic training does to turn an ordinary bloke into a soldier.'

'I thought it was to train them to win battles,' Phyl said, sitting down to do up her shoes.

'Oh, it is. It trains them to wins battles of who's got the nattiest uniform or who can blanco a belt the quickest.' Shirley spoke without a glimmer of a smile, but the girls were getting used to this by now. She was the only one of them who could pull someone's leg without getting the giggles. 'If there is a war, they'll probably just line up the troops and inspect 'em and say the smartest one wins. The cleanest gas mask or the shiniest buttons. That's all it's about, really.'

'Well, I don't think six weeks' basic training is going to make my Tom forget what honeymoons are for,' Maggie said with a grin. 'Even six *years*' basic training wouldn't do that! And I reckon we'll have better things to do on our wedding night than fold clothes.'

'What sort of dress are you going to wear?' Jo asked, thinking about her own engagement. She and Nick weren't planning to get married for at least two years, to give them time to save up. They'd have to go into rooms even then, until they could afford somewhere to rent, but there were still all sorts of things you needed when you started out – bits of furniture, kitchen equipment, sheets and blankets, that sort of thing. Even second hand it would cost quite a lot. And there was a lot of expense to the wedding itself, with the dress and bridesmaids and everything.

'Yes, have you chosen your frock yet?' Phyl asked eagerly. 'What'll you have, lace or brocade? I'd fancy a nice slipper satin myself. Will it be white or ivory?'

'White!' The girls turned in surprise to see Irene, who hadn't said a word so far, standing by a mirror putting on her cap. 'I wouldn't have thought she'd have the nerve to wear white. Everyone knows she and that gent's floorwalker have been gaying it for months now.'

There was a short silence. Maggie flushed a deep red and looked about to burst into tears. Jo moved towards her as if to protect her, and Phyl jumped indignantly to her feet. To their surprise, however, it was Etty, who had been sitting quietly on a chair listening, who spoke up.

'I don't see as that's any of your business, Irene Bond. And maybe you don't know as much as you think you do.' Irene stared at her, as stunned as if a hand had reached out from the mirror and slapped her face. The others looked at each other, and Phyl sat down slowly, covering her mouth to hide a grin as Etty went on, 'Anyway, she don't even *need* to wear white. She's got something much better to wear, haven't you, Mag? It'll be a Pearly wedding, won't it?'

'Yes.' Maggie gave her a grateful look. 'Yes, it will. Everyone will be in Pearly costume. Except for Tom, of course. He'll be in uniform.' She looked from Etty to Shirley and laughed suddenly. 'And I bet you he'll be the smartest soldier in England that day. After all – he'll have had the training for it!'

It was time to go through the tunnel to the Corner House to start work. Phyl found herself walking beside Irene, a little behind the others. Since the fight in the dressing room the two had avoided each other and only spoken when it had been absolutely necessary, but now Phyl said, 'Why did you have to be so nasty about Maggie? Couldn't you see she was all happy and excited? You didn't have to go and spoil it for her.'

Irene snorted. 'Spoil it! I didn't spoil it. Anyway, I only said what was true. She and that Tommy have been going together for ages. I wouldn't mind betting they've *got* to get married. Probably got a bellyful of arms and legs this very minute.'

'That's an awful thing to say!' Phyl told her angrily. 'Maggie and Tommy have decided to get married because he's going away in the Army, and that's all there is to it. There's no need for you to start spreading nasty stories about her. If you ask me, you're just jealous.'

'Jealous? Why should I be jealous of that fat tart?'

'Because she's got a nice bloke who loves her,' Phyl said frankly, 'and all you can find is greasy old men like that Herbert Lennox from the warehouse. And that's all you ever *will* find, Irene Bond, because no decent boy is going to want to marry a sharp-nosed, dirty-minded, spiteful little cat like *you*!'

She strode ahead, back straight and head up, trembling a little with indignation. Irene stared after her. Her nose was white and pinched, her cheeks burning and her eyes and

260

mouth narrowed with fury. She paused and stamped her foot on the ground.

'Hoity-toity!' she exclaimed, loud enough for Phyl to hear. 'Hoity-toity! Just because *you've* all got to grab the first man that comes along – just because there's none of you got the taste to aim for something a bit better. *Jealous?* Just you wait a bit, Phyl Jennings – we'll see who's jealous in the end, just you wait and see.'

Irene spent the rest of that day ostentatiously avoiding the other girls. The restaurant was busy and she worked hard, marching briskly between her station and the kitchen. She refused to meet their eyes as they passed, and during their tea-break she went to sit with some of the other Nippies. Jo watched her curiously.

'What's got into Lady Muck? She's been dashing about as if she's got ants in her pants, and when I asked her a civil question just now she just about bit my head off. Someone poked a stick in her eye?'

'It was me,' Phyl said. 'I gave her an earful for saying what she did about Maggie. She'll probably never speak to any of us again.'

'Oh, dear. What a shame. I shan't be able to sleep for worrying about it.' Jo wriggled her eyebrows and grinned. 'Well, that's one less you'll have to invite, Maggie.'

'I wouldn't have asked her anyway, nasty little baggage.' Maggie had recovered her good humour. 'I want people to enjoy themselves. Look, I don't know what you're all expecting – it won't be a posh do, you know. We hadn't even thought about a reception or anything, it'll just be a party at home. I mean, you can all come – course you can – but there won't be no champagne.'

'Well, that's a relief,' Shirley said. 'I was just thinking we'd need some training in how to hold those funny glasses. Do we need to buy posh hats and smart frocks?'

'You won't be allowed in without them,' said Maggie, who could be as poker-faced as Shirley on occasion. 'I'll have people on the door to keep out anyone not properly dressed.'

'That lets me out, then,' Shirley returned. 'I was thinking of wearing the grass skirt my Uncle Ted brought back from Hawaii. He says they're all the go there at weddings.'

The girls squealed with laughter and Irene, sitting silently at another table, looked across at them with a scowl. Her gaze rested particularly on Phyl's merry eyes. I'd like to wipe off that smirk and make her laugh on the other side of her face, she thought. And somehow I will. I'll make her sorry for saying those things to me if it's the last thing I do.

Irene began to take revenge almost at once.

At first it was little things. One of Phyl's shoes would be missing, or her cape mysteriously moved to another peg so that she had to waste time searching for it. Then she put on her apron one morning and found it stained with something that looked like tea, which she knew couldn't have been there the evening before. Her cap was torn, or a button missing from her uniform – all things that could be put right, but annoying and likely to make her late on duty, or less than her usual smart self.

'It's like there's a jinx on me,' she told Jo when she found a ladder in her stocking one morning, minutes before they were due to line up for inspection. 'I know for a fact it was all right this morning. But there's something every day. I tell you, it's beginning to get me down.'

'I don't think it's a jinx,' Jo said grimly, lending Phyl a needle so that she could make a hasty darn. 'I think it's our dear friend Irene.'

'*Irene?* D'you really think so? But—'

'I'm pretty sure I saw her snag your stocking while we were having our breakfast. She was sitting next to you, wasn't she, and she scraped back her chair and felt about for something on the floor. I reckon she did it then.'

'I *did* feel something scratch me,' Phyl said, remembering. 'But it wasn't much more than a tickle – I never even thought . . . And d'you reckon she did all those other things, too?'

'Why not? We know she's got it in for you, and she's just the sort. I'd keep an eye on her if I were you.'

'Nasty cat.' Phyl finished cobbling together the edges of the lisle stocking and straightened up. 'Well, she needn't think she's going to bully *me*! I might be little but I can stand up for myself as good as the next chap!'

As if aware that she'd been rumbled, Irene stopped tampering with Phyl's clothes and turned her attention to more serious matters. The next day, as Phyl presented the bill to one of her customers, she was astonished to see a frown on his face. He looked hard at the figures, then gave her a suspicious stare.

'This isn't right.'

'Isn't it, sir? I'm sure it is. Let me see.' Phyl took the bill and added up the figures quickly in her head. 'No, that's right, five shillings and eightpence.'

'But it shouldn't be five-and-eightpence at all. It should be four-and-six. Look, you haven't put the right prices against what I had. Sausage and egg and chips are one-and-six, not two-and-three, and apple crumble's ninepence. You've put one-and-three. You've overcharged me by one shilling and threepence!' He rose to his feet. 'I think we'd better talk to the manager about this.'

Phyl stared at him in dismay. How such a thing could have happened, she had no idea, but she knew perfectly well that she would never have done such a thing on purpose. She could hardly believe she'd done it by mistake, but there the figures were, plain to see. 'Sir, I'm dreadfully sorry, I can't think how – I'm *sure* I wrote down the right prices. I'd never—'

'Well, it's quite obvious you didn't.' He was marching across the big room now, threading his way between the tables while Phyl almost ran to keep up with him, scarlet-faced and almost in tears. Other diners turned to stare as they passed and she felt as if the whole room had fallen silent to watch and wonder what was happening. By the time they arrived at the desk, Mr Carter himself had noticed what was going on and appeared at the same moment.

'Phyllis! What's the matter?' He looked at the indignant diner. 'Is something wrong, sir?'

'You could say that.' The man was big and well-dressed, a

businessman who had been coming into the Corner House regularly for quite a long time, although he had never sat at one of Phyl's tables before. 'This young woman has been trying to cheat me.'

'*Cheat* you? *Phyllis?*' Mr Carter turned to Phyl in astonishment. 'I can't believe . . .' He turned back to the customer. 'Perhaps you'd like to come into my office, sir, and we can discuss this. You, too, Miss Jennings.'

Her heart beating fast, Phyl followed the two men into the little office which was Mr Carter's own domain, at the back of the big dining-hall. Mr Carter indicated a chair for the businessman and went to sit behind his desk, leaving Phyl standing miserably by the door.

'Close the door, Miss Jennings.' The senior staff scarcely ever called the girls by their surnames, preferring to use their first names, and Phyl knew that this meant real trouble. If she were proved to be cheating the customers, she would be sacked without a moment's notice and without a reference. She felt the tears smart behind her eyes.

Mr Carter looked at her gravely, then turned to the customer.

'I can't tell you how sorry I am that this should have occurred, Mr . . . ?'

'Glossop,' the man said curtly. 'And I'm afraid I'm not interested in mealy-mouthed apologies. The girl tried to cheat me – she tried to *steal* from me – and that won't do. It's not what you expect from a Lyons Corner House.'

'Indeed it isn't.' Mr Carter's mollifying tone cooled a little. 'And I can assure you that Lyons would take any such incident very seriously indeed. In fact, from my own point of view I can tell you that any girl found doing so on my floor will be out of here so fast her feet won't *touch* the floor. All the same, I am not prepared to take action without knowing the full facts of the matter. Could you tell me, sir, exactly what happened?'

'Well, what do you *think* happened?' The man was clearly irritated by Mr Carter's measured tone. 'I gave the girl my order, she brought me my meal, and after I'd finished I asked

264

for the bill. When I checked it I found that I'd been overcharged. *Deliberately* overcharged – there was no possibility of a mistake.'

'Can you explain that, sir? Mistakes do occur in addition. Even the best of my girls—'

'There was no mistake in the addition,' Mr Glossop said brusquely. 'That was perfectly correct. The *mistake* was in the prices charged. Two of the items were charged at a much higher price than they should have been.' He flung Phyl a scathing glance. 'I suppose she thought she was being clever, but if she thought that she chose the wrong man.'

'Sir, I never—' Phyl began. 'I didn't – I *wouldn't*—'

'All right, Phyllis. I'll hear you in a moment.' Mr Carter held his hand out for the bill. 'If I might just . . . ?'

'There you are. See for yourself.' Mr Glossop handed the bill over the desk and jabbed at it with a thick forefinger. 'There. And there. Those two items have been overpriced. It's quite deliberate.'

'I see.' Mr Carter stared at the slip of paper. 'Yes, I do see.' He raised his eyes to meet Phyl's imploring gaze. 'Well, Miss Jennings, what do you have to say?'

'I didn't do it!' she exclaimed. 'Honestly, Mr Carter, I wouldn't dream of doing such a thing – you know I wouldn't. I've been brought up to be honest, I wouldn't steal a penny, never. And I'm sure I wrote the prices down right. It wasn't a mistake.'

Mr Carter raised his eyebrows slightly and glanced at the customer. 'That's an interesting point,' he murmured. 'If Miss Jennings were indeed trying to cheat you, isn't that just what she would claim – that it *was* a mistake?' He shook his head. 'I have to say, this young lady is one of our best Nippies – she's quick and bright, and cheerful. The customers like her.' He chewed his lip. 'You're a regular customer, aren't you, Mr Glossop? Have you ever been served by Miss Jennings before?'

The man shook his head. 'No. I usually sit nearer the door. That tall, dark-haired girl serves me. Thin face, green eyes.'

'Irene,' Phyl said before she could stop herself, and then, more slowly, '*Irene* . . .'

Mr Carter gave her a sharp glance. 'What is it, Phyllis?'

He'd used her name again. Phyl's heart leapt, but she reminded herself that it meant nothing, that he had probably just forgotten . . . 'Nothing,' she said quickly. It wouldn't help if they thought she was trying to cast blame on another girl. And in any case, how could Irene possibly . . . ? 'Please,' she said, holding out her hand, 'could *I* see the bill?'

'I should have thought you'd already seen it enough,' Mr Glossop said nastily, but Mr Carter handed it over and Phyl scanned it. The two items were, as she already knew, wrongly priced – and yet there was something odd about the figures . . .

'Why,' she said slowly, 'they've been scratched out and written in again. Look.' She held the bill out to Mr Carter. 'Someone's done that while it was in my pigeon-hole. Someone's been trying to get me into trouble.'

'Surely not . . .' But Mr Carter took it back and studied it with attention. Finally, he looked up at the increasingly impatient Mr Glossop. 'I think she's right, sir. The paper's definitely been scratched there, you see? As if with a sharp penknife or something of the sort.' He sighed. 'I really don't think I can discipline Miss Jennings while there's any doubt at all that she did this. I have to repeat, she's shown herself to be honest, willing, and very hard-working – indeed, she's already been marked down as a possible future manageress.' Phyl stared at him in astonishment, feeling the blood rush to her cheeks. 'I can only assure you that we'll do everything possible to trace the real culprit, and in the meantime I'd like to offer you your next meal at this Corner House absolutely free, as a sign of our goodwill and regret that this should have happened. And please,' he said with a smile, 'don't ask for sausages and chips. I'd like you to enjoy something rather more exciting than that!'

Mr Glossop looked from Mr Carter to Phyl. Phyl met his eyes, willing him to believe in her innocence, and at last he gave a shrug and a 'Hrmph!' and said, 'Well, I suppose I'll have to leave it at that. I can see that there's some doubt and since you seem to trust the girl . . . I hope she doesn't let you down, that's all. And I hope you won't forget that even if you can trust this one, there must be another out there that you *can't* trust. This sort of thing's quite unacceptable, you know. Quite unacceptable.'

'I agree absolutely.' Mr Carter rose and held out his hand. 'And I assure you again, we'll do our utmost to get to the bottom of the affair. And I'm most grateful to you for being so understanding. Now, let me see you out . . .' He turned back to Phyl. 'Wait here for me, Miss Jennings, I'd like a further word with you.'

Phyl waited in the office, her heart sinking again. Was she going to get the sack after all? Perhaps Mr Carter didn't trust her quite as much as he'd said . . . Her mind went back to his words about her being marked down as a future manageress. He *couldn't* have meant that, surely! He'd just said it to soothe the irate customer, and now he was coming back to tell her to collect her cards . . .

Mr Carter came back into the office and sat down again. 'I've asked Jo to take over your station for the time being. We can't have your other customers complaining that they're being neglected!' He smiled, but Phyl could only stare at him despairingly, convinced now that he was about to dismiss her. 'Now, don't look so woebegone. I'm quite sure it was as you said and someone else has altered the bill. But what I need to know now is who would have done such a thing? And why?'

Phyl was pretty sure she knew the answer to both questions and for a moment she was strongly tempted to tell him. But something held her back. Suppose it hadn't been Irene. There were a score or more Nippies working on this floor, and almost any one of them could have had the opportunity. It looked very suspicious – even Mr Carter must be able to see that – that Mr Glossop normally sat at Irene's table, and that she probably knew quite well that he always checked his bill carefully and was likely to complain if it were wrong. But that still didn't mean . . .

'I don't know,' she said in a low voice. 'Please, Mr Carter, can I go back to work? You – you're not going to sack me, are you?'

'Sack you? Of course not! I thought I'd made that clear.' He looked thoughtfully at her. 'But you must see we can't have this kind of thing happening. I simply have to find out who is responsible.' He put his head on one side and regarded her. 'I think you know, don't you? Or you have a strong suspicion.'

'I *don't* know,' she said desperately. 'Not for certain . . . Mr Carter, it won't happen again, I'm *sure* it won't. I'll check my bills extra carefully from now on and make sure they're all right. I *promise* it won't happen again.'

'I don't see,' he said very gravely, 'how you can possibly promise that if you don't know who did it . . .' Their eyes met and Phyl saw that he understood perfectly, and probably that he also had a very good idea as to who the culprit was. Then, after a moment's thought, he added, 'But very well. I'll do nothing this time. But if it ever happens again – and I mean this, Phyllis – I shall take it very seriously indeed. Lyons have a first-class reputation and we can't allow anything – anything at *all* – to sully that reputation. And it rests largely in the hands of you Nippies. We do our best to give you a happy working atmosphere, and if there are any problems they'll inevitably reflect in your work. Do you understand me?'

'Yes, Mr Carter,' Phyl whispered.

He rose to his feet. 'Good. And I'll be glad if you'll pass the message on to anyone else you think might need to hear it.' Their eyes met again. 'I shall be mentioning the matter in my little talk tomorrow morning, and after that we'll consider it closed. *Unless* it happens again.' Then, to Phyl's astonishment, he reached out and patted her shoulder. 'Now, run – *nip* – along back to your work. And I did mean what I said about your having been noticed, you know. Don't let anyone else spoil it for you!'

Scarlet-faced again, with tears in her eyes, Phyl came out of the office and went back into the restaurant. The lunchtime rush was over and it was quieter now, and the first person she saw was Irene.

Irene looked at Phyl's face and smirked, then hid her smile with a look of false concern.

'Oh, dear. You do look upset. Not in trouble, are you?'

Phyl felt her temper rise, but before she could tell Irene what she really wanted to say she remembered Mr Carter's words. *If there are any problems, they'll reflect in your work . . . Pass the message on . . .* She clenched her hands tightly and lifted her chin.

'No, I'm not, as it happens, although someone else might be. You want to be careful, Irene.' And then, as the other girl opened her mouth to retort, 'You don't happen to have a small, sharp penknife I could borrow, do you? I want to make some alterations . . . to a bill . . .'

Irene's face reddened. She cast a quick look to either side, but Phyl said softly, 'I wouldn't. Whatever it is you're thinking of doing – I wouldn't. I didn't tell on you, but Mr Carter knows all the same. He's not a fool, Irene, but you'll be one if you go on the way you have been. So – no more messing about, see? Either with my things or my bills. Because next time I *will* tell.'

Quivering with fury, she turned and marched away, leaving Irene gasping like a stranded fish. She stalked over to her tables and began rapidly to clear them. Jo, who had already started the job, stared at her in astonishment.

'What on earth's happening, our Phyl? You look like you're ready to commit murder. And what was the trouble with that fat bloke?'

'I'll tell you later,' Phyl muttered, sweeping a pile of used cutlery on to her tray. 'But I'll tell you this now, Jo – we won't be having any more trouble with that Irene Bond. At least—' The thought struck her that Irene wasn't so easily brushed aside '—I *hope* not.'

Preparations for Maggie's wedding began at once. All the Pearlies looked out their costumes and examined the buttons to replace missing ones and make sure the rest were all secure. Ivy Pratt seemed to spend all her days sewing and even her mother-in-law Ada laid aside her dark grey knitting

– socks for Sam – and gave a hand. She was a Pearly, too, and as the two women sewed she kept up a steady reminiscence of earlier Pearly festivities.

'I knowed young Henry Croft,' she said, as she had said a hundred times. 'Knowed him from when he was first down the Market. My old dad was in Somers Town, see, and when young Henry come to work there our Bert's place was the first one he cleared out of rats. Little bloke, he was, but quick as a ferret and always had a grin on his face. My dad always reckoned he was so glad to be let out of the workhouse, he'd be happy in a sewer.'

Ivy had heard it all before but she listened as if it was all new. A lot of people had known Henry Croft, of course, but nobody else could claim to have given him his first job. Fred and Sal Pratt had given him more than that, too.

'Used to come round our place for fish and chips of a Friday night,' Ada went on, peering at her needle as she threaded the fine silk through it. 'I dunno what they does to these needles these days, our Ivy, they just don't seem to make the eyes proper. I can't get this through nohow . . . You see if you can do it, girl.' She handed the needle and thread over and Ivy pushed the thread through and handed it back. 'Yes, every Friday night, young Henry Croft come round to us for his supper, and Ma often used to put a bit of extra in Dad's dinner-box for him to give the nipper. That's all he was to us, see, just a nipper like any other. Didn't have no real home, used to doss down on a pile of sacks in one of the sheds, but he never piped his eye about it. Thought he was lucky to be where he was, and that's why he started up the Pearlies to raise money for other people what needed it.' She fixed Ivy with a glare with her small, black-button eyes. 'Pity some others what I could mention don't follow his example. World'd be a better place if people went round with a smile on their faces instead of looking like they'd lost a shilling and found sixpence.'

You can talk! Ivy thought, biting her lip so as not to laugh. Sam's mother only smiled on special occasions, and even then you had to put in a request six weeks ahead of time. It was touch and go whether she'd manage it for Maggie's wedding, but at least her heart was in the right place, or she wouldn't be helping to sew on all these buttons. Ada Pratt had had a lifetime of doing what must be done, usually in difficult circumstances, and now that she was in her seventies she never lifted a finger if she didn't want to.

Maggie was in a constant flurry. There were all kinds of things to arrange – the calling of the banns at her church, reminding Tommy to get them called at his, organising the service itself and, although she'd told the girls there wouldn't be a smart reception, there was certainly going to be a party with the whole street coming as well as Pearlies from other boroughs. Everything had to be ready in good time to give her and Evie and Mum the chance to do all the food at the last minute.

'It's lovely the way Lyons give their staff a wedding cake,' Shirley said. 'At least you don't have to worry about that. They're smashing cakes, too, three-tier and iced with trellis decorations and little roses and silver balls, the lot. *And* got a little figure of a bride and groom standing on the top.'

'Well, you wouldn't want a stork carrying a little bundle in its beak,' Maggie said with a grin, and then blushed. The other girls remembered Irene's remarks and glanced awkwardly at each other. They all knew that Phyl had bitten Irene's head off for suggesting Maggie might be expecting, but they also knew that it could well be true. Jo even found herself glancing surreptitiously at Maggie's waistline – or the place where her waistline would have been if she hadn't been so plump.

Maggie laughed suddenly. 'It's all right – you don't need to look so embarrassed. I'm not in the family way. Me and Tom's too careful for that.' This remark, making plain what they'd all half suspected, had the effect of embarrassing them even more. 'Mind you, we might chuck all that out of the window once we're spliced – Tom says it's like going to bed in an overcoat, and pricey too.'

'I wonder how they do that trellis icing without breaking it,'

271

Shirley said rather loudly. 'I mean, it's so delicate, you'd think it would snap while they were putting it on the cake.'

'They do it on the cake, twerp,' Jo said, thankful to have a change of subject. 'It's not like putting up a garden fence.'

'I saw someone with that sort of trellis in a garden once,' Etty joined in. 'Ever so pretty, it was, with all roses growing up it. Can't you ask them to make roses grow up yours, Maggie – icing ones, I mean?'

Maggie surveyed them and grinned. Not one of them had ever gone all the way with a boy, and they were somewhat shocked that she and Tommy had. Maggie wasn't ashamed, however. She felt more grown-up, more worldly-wise. She knew things they didn't, things that – if truth were told – they were dying to ask. She felt her body grow warm as she remembered Tommy's love-making in the park, in one of the secluded spots they'd made their own. It would be even better in a bed, she thought, even better when you had all night. And the next night, and the one after that, for the rest of your lives . . .

Except that they wouldn't. The realisation came like a tiny stab of ice in her heart. For Tommy and herself, it might only be for a few nights before he went off to war.

Irene kept herself apart from the others. Since the failure of her attempt to get Phyl into real trouble, she had stopped her campaign – for the time being. Unknown to Phyl, Mr Carter had drawn her aside one day and given her a severe lecture about what it meant to be a Nippy, and what high standards Lyons expected from all their staff. He never accused her directly but Irene knew that he was giving her a warning, and she knew, too, that he was watching her in the restaurant. She had even seen him check her bills once. Irene burned with resentment. As if she'd be fool enough to overcharge her own customers!

Instead, she took pains to carry out her work even more efficiently, never pausing for a quick word with any of the others, but hurrying back and forth as if her life depended on it. And in the staff dining-room she sat at another table. She

272

didn't even look at Phyl and the others, and she told herself she didn't care what they thought, or what they said.

Anyway, their talk was all of Maggie's wedding, and it made her sick. She couldn't understand Maggie throwing herself away on a boy like Tommy, with no real job – you couldn't count working in a gents' outfitters as a proper job – and now a private in the Army. Lowest of the low, they were, and if there was a war – and Irene and her dad-in-the-Civil-Service still didn't believe there would be – he'd probably be one of the first to get killed. Or lose his legs, like that revolting old man who'd been at the Somme and now sat on a little cart outside Charing Cross station selling matches. Being married wouldn't seem such a good idea when Maggie had a useless hulk like that to look after for the next fifty years.

When Irene got married, it would be to a bloke who had a career ahead of him, someone with a bit of class who could see how daft all this war talk was and wasn't going to go and chuck it all up just because of some silly idea of patriotism. Irene loved her country, naturally – although it might have been more true to say that she just took it for granted that it was better than anywhere else, just because it was her country – but she didn't see the sense in throwing your life away for a lot of foreigners you were never going to meet, specially when half of them were Jews. Jews were the cause of half the trouble in the world, her dad said, and had been ever since the year dot. No, Irene was looking for a chap who knew his duty to his wife and family, a chap who would be a good provider, work hard to bring home a decent pay packet and keep out of the pubs.

She went to the dance at Sudbury the next Saturday. Phyl wasn't there – she'd said earlier on that she and the others were going to the pictures. Irene knew that Phyl had several boyfriends – Mike, of course, and that Sandy Smith, and the tall young floor supervisor, Richard Godwin. In her opinion, Richard was the best of the lot and it was a wonder to her that a common little piece like Phyl Jennings could take his eye. But tonight Phyl wasn't there and Richard was. Irene's eyes gleamed and she went to the ladies' to put on a bit more

273

Cherry Pink lipstick, then chose a seat opposite him, where he couldn't help but see her. She glanced across until their eyes met and she gave him her sweetest smile.

As the music for the first dance ended, he got up and came over, just as if she'd pulled a piece of string. Irene glanced away, pretending not to notice, and gave a little start when he stopped in front of her and spoke.

'Would you give me the pleasure of the next dance?'

Oh, he had lovely manners! Not like those awkward boys who turned red and stammered and didn't know how to ask a girl on to the floor. Irene looked up and smiled graciously.

'Don't mind if I do.'

She stood up and went into his arms. He held her firmly but not too tight, and his hands were slender and cool, not like the big clumsy hands some boys had, or hot and sweaty like Herbert Lennox's. Irene felt a little quiver of excitement. She thought of Phyl and her excitement was touched with satisfaction. It's your own fault, she told Phyl silently, you ought to have been here. I'm blowed if I'd let a chap like this out on the loose if he was mine!

The dance was a foxtrot. A lot of boys couldn't do a foxtrot well, they thought it was too tricky and fell over their own feet and trod on hers, but Richard Godwin could do it to smooth perfection. He whirled her round the floor with lots of fancy turns, and when it finished Irene smiled at him, showing her white teeth.

'That was smashing. You're ever such a good dancer.'

'So are you.' He smiled back. He had good teeth, too, she noticed, and he was definitely film-star material with that corn-coloured hair and those deep blue eyes. She let her fingers remain in his, and they walked back to her chair hand in hand.

'I suppose you're all booked up for the rest of the evening,' he said a shade wistfully. Irene felt a small leap of triumph. She shook her head.

'I'd only just arrived when you asked me to dance. I haven't booked any dances yet.'

'Well, how about letting me have a few more? Or have you

got a queue of admirers waiting to ask you?' He smiled again, slowly, and Irene's heart turned over.

'Oh, there's probably a few here,' she said carelessly, glancing around, 'but I don't like to have a regular partner. Boys can get silly, you know – all jealous if they think you're dancing with someone else when you ought to be dancing with them. I don't want that sort of thing.'

'And would you call me a "boy"?' he enquired with a quizzical look.

Irene turned her head and studied him. She looked at his deep blond hair, carefully waved and kept shiny with Brylcreem, at his blue eyes and the firm, smooth planes of his face. He was smoothly shaved, and his tie and shirt were immaculate beneath a dark blue blazer. She guessed he was about twenty-six.

'Oh, no,' she said, letting her dimples show, 'you're not a boy. You're a man.'

'So you don't think I'd get silly – even if we spent the whole evening dancing together?' He had moved very slightly closer, so that his arm touched hers. She could feel the fabric against her bare skin.

'I don't think so,' she whispered, giving him an upward glance from beneath her lashes. 'I don't think you'd get silly at all . . .'

Chapter Eighteen

Phyl was sitting next to Mike in the back row at the cinema. They'd come to see a Roy Rogers film, but as usual there was a *Pathe Pictorial* first, filled with pictures of what was happening in Europe. There were shots of Hyde Park, too, with the trenches that were being dug, and of ordinary people building Anderson shelters in their back gardens. She watched with foreboding and felt for his hand in the darkness.

'Oh, Mike . . .'

'It's all right,' he murmured in her ear. 'It's all right, Phyl. It won't come to nothing. And if it does – well, we'll be ready for it. That's all we're doing – getting ready, just in case.'

'But what if there *is* a war? They say there'll be thousands of bombs dropped on London, thousands. We'll all be blown to bits.'

'No, we won't.' He gave her hand a comforting squeeze. 'Don't forget the Air Force, Phyl! That's what me and Charlie will be doing – up there in our planes, driving 'em back over the Channel. They're not going to get near enough to London to drop bombs.'

He drew her into his arms and kissed her ear. Phyl turned her face to him and met his lips with hers. She clung to him, feeling suddenly shaky. The prospect of war seemed all at once very real.

'We've had shelters delivered back home,' she whispered. 'Dad and Uncle Bill and the boys had to dig great big holes to

276

put them in. It proper messed up Uncle Bill's spuds. If there's an air raid, they've got to go down there and stay put till the "Raiders Passed" signal goes. It could be *hours*. It's going to be awful, stuck in those things for hours, hearing bombs drop overhead. And Jo and me'll be at Auntie Holt's, and she hasn't got a shelter at all, there's no garden to put it in, so we'll have to go down the street. In our nighties and all! And we won't know what's happening at home. It's horrible.'

'It won't come to that. I just told you, we won't let 'em in. Look, Phyl, don't get yourself all worked up. It may never happen, and if it does it'll all be over by Christmas. We'll tan Hitler's backside for him, you see if we don't. He'll know better next time than to mess with the British.'

Phyl allowed him to comfort her. The thought of what might lie ahead was too awful to contemplate and she let herself drift away on his kisses, thankful that they'd got back-row seats and weren't going to be poked on the shoulders and told to behave themselves. Perhaps he was right. Only that afternoon she'd seen a shoe shine boy sitting on the pavement with his blackboard beside him, and instead of his charges he'd chalked the message: CHIN UP, DON'T WORRY ABOUT TOMORROW, NUFFINS APPENED YET, KEEP SMILIN. And in Hyde Park, despite the trenches, there had been mothers with their babies in pushchairs, sitting on the grass in the sunshine, laughing and joking and playing with their kids . . .

'We're not going to let him beat us,' Mike said. 'We're not going to let him scare us. He's just a silly little bloke with a silly little moustache, and if he tries to come over here we'll let him have what for. Bombs! Just let him try, that's all.'

Jo had taken Nick home for the weekend. They'd arrived at teatime and sat down round the table with the family. Freddy was there, getting ready to take his latest girl to the pictures, and Alice was worrying about Roberston, who had been in a fight with the black and white tom three doors down and had a torn ear. She showed it to Jo.

'Look, it's all scabby. It was bleeding all over the place when he came in this morning.'

'That means it's getting better,' Jo said, examining the big ginger cat. 'Scabs are when the bleeding stops and it all dries up so that dirt can't get in. He'll be all right, Ally.'

'The other chap must be a bit of a bruiser,' Nick observed, squatting down to stroke the furry back. 'It takes a brave cat to tangle with old Robbie.'

'Oh, he's *much* worse,' Alice said with satisfaction. 'Mrs Hutchins had to take him to the vet and have stitches. She came round to complain.'

'And I had to offer to pay something towards the vet's bill,' her father said ruefully 'otherwise she'd have had half the street out with her shouting the odds. I told her, you can't be responsible for what a cat does and anyway it was likely her Blackie started the fight, but she wouldn't have it. Cost me eighteenpence, that did.'

Jo carried in the big cottage loaf she'd brought home with her. It had a crusty round top, half sunk into the big base, and she knew everyone would want a bit of the flaky crust. She pulled the top off, revealing the softness of the bread within, and started to slice it up.

'What's it like up in London now?' Freddy asked, appearing in a fresh white shirt and Fair Isle pullover and sitting at the table. 'People getting twitchy about the war?'

'Now then,' Carrie said, coming in from the scullery with a dish of beetroot to go with the ham already laid out on a plate, 'we don't want none of that talk. Nobody's said for definite there's going to be a war yet, as far as I know.'

'Nobody's said there's not going to be,' Fred said inaccurately. People were saying both things all the time, and the truth was nobody knew for certain. It was just like a huge black cloud hanging over the country, a cloud that might suddenly explode in a terrible, destructive storm of thunder and lightning – or might just slip away and disappear. But while it was hanging there, everyone had the same uneasy feeling that you got before a real thunderstorm – a heavy foreboding, an oppressive sense of doom.

'We had rehearsals at school before we broke up,' Alice said to Jo as they began their tea.

'Rehearsals? I didn't know you were going to be in a play.'

'Not for a play, silly. For the evacuation. We all had to line up with our gas masks and the teachers tied luggage labels on us with our names on, in case we got lost, and then we marched along the road and down to the station. They wouldn't tell us where we're going.'

Jo stared at her. 'When's this going to happen?'

'Not at all, we hope,' Carrie said. She had gone very pale. 'It's just a part of all these preparations. Shelters and ration books and evacuation . . . I must say, it looks serious, but there's still some hope . . . isn't there?' Her voice broke a little and Jo looked at her, alarmed. She saw the glitter in Carrie's eyes and had a sudden flash of insight. It would be awful for her – for all mothers – to have to stand by and watch their children go away to a strange place, to live with strangers, not knowing when they'd come back. She reached out suddenly and touched her mother's hand.

'Of course there's hope. There's always hope.'

'I don't know . . .' Carrie gave her a wavering smile and then turned away, fishing in the sleeve of her cardigan for a hanky. She blew her nose and said more briskly, 'Anyway, we've sorted out what's to happen to Robbie if this evacuation thing goes ahead. He's staying here to keep me and your dad company.'

Jo glanced at Alice. Her head was bent over her plate and her fair hair had come loose from its slide and hung down to hide her face. Jo could guess at her expression – set and mutinous, her bottom lip jutting out enough, as Bill often said, to rest a threepenny bit on. Mum and Dad might think they'd sorted out what was to happen to Robbie, Jo thought, but she'd put money on Alice having different ideas.

'I reckon home's the best place for a cat,' Nick said. 'Specially one like Robbie, who knows his way around so well. He wouldn't like being out in the country, with fields and trees and – and—' He faltered, evidently realising the nonsense of what he was saying. Alice realised it, too, and lifted her head to give him a look of ineffable scorn.

'Don't be silly, Nick. Cats *like* trees and fields and grass.

They like catching birds and mice. I bet Robbie could even catch rabbits if he wanted to. He'll want to come to the country with me. He'll be miserable, left here on his own with no one to love him.'

'Well, thank you very much,' her mother said, half-amused. 'So your daddy and me don't count, and you don't think we'll love him. That puts us in our place, doesn't it?'

'I know *you* love him, Mum,' Alice said, 'but I don't think Daddy does much. He calls him "that cat" and last week he said Robbie drank too much milk.'

'For heaven's sake——' Carrie began, but Bill broke in. He, too, was more amused than indignant and trying hard to keep a straight face. He looked at his daughter and spoke in a hurt tone.

'I just don't know what I've done to deserve this. I looked after *that cat's* mum at work, made a bed with my best work pullover for her to have her babies on, carried the kitten all the way home in me dinner-box, and you say I don't love him! What about all the bits of bread and fish paste I give him at teatime, eh? Isn't that loving him? What about the fish I caught down the docks and brought home special for him? Don't that count? And now you're going to go off to the country and take him away from me, so I'll have nothing to remind me of you. It's a bit hard, that's all I can say, it's a bit hard.' He heaved a great, shuddering sigh.

'Don't, Dad,' Jo begged. 'You're making me cry.'

'Making *you* cry?' he said. 'What d'you think it's doing to me? Eh?' He wiped the back of one hand across his eyes.

Alice looked at him in alarm. Her face reddened and the mutinous bottom lip began to tremble. Her blue eyes filled with tears.

'I didn't mean——' she began, and then stopped as the family's composure broke down and they all collapsed with laughter. Alice stared at them indignantly and then turned to her mother. 'Mummy, they're *laughing* at me!'

'They're not, they're laughing at Daddy.' Carrie gathered her daughter hastily into her arms. 'He's just being silly, so they're laughing at him. You get on with your tea and take no notice. They're all being silly.'

Alice cast the rest of the family a doubtful look. Then she picked up her knife and fork and applied herself once more to her meal. Her face had regained its determined look.

'Anyway,' she said, 'I still think Robbie would like it out in the country. And if Daddy wants another kitten, he could easily get one. Uncle Stan told me the other day that Robbie's mum had had another family and one of them's ginger, just like Rob. That would remind Daddy of me, and it would be nice for Robbie to have a little brother at home to come back to when the war's over.'

Carrie and Jo glanced at each other and sighed. You couldn't win an argument with Alice. Nobody ever had, not since she'd first learned to speak. You just had to hope that eventually she would see reason.

Obviously, the question of Robbie and evacuation was very far from sorted out. But saddest of all, Jo thought, was the matter-of-fact way in which Alice had spoken of the war. Only nine years old, and she seemed to take it for granted that there was going to be one, and that she would have to leave home to escape the danger.

It wasn't fair.

'What will they do about people like our Jack?' Annie Wood asked tearfully. Shirley had come home to find her poring yet again over the mass of leaflets that had been dropping through the letter-box over the past few weeks. 'I mean, they're talking about evacuating children and blind people, but what about people like Jack? He's not a child, he's nineteen years old, but you know as well as I do he might as well be six. He can't go to strangers, so what's he got to do, stay here to be bombed? He'll be frightened out of his wits.'

Poor Jack hadn't got many wits to be frightened out of, Shirley thought wryly, but she knew her mother was right. Jack was afraid of loud noises and terrified of thunder. If ever there was a storm, he would go and hide under his bed, like a dog or a cat. He'd never be able to stand up to bombing.

'Have you asked about him? Can't you go with him, like mothers with babies? Surely there's some arrangement.'

Annie shook her head. 'I can't get no sense out of that woman down the Office. She don't seem to understand about people like Jack. She just says he's too old to go as a child, but there's special arrangements for blind and people like that. But Jack's not like that. Someone his age who's blind might be able to do everything for themselves just the same, but Jack needs his mum and the special arrangements don't come into it. She says they're getting Homes organised but he can't go to one of those places. He'd die.'

It sounded dramatic, but Shirley knew it was probably true. Jack suffered terribly if he was taken away from his family. A few years ago, he had had to go into hospital to have his tonsils out, and he'd almost faded away before they got him home again. It was like pulling a flower up out of the ground and leaving it to wilt.

'Another woman came in then,' Annie continued, 'and she looked at the papers and said Jack would be called up anyway and have to go into the Army. I said he couldn't, he's a Mongol, and do you know what she said then? She said if he was a foreigner he'd probably have to be interned!'

Shirley stared at her. Lots of people didn't know much about Jack's condition, but for someone working in an office to be so ignorant was almost beyond belief.

'The stupid woman! She ought to be given the sack. What did you say, Mum?'

'I didn't say anything. I couldn't. I just looked at them both sitting there so smug in their suits and pearls, and I turned on my heel and walked out. It was all I could do.'

And came home and had an asthma attack, Shirley thought. It had been obvious when she came in that her mother had been poorly, and she was still lying on the sofa, pale and exhausted. Never mind our Jack, she thought with sudden bitterness, how's our Mum going to get through a war? And what about all the other people who aren't strong or got something wrong with them? It's going to be a proper mess.

'I suppose he'll just have to stay here with me,' Annie said dispiritedly. 'Goodness knows how he'll stand up to it, but we can't afford to go away without the proper billeting. They pay the country people to have evacuees, see, and the Government pays seven-and-six towards the cost, but if we went on our own it'd be much more. We can't afford that, not on your dad's pay. I don't see how I could go anyway. There's your dad to be seen to, and you. And we're used to everything around here, me and Jack. I don't know how we'd go on out in the country, with all them cows and things.'

Shirley looked at her thoughtfully but said nothing. She went out into the kitchen to fill the kettle, and was just setting it on the gas-ring when her brother Donald came in.

Donald was wearing his Army uniform as usual. He was proud of it and wore it well, walking tall and upright with all the buttons gleaming and his belt as white as snow. He was on leave now and had done a few jobs around the place, and when he went away again he would be missed.

'Hullo, Sis,' he said. 'If you're making some tea, I'll have mine strong with three spoons of sugar.'

'Please,' she said. 'Don't they teach you to say "please" in the Army?'

'Only when we're just going to kill someone,' he said, and saw the shock on her face. 'Sorry, Shirl, I didn't mean that. *Please* can I have a cup of tea, strong with three spoons of sugar? Mind you, I'd like to see the sarge's face if I said please to him! Not that he's ever likely to make me a cup of tea,' he added with a grin.

Shirley got out the cups and took the teapot from its shelf. She stood by the table with its covering of green American oilcloth, and regarded her brother.

'I want to talk to you, Don.'

'Well, you don't have to make an appointment. Fire away.'

'It's about Jack. And Mum. Have you heard what happened down the Office when she went to see about evacuation?'

Don nodded and frowned. 'Bit poor, if you ask me. They just weren't interested.'

'I think Jack ought to be out in the country,' she said. 'He'll die of fright the first time there's a bombing raid. And Mum's going to be worse than ever with all the worry – you know what it does to her. They both ought to be sent away if the war starts.'

'When,' he said. 'Not if. It's going to happen, Shirl.'

'So we'd better put on our thinking caps. Jack can't go without Mum and the evacuation people won't pay for her as well. Dad can't run to it, not with all the extra Jack costs anyway. So that leaves you and me.' The kettle's whistle shrilled and she poured boiling water into the teapot, swilled it around and tipped it down the sink. She opened the tea-caddy and spooned tea into the pot, then poured in the rest of the water. 'I think we ought to chip in, Don.'

'You mean pay for Mum and Jack to be evacuated?'

'Yes. Mind, I don't know how much it'd cost, and I don't know how we'd arrange it, but I think we ought to try. If you and me and Dad could all put a bit together, it might be enough. And Dad wouldn't be on his own. I'm home every night so I can keep an eye on things here.'

'Well, I don't mind helping out,' Donald said thoughtfully. 'I reckon you're right. Jack would have kittens, and Mum'd be exhausted trying to look after him. I just wonder who'll be willing to take 'em in. Still, it's worth a try.' He paused, chewing his lip. 'You know, what we ought to do is think of someone we know out in the country, someone who'd help us find a billet for them. I might ask round the blokes in the barracks. What about you, Shirl? Isn't there anyone you know up at the Corner House or at that club you go to? There must be someone who comes from the country.'

'Yes.' Shirley stared at him, her mind ticking over furiously and coming to rest, like a pointer, against one name. 'Yes, there is . . .'

'You mean you want your mam and Jack to go and stay in our village?' Owen stared at Shirley. 'D'you have any idea what it's like in the valleys? There's nothing posh about mining country, you know.'

'I know that. I saw some pictures once, on *Pathe Pictorial*. The Duke of Windsor – well, he was Prince of Wales then – going round and saying something must be done. But it must be better than that now.'

Owen gave a short laugh. 'Don't you believe it, *cariad*. That was just talk, see – once he got back to Buckingham Palace he forgot all about the mines. He was only interested in Mrs Simpson, wasn't he? I tell you, miners live hard. There's not much comfort in miners' cottages, except for the free coal to keep them warm.'

'They'll be safer than London, though,' Shirley said. 'There's not much point in bombing coalmines.'

Owen wasn't so sure, but he thought it was unlikely the German bombers would go as far as South Wales. Even places like Plymouth weren't part of the evacuation programme because of their distance. He thought of the valleys, and the mountains around them. There was dirt underfoot, the crunching dirt of coal, and the air was filled with black grit and the noise of the machinery, but up on the mountains there was peace and green grass, and you could lose yourself amongst the hills. He had once walked for miles beside a clear, glittering stream, watching the spray as it tumbled over sudden cliffs in a flurry of rainbow colour. He had seen birds such as were never seen in the valleys – a green wagtail, a wheatear, a kingfisher – and had sat for hours beside a still, deep pool in what seemed to him to be a fairy glen, wondering at the smooth roundness of the rocks at the foot of a wide, shallow fall. Some of them had been caught in natural rock basins polished by years of swirling water . . . He felt a sudden rush of homesickness.

'My Auntie Mair might have room,' he said. 'She don't live down in the valley – she married a farmer, see, they live away from the village. I could ask Mam what she thinks, write a letter to her.'

'Oh, please,' Shirley begged, gazing at him. 'You see, I honestly don't think Jack or Mum would survive if it's going to be as awful as they say. The rest of us, we'll get through somehow, but Jack would scream his head off if he had to go in an air-raid shelter, he's so frightened of being shut in. And there'd be the noise, too – he's terrified of bangs. But he's no trouble otherwise,' she added hastily, afraid that she might be putting Owen off. 'As long as he can have quiet and he's got Mum around, he's a lamb.'

'I know. I've been to your house often enough. Jack's a smashing boy. I'll talk to me Mam,' Owen promised, 'and ask her to write to Auntie Mair. She'll probably have to have evacuees anyway, so I expect she'd rather have someone she knows, like.'

'What about your dad?' Shirley asked. 'Will he be going?'

Owen shook his head. 'Says there's no point and he won't take a place away from someone who really needs it. And Mam couldn't go, see, because of the shop. She does most of the work there now – Uncle John leaves it to her. He's not too well himself – got a dicky heart.'

'I'd be really grateful if you'd write to your auntie,' Shirley said. 'I'm worried about Jack and our Mum. They'd be better off out of London before it even starts, if it's going to.'

He nodded. 'I'll talk to Mam tonight.'

For a few moments they were quiet. They were walking hand in hand along the Embankment and paused beside Cleopatra's Needle. The stone obelisk pointed skywards, like a warning finger. Shirley looked up at it.

'I read about this once. They towed it here from Egypt behind a ship, only it broke away in the Bay of Biscay and got lost. After a while, someone found it again and brought it the rest of the way. It's funny, isn't it, to think of a thing like this floating? You'd think it would sink.'

'I suppose they had floats all around it, like a sort of rubber dinghy.' Owen lifted Shirley's hand and examined it, stroking the fingers. 'Shirley – there's something I want to ask you.'

Shirley stood very still. Her heart began to thump. She remembered the other occasions when she had thought Owen might be about to propose and how she'd headed him off and been relieved when he seemed to understand. Tonight, she could think of nothing to say. She gazed at him dumbly.

'I know I said I wouldn't press you, like,' he said, speaking rapidly as if he were afraid she would interrupt. 'I know I promised I wouldn't rush you. But – well, with all this talk about war I don't feel like I can wait much longer. We don't know what's going to happen to us, do we? In a few weeks we could be anywhere. I could be in the Army, or learning to fly a plane, or steer a ship, or—'

'Owen, don't,' she begged. 'Don't talk about it. I can't bear to think of it.'

'Neither can I, really,' he said honestly. 'But there's one thing I do want you to think about, Shirley. I want you to think about whether you could ever, well, marry me. If you could ever be my wife.' He was holding both her hands now, gazing deeply into her eyes. 'I love you, Shirley. I fell in love with you that first time we met, when we danced together, and I've loved you more every day since. I'm going to go on loving you till the day I die. So – if you think there's a chance – if you could ever love me – well, what do you say? Will you? Will you marry me?'

'Oh, *Owen*,' she breathed. The emotion in his stumbling words had almost stunned her. It poured out of him, immersing her in the warmth of his love. The tears sprang hot to her eyes and she could barely speak. She stood with her hands in his, her eyes brimming, and shook her head helplessly until at last she could speak again. 'Oh, Owen. Oh, yes. I've loved you, too – all that time.' The truth of it burst upon her, like a sunrise out of midnight. 'Oh, yes, I'll marry you. I *want* to . . . But not straight away,' she added. 'I don't want a rushed wedding. I want to be engaged for a while – like Jo Mason and Nick Laurence. And I want to make sure Mum and Jack are settled and happy somewhere before I think about myself.'

'It wouldn't be just you,' he pointed out, grinning with happiness. 'It's me, too, in this engagement, Shirley Wood! Oh, *cariad* . . .' He caught her against him and began to cover her face with kisses. 'Oh, you don't know how happy you've made me. I never thought you would, see – I thought no, she's far too good for me, she'll never be interested in a poor

Welsh boy from the valleys. But I had to try, didn't I? You never know what you can do if you don't try, that's what my dad always says.'

'I'm glad he does,' Shirley said fervently. 'Me, too good for you? Don't be daft, Owen Prosser.' She paused and laughed suddenly. 'I've just thought – I'll be Shirley Prosser, won't I? Mrs Shirley Prosser!' She laughed again.

'What's so funny about that?' he asked, smiling at her laughter. 'It sounds all right to me.'

'It sounds all right to me, too. It sounds lovely. And there's nothing wrong with it. Nothing at all. Mrs Shirley Prosser!'

Her laughter was infectious. Owen, hardly knowing what he was laughing at, joined in. Passers-by heard them and recognised their joy. They turned their heads and smiled, walking on with happier faces. But Shirley and Owen didn't even notice them. There, at the base of Cleopatra's Needle, they were in their own private world, and Shirley thought it was the most romantic place she had ever known.

Chapter Nineteen

Etty was overwhelmed when Maggie asked her to be a bridesmaid.

'But don't you want your own friends? And your family – Evie and Ginnie and your cousins, don't you want them? And what about me not being a Pearly? I mean, what will I wear? I haven't got the costume or nothing—'

Maggie laughed. 'Don't you worry, girl. We'll find you something to wear. I'd just like you to be there, that's all. After all, you're one of the family now.' She winked. 'Likely to be *properly* one of the family before long, if my eyes don't deceive me.'

'What d'you mean?' Etty recalled Irene's spiteful comments about Maggie herself and blushed furiously. 'Me and Jim have never—'

'Gawd love yer, girl, I never meant nothing like that.' Privately, Maggie had wondered more than once why Jim was so slow off the mark. He needed a few lessons from her Tom! 'I only meant anyone can see our Jim's sweet as sugar on you and you're just as smitten with him. Matter of fact, me and Tom were wondering whether to suggest making it a double wedding – but I suppose it's too late now, what with having to get the banns called and all.'

Etty looked at her doubtfully. Unconsciously, she raised a finger to touch the little golden brooch Jim had given her. To each of them it meant just the same as an engagement ring, but because it was a brooch nobody else knew it. They didn't want anyone else to know, not yet. It was their secret, hidden close in their hearts and cherished like secret treasure.

'I don't know,' Etty said uncertainly. 'We haven't known each other all that long.'

'As long as me and Tom, near enough. Mum and Dad'd be pleased, I can tell you that. And you don't have to ask no one's permission, do you?'

'I don't know.' Etty had never thought about it. No doubt she'd been told when she left the orphanage, but if so she hadn't taken much notice for she had no memory of it now. 'I'm probably supposed to ask the court. I think they decide things like that.'

'You mean you'd have to go to court just to ask if you could get married?' Maggie stared at her in amazement. 'Well, if that don't beat the band! Anyone'd think you were a criminal.'

Being an orphan wasn't so very different from being a criminal in some ways, Etty thought. But she was out of it now and, as Maggie had said, almost part of a proper family. Perhaps one day soon she'd be really part of it, their name hers. Mrs Jim Pratt. Etty Pratt. It might not be the most exciting name in the world to some people, but to Etty it sounded like a chime of bells.

'I don't think we'll have a double wedding,' she said to Maggie. 'It'd be stealing your thunder. You have your wedding all to yourselves, Mag, and I'll be your bridesmaid. Then you can be mine.'

'Matron of honour,' Maggie corrected her, putting on a refined accent. 'Matron of honour, that's what it is when you're a married woman. Sounds ever so posh, don't it?' she added, reverting to her normal Cockney. 'Our Evie's being my *matron of honour*, and Queenie's going to be the smallest bridesmaid. Ma's making her costume now, she's going to look just like a little doll in it.'

'It's all going to be smashing,' Etty sighed. 'Just like on the films. D'you know, I've never been to a real wedding before.'

Maggie looked at her. 'No, I suppose you haven't. Well, there's weddings and there's weddings, young Etty. Some of them posh society dos up the West End, you wonder if they got any idea how to enjoy theirselves proper, all dressed up in their fancy hats and rattling with jewellery. We might not have much money down our way, but we gives it all we got and has a real good time. You wait and see.'

Despite having what seemed like thousands of pearl buttons to sew on the various costumes, Ivy Pratt agreed at once to 'run up' something for Etty. 'It won't be a Pearly costume,' she warned, 'nor it won't be nothing you'd wear to visit the King, but you'll look all right, girl. There's a frock of our Evie's, wore it when she was carrying Queenie. That might do—'

Maggie gave a hoot of laughter. 'Evie's tent! Everyone'll think it's Etty getting spliced, and just in time, too! You can't make her wear that, Ma.'

'I'd take it in a bit first,' Ivy said indignantly. 'Goes without saying I'd do that.'

But Maggie was still snorting with laughter. 'You'll need to take it in more than a bit. There's room for Etty and our twins and half a dozen others in there. Evie was like the side of a house.'

'It'll look all right,' Ivy repeated. 'Pretty shade of pink, it is – bring out Etty's colouring. You stop that silly giggling, our Maggie, and go and get it. It's in my cupboard.'

Maggie, still shaking with mirth, went upstairs. Etty could hear her opening and shutting doors in her search. She sat watching Ivy sewing tiny pearl buttons on a waistcoat. It was almost like a separate layer of fabric, she thought, they were so thickly crowded together. The waistcoat was stiff with them, glowing and glimmering in the warm gaslight.

'That's lovely,' she said. 'But it must take hours making all these costumes.'

'It does, love. Sometimes I think I'm doing it in me sleep. But, there, they've all got to be just so for our Maggie's wedding.'

'I could help if you like,' Etty offered.

Ivy laid the waistcoat in her lap. 'You? Sew on all these buttons?'

'Well, some of them.' Etty gave a rueful smile. 'That's one of the things they taught us in the orphanage – how to sew on buttons and darn socks and all that sort of thing. We never made anything pretty or fancy, but I can do all plain sewing. I could come round every day after work, that's if – if I wouldn't be in the way,' she finished shyly.

'In the way! You'd be a jewel. A real little jewel. I mean, I'm not doing it all on me own. Evie's doing her turn and Sam's ma when she can see to thread the needle, and even our Ginnie's doing some, but an extra pair of hands – well, I don't know what to say.' Ivy beamed at her. 'I'll say this, though, our Jim picked a real little winner when he chose you. You coulda bin brought up with us, you've fitted in so well.'

Etty blushed scarlet. Jim hadn't 'chosen' her any more than she'd chosen him, and there hadn't been any real proposal – only the way they'd looked at each other when he gave her the brooch – but everyone seemed to assume they'd be getting married one day, and somehow Etty no longer felt it was necessary to put them right. Maybe they *were* right, she thought with a tiny inward quiver of delight. Maybe there wasn't any need to say any more. Maybe she and Jim really had 'chosen' each other, that first day he'd taken her out on his bike, when they'd stood leaning over the gate and watching the cows.

Maggie erupted back into the room, her arms filled with yards of soft pink material. 'Here it is, Ma. It's even bigger than I thought! We could go camping in this.'

'Don't you be so cheeky,' her mother said, lifting the dress from her arms and holding it up. It did indeed look like a tent, but the fabric was like satin and the colour that of a rose. 'You'll be wanting a frock like this yourself before long. Perhaps we shouldn't be cutting it up . . .'

'Don't be daft, Mum. You know I don't wear pink. Anyway, me and Tommy aren't in any hurry to start producing kids, so don't think you're going to get presented with any more grandchildren for a while. This'll do smashing for Etty's frock, and there'll be enough left over for Queenie to have one, too. She won't want to stay in her Pearly costume all through the party.'

The front door opened and slammed and Sam Pratt came into the room, looking enormous as usual in his costermonger's coat and trousers, his tall hat perched on his head. He pulled it off and threw it on top of the piano, then gave his wife a smacking kiss.

'Here we are, Ivy old girl. Not much doing down the Market today so I come home early.' He kissed his mother and daughter as well, then stood in front of Etty, now swamped in the pink dress Maggie had dumped on her lap. 'And if it ain't my favourite mother of pearl! That's a nice almond rock you got on your lap, sweetheart. Looks like the one our Evie wore when she was carrying.'

'It is,' his wife told him. 'I'm going to alter it for Etty to wear at the wedding. She's going to be one of the bridesmaids.'

'*One* of 'em? The way our Mag's going, we're *all* going to be blooming bridesmaids! You'd think no one had never got spliced before,' he told Etty. 'My Ivy and our Evie can't talk about nothing else. Well, so long as all I got to do is get the pig's ear in, I don't mind what they do. Any excuse'll do for a bit of a knees-up.'

Etty looked at him cautiously, then glanced towards Maggie. She was getting used to Sam's rhyming slang now but she hadn't heard 'pig's ear' before. Maggie saw her look and laughed.

'Beer. That's what he means. He's been talking about getting in a whole barrel.'

'Well, why not?' demanded her father. 'It's not every day my favourite bricks and mortar gets herself wed. And there ain't much else to have a party about these days.'

'You'd better not let our Evie hear you say I'm your favourite. Ma's depending on her to help with the sewing.'

'I only says it to you. When I'm talking to Evie, I says she's my favourite. That way, everyone's happy.' He winked at Etty. 'You wouldn't believe what I has to do to keep these girls happy. It's a hard life, being a husband and father, that it is.'

'Pass me your hanky,' Maggie said. 'I can't control me tears.'

After tea, they spread the pink frock out and began to unpick the seams. It was big enough for them all to do it together, even Gran, and it wasn't long before the garment had been reduced to a pile of loose pieces. Ivy rooted through a drawer and found a pattern for a long dress with a high waist and puffed sleeves.

'There you are. It's what I made for Jenny Birch down the road when she was bridesmaid to her brother and that girl from Finsbury. It'll do nice for our Etty. All I need is your measurements, love, and I can get started.'

Etty, who was sewing pearl buttons on to Jim's waistcoat, looked at it with awe.

'It's gorgeous. I've never had a frock like that in my life.'

'You'll look a real stunner,' Maggie assured her. 'Put that waistcoat down and stand up. Let's hold it up against you, get an idea what it'll look like.'

Etty did as she was told. Ivy draped the material around her, hiding the plain skirt and blouse she wore, and Maggie went to fetch a mirror from the front room so that she could see what she looked like. Etty stared in amazement.

'It's lovely . . .'

'It really suits you, that colour,' Ivy said with satisfaction. 'I knew it would. You'll look really pretty in that, our Etty.'

Our Etty. It was the second time she'd said that. Etty turned towards her, her eyes bright with sudden tears, but before she could speak the door opened and Jim came in, still in his overalls, covered in grease and oil from his day's work.

He stopped abruptly in the doorway and they stood gazing at each other.

'Etty,' he whispered, staring at the brightness of her eyes, the colour brought to her face, the slender lines of her body swathed from shoulder to toe in the rose-pink satin. 'Oh, Etty . . .'

★

Richard had behaved impeccably when he took Irene home after the dance that first time. He had nodded when she told him she usually went by taxi, as if it were no more than he would expect of a girl like her, and when they reached her station he handed her into the cab as though she were a princess, taking it upon himself to tell the driver her address and – even more impressive – giving him the fare. Irene sat back, smiling graciously, and then as he leaned in to say goodnight, she moved forward and gave him an impulsive kiss on the cheek.

'Thank you for a lovely evening.'

'We'll do it again, won't we?' he said. 'You'll be at next Saturday's hop, like you promised?'

'Did I promise? Well, I dare say I will, then.' She gave him another smile and sat back as the taxi began to move. 'Goodnight, Richard.'

Turning her head slightly, she caught a last glimpse of him standing on the pavement, his hair gleaming gold under the gas lamp. With a smile of satisfaction, Irene settled in her seat and thought about the evening.

Richard Godwin was a catch, no doubt about that. As a floor supervisor at Coventry Street, he had a good career in front of him. And he was good-looking, too. A lot of girls would envy her if she landed him.

At the moment, there was only one girl Irene wanted to envy her, and that was Phyl Jennings. Irene knew that Phyl had been going around with Richard, and she was also well aware that he'd spent a lot of time that evening looking around the dance-hall for her. He'd been interested in Irene herself, there was no doubt about that, but he was more interested in Phyl, and he'd even asked Irene about her, casually of course.

'You know Phyl Jennings, don't you?' he'd asked as they waltzed to one of Sinatra's songs. 'She's okay, I suppose, is she? I haven't seen her here the last couple of weeks.'

'Oh, she's fine.' Irene pretended not to know that Richard and Phyl had been going out together. 'But you know Phyl –

got so many boyfriends, she has a job keeping them all dangling on her line.'

'Oh? Bit of a goer, is she?'

That was the word Herbert Lennox had used about Irene. She hadn't liked it, but she had no objection to it being used about Phyl. She shrugged.

'I don't know about that. Bit of a tease, I'd have said – you know, the sort to lead a boy on and then leave him flat. And I don't know that it's right to talk about them the way she does – you know, telling the other girls things. Mind, I don't know her all that well, she's not a particular friend of mine.'

They danced for a while in silence and when Richard next spoke it was to comment on the band. The dance came to an end and he took Irene to her chair and went off to buy her an ice. When he came back, they sat together, companionably spooning the ice cream from the little cardboard cartons, and chatted about other things. It was some time before he returned to the subject of Phyl.

'You surprised me, saying that about Phyl Jennings.' They were doing a quickstep now, and Irene was pleased to find that Richard's footwork was as fancy as her own. She'd had lessons from the age of fourteen because her mother said that dancing was an accomplishment that would last you for life, and she wondered where Richard had learned his dancing. She turned her head to look up at him enquiringly when he mentioned Phyl again.

'Why are you surprised? Didn't you know she was like that?'

'Oh, I've *heard* things, of course,' he said dismissively, as if he hardly knew Phyl at all. 'But I always thought she was rather a nice kid. Sparky, you know.'

Irene felt annoyed. 'You can't always go by appearances,' she said sharply. 'Anyway, why are you so interested in her? She's only a Nippy when all's said and done.'

'I'm not interested, not particularly. I've just seen her here a lot, you know, and danced with her a bit. I just wondered if she was ill or anything.' He gave Irene an engaging grin. 'And what's wrong with being a Nippy? *You're* a Nippy and I'm not complaining about that!'

'Yes, but I'm not going to stay one all my life,' Irene said loftily. 'Manageress, that's what I mean to be.' She paused, then added carelessly, 'I wouldn't worry about Phyl Jennings if I were you. She's got this big romance going with a boy who comes into the Corner House every Saturday and sits at one of her tables. They've been going out for months, and I wouldn't be surprised if they get engaged soon.'

The dance came to an end and Richard stood still for a moment before leading Irene back to the chairs. 'Well, that's all right, then,' he said offhandedly, keeping his arm around her waist. 'So long as she's okay.'

In the back of the taxi, Irene smiled to herself with satisfaction. Richard knew now that Phyl had been two-timing him – not that she'd ever made any secret of the fact that she had several boyfriends, but Irene had made sure he knew that Mike was a serious one. In fact, Irene herself knew nothing of the sort, but what she did know was that Phyl had always looked extra bright and 'sparky', as Richard had called her, when she was dancing with the handsome young floor supervisor, and it gave Irene considerable satisfaction to put a possible spoke in her wheel.

What was more, Richard was well worth considering for herself. It would be even more satisfying to land a good-looking Lyons employee with his feet firmly on the rungs of the ladder. Better than a warehouseman, any day of the week!

Irene was able to further her plan to take revenge on Phyl the next Saturday afternoon, when Mike came into the Corner House to find all Phyl's tables taken. For a moment he stood, uncertain where to go, and Irene, spotting him, nudged the nearest Seater and jerked her head in his direction.

'Put that one on my table. I know him.'

Obligingly, the Seater bustled forward and showed Mike to a table in the corner, behind a huge potted palm. Even better, Irene thought gleefully. When Phyl came out of the kitchen, she wouldn't even notice him, and he'd be unable to attract her attention. Smiling, she crossed the floor, and stood in front of him.

'Good afternoon, Sir. How can I help you? Oh—' She gave a start. 'It's Mike, isn't it? Phyl's Mike? Why didn't they put you at one of her tables?'

'Already taken,' he said ruefully. 'You're Irene, aren't you?'

'That's right.' She wondered what Phyl had told him about her. Nothing flattering, that was for sure. With a conspiratorial smile, she said, 'I'm not Phyl's favourite person, I'm afraid.'

'Oh? Why's that?'

'Well, you know how it is.' Irene cast down her eyes, then lifted them to look at him through her lashes. 'There's always a bit of rivalry between girls for the best-looking boys, and, well, I'm afraid Phyl's a bit cross with me over taking her favourite chap away from her.'

'Oh?' Mike said again.

'Yes. Well, maybe I shouldn't be telling you this – but after all she never makes any secret of the fact that she's got plenty of boys. Safety in numbers, I suppose. But there was one that she liked specially – Richard, his name is. *Very* good-looking.' Irene rolled her eyes. 'Works at Coventry Street Corner House. Sort of chap any girl'd be pleased to have after her. Phyl used to go dancing with him a lot – when you couldn't make it to the pictures, I suppose. But last Saturday – well, she wasn't there and I was, and—' Irene shrugged again. 'You know what they say. All's fair in love and war. I'm afraid he was, well, smitten.'

'I see.' Mike's face was unreadable. Irene picked up the menu, so that if any of the supervisors were looking this way they'd think she was simply discussing the menu with her customer.

'Phyl's not very pleased with me,' she confided. 'She was hoping to make her number with him, you see – thought he was going to put a ring on her finger. Well, he'd be a catch for her, wouldn't he – supervisor already, he's obviously going to get good promotion. Yes, she really thought she'd got him hooked . . . Not that it stopped her having her fun with the other boys!' She gave him a you-know-what-I-mean look. 'Quite a little goer, our Phyl is.' Then, without giving him time to respond, she laid down the menu and said briskly, 'And what would you like to eat? Something special? We've got some really nice things on this afternoon.'

'Pot of tea,' Mike said in a flat tone, as if he were thinking of something quite different. 'And poached egg on toast. And make it snappy, would you? I'm in a bit of a hurry this afternoon.'

Irene walked briskly away, a tiny smile tugging at her lips and a fierce satisfaction in her heart. That's two down, she thought triumphantly, and Phyl Jennings will never know why. That'll teach her to call me a sharp-nosed, dirty-minded little tart!

'South Wales?' Annie Wood echoed. The afternoon had been full of surprises. First, Shirley and young Owen coming in with their eyes like stars, saying they were engaged – and without a word to Shirley's father or mother about whether they had permission! – and then this idea that she and Jack should up sticks and go to live on a farm in Wales. It took a bit of thinking about.

'Only if there really is a war,' Shirley said earnestly. 'You know what they said down the Office about Jack. Well, Owen's auntie lives on this farm near Merthyr Tydfil, and he's asked her and she says she'd be pleased to have you both there. You'd be safe from the bombing and everything. And think how Jack would love it – the chickens and ducks and all the baby animals.'

'And what about the big animals?' Annie said doubtfully. 'The bulls and cows and pigs. Pigs can be real nasty, so I've heard.'

'Auntie Mair don't keep no pigs,' Owen said. 'Well, just one for the house, like, but he's as soft and gentle as a lamb, comes in and lays by the fire and everything.' He saw Annie's face and realised this might not be the most encouraging thing to say. 'Well, perhaps he doesn't now,' he added hurriedly. 'That was just the one I saw – they have a new one every year, see, and they're only piglets really, not full-grown pigs at all.'

'Why's that?' Shirley asked with interest. 'What happens to them?'

'Never mind that,' her mother said, saving Owen from having to explain the fate of a piglet who was so much a part of the family that he lay on the hearthrug with the cats. 'It's very kind of your auntie, Owen, and kind of you, too, to think of asking her, but we can't say yes just like that. It wants thinking about, and I'll need to talk it over with Shirley's father. Just as you ought to have talked over this engagement you've sprung on us,' she added, trying to sound stern. In truth, she was delighted. Owen was a fine young man, even if he was Welsh, and knew how to pull his weight around the house. 'And I'm not all that sure that Jack would settle out in the country. He's used to the streets and houses and plenty of people about.'

'Oh, Mum, you know how he loves going to the park and watching the birds. Honestly, he really would like it.' Shirley sat with her hand in Owen's, a picture of radiant happiness. 'And me and Owen would come to see you as often as we could. I think it sounds like a bit of paradise!'

'And there's the cost to think about, too,' Annie said feebly. 'Train fares, and paying for our keep . . . It's not as simple as you might think, our Shirl.'

'Auntie Mair wouldn't want much keep,' Owen said. 'Most of their food comes off the farm, see, and there's always plenty to go round. Butter and milk from the cows, eggs from the hens, pork—' He stopped abruptly, not wanting to bring up the subject of the piglet again. 'Anyway, she says if you and Jack could give a hand around the place, they wouldn't ask anything much at all. She and Uncle Dafydd think that if there's a war all the young men will be wanted, see, either in the Army or down the mines, so they'd be pushed to keep the work done on the farm.'

'Work on the farm!' Annie exclaimed. 'Oh, Shirl, I don't know about that. I don't, really. I mean, I don't know nothing about animals and that. I couldn't milk a cow to save me life.

300

And our Jack, well, you couldn't expect him to do much. I've seen pictures of men on farms – using great big scythes, or ploughing with those huge horses. He couldn't do that. He'd cut his legs off the first minute with a scythe, and if you put him near those big carthorses he'd get bitten or trodden on. Seems to me it'd be more dangerous there than in London!'

'Oh, Mum, you're just making excuses. Jack loves horses – look how he always feeds the baker's horse, and the coalman's, and all the rest. He's good with all animals, he's so gentle. And there's lots he could do, isn't there, Owen? Feeding hens, collecting eggs, all that sort of thing. He'd have a lovely time, and be a help, too.'

'He would,' Owen nodded. 'And so could you, Mrs Wood. There's plenty to do around the place, but Auntie Mair wouldn't want you to be a servant. It's all hands to the pump at Nant-ddu Farm.'

'Nant Thee?' Annie shook her head. 'That's another thing – we can't speak Welsh. I couldn't even pronounce all those names, and what would we do if they didn't understand us? I'm too old to learn a new language and Jack would never master it.'

'It's all right,' Owen said, laughing. 'You won't have to speak Welsh, and everyone will understand you. Well, almost everyone,' he added thoughtfully. 'There's a few old farmers out in the mountains who don't bother with English, but I don't suppose you'll ever come across them.' He gave Annie a look of understanding. 'Look, you just think about it, that's all you have to do, see. It's only if there's a war anyway. I remember my mam, she was just the same when we came to London, but she settled in fine. People are people wherever you go.'

'That's true enough,' Annie agreed. She sighed and looked out of the window into the street. Half a dozen children were playing What's the Time, Mr Wolf? and a few little girls were leaping about on chalked hopscotch squares. 'And like I said, it's really kind of you and your auntie to offer. It's just that this is what I've been used to all my life. I don't know what it would be like, living on the side of a mountain with only fields to look out at, and animals. Here, I can go out of the door any time of day and have a natter with someone I know. I can't help feeling it'd be lonely down there in Wales.'

'But better than being blown to pieces by a German bomb,' Shirley pointed out. 'And better for Jack than being frightened to death by aeroplanes and noise.'

'Yes. I know.' Annie sighed again. 'Oh, Shirl, what's the world coming to? Why do we all have to be dragged into a horrible war? We ought to be able to live the way we always have, just ordinary – bringing up our families, having a bit of a party now and then, just *ordinary*. I don't know why we've got to start thinking about bombs and being evacuated, and rationing and all that. I don't, really.'

Neither did Shirley, nor Owen. They sat silently together, trying to look into a future that none of them could really imagine. A future that should have been shining and happy, and instead was as murky as a London fog.

Chapter Twenty

Mike left a message for Phyl that afternoon, saying that he wouldn't be able to make it to the pictures that evening. Irene gave the message, hiding her glee behind a mask of concern. Phyl listened in dismay.

'Did he say why?'

Irene shook her head. Mike had told her his mother was poorly and he had to go home to be there while his dad went on night shift, but she didn't bother to repeat that. 'Just said he had something else to do,' she said, leaving the impression that the 'something else' was in fact 'something better'. 'Anyway,' she continued offhandedly, not wanting to arouse Phyl's suspicions by being too friendly, 'I've got better things to do than run errands for you, Phyl Jennings.' And she walked off, leaving Phyl feeling let down and disappointed.

'Well, come to the dance with me and Owen instead,' Shirley suggested when she heard, and Phyl thought she might as well. There were plenty of boys to dance with at Sudbury and it would while away the evening. Jo would be out with Nick and to sit at home on a Saturday evening was unthinkable. She went back to Elmbury Street and put on her best frock, just to show that she didn't care.

All the same, she was hurt by Mike's apparent rudeness. He'd never treated her like that before – sitting at a different table, leaving a vague message (and with Irene Bond, of all people!) and not even suggesting another date. Phyl wasn't to know, of course, that he'd asked Irene to tell her he'd be at the bandstand in Hyde Park on Sunday afternoon, or that if his mum was still poorly next week he might not be able to come to the Corner House at all. The impression she was left with was that he had cooled off – perhaps even found another girl – and she knew that the only thing to do was go out and try her best to enjoy herself. Sitting at home, brooding, wasn't going to do any good at all.

She arrived at the dance looking her best. Her yellow frock showed up the brightness of her eyes and set off her dark brown, curly hair. She put on fresh lipstick in the ladies' cloakroom and marched out into the dance hall, her chin up, looking for Shirley and Owen.

The first person she saw was Richard Godwin, and he was dancing with Irene.

Phyl sat down and watched them. Richard was holding Irene very close and she was resting her head on his shoulder as they waltzed to a Victor Silvester theme. You couldn't deny it, they danced well together, their steps in perfect unison. Almost as if they'd been doing it for years . . .

Phyl felt a sudden quiver of misgiving. There was nothing wrong with Richard dancing with other girls, and after all he hadn't known Phyl was coming this evening. But there was something in the way he was holding Irene, and something in the triumphant angle of her head . . . and there was *definitely* something in the way her eyes flashed when they whirled close by the chairs and she caught sight of Phyl, sitting alone in her yellow frock.

Phyl watched as she murmured something in Richard's ear and he laughed down at her. Had Irene said something about Phyl that amused him? Surely – *surely* – they couldn't have been talking about her behind her back? And how was it they seemed to know each other so well? What had been going on these past few weeks?

Shirley and Owen appeared beside her and sat down. Shirley was looking cool and pretty in a blue dress sprinkled with white daisies, and white shoes. She followed the direction of Phyl's gaze.

'Just look at Lady Muck! Doesn't she think she's someone?

Here, isn't that that chap from Coventry Street you used to dance with? Richard someone?'

'Richard Godwin,' Phyl answered, her eyes still on the dancers. 'That's right. Pally, aren't they?'

Shirley gave her friend a quick glance. 'A bit more than that, I'd say. Did it cool off between the two of you, then?'

'It wasn't ever all that warm really,' Phyl replied, uncomfortably recalling Richard's champagne kisses. 'You know me, I don't let any of them get too serious.'

'That's the best way,' Shirley agreed. 'Until the right one comes along, anyway.' Her eyes strayed to her left hand.

Phyl looked down and saw the tiny diamond winking up at her. 'Oh, Shirley! I'm a selfish pig – I haven't even said congratulations. I didn't know till yesterday and there didn't seem to be a proper chance. I'm ever so pleased.' She smiled at Owen. 'You mind you look after her, or you'll have all Marble Arch Corner House on your tail!'

'Oh, I'll look after her all right,' he said, putting his arm round Shirley's waist and giving her a squeeze. 'I know when I'm on to a good thing!'

Phyl looked at their happy faces and felt suddenly lonely. All at once, her life seemed empty and uncertain. Only a week or two ago she'd been dancing through the days, enjoying her work as much as she enjoyed her leisure, with three or four regular boys to go about with and others to pick and choose from should she feel like a change. None of them had been 'serious' and they'd all known there were others – she'd never led any of them to think he was her only boy. But then she'd sat with Mike at the picture palace and watched that awful *Pathe Pictorial*, and since then everything had seemed different. She'd been much more aware of her feelings for him. Mike *was* special – just how special she still wasn't sure, but she knew she didn't want to lose him. Yet today he'd come into the Corner House and sat at a different table, leaving her a message that was so casual it was almost rude, and now when she came to the dance to try to forget that, here was Richard dancing with Irene Bond as if they'd been welded . . .

Well, she couldn't let it go that easy. Probably when the dance finished he would come over to say hullo and book a dance with her. She watched as the music ended, and saw him escort Irene back to her chair on the other side of the room. But instead of leaving her there, he sat down beside her and Phyl saw him slip his arm around her waist.

To her relief, another boy she knew came and asked her for the next dance, looking surprised and gratified at Phyl's response. He wasn't a bad dancer, but somehow they couldn't get their steps in tune and he trod on Phyl's toes several times. Blushing furiously, he apologised but Phyl shook her head.

'My fault,' she said. 'I'm not really in a dancing mood tonight. Ought to have stayed home and washed my hair, I think!' She spoke absently, her eyes moving past him to search for Richard and Irene. They were at the far end, doing some really complicated steps, and Phyl felt a stab of jealousy. Dancing was one of her main delights, and a good partner who could try out all the latest steps was what she came for. Until now, Richard and she had fitted together like a dream.

'Maybe we'd better go and sit down,' the boy offered miserably, and Phyl returned her attention to him, feeling suddenly guilty at having committed such a breach of manners. Really, he wasn't bad at all, and all the mistakes were her fault for not paying attention. She shook her head again.

'No. I'd like to go on dancing. Look, let's go down to that corner where there's a bit more room and try out a different turn. I learnt it last week. What you do is . . .' They twirled down the room, more confidently now that Phyl was taking more care, and secured a space for themselves, far away from Richard and Irene. By the time the music stopped again they were laughing.

'There! It's easy really.' Phyl let the boy take her back to her chair and smiled at him. 'Let's have another dance later on. I've got someone to see now.'

'All right.' He looked half disappointed and half pleased. Phyl watched him go, feeling mildly sorry for him – he was a nice chap and another time she might have considered adding him to what Jo called her 'string', but tonight she was more concerned with other matters. She waited until she saw Irene go to the ladies' and then made directly for Richard.

'Hullo, Richard.'

He turned quickly and she saw his face colour. 'Phyl! I didn't know you were coming tonight.'

'Nor did I,' she said, smiling at him. 'It was a last-minute decision. Aren't you going to ask me to dance?'

He looked embarrassed. 'Well – the thing is – you see, Phyl, I didn't know you'd be here and I – I've—'

'You've got someone else.' She went on smiling. 'Well, that's all right. She won't mind me dancing one or two with you, I'm sure.'

'Oh, but I'm afraid she will.' Irene was beside them, her hand laid possessively on Richard's sleeve. 'She'll mind a lot, Phyl. You see, Richard's asked me specially to promise him all my dances, and if you take him away that'll mean I'll have to sit out, won't it? And that would be rude.'

'It doesn't hurt to sit out now and then,' Phyl said, looking at Irene's red fingernails against the dark blue of Richard's blazer. 'I've done it.'

'Well, it doesn't suit *me* to sit out. Anyway, you don't even know as Richard *wants* to dance with you.' Irene moved closer to him. 'From what he's told me, he's had just about enough of you following him about.'

'Irene!' Richard protested. 'I never said—'

'Didn't you, Dickie?' She turned her face up to his. 'Didn't you say to me that Phyl Jennings was all right in her way, but a chap needs to be able to breathe now and then? Or did I make a mistake?'

'I'm sure I—' Richard began, but it was too late. Phyl, scarlet to the roots of her hair, spoke over him, her voice brittle and angry.

'It's all right, Richard. You don't have to say anything. I'm not a fool – I can see the writing on the wall. I won't *follow you about* any more.' She turned and stalked away across the floor, ignoring the dancers who were crowding on for the

307

next foxtrot. The boy she had danced with earlier, thinking that she was approaching him, got up with an eager smile but she walked straight past, leaving him baffled and disappointed. Shirley and Owen, just about to dance themselves, caught her as she picked up her bag.

'What's the matter? What's happened?'

Phyl gave them a bright-eyed glance. 'Nothing. I'm just going home, that's all. I shouldn't have come tonight. I should have stayed at home with a good book. I'd have had more fun.'

'But, Phyl—' Shirley began.

'Ask Lady Muck, if you want to know any more,' Phyl said, jerking her head towards Irene and Richard, now moving smoothly into the dance. 'Ask her what she's been saying about me. Not that she'll tell you, not in a million years – the nasty, spiteful little toad! *Dickie!* ' she added bitterly. 'He told me he *hated* being called Dickie!'

She shook them off and marched out of the hall. It was so early there were still people arriving, but Phyl took no notice of them. She collected her coat and went to catch the train back to London.

It was only as she was sitting there in the empty carriage that it occurred to her to wonder whether Irene had been talking to Mike as well, and if that was why he'd left the Corner House without bothering to leave her a proper message.

Irene saw Phyl leave and smiled to herself. She smiled at Richard as well, and made no objection when he held her more tightly. They danced the tango to 'Jealousy', with more abandon than Irene had ever shown before, and followed it with 'I'll See You In My Dreams'. Then Richard took her back to her seat and asked if she'd like an ice.

Irene nodded. 'That was a lovely dance, Richard,' she said when he'd fetched them both ice creams. 'I think that last tune they played is ever so pretty, don't you?'

'It used to be Sydney Lipton's signature tune,' he said. 'I heard him play once.'

Irene stared at him. 'In real life, you mean? Isn't he at one of the posh hotels?'

'The Grosvenor House,' Richard nodded. In fact, he had only heard Sydney Lipton on the wireless, as had everyone else in the room, but the look of adulation on Irene's face wasn't something he was prepared to forgo easily. 'I'll take you there one day, if you like,' he offered carelessly.

Irene gazed at him. The Grosvenor House Hotel! None of the other Nippies had ever been there, or were ever likely to. Irene Bond, she told herself gleefully, you're on your way up.

They danced again, to another Sydney Lipton favourite, 'There's a Rainbow Round My Shoulder' and then to a Joe Loss number, 'A-Tisket, A-Tasket'.

'I suppose you've been to the Astoria to hear him as well,' Irene said provocatively as Richard whirled her to a stop, and rolled her eyes when he nodded. 'And did you see Vera Lynn, too? What did you think of her?'

'She's all right,' he said offhandedly. 'Quite pretty, really. Not as pretty as you, though.' He bent and nuzzled her neck. 'What d'you say we slip off early?' he whispered. 'I'll come back with you in the taxi and we'll have time to say a proper goodnight.'

Irene squealed. 'Richard Godwin! I don't know what you're suggesting! I'll have you know I'm a respectable girl.'

'I never thought you were anything else,' he declared. 'I wouldn't have suggested it if you weren't. I'm not interested in tarts.'

'You went out quite a bit with Phyl Jennings,' Irene suggested slyly.

Richard gave her an odd look. They both knew that Phyl was as respectable as any mother would want, but neither was quite sure what the other knew. After a minute or two, he shrugged and said, 'Well, that's all in the past, isn't it? It's you I'm going out with now. So what d'you say? Shall we slip off now, before they play the National Anthem, and have the train to ourselves?'

Irene pretended to consider. 'Well, I really wanted to do the last waltz . . .' she said slowly, and then looked up at him

309

with a quick, sudden smile. 'Oh, all right. Let's do that. It'll be nice to have a bit of room in the train and not be pressed up against all those sweaty bodies anyway.'

'There's only one body I'd like to be pressed up against,' he murmured daringly, making her squeal again, 'and that's not sweaty at all. In fact, it's wearing some very nice scent.'

'You're a cheeky monkey, Richard Godwin,' Irene told him severely, 'and I'm not at all sure I ought to be going anywhere with you. Specially not where it's all dark, and there's no one else about. Why, I don't know *what* you might get up to!'

'Neither do I,' he said with his engaging grin, 'but I never stop hoping.'

The train was half-empty, as they'd expected, but there were no empty compartments and eventually they found themselves sharing with another young couple, who made no bones about behaving as if they were entirely on their own. Irene glanced at their entwined bodies with disapproval, and drew away when Richard made to slip his arm around her waist.

'Dickie! Not in public.'

'I wouldn't call this in public,' he murmured, sliding his hand behind her waist and squeezing her against him. 'Those two wouldn't notice if the carriage caught fire – and it might do, the way they're carrying on.' He looked over at the two squirming bodies. 'Come on, Irene, don't be stand-offish. Give us a kiss.'

Irene held back for a moment longer, then gave way. She lifted her face and let him kiss her lips. It wasn't the first time she'd been kissed, but none of the other boys had even set up so much as a tingle. And neither, she realised with disappointment, did Richard.

'Come on, Irene,' he muttered again, pulling her closer. 'Give us a proper kiss. Or an improper one,' he added wickedly. His lips pressed against hers, his mouth half-open. She could feel the wetness of his tongue, and a shudder ran through her. Unable to help herself, she pulled away.

Richard stared at her. 'What's the matter?'

'I don't know. I don't want to do that – not here.' She glanced towards the corner again. It was doubtful whether the other two were even aware of their presence. 'They're putting me off.'

Richard sighed and sat back. He had gone a little pale and there was a tautness about his lips. He kept his arm around Irene's waist, his fingers digging in a little.

'Let's hope there's no one else in the taxi, then,' he said coolly.

Irene gave him a doubtful glance, and decided to take his remark as a joke. She giggled uncertainly. 'You're a one, you are, Dickie Godwin. Just because Phyl Jennings let you paw all over her—'

Richard's face stiffened. 'I'd rather not talk about Phyl Jennings, if you don't mind. And I didn't *paw all over her.*' He paused, then added, 'And as a matter of fact, I'd just as soon you didn't keep calling me Dickie. I prefer to be called Richard.'

Hoity-toity! Irene thought, but she said nothing. It was obvious he was annoyed, and she didn't want to make matters worse. Richard Godwin was too good a catch to let slip through her fingers. I'd better let him have a few kisses in the taxi, she told herself, curbing an involuntary shiver of distaste. It's what they all want after all, and it won't kill me. You have to do a lot worse than that when you get married.

Irene's experience of men and marriage was limited to the relationship between her father and her mother. Henry Bond was a cold, distant man whose life revolved around the office where he worked in Whitehall. He seldom talked about his work, reproving anyone who enquired with the information that it was 'government service', but occasionally he made categorical pronouncements – such as the fact that there would be no war – which his family, thinking him to be in the confidence of all Parliament, believed. In fact, he was quite a lowly civil servant and privy to almost nothing. It was only in his own home that he wielded any power and, to a lesser extent, at the bowling club where he was treasurer.

Henry took even less interest in Irene than he did in his

311

wife, Sylvia. The first ten years of Irene's life had been spent trying to win his approval, if not his love. She thought she had managed it, first with her ballet and music lessons, then by passing the Scholarship to the local grammar school, but only a month or two later her brother Bobbie had been born, and she knew that she would never, now, count for anything in her father's eyes.

Her mother was almost equally relegated to a back shelf. She had never been more than a housekeeper and breeder for her husband, and had more or less failed in both, first by being in constant low health, suffering several miscarriages and unable to work about the house so that a 'daily' had to be employed, and then by producing a daughter. Irene had been her only comfort, indiscriminately spoiled when her husband wasn't looking, but when Bobbie arrived she was so thankful to have borne a son at last that she transferred all her affection to him and Irene found herself not only left out in the cold but expected to dance attendance on this new male interloper.

What went on behind her parents' bedroom door Irene didn't know, and didn't want to know. Once, passing it on her way to the lavatory at night, she had heard strange noises coming from within. A peculiar, high-pitched giggle that must have been her mother's, and the same unfamiliar voice begging for something or someone to 'stop, please stop' – and then a guttural groaning noise that sounded as if it were her father in deep distress, even pain. Irene had stood frozen and then scurried back to bed, where she had lain for the rest of the night, holding herself so that she wouldn't wet the bed, convinced that when morning came she would find that one of her parents, if not both, were dead, murdered. But to her amazement, both had seemed just as normal, other than that her mother looked more tired than usual and her father grimly satisfied, and when she had heard those noises again – as she did, on occasion – she had merely pulled the bedclothes over her head and closed her eyes tightly, her hand straying between her legs.

If she had thought about it now, she would have known

what had been happening. But Irene didn't want to think about it. She hadn't heard the noises for a long time now and she pushed away the memory with the same shiver of distaste as when Richard had kissed her. She didn't want to know about *all that*. It might be necessary when she was married – though no more often than she could help – but until then no man was going to get past her defences.

A few kisses, though, would keep Richard happy while she decided whether he was the one she wanted to marry. Meanwhile, she'd better take that taut, annoyed look away from his face. She didn't want him shoving her in a taxi and sending her home on her own – not after the evening had begun so promisingly.

Irene thought about Phyl again. The look on her face when she'd come into the dance-hall and spotted them! Irene had hardly known where to put herself for glee. On top of her disappointment over Mike that afternoon, seeing Irene with Richard must have really been one in the eye. Served her right, too, Irene thought maliciously, swaggering about making up to all the boys. Thought she was the cat's whiskers! Well, she'd got another think coming now. Irene hadn't missed seeing her slip away early on her own.

The thought of Phyl drove away her distaste for Richard's kisses and she snuggled up to him, feeling warm and relaxed. She laid her head on his shoulder and peeped up through her lashes.

'I'm sorry, Richard,' she whispered beguilingly. 'It's just, well, kissing's a private sort of thing to me. It's too – too *precious* for other people to see. Or am I just being a silly little girl?'

He glanced down at her. She was looking especially winsome, pressing her lips together in a little pout so that her dimples showed. Maybe she could be fun after all. He'd begun to wonder if she wasn't a bit of a tease, but if she was she was certainly laying it on thick now, and she'd soon find out what happened to girls who did that and then tried to back off.

'You, a silly little girl?' he said lightly. 'Perish the thought!

And just to prove it, give us a kiss now, just to be going on with. Those two are never going to notice.'

Irene lifted her face and closed her eyes. She felt Richard's open mouth on hers and once again the little shudder ran through her. But she knew how to deal with it now. Think of Phyl Jennings, she told herself firmly. Think of Phyl Jennings, going home on her own with nobody to kiss. And, to her delight and Richard's pleasurable surprise, a tingle ran through her and she found herself returning his kiss. So it was as easy as that!

On Sunday afternoon, Irene stayed at home to finish making herself a new dance frock. Her father had gone to the bowling club and Bobbie was at Sunday school, so for once she had her mother to herself. They sat sewing in the front room, Irene stitching on the Singer treadle machine and Sylvia embroidering a tablecloth.

'You come home a bit late last night,' Sylvia observed. 'Was that a taxi I heard turn the corner at nearly midnight?'

'Course it was. I wouldn't come home that late any other way, would I?'

'Did a young man bring you home, then?' Sylvia asked, carefully casual.

'Yes, as a matter of fact. Floor supervisor, he is, name of Richard Godwin. Good job, that is, and he's young for it. Manager he'll be before long if I'm any judge.'

'Sounds a nice, suitable young man,' Sylvia said, having heard nothing at all about him. 'All the same, you be careful, our Irene. You know what men are, there's not much difference between any of 'em when it comes down to it.'

'It's all right. Mum,' Irene said easily. 'Richard's a decent bloke. He won't try nothing on, and if he did I'd soon smack his face for him.'

They went on sewing, each looking ahead to a future that they believed would be exactly as they willed it. A husband with a bit of class and a good job, who wouldn't expect too much in the way of 'rights', and a nice little house with an indoor lavvy and proper bathroom. Once that was all secure,

Irene could leave her job and spend her days as she pleased. All she had to do was make sure Richard was the right one and then ensnare him. Shouldn't be too difficult.

Irene thought of Phyl again, and felt the same tingle in her stomach that she had felt last night, and which had helped so much when Richard kissed her.

At Shirley Wood's house, Owen played Snakes and Ladders with Jack while Shirley and her mother got tea ready. Donald was away again and Alf was snoring in his chair, the *Sunday Express* spread over his face. Owen glanced up and caught sight of the headline. As usual, it was full of speculation about the war and he felt a sinking in his heart. I don't want to go away to war, he thought. Shirley's brother Donald was already back at camp and they didn't know where. It was as if it had already begun.

He looked at Jack's round face, furrowed with concentration as he shook the dice in its little cup until Owen began to wonder if he would knock off all the spots. It's time we thought about making proper arrangements for him and Shirley's mum, he thought. It could happen all of a sudden, and it'd be too late then.

Etty sat with all the female members of the Pratt family, feverishly sewing on pearl buttons. When this is over, she promised herself, I'll never touch another pearl button in my whole life. But she'd have to, of course. If she married Jim, she'd have his costume to look after, and maybe even one of her own. And – a bit later – some smaller ones to make for their own little princes and princesses . . .

A giggle rose like a bubble to her lips. She, Etty Brown, who didn't even know who her own mum and dad were, thinking of her own kiddies being princes and princesses! She looked across at Maggie and they grinned at each other.

Phyl was sitting at home, pretending to read. She hadn't turned a page for half an hour. Her mind was filled with pictures of Richard Godwin dancing with Irene – and, worse than that, of Mike sitting at Irene's table and leaving without a word to her. Her eyes kept filling with tears, and she had to brush them away. She threw the book away and flung herself down on her bed, burying her face in the pillow.

Mike waited for an hour at the bandstand in Hyde Park, and then he had to go home. His cousin had come to sit with Mum while he went to meet Phyl, but he'd promised to be back by four. He'd hoped to be taking Phyl with him. But suddenly it seemed as if she wasn't interested any more.

Chapter Twenty-One

Everybody now accepted that there would almost certainly be war.

'Nothing can stop it now,' Bill Mason said gloomily. 'That man's bent on taking over Europe. Something's got to be done about it, and there's nothing else he'll understand.'

Carrie poured him a cup of tea. She hardly knew what to say. All during their marriage the shadow of Bill's experiences in the Great War of 1914–18 had lain across their happiness, waking him at night with terrible dreams, sickening him when he thought of the whole dreadful business happening again. He'd tried to believe it never would, refused even to entertain the possibility – but now, like the rest of the nation, he was having to face up to it.

'It's our boys I'm worried about,' he said, ladling in sugar and stirring as if his life depended on it. 'Our Freddy and young Eric, and your May's nippers. I don't want to see what I saw last time, Carrie, I don't want to see it happening to our boys, I just don't.'

'But surely they're too young,' Carrie said in dismay. 'Our Eric's not turned seventeen yet, and he's got that weak chest, you know how easy he catches cold. And Ronnie's only a few months older.' She fell silent, thinking of the two older boys – Freddy at twenty-two and Norman a year older, were certainly old enough to be conscripted. 'You don't really think they'll call them up, do you?' she asked tremulously. 'I mean, there's plenty of young chaps joined up this past year, and if it's all going to be over by Christmas . . .'

'That's what they said last time,' Bill said heavily. 'No, Carrie, we got to face it. They haven't been issuing all them gas masks and Anderson shelters for nothing. And I don't reckon as they'll take a few colds as an excuse. They're getting ready for a long do, and there's no use us thinking otherwise.'

'Bill, I can't bear to think of it,' she said, her voice trembling. 'Our Freddy and Eric going off to foreign countries and having to fight in trenches dug in the ground . . . It's not what we brought them up for. We wanted them to live ordinary lives, like us, with jobs that'd bring home a wage they could raise their own families on. Isn't that what life's supposed to be, Bill? Isn't it?'

'It's what I reckon it ought to be,' he said, 'but when someone like that bloke Hitler comes along, wanting to take over everything, we all has to stand up on our hind legs against him. It's like kids in a playground, see, all quite happy till the school bully comes and smashes up their game. You can't let him get away with it.'

'It's awful,' she said, and then thought of something else. 'There's our Jo, too, and her Nick – suppose he's called up? She'll break her heart if anything happens to him.'

'I know. But there's nothing we can do about any of that, Carrie.' He hesitated. 'What we've got to think about is our Alice and that ruddy cat of hers.'

'I know. She's going to have to go. There's quite a few already gone, you know – people who've got relations in the country mostly. Mrs Harper from number seventeen, she went to Somerset last week, and that whole family from up the corner have gone to Yorkshire, to her sister's.' She got up and opened the bureau that Bill had made, and fished out a bit of paper. 'This is the registration form. We've got to fill it in and give it back so they know Alice is registered for evacuation.' She looked at it unhappily. 'She's not going to be able to take Robbie, you know.'

'Well, of course she isn't! We all know that. I just wish we

318

could get her to see it.' Bill sighed. 'I'm beginning to wish I'd never brought that cat home. She don't think of nothing else.'

'She loves him. She always wanted a ginger kitten, and when we saw her face that Christmas morning – well, you'd not deny your child a thing like that, would you?'

'No, I wouldn't do that. But she's got to see sense over leaving him behind. It's not as if he won't have a good home here after all. What does she think we're going to do to him?'

Carrie gave him a wry look. 'I suppose she thinks if it's not safe for her, it's not safe for him either. And you know they're telling people to get their pets destroyed if they've got nowhere to leave them? Someone at school told her that the other day and she came home crying her eyes out. I mean, we'd never let that happen to Robbie, but she can't believe a policeman won't come one day and take him away.'

'That's daft! They'll have more to worry about than taking cats away. Anyway, why should they? It's only if people are going off and got no one to leave them with.'

'It's that boy at school who tells her things. I keep telling her to take no notice, but there you are, they always take more notice of other children.'

'Well, you tell her cats will have important war work to do,' Bill said. 'Same as in the dockyard. They'll be wanted to keep down rats and mice, and we needs Robbie here to look after *us*. There's plenty of cats out in the country to see to their vermin.'

Evacuation was the subject of conversation in the Woods' household, too. Owen had come round to tell Annie that his aunt was waiting to receive her visitors. 'She's got bedrooms ready for you, see, but the local billeting officer's been round and told her if she can't say for certain you're coming she'll have to take in school evacuees. They're saying the children will be going pretty soon. Things are boiling up over there, see.'

Everyone knew that 'over there' meant in Germany. Hitler was threatening to march into Poland, and if he did that war was inevitable. Everyone was hanging on to a slender thread of possibility that he'd change his mind, but the thread was getting thinner and more frail with each passing day.

Annie gazed at him and then looked helplessly towards her husband. 'I don't know what to do for the best . . .'

Alf Wood rubbed his hand over his face. 'It's up to you, love. You've got our Jack to think of, as well as yourself—'

'Oh, it don't matter about me!' Annie made an impatient gesture. 'It's Jack that's important. I went down the Office again today and they said what we could do is send our Jack along with others what're handicapped, and he'd go to a sort of Home. But he'd be frightened to death amongst a lot of strangers. He's used to being at home with his mum and dad.'

'Well, then, it looks like you've got to take up Owen's auntie's kind offer and go to Wales, don't it?'

'But what about you? You're my husband – I can't go off like I'm going on holiday for goodness knows how long. You need someone to look after you, see to your meals and your washing and that. Those things are my job, I can't just leave you to manage by yourself.'

'I'll be here, Mum,' Shirley said. 'I can look after Dad.'

Annie looked at her. 'How can you? You've got your own job to do. Look at the hours you work up at that Corner House, look how tired you get sometimes. Why, you've been so tired sometimes your dad's had to practically carry you home from the Underground. How can you turn round and do his washing and dinners and all that as well?'

'We're all going to have to make a bit more effort, Mum, one way or another. Looking after Dad won't be half as bad as what some people are going to have to do. I'll manage.'

Owen had been listening quietly from his chair in the corner. Now he spoke up, rather diffidently, as if none of it was really any of his business.

'Auntie Mair says she really will have to know soon, Mrs Wood. They're making lists, see, of all the people in the village who've got rooms. Once they've told you you've got to take evacuees, you can't alter it – at least, I don't think you can.'

Annie sighed and stared at her hands, twisting themselves

320

together in her lap. From somewhere in the back of the house they could hear the strains of Jack's mouth-organ. He was playing 'There'll Always Be An England'. Shirley thought how quiet the house was going to seem if he went away, and felt unexpected tears in her eyes. She reached out and touched her mother's twining fingers.

'Look, Mum, why don't you just try it for a bit? Take Jack and see how you think you'll like it. You don't have to stay – if you decide to come home, Owen's auntie can just tell the billeting people she's got a room after all. Just think of it as if you're going away for a bit of a holiday.'

'A *holiday*?' Annie said, with a sharp-edged laugh. 'Me and your dad have never had a holiday in our lives. It seems a funny way to start.'

Shirley said nothing. She kept her hand over her mother's, trying to pass back to her some of the warmth that she'd received all through her life. She knew just how torn Annie was feeling, between Jack on the one hand and herself and her father on the other. She knew, too, that her mother was probably feeling nervous at the thought of going all the way to Wales on her own, to live with strangers in a completely strange place. Annie had spoken the truth when she'd said she'd never had a holiday. The furthest she had been was to Brighton for a day at the seaside, and a couple of years ago to Portsmouth so that Jack could see the ships of the Royal Navy in the Review of the Fleet at Spithead. The idea of going to Wales, not just to stay for a few days but to live, perhaps for months, must be terrifying.

'Tell you what,' Owen said suddenly, 'why don't me and Shirley come with you? We're both allowed some holiday – we were thinking of having a few days out, weren't we, *cariad*? – but we could come on the train to Wales and see you and Jack settled in, like. It might make it easier, and I can take Shirley to meet some more of the family.'

Annie looked up, her eyes brighter. 'Would you really, Owen? Oh, that would be a real help. It's not that I'm scared of going all that way by myself, mind, it's just that – well, with

Jack and everything, it'd be ever so much easier.' She looked towards her husband again. 'What d'you think, Alf?'

Alf Wood sighed and rubbed his face again, his hand moving slowly as if he wanted to hide his expression. His voice was heavy and tired. 'I reckon you ought to think about it, love. Tell the truth, I don't want you to go at all, and that's the top and bottom of it, but it's like our Shirl says, we've all got to make a bit more effort. And I'll sleep easier knowing you and our Jack are safe. I just wish our Shirl could go, too.'

'Well, I can't,' Shirley said quickly, before the idea could take root. 'You know I've got my job, and I want to be here for you anyway. And I don't want to leave Owen either,' she added, turning to him and tucking her hand in his. 'As long as he can be in London, that's where I want to be, too.'

As long as he's in London . . . The words hung in the air. None of the young men could be certain of their future. All of those over eighteen were likely to be called up sooner or later, and some – like Mike and Tom and Charlie – had already taken the King's shilling. It wouldn't be long before they were all in the Forces.

'I'll go,' Annie said with sudden decision. 'I'll go down the station first thing tomorrow and find out about train times and all that, and we'll go as soon as you and Owen can get your holidays arranged. You write to your auntie, Owen, and ask her if that's all right, and tell her I'll let her know when we'll be arriving. And in that case, I'd better get a few jobs done – there's a huge pile of socks wants darning, and those back windows have got to be washed and I'll get some more whitening for the step – you'll have to keep that done nice, our Shirl – and there's that cupboard under the stairs wants clearing out, I bet it's full of spiders. Oh, and you'll have to get that garden fence mended, Alf, there's a hole big enough for Mrs Jenkins's dog to get through, he'll be all over your tomatoes. And—'

'Hang on,' Alf protested. 'That fence has bin waiting three weeks now. I don't see why it's got to be done before you goes away. And it won't matter if the windows aren't clean or the step not white if we've got bombs dropping on us.'

322

'I'll have no one saying I left my house in a mess,' Annie said sternly. 'And that's enough about bombs. I won't be able to sleep easy in my bed, even if it is halfway up a mountain, if I'm thinking of you and our Shirl being bombed . . .'

Her voice shook suddenly and she reached out both her hands. 'Oh, Alf – Alf. I can't bear to think of it – us all those hundreds of miles away and you here having to fetch for yourselves, and *bombs* . . . Tell me it's not going to happen. Tell me it isn't true . . .'

Alf leant over and gathered her into his arms. She rested against him, sobbing, while Shirley looked on, the tears rolling down her own cheeks. Owen pulled her close and held his palm against her wet face. Dread swept over them all; they sat without speaking as Annie fought to control her sobs. And then, into the silence, there came from the back garden the soft, sweet strains of Jack's mouth-organ.

Annie lifted her head and listened. 'That's a new tune,' she whispered. 'He's never played that one before.' She waited, letting the music drift in as she concentrated on the tune. 'What is it?'

Owen looked at her and smiled. 'I know what it is, Mrs Wood. It's "Land of My Fathers". I was singing it last time I was here, and he's remembered it, see. Why, it's practically the Welsh national anthem, that is.'

' "Land of My Fathers",' Annie whispered. 'Well, that settles it, then, don't it? Our Jack wants to go to Wales – so to Wales we shall go!'

Tommy came into Maggie's house just as she and her mother had started making some alterations to the wedding dress Maggie was borrowing from another Pearly girl. It was made of ivory satin and covered with tiny pearl buttons, and whenever Maggie looked at it she remembered Irene's spiteful comments. She was right, all the same, Maggie thought ruefully as she threaded her needle. I'm not really entitled to wear white. So – she grinned suddenly – it's just as well this one's cream, isn't it?

'What are you laughing at, our Mag?' her mother asked,

but before Maggie could answer the front door opened and Tommy's voice called out. Panic-stricken, the women gathered up the yards of satin and Maggie made for the stairs.

'Don't you come in here, Tommy Wheeler, I'm not respectable!'

'In that case, I'm coming in at once,' he retorted, but he gave her a minute or so for appearances' sake before pushing open the door to the back room. Maggie was out of sight by then and when she came back he was talking to her grandmother, sitting as usual in her corner.

'I remember the lasht lot,' the old woman was saying through her gums. She always took out her teeth after tea, when there was no more chewing to do. 'My Sham was in that. Come 'ome wounded, he did, bullet-'oles all over him, they never thought he'd live. But us Pratts is tough. We got through that and we'll get through this.'

Tommy had never heard her make such a long speech before, or such an optimistic one. He looked at the old woman, scowling up at him with her lips crimped together like a Cornish pasty, and thought it was a pity Mr Chamberlain hadn't had her with him the day he'd gone and got that piece of paper signed at Munich. Hitler would have thought twice about invading Poland, or anywhere else, if he'd met Ada Pratt.

'She ought to be our secret weapon,' he told Maggie later on, as they sat cuddling in the front room. 'One look at her and the German army would turn and run. Specially after tea when she's got her teeth out.'

'We could just send her teeth,' Maggie suggested. 'I've been frightened myself once or twice, coming across them unexpected. She don't care where she leaves them – it's like a horrible grin, leering at you from a shelf or the corner of the sideboard. Our Queenie used to be scared stiff of them.'

'I don't blame her.' Tommy was quiet for a few minutes, then said, 'Maggie, there's something I want to ask you. Me and Charlie are a bit worried about Mike – he's proper down in the dumps just lately. Have he and Phyl had a bust-up?'

After all their talk about joining the RAF, Mike and Charlie had joined the Army with Tom.

Maggie sighed and shook her head. 'Nobody knows what's happened there, Tom. She won't say nothing, but we all know there's something wrong. It all started when he come into the Corner House one Saturday and sat at a different table – one of Irene's. And I wouldn't be surprised if she didn't have something to do with it, because he's never been in at all since and Phyl and Irene won't address a single word to each other now.'

'What d'you think happened?'

'I don't know, I tell you. But whatever it is, it's really upset her. She's not the same girl any more. I dunno what to do about it. Even Jo don't know what to do, and she's her cousin.'

'Well, I'll tell you what Charlie told me. He says Mike's as miserable as sin and *he* won't say why neither. Whatever it is, they're both pining for each other and me and Charlie think it's up to us to do something.'

'Us?' Maggie stared at him. 'You and me, you mean?'

'No, you twerp, not just you and me – all of us. We're all mates, aren't we? Had some good times together? And there's us happy as sandboys, and Jo with her Nick, and Etty and your Jim – well, it's a poor do if we can't do something to help Phyl and Mike, that's what I think. We got to get 'em together again. Like we got Jo and Nick Laurence together in the first place.'

'I'd like to,' Maggie said thoughtfully. 'But I don't see what – hang on!' Her eyes sparkled and she grinned at him and then landed a smacking kiss on his lips. '*I* know what we'll do.'

'What?' he asked. 'What's the idea?'

Maggie shook her head and laid her finger alongside her nose. 'Never you mind, Tom. But you can go back and tell Charlie it's as good as fixed. Just you leave it to your Auntie Mag . . .'

Phyl was sitting in a pub with Sandy Smith. He brought their drinks over – a pint of bitter for himself and a port and lemon for Phyl – and set them on the table, then clicked his fingers in front of her eyes.

'Wake up, Phyl. I know I'm not your favourite boyfriend, but you could at least throw me the odd word while you're out with me. What's the matter?'

Phyl shook her head and flushed. 'Sorry, Sandy. I was just thinking . . .'

'Oh, is that what it was? I thought you were in pain. Who's the lucky bloke, then?'

'The lucky bloke?'

'The one you were thinking about,' he said with exaggerated patience. 'It don't take a Houdini to know it's a bloke you were thinking about.'

'A *Houdini?*' Momentarily diverted, she stared at him. 'What are you on about?'

'That clever bloke, you know, the one that does all the sums. Isn't that his name, Houdini?'

Phyl rolled her eyes. 'That's Einstein, you dope! Houdini's the one they tied up in sacks and chucked in the river.'

'Was he? Why would they want to do that, then?'

'To see if he could get out. It's what he did. He got people to chain him up and put handcuffs on him and all sorts, and then he made them put him in a box and strap it up all over the outside, and then he tried to get out—' She broke off and stared at him suspiciously. 'You know all this, Sandy, you're just having me on.'

'Well, at least it's made you think about something else for a minute or two,' he retorted, and ducked as she swung her hand at him. 'Seriously, Phyl, what is the matter? I know you got other blokes – one of 'em's serious, isn't he? Is that what's the matter? Are you trying to think of a way to give me the brush-off?'

'No, of course I'm not!' Phyl hesitated, then sighed and flipped her hands. 'Well, you're right in a way. I thought he was starting to be serious. I didn't really want to get serious about any of them – any of you, I mean. But, well, with Mike I just found out it had happened, without me noticing,

326

somehow. And then he stopped coming to the Corner House and stopped asking me out and – well, I don't know what to do.'

'Hasn't he told you why?'

'He hasn't spoken to me. He hasn't even written me a note. I can't understand it, Sandy. He knew how I felt about him, I'm sure he did.'

'You don't think he's got another girl?'

'I don't know. I don't know what to think.' She raised her eyes, regardless of the tears brimming in them. 'That's the worst part, in a way. If only I knew . . . It might be something I've done, or something I've said, and if I don't know, how can I ever put it right?'

'Well, you could ask him,' he said reasonably, but Phyl shook her head.

'No. It's for him to say. He's the one that stopped coming, not me. I won't push in where I'm not wanted.'

'But you don't know you're not wanted. If it was some sort of misunderstanding—'

'There was nothing to misunderstand,' Phyl declared flatly. 'We didn't have a date that weekend, so I couldn't have stood him up. He just . . . stopped coming. How could there be a misunderstanding?'

'Perhaps he's ill.'

'No. One of his mates would have told me. He'd have let me know.' She shrugged and gave a bright, artificial smile. 'Well, it's better to find out sooner than later, I suppose. Whatever it is he's taken the huff about, it's nothing I've done deliberately. I just – well, I just never thought he was that sort, that's all.' Her voice trailed away miserably, and then she added with more energy, 'I just think I'm entitled to an *explanation*. Not to be dropped, like – like an old glove.'

'The thing about gloves,' Sandy said after a pause, 'is that they're meant to be in pairs.'

There was a short silence. Then Phyl said with a touch of irritation, 'I don't know what that's supposed to mean. Of *course* gloves are meant to be in pairs. The thing about *old* gloves is that it doesn't matter if you chuck one out because

327

you're not going to wear them anyway – oh, for goodness' sake, why are we talking about gloves? First it's Houdini and then it's – honestly, Sandy, you'd make an argument out of anything!'

'I'm sorry,' he said meekly. 'I didn't mean to start an argument. I was just trying to help.'

'Well, I don't know how talking about old gloves is meant to help,' Phyl said in a disgruntled tone. She sighed. 'Oh, I'm sorry, Sandy. I'm not very good company tonight. Perhaps I'd better go home.'

'Finish your drink first,' Sandy said peaceably. 'There's no point in leaving it.'

'I warn you,' Phyl said with a shaky smile, 'you're liable to get your head bitten off if you talk to me.'

'That's all right. I don't mind having my head bitten off.' He glanced at her and then fiddled with his glass. 'To tell you the truth, I'd rather be here with you, having my head bitten off, than not with you at all.'

'Oh, lor,' Phyl said after a pause, 'not you as well.'

'Look,' he said, 'you can't blame us. You're a smashing girl, Phyl. Anyone who goes out with you is going to get smitten. Probably a lot who never go out with you are as well. Half the Corner House and its customers would like to be where I am tonight. But they're not, and I am, and I think it's time you knew. I know I haven't got a chance, not while you're still mooning after this other bloke, but, well, if you ever feel like considering me for the job, you just let me know, okay?'

'What job?' Phyl asked, trying to sound joky. 'What are you burbling about now?'

'The job of – of boyfriend. Sweetheart. Whatever you like to call it.' He looked at her, the smile gone from his eyes. 'I mean it, Phyl, so please don't laugh at me. I think a lot of you. I wish you could think something of me, too.'

Phyl looked down at the table. Sandy was still fiddling with his glass and she reached across and laid her hand over his. 'I'm not laughing at you, Sandy. I appreciate it, I really do. And I do think something of you. But I don't think—'

'You don't think you want me as a sweetheart. Well, all right. So long as you don't drop me altogether.' He grinned at her. 'You'll never get rid of me, you know. I'll always be around, just in case you change your mind.'

I wish I could, Phyl thought. Sandy was funny and cheery, always ready with a joke and yet, as he had just shown, with a sensitive side as well. Why couldn't she have fallen in love with him instead of Mike? Yet as she looked at the fair, freckled face with its boyish grin and dancing eyes, it was Mike's dark looks that she found herself longing for, and the pang of loneliness was almost more than she could bear.

'Thanks, Sandy,' she said, giving his hand a pat. 'I'll remember. And I won't drop you – ever.' She picked up her glass and finished her drink. 'But I think I'll go home now all the same. I'm really tired. I need a good night's sleep.'

Sandy pushed back his chair. 'Okay, Phyl. Let's go. And if I run into that other bloke, I'll tell him he's a proper twerp, letting a girl like you go. Some people don't know they're born!'

He walked her back to Auntie Holt's and left her on the doorstep. Phyl stood for a moment, watching him walk away down the street. At the corner he turned and waved and she waved back and blew him a kiss.

I don't know why we can't fall for the right people in this world, she thought sadly, putting her finger on the doorbell. I really don't.

Chapter Twenty-Two

It was the middle of August when the Wood family set off for Paddington railway station. All Annie's and Jack's luggage was packed into two large suitcases, borrowed from a neighbour, while Owen and Shirley carried two smaller bags. They would bring the cases back with them to return to their owner. Alf Wood accompanied the party, rather silent. Annie had begged him to come to Wales, too, but he hadn't been able to get time off work.

He bought a penny platform ticket and followed them glumly down the platform. Jack wanted to see the engine, and while Shirley and Owen took him to pat its gleaming sides and talk to the engine-driver, Alf and Annie stood and looked at each other.

'Now, you will make sure you get your proper meals, won't you?' Annie said, trying to sound brisk. 'Vi Watkins next door says she'll give you a bit of Sunday dinner, and she'll see you right next week, and then our Shirl'll be back to see to things. There's only your breakfast to do and your sandwiches. And see you change your pants regular, and take the bottom sheet off the bed every Sunday morning and put the top one to the bottom so our Shirl don't have too much washing to do. And – and – oh, Alf—' Her trembling voice broke. 'I'm going to miss you so bad!'

'I know.' Clumsily, unused to embracing her in public, he put both arms around her. 'I don't know how I'm going to manage without you, Annie, straight I don't.'

'Now, then.' She brushed her hand fiercely across her eyes and sniffed back her tears. 'Don't start me off again.' For the past three or four days, all the time she'd been frenziedly cleaning cupboards and washing windows, Annie had been weeping gently, and she looked completely worn out. 'For two pins I'd turn round and go straight home. If it weren't for our Jack—'

'That's it,' he said. 'It's our Jack that matters. We've got to keep him safe. You go off now, Annie, and look after him. And when it's all over, you can come home and see just how well me and Shirl can manage on our own. The place'll be like a new pin.'

'You'll probably manage so well you won't want me back at all,' she said, trying to smile. 'You'll have settled down to being a bachelor again.'

Alf stared at her and then, uncaring now who might see them, caught her hard against him and kissed her roughly. 'No, I won't. I won't ever get used to being a bachelor. There won't be a minute when I don't wish you were back home where you belong. You come back the second it's all over, Annie, see, or I'll be coming to Wales quick enough to fetch you!'

The engine suddenly let off steam and there was a shrill whistle. The guard began to wave his flag and shout for the doors to be closed, and Shirley and Owen came hurrying back down the platform, towing Jack behind them. Half bewildered, half excited, he was clutching a stick of rock in one hand and his beloved mouth-organ in the other. Alf gave him a quick hug and then pushed him up into the train with Owen and the suitcases, then turned to his daughter.

'I'll see you next week, then, Shirl.'

'Yes.' She stood uncertainly. Alf had never been a demonstrative father, yet she was in no doubt that he loved her, as he loved all his family. She looked up at him. 'Cheerio, then.'

'Come on,' he said roughly, 'give your old dad a kiss, can't you? And mind you look after your mum, see, and young Jack. Make sure they're settled in before you come back.'

'I will.' Shirley emerged from his embrace, breathless. She scrambled up behind Owen and they went to find a compartment. Alf turned back to his wife.

'Cheerio, then, Annie. Mind you take care of yourself and our Jack now, and write regular.'

'I will. And you remember what I said. Eat proper meals, and—'

'And change my pants regular.' He gave her another smacking kiss and a broad grin. 'All right, I heard you, and so did half Paddington, I wouldn't wonder. Now, you get in or you'll be left behind, and what am I going to do then about that little popsy I've got waiting for me . . . ? Cheerio, Annie, Cheerio, love.' He watched her climb aboard the train and slammed the door shut after her. She turned and leaned from the window, the tears once again streaming down her cheeks. 'Don't go piping your eye now. It's not going to be for long. Just a holiday, see. A nice country holiday . . .'

His words were lost in the snorting and chuffing of the great engine. Steam and smoke billowed once more about him, and he stood back and watched as the long line of carriages moved slowly away, picking up speed as they left the station. Above him in the great soaring arches of the roof, pigeons whirled and settled again. All around him other people were watching the train disappear, some as saddened as himself, some anxious and frightened, all saying a kind of goodbye.

Alf Wood turned and walked back along the platform. He felt very alone. There was an empty house for him to go back to, and even though Shirley would be back in a few days, and Owen and Donald would come and go, he knew that for him it would continue to be empty until the coming war was over and his wife could be with him once more.

The journey to Wales was long and, after the first half-hour, tedious. Jack sat entranced, his flat nose pressed against the window, watching first the houses and then fields, woods and rivers pass by. At the first sight of a herd of cows he crowed with excitement, pointing and hammering his fist on the glass, and sheep and horses produced the same response. But for the others it was a weary day and they were all thankful when at last the train drew into the final station and they were able to climb down and set their luggage on the platform.

'Look at that!' Annie said, awed. In the distance were mountains, purple with heather like an emperor in his robes, but nearer at hand the land was black with coal dust and the mountains were of slag. Even now, late in the evening, the rattle and grind of machinery could be heard working, and as the little party walked out of the station a small crowd of miners passed them, their eyes showing white against the grime of the pit.

'They're just going off shift,' Owen explained. 'The next lot will be already there, going underground.'

'They work all night?' Shirley asked, horrified, and he grinned.

'Don't make much different whether it's day or night down the pit, *cariad*. And the coal's got to be dug out, see, so what's the point of stopping?' He glanced around the narrow street and the small, grey-faced houses in their serried rows. 'This is where we used to live – that street there, see? The house on the corner, that was ours. Now, Uncle Dafydd said he'd meet us here, borrow a van off one of the neighbours, so we'd better not go any further. There's a bit of a wall you could sit on, Mrs Wood.'

'I've been sitting down all day,' Annie protested, but she sank down on to the wall all the same. 'Funny how it don't seem like sitting down when you're on a train . . . Is it far to your auntie's, Owen? I'll be thankful to get there, I can't pretend otherwise.'

'Here he comes.' An old black van was rattling along the cobbles towards them. Owen waved and it drew shakily to a halt. A small, bow-legged old man with a straggling grey moustache and bright blue eyes jumped out and gripped Owen's hand, pumping it up and down as if he expected to draw water. 'Hullo, Uncle Dafydd, how are you?'

'Owen, boyo, good to see you, it is.' His voice was much more Welsh than Owen's, squeaky and high-pitched. 'And this is your young lady, is it? Shirley, is that right? My old woman, she told me to be sure not to forget what your name was. And Mrs Wood, it's glad I am to welcome you to the valleys, and your boy Jack, too, poor fellow. Look at him now, tired out with all the travelling in that old train. Now, you all get into old Ivor's van, he cleaned it out specially this afternoon, made a good job of it, too, you'd hardly know he'd ever had a pig in it . . . Mrs Wood, you can sit by me, and the young folks can make themselves comfortable on those old cases in the back. We'll have you back at Nant-ddu in a jiffy, and my Mair's got a nice supper waiting for you, and a big pot of tea and some bara brith. You'll be glad of that, I know.'

He scarcely drew breath as he settled them all in the van, then jumped in himself and crashed it into gear. With a jerk that almost sent Annie through the windscreen – and no doubt would have done, had the van possessed one – he set off along the road, the wheels bouncing on the cobbles. In the back, Shirley clung to Owen while Jack, refreshed by a long nap in the train, shouted with delight.

Uncle Dafydd's idea of a jiffy was more like an hour, but at last they left behind the gritty air and grimy streets of the mining villages and began the steep climb up the flank of the mountain. Here, there were still mines and open-cast workings, but they petered out after a while and the rough road wound its way through grass beginning to show real green, and then, at last, into swathes of the purple heather. The noise of machinery fell away below them and, when the van finally squealed to a halt and the engine stopped, Shirley could hear the richest silence she had ever known.

Yet it was not silent at all, she thought as she scrambled down and stood in the farmyard, drawing in great lungfuls of cool mountain air. There was plenty of sound to be heard – it was just that the huge bowl of sky, the vast open spaces all around them, were big enough to soak it up and absorb it. And the sounds seemed to fit the landscape – that clear, bubbling sound, which must be a bird of some kind, was almost a part of the crystal stream that sparkled along one side of the yard, while the soft bleating of sheep in some distant pasture was like the rustling of the breeze in the bushes that sheltered the tiny, flower-filled garden by the door.

'It's lovely,' she said, gazing about her and lifting her face towards the reddening sun. 'Oh, Owen, it's lovely.'

'I know.' He took her hand. 'I'd forgotten just how lovely it was, *cariad*. I'd like to come back here one day to live. It's so peaceful like, and so quiet ... I'll show you round everywhere, Shirley. I'll take you to all the places I used to know.'

Annie was beside them, holding Jack's hand to stop him tramping off on his own. Shirley turned to look at her. 'D'you like it, Mum? D'you think you and Jack will be all right here?'

'I hope so, love. It seems funny, though, just one house on its own with no others around. Doesn't your auntie get lonely, Owen?'

'I don't think she has time,' he said with a grin, 'but you can ask her yourself if you like. Here she comes now.'

Mair Prosser had opened the back door as soon as she heard the van arrive, and came stumping down the garden path to meet them. The garden opened straight out on to the yard and was evidently her pride and joy, filled with flowers that wouldn't be expected to grow halfway up a mountain. The hens which had been scratching about in the yard and immediately rushed for the gate were shooed firmly back, and Owen's aunt, as round and rosy as an apple, shut the gate behind her and came over to the tired little group by the van.

'There it is you are, then!' Her voice was like a song, and her hair as bubbling and white as the foam on the dancing stream. 'I thought it was lost Dafydd had got, him not being used to going to the big town, see. Now you come along in, all of you, you must be parched. I've a pot of tea waiting and some of my own Welsh cakes and bara brith, and when you're feeling a bit better there'll be supper on the table. Cock-a-leekie, Owen told me when he wrote, so I hope that's all right for you, is it?' Her voice lifted at the end of each sentence and she looked at them with eyes as bright as a bird's.

Without any warning, Shirley felt tears in her eyes. She

wanted to rest her head on the round bosom and cry with tiredness. She wanted to be undressed and put to bed like a little girl in one of the bedrooms whose windows must be those just under the eaves, with roses growing almost to their sills. She wanted to sleep with the scent of those roses wafting in through the open window, and the call of that wonderful bird bubbling in her dreams . . .

'Poor girl,' she heard a voice say from a long way off, 'she's worn out with it all. Bring her in, Owen, there's a good boy, and let's give her a cup of tea. It's all right, *cariad* . . .' The voice was in her ear now, soothing and murmuring. 'It's all right. You're home now, see? You got nothing to do but rest . . .'

For the first few times he and Irene had been out together, Richard Godwin had indeed been – more or less – satisfied with a 'few kisses'. But now he was becoming restless, wanting more.

'Come on, Irene,' he whispered, starting to unbutton her blouse in the back row of the Odeon. 'You know you like it really.'

Irene knew nothing of the sort. As always, when he started to kiss her, she conjured up the picture of Phyl's face when she'd first seen Richard and Irene dancing together. She was still able to feel the thrill of that moment, but it was fading now and she needed something else to help her enjoy Richard's caresses. She thought of Etty and her small, slight body and hurt face when Irene had told the others about her mother, and relaxed in Richard's arms. It couldn't do any harm to let him go a bit further, not here in the back row of the pictures with lots of other people around.

It gave her a thrill, too, she'd discovered, to lead him on a bit and then slap him down. It made her feel powerful. She snuggled against him, making little whimpering noises as his fingers slid inside her bra and touched her nipple, and she could feel the excitement in him. She lifted her face a little and, as if a button had been pressed, he laid his lips on hers. His mouth was open and wet and it was all she could do not to shrink away, but instead she whispered his name. 'Richard . . .'

'You see?' he muttered hoarsely. 'I told you you'd like it . . .'

The usherette's torch flashed their way. Mostly, the back row was left alone to its entwined couples, but every now and then a light shone along to remind people where they were. Irene quickly pulled out of Richard's embrace and they sat decorously holding hands for a while, until he slipped his arm around her and began to explore inside her blouse once more.

After the film, they walked down to Hyde Park. One of the gates was still open and Richard drew her inside.

'No – we'll get locked in . . .'

'They won't shut this gate yet, they never do. It's always the last one. Come on, Rene – just a few minutes, so I can kiss you properly.'

She went with him, unwilling but knowing that he would demand his ration of kisses before taking her home. You had to tread a very careful line between keeping a chap dangling and slapping him down just that bit too much so that he got tired of trying. Richard was still the best catch Irene had had a chance of so far, and she didn't mean to lose him. She walked beside him into the darkened park and when he slid his arm around her waist she snuggled up to him and slipped her arm around him.

'It's a lovely night, Richard. Ever so romantic.'

'I'm glad you think so, Rene, because I'm feeling specially romantic myself tonight.'

Irene didn't know quite how to answer this, so she giggled softly and rested her head on his shoulder. Richard stopped walking and turned her into his arms. He kissed her lingeringly and she thought hastily of Phyl and then of Etty. He let his lips trail down her cheek and into the neck of her blouse, and slid one hand up to cover her breast.

'Richard!' she whispered. 'You mustn't.'

'Why not? You let me in the pictures.'

'That's different.' They'd been surrounded by other people there. Here in the park, she was uncomfortably aware of how lonely it was. There was no one else around – or, if there were, they were all hidden in the bushes, and not the slightest bit interested in Richard and herself. 'I think we ought to be going home now, Richard.'

'In a little while.' He kissed her again, more urgently. 'There's a seat over here. Let's sit down for a few minutes.'

Irene allowed him to draw her along and they sat down. Instantly, his arms were around her again and he began to cover her face with kisses. At the same time, while one arm held her firmly against him, his other hand was busy with her blouse, tearing the buttons open and fastening upon her breast. Irene felt her bra strap tug uncomfortably and gave a little cry, but he either ignored or misunderstood it. She was suddenly reminded of her mother's cries in the night: '*Stop it – please, stop it . . .*'

'Richard—'

'Irene,' he muttered against her skin. His face was buried between her breasts now. 'Oh, God, Irene . . .'

'Richard, no!'

'Don't try and stop me – not now. Oh, God, Irene, you don't know what it's like – sitting beside you all evening, wanting you – wanting this—' His hand slid down over her stomach, thrust itself between her thighs. Irene gasped with horror and grasped his wrist, trying to pull his hand away, but Richard's arm was like a steel post, strong and immovable. His fingers scrabbled painfully against her flesh and she cried out again.

'No – no, Richard, stop it, *stop it* . . .' She knew now what she had tried not to know, what had been going on in the bedroom all those years ago, and she almost retched with disgust at both the memory of those nights and the reality of now, of Richard's mouth on her body, his scrabbling fingers between her legs. He was thrusting his body against her now, forcing her back on the bench, and for a moment his hand left her body to fumble with his own clothes. 'Stop it, Richard, *please*!' Her voice rose to a scream.

'For God's sake, Irene!' He had been jerked out of his passion and she cried out again as his hand slapped her roughly across the face. 'Shut up! You'll have the cops here. Stay still, for God's sake, and stop that bloody noise!' He bent her back and laid himself on top of her, and she could feel the strange, hard protuberance that sprang from his trousers against her bare legs. As if a spider had suddenly assaulted her, she screamed again and tried frantically to wriggle free.

'I can't,' she sobbed. 'Please, Richard, don't do it. Don't touch me there. Take me home, please, please take me home.'

'When you've given me what you've been dangling in front of me all these weeks,' he growled, sliding his hands beneath her buttocks to lift her hard against him. 'I told you what I thought of cock-teasers, didn't I? First Phyl and now you – except that she never went so far as you did, leading me on, letting me think you were game for it . . . You're all the bloody same. All love and kisses as long as you've got a bloke who's willing to pay for you all along the line, but the minute he wants something more it's, *Oh, no, I can't, Mummy wouldn't like it* . . . Well, you know the answer to that, don't you? Mummy's not getting it! *You* are.'

'No! No! I won't – I won't let you.' Irene was fighting him in earnest now. She squirmed beneath him, unaware that this was exciting him all the more, and then managed to get one hand free and dragged her long, scarlet fingernails down his cheek. With a yelp Richard released his hold and jerked away from her, and Irene was instantly off the bench and on her feet. She had dropped her bag somewhere during the struggle, but she didn't stop to find it. She shot off along the path, back towards the gate, frighteningly aware that Richard was already in pursuit, and managed to reach the pavement outside just as he caught up with her.

To her infinite relief, a policeman was strolling down the road towards them. He glanced at them curiously and stopped.

'You all right, miss?'

Irene almost threw herself into his arms. However, a shred of self-preservation remained with her and she knew that if she told the policeman what had been happening, it could only lead to embarrassing questions and a probable warning to her to be more careful in future, not to mention a stern warning to Richard, for which he would not forgive her. She gulped and nodded.

'I've lost my bag. We – we were walking through the park and I – I dropped it somewhere. We looked for it, but it's so dark . . .' She lifted her eyes towards the big policeman, putting on her most appealing expression. 'If you could just come and help – with your torch – I'd be ever so grateful.'

The policeman looked at her doubtfully. With her carefully waved hair all tousled, her blouse undone and half out of her skirt, and the tears on her cheeks, it was quite obvious that she'd been doing more than looking for a lost handbag. And the blood on the young man's scratched face completed the tale. But if the young lady didn't want to make a complaint, it wasn't for him to interfere. Another foolish young miss who'd led a man on and didn't know what she was getting herself into, he thought, and set off into the park to look for the dropped handbag.

It was quickly enough found. The policeman, however, wasn't willing to let Irene go off again with the young man who had obviously gone too far and might do so again, by the look of his sullen face. He asked Irene where she lived and if she had enough money for the taxi fare. On being assured that she had, he hailed a cab and saw her into it. He and Richard stood on the pavement watching it disappear along the gas-lit street.

'I suppose it's all right for me to go now?' Richard asked, sullenly sarcastic.

The bobby looked down at him and felt a small twinge of compassion. The chap was only young, and too good-looking for his own good. He'd been led on, no doubt, and probably didn't even know his own strength, or the strength of his natural urges. There was many a young chap been caught by a girl in a similar situation, and found himself on the church steps, or worse, as a consequence.

'That's right, sonny,' he said. 'You get off home. And think yourself lucky to get away with a few scratches. That young woman could have been going home with a bun in the oven tonight, and you know what that would have meant.'

'I didn't—' Richard began, and caught the policeman's eye. 'Well, maybe I would have. But she's been asking for it for weeks.'

'I know,' the bobby said. 'But if you're wise, you won't give it to 'em, see? It's the ones who *don't* ask for it that you want to look for. Or the ones that know what they're about and just want a bit of fun, same as you. Not young women like that one, respectable as the Queen Mother and frozen up as yesterday's ice cream.'

He strolled on up the road, continuing his beat, and Richard watched him for a moment then turned and walked off in the opposite direction. His usual air of suavity and confidence had deserted him. He felt suddenly very young and very uncertain.

By the time she arrived home, Irene had managed to pull herself together. Sitting in the back of the taxi she had first given way to her tears but, noticing the driver glancing curiously at her in his mirror, she blew her nose fiercely and drew in a deep, shuddering breath.

'You all right, love?'

'Perfectly,' she answered frostily. 'I just had a bit of bad news, that's all. Someone in the family took bad. That's why I've got to get home quick.'

'Sorry about that,' he said, sounding unconvinced, but he asked no more and Irene sat back in her seat, staring out of the window, oblivious to all that they were passing – the gas-lit streets, the noise of singing and laughter in the pubs, the glow of light spilling out on to pavements as the Saturday evening drinkers came roistering out.

Oblivious, too, to the preparations for war – the notices on the walls, the trenches dug in Hyde Park, the Anderson shelters in people's gardens, the larger community shelters in the streets.

Irene, her mind totally absorbed with her own feelings, saw none of them.

How dared Richard try to take advantage of her like that? How *dared* he? Time and again she'd impressed upon him that she wasn't *that sort* of girl. She'd *told* him she was respectable, that a few kisses were all that he could expect. Anything else – the snuggling up, the flirting with her eyes, the cuddling in the back row of the pictures – all that was just a bit of fun. It was natural. It was what boys expected. It didn't *mean* anything.

It didn't give him any excuse to – to *attack* her like that.

He'll never get another chance, Irene vowed. I'll never go out with him again. I wouldn't even walk through a doorway with him! He's disgusting – that's what he is. *Disgusting*.

In fact, when you came to think about it, all men were disgusting. It was true what people said, that they were all after only one thing. Friendship and a few kisses weren't enough – they all wanted to go further sooner or later, mostly sooner, and when a girl tried to say no they just took no notice. And when you came to think of it, what they were after was just – well, *disgusting*. There was no other word for it.

A few kisses – although Irene had to think hard about Etty Brown or Phyl Jennings even to begin to enjoy them – were one thing. But all that mauling about and slobbering and – and the other thing – *ugh*.

What I want, Irene thought, is a man who's past all that. Someone with a bit of money and a bit of class, who's more interested in having a smart wife to keep house for him than in *all that*. Someone a bit older – say forty or so – who just isn't interested any more.

The taxi turned the last corner into her street and Irene found the money to pay the fare. She handed it over with resentment. Richard ought to have paid that, she thought, and didn't bother with a tip, just to show the driver what she thought about men in general. He scowled at her and drove off, revving the engine so that half the street would be woken up.

The light was still on in the front bedroom window where her parents slept. Irene glanced up at it and thought of the

342

noises she used to hear at night. It was quite a long time since she'd heard that pleading voice and those heavy, groaning grunts. Obviously her father had lost interest at last, and left her mother in peace.

I'm never going to let that happen to me, she promised herself. Never, never, never.

Chapter Twenty-Three

Tommy, Mike and Charlie were all home on leave
together. It was only for a weekend, but it rarely
happened these days and they wanted to celebrate.

'Well, there's only one place it can be, isn't there?' Tommy
said. 'The Corner House!'

'It'll be like old times,' Charlie agreed. But Mike hung back,
his mouth screwed up ruefully.

'Can't we go somewhere else for a change? Anyone'd think
there wasn't anywhere else in London.'

'There isn't, as far as I'm concerned.' Tommy looked
exasperated. 'For God's sake, Mike, you're not still carrying a
chip on your shoulder over Phyl, are you?'

'It's not a chip. She's made it pretty clear she's not
interested any more. She's just the same as the rest of them –
out to feather her own nest. That Godwin bloke's got a better
job than me – he's not joining up, so he won't get sent away,
he'll be around to take her out – and he looks like a bloody
film star. He's a better catch than I'll ever be. I'm best off
trying to forget all about her, and going to the Corner House
isn't going to help.'

Tommy stared at him. 'You're daft, Mike. Phyl Jennings
isn't like that. She's a smashing girl. Why, if I wasn't getting
spliced to my Maggie I might even try my luck with her
myself! Anyway, she's not going out with Richard Godwin
any more. He's been taking that Irene Bond out.'

'*Irene?*' Mike stared at him. 'I didn't know that.'

'Well, I didn't myself till Maggie told me the other night. Apparently she really set her cap at him and he fell for it – the sucker. They've been dancing out at Sudbury, and gone to the pictures together and all sorts. Maggie reckons it's serious.'

Mike thought about this for a moment or two. 'Well, that still don't make any difference to Phyl and me. She still doesn't want to know, or she'd have got in touch. And why'd she stand me up that Sunday afternoon when I asked her to meet me by the bandstand in Hyde Park, eh? Tell me that. She never even sent a message to say she couldn't come.'

Tommy sighed. 'I don't know, Mike. But I'm sure there must have been a reason. Why don't you give her another chance, eh? Come down the Corner House and try and make it up.'

'There's nothing to make up. We never quarrelled. She just stopped seeing me, and it's up to her to make the first move. You and Charlie go. I'll stop home. My mum's not too well again anyway, she'll be glad of some company.'

Tommy and Charlie glanced at each other and shrugged. 'Well, if that's the way you feel . . . But you'll have to see her at the wedding next week, you know. She'll be coming to that. I don't want no bad feelings that day.'

'I might not be able to get leave—'

'Listen, mate,' Tommy said in a threatening tone, 'that day, *everyone's* going to have to get leave. I'm not taking no excuses, see? You're going to be at my wedding and Phyl's going to be at Maggie's, and since it happens to be the same wedding you've got no choice. You've got to be there.'

Mike sighed. 'Well, I suppose we don't have to talk to each other. We can sit at opposite ends of the room.'

'I told you, I don't want no bad feelings.'

'There won't be any, Tom. But you can't expect us to be all lovey-dovey, not after the way she chucked me without a word. I'll come, and there won't be any bad words, I'll promise you that, but you can't tell me what to feel.'

Tommy heard the edge in his voice and wisely decided not to pursue the matter. He and Maggie had talked about it the other evening and both were baffled by what had happened. The trouble was, neither Mike nor Phyl was willing to talk about what had gone wrong, and neither was willing to make the first move to put it right. Both insisted that the friendship was over and they didn't want it to start again – and yet it was clear that both were miserable.

'They're a couple of twerps,' Maggie had said, 'and if you ask me, all they got to do is see each other again to realise it for themselves.'

Maybe at the wedding they would do that.

Shirley and Owen came back to London, leaving Annie and Jack at Nant-ddu. They sat on the train, watching the mountains fall away behind them, to be displaced first by the gritty, black mining valleys and then the softer countryside of England. For a long time they didn't speak. Shirley's face was wet with tears and Owen held her hand, comfortingly stroking her fingers.

'They'll be better off there, *cariad*,' he said at last. 'You could see how Jack took to it all, and my Auntie Mair and your mam got on like a house on fire. They'll be all right, Shirley.'

'I know. I'm not worrying about them – it's just me and Dad.' She gave him a watery smile. 'I'm being selfish, I suppose, but we're going to miss them so much.'

'Course you are,' he said. 'Course you are. And it's going to mean a lot more work for you, too.'

'It's not that. I don't mind doing a bit of cooking and cleaning the house and getting the washing done. We've all got to do our bit after all, and Dad'll help when he can. But – not having Mum there, to talk to when I come in from work and have a laugh with. And not hearing Jack's mouth-organ about the place . . . It's going to seem so empty, Owen.' She was silent for a few minutes, then said with an attempt at cheerfulness, 'It's a lovely place, though, Nant-ddu. I've never been anywhere like it before – never thought I would. It's the sort of place you see at the pictures, in those nature films. And Jack took to it like a duck to water, didn't he?

Feeding the hens and helping with the milking – I reckon he's going to be a really useful chap on the farm.'

Owen laughed. 'Did you see him playing the mouth-organ to the cows? I swear they were listening to him. And he'll love the lambs when they come along in spring, they're a comic turn in themselves.'

Shirley stared at him. 'In *spring*?' Her voice was small and cold. 'You don't really think they'll still be there in spring, Owen, do you? I mean, even if there is a war, it's not going to last that long, is it? Don't they say it'll all be over by Christmas?'

Owen bit his lip. He squeezed her hand tightly. 'I'm sorry, *cariad*. I wasn't thinking what I was saying. Of course it won't last till spring. It'll be just like a holiday for your mam and Jack. They'll be home by Christmas, of course they will. It'll all be over long before then.'

All during those last days of August, the tension mounted. No one could doubt now that the country was facing war. Everything was ready – troops in position, air-raid shelters in streets and gardens, the evacuation rehearsed over and over again, ration books printed and ready for issue. Everybody had a gas mask in a brown cardboard box and had practised putting it on. Babies had their own and had been thrust, many of them screaming, into the rubbery containers.

'It's the smell they don't like,' Ivy Pratt said. Evie's youngest, six-month-old Freddy, had almost bellowed the place down when she tried to get him into his. 'It's horrible, that rubber smell – it's no wonder they don't like it. And he doesn't understand, poor little mite.'

'I don't understand meself,' Evie said. As usual, she was at her mother's for the afternoon, Queenie, now a sturdy toddler, and her brother Billy were outside in the street, sitting on the kerb making sticky balls with the melting tar. 'I don't understand how anyone could drop that awful gas on little babies like Queenie and Freddy.'

'They only dropped it on the soldiers last time,' Ada Pratt mumbled from her corner. She'd taken her teeth out after dinner – they seemed to hurt her gums more than ever these days, and if Ivy made a cup of tea in a minute she could dunk her biscuit in it so didn't really need them in till teatime. 'My hubby's brother caught it bad. He wasn't never the same again afterwards and died at forty, and he told us some of the chaps in his unit just turned to froth when they got it. Turned to froth.'

'I don't think I want to hear about that, Gran, if you don't mind,' Evie said, turning white. 'I don't want to think about my little ones turning to froth ... How about this wedding, Ma? What happens if Tom can't make it?'

'Well, he's got to, ain't he? Can't have a wedding without the groom. And I don't see why he can't have his leave what's bin promised him – after all, we ain't at war yet, nor likely to be by then. It's only a week off.'

'Well, if it was me,' Evie said, 'I reckon I'd be round seeing the vicar now, getting it brought forward. It'd be a shame for our Mag if she couldn't get wed after all.' She grinned. 'Could be a bit embarrassing in a few months' time an' all!'

'Now, then. Don't you go casting nasturtiums at your sister. She's a good girl, our Maggie is. You don't really reckon there'll be any problem, do you? About the wedding, I mean?'

Evie shrugged. 'I dunno, do I? I only know my Joe says they're ready to declare war any minute. We're right on the edge of it, Ma.'

Ivy looked upset. 'After all the trouble we bin to with the frocks an' all. We can't be having to cancel it, not after all that.'

'It's going to mean a lot more than a few cancelled weddings, Ma,' Evie said soberly, and hugged Freddy close against her. 'Me and Joe are wondering about evacuation. I'm entitled to go too, see, with the little 'uns being under five. What are you going to do about our Ginnie?'

'Ginnie? I'm not having her evacuated!'

'She'd be a lot safer out in the country, Ma.'

Ivy shook her head. 'Me and your father have bin all through it. There's the wedding, for one thing – we're not sending her off before that. Set her little heart on being bridesmaid, she has. And she'd never settle in the country, with all them great big fields and woods, and owls hooting and that. You know what she's like about noises. And there's wild cows and pigs and all sorts. She'd be frightened to death.'

'She'd be with all her mates, and the teachers at school.'

'You know what she thinks about them! Ginnie don't like school. No, she'll be happier here with me and her dad. You go if you like, Evie. I wouldn't blame you with three little 'uns, though I won't say I won't miss you, but me and your gran and Ginnie, we're stopping here. Them old Germans ain't going to shift *us* out of our own home!'

On the other side of London, Carrie and Bill Mason were discussing the same problem. Alice was still firmly set against going anywhere without Robbie, even though the schoolteacher had been round to tell them of the arrangements that had been made.

'All they got to do is say the word,' Carrie said, 'and you'll be off next day. There won't be no time for mucking about, Alice.'

'I'm not mucking about. I'm just not going – not without Robbie.'

Bill frowned. He was seldom heavy-handed with his children, but he was getting tired of Alice's obstinacy, and he was frightened and worried as well.

'Now, you look here, my girl. You're not being given no choice in this, see? If we say you're to be evacuated, evacuated you'll be, and no palaver about whether you take a blooming cat along as well. We bin through this and through it until I'm sick to death of hearing about it, so for once and for all, you're *going*. And Robbie isn't.'

Alice's face set mutinously. She gathered the big ginger cat in her arms and stood staring at her mother and father. Then, without a word, she turned and marched out of the back room and through the scullery into the back yard.

'Oh dear,' Carrie said with a sigh. 'She's ever so upset about it, Bill.'

349

'I can't help that. A cat's only a cat, when all's said and done, and she's our daughter, Carrie. I'm not taking no risks with her life, not for the sake of a cat. There's going to be *bombs*, Carrie. What good is it going to do that cat if our Alice is blown to bits? She can't do nothing to *save* him.'

'Don't talk like that, Bill! I can't bear it.'

'We're going to have to bear it, girl,' he said seriously. 'It's going to be happening all around us. We're not going to be able to turn round and say we can't bear it.'

'I know. It's just the thought of our Alice . . . You're right, Bill, she's got to go, but if we make her go without Robbie she'll just hate us for it.'

'Better that,' he said, 'than let her get killed by a bomb.'

'What do you mean, not going? Of course you've got to go.'

Jo and Phyl were in their bedroom at Auntie Holt's, getting ready to go to work. As usual on a Monday morning, they were in a rush, searching for clean caps, unladdered stockings and red cotton in case any buttons had mysteriously come loose since Saturday. It was less than a week now to Maggie's wedding, and with that and the threat of war hanging over them like a huge black shadow, tempers were getting short.

'I can't believe you could be so blooming selfish,' Jo stormed, not pausing as she hastily dragged her bedclothes together. 'Maggie's depending on us all to go and give her our best wishes. Just because you've had a stupid row with Mike—'

'I haven't. We never had a row at all.'

'*Well*, then. It's even *more* selfish. And daft into the bargain. What happened between you two, anyway? We all thought you were going to be the next one with a ring on your finger.'

'Yes, well, you all thought wrong, then, didn't you?' Phyl was ready. She snatched up her bag and whisked out of the door. Jo followed, stopping to give their landlady a hug and kiss before she ran down the street after her cousin. During the time they had lived in her house, Mrs Holt had indeed become like a member of the family, an 'auntie' to them both.

Not much that they did escaped her, and she was as concerned as Jo about Phyl's unhappiness lately.

'Don't you try telling me she isn't moping about that boy,' she'd said to Jo only the evening before. 'Thought the world of him, she did, and it's plain as the nose on your face that she's still hankering after him. Whatever's gone wrong, it's my bet it's something that could be put right, if only one of 'em would swallow a bit of pride.'

Jo caught up with Phyl at the corner. One look at her cousin's face told her that more advice and discussion would be unwelcome, but she plunged on just the same.

'You're not really going to stop away from Maggie's wedding, are you? She'd be ever so upset.'

'She wouldn't even notice. You've been to Maggie's place, Jo. There's hundreds in that family, and what with most of their street going, too, and then all Tommy's lot, they won't know who's there and who's not. It won't make a scrap of difference to Maggie if I don't go.'

'It will. She'll be hurt. Think about her feelings, Phyl.'

'And who's thinking about mine?' Phyl demanded. She stopped dead on the pavement and faced her cousin. 'Jo, don't you realise what it'd be like for me to be there and see Mike and know what he's done to me? What am I supposed to do, eh? Waltz up to him with a big smile on my face and pretend nothing's happened? He *dropped* me, Jo, just when we were getting really close. *I'm* the one whose feelings have been hurt.'

'I know,' Jo said more softly. 'I know, Phyl. It's rotten for you. But you can't let it stop you from living your life. You want to go to the wedding, don't you?'

'Well, of course I do. Don't be daft, Jo. I've been looking forward to it as much as anyone.'

'Well, then, *go*. You can't go through life frightened to go to places because you might meet someone you don't want to meet, Phyl. You'll turn into a blooming recluse.'

'Well, thanks very much,' Phyl said, walking on. 'How many people do you think I'm going to be frightened of meeting? I thought I was an ordinary sort of girl but you're turning me into a sort of monster.'

'No, I'm not,' Jo said, beginning to laugh despite herself. 'But honestly, Phyl, nobody's asking you to sign your life away. Like you said, there'll be hundreds of people there – you probably won't even get near Mike, even if you wanted to. Look, me and Nick will stick around near you and if it does look like getting awkward we'll come and help. How will that be? Only, please come. It's not just Maggie who'll be upset if you don't, it's all the rest of us, too – specially me. Hmm?'

Phyl looked at her and blew out a long breath. 'Oh – all right, then. I'll come. But mind you stay by me all the time, all right? I just don't want to have to talk to him. Not that he'll want to talk to me anyway,' she added in a depressed tone. 'He's made that clear enough.'

'Oh, Phyl, I *am* glad!' Jo exclaimed, swinging her round on the pavement. 'Not about what you said about Mike – you know I don't mean that – but about you coming after all. And Maggie'll be pleased, too. She really has been upset about it, you know. She'll be tickled pink you're coming after all.'

'All right, all right, don't make a song and dance about it!' Phyl extricated herself, laughing. 'Not here in the street anyway. And – oh, lor, Jo, there's our bus! We'll have to run for it – come on.' She set off along the pavement with Jo in hot pursuit.

They scrambled aboard with seconds to spare. An old man who had been hobbling behind them on the pavement, observing their antics, watched as they flung themselves up the step and collapsed laughing on the first available seat.

'I don't know what young girls is coming to these days,' he remarked lugubriously to a stout woman in a flowered pinafore, scrubbing her step. 'They was never like that in my day.'

The stout woman looked up at him. It was difficult to tell, she thought, whether he was disapproving or just plain envious.

*

352

Getting a home organised when you had to go to work each day wasn't as easy as Shirley had thought.

Poorly though her mother had been, she still did more than anyone had realised. There was always a dinner on the table to welcome Shirley and her father, their clothes were kept clean and the house spotless. Shirley did a good deal of the work at weekends, but it was astonishing how much there seemed to be to do during the week. Annie had got to the shops most days and always had her washing on the line before nine o'clock. For Shirley, shopping was a real problem and the washing had mounted up into a huge pile before she knew it.

'I know I get my clothes dirty at work,' Alf said apologetically. 'I can't help it, Shirley, love.'

'I know, Dad. And it's only our things, after all – I ought to be able to manage it. I don't seem to be able to catch up somehow.'

'You'll get used to it,' he said. 'I could do me own bits and pieces, come to that. And we can send the sheets to the laundry.'

'I suppose we could do that. But I'm not having you do your own washing, Dad, not when you've done a hard day's work down the building site. I'll do them in the evening, then they'll be ready to hang out before I go to work. Mrs Watkins'll take 'em in if it rains. And if you could get in a few veg on your way home, that'd be a help. I can get them done in the morning, too, ready to cook when I get home.'

'It don't seem right,' he said, 'you having to do all the work.'

'It's not that much, Dad. There's only the two of us after all, and Donald can do a hand's turn when he's home. It's just a question of getting used to it, like you said.'

It wasn't easy, all the same. In the first few days, Shirley forgot to turn on the gas under the potatoes so that they were still raw when the rest of the meal was ready; she boiled the cabbage dry and had to spend all evening scrubbing the saucepan; she left half a pound of liver out of the meat safe so that it went dry and the flies got on it and laid eggs; she forgot to boil the milk overnight so that it was sour by next morning; and she scorched her father's best shirt through trying to do the ironing at the same time as frying his breakfast.

'I'm ever so sorry,' she said, gazing in dismay at the brown triangle right in the front. 'I'll buy you another one out of my Christmas money.'

'It's all right, girl. You don't need to do that. I don't suppose there'll be many chances to wear me best shirt anyway, not if this war starts. Unless it's to welcome the Jerries as they come marching down the street.'

'Don't say such things, Dad!' Shirley began to search frantically for her handbag. 'Now, you know I'll be a bit late home tonight. Owen's coming to fetch me and he don't get off till six, but I'll get dinner on the table for seven so you can do a bit of work on the allotment if you want to.'

'Make it later if you like,' he said. 'The evenings are drawing in and I don't like stopping before it's dark. I'll make meself a bit of bread and jam to be going on with.'

As it turned out, they were all late getting home that evening. The word had gone round the Corner House that people were going along to Downing Street, where the Prime Minister lived. Things were looking really serious, and some sort of announcement was expected at any time.

'Let's go down after we come off shift,' Jo suggested. 'I know it won't make any difference, but I just want to be there. We can walk through the park.'

Maggie said she had too much to do at home, but Phyl and Etty agreed to go and, after a brief hesitation, Shirley said she would follow with Owen. They caught the others up as they crossed Hyde Park Corner to Green Park. There were people outside Buckingham Palace, too, crowding round the big iron gates. The Royal Standard was flying from the roof, showing that the King was at home.

'I wonder what he's thinking,' Jo said as they paused to look up at the balcony. 'He must be ever so worried. Remember how we stood here and cheered on Coronation Day, Phyl? We never thought we'd be standing here thinking about a war, did we?'

They walked down the Mall, thinking of the difference between that day and this – the night spent camping on the pavement, the fat woman with her Thermos flask, the rain. It had been a happy day, despite the weather, and it had been the day she and Phyl had first got the idea of being Nippies. It was a good idea, too, she thought, the best we ever had. We've had a lovely time. It's a blooming shame the Germans have come along to spoil it all.

The ducks were sprinkling the lake in St James's Park with colour and people were picnicking on the grass, to all appearances as if nothing were wrong at all. But there was a tension in the atmosphere just the same, and a brittle edge to the laughter.

The usual little knot of people in Downing Street, hoping to see some important person coming or going, had swelled to a crowd. The girls and Owen joined them, standing opposite Number Ten, rising on tiptoe whenever a car drew into the street. There was a policeman on guard outside, and men with briefcases and serious faces hurried in and out. The crowd was quiet, waiting.

'I bin here since ten o'clock this morning,' one man told Jo. 'My day off, see, so I come down to see what was in the wind. It won't be long now, you mark my words.'

'There's bin an order gone out about evacuation,' a woman nearby chimed in. 'The kiddies are all going on Friday, and the blind people and mothers with babies on Saturday. They must be expecting something soon.'

'Evacuation!' Jo exclaimed, clutching Phyl's arm. 'Our Alice! Oh, Phyl . . .'

'It looks as if we got your mam and Jack out just in time,' Owen said to Shirley.

Etty had turned pale. 'But what about the wedding? They'll be stopping leave. Suppose Tommy can't get home—'

'He'll make it, don't you worry,' Phyl told her. 'Tommy's not going to pass up the chance of marrying Maggie, and if he doesn't get there Maggie'll be round at the camp hauling him out by force, and I wouldn't like to be the man who tried to stop her!'

'We ought to send her over to Germany to sort Hitler out,' Jo agreed, much as Maggie had suggested sending her old grandmother.

After a while, they wandered reluctantly out of Downing Street again. You could stand there for ever, Shirley remarked, and the pile of ironing at home would just get bigger. They walked down to the Houses of Parliament and stood for a few minutes below the clock tower, looking up at the white face and listening as the bell of Big Ben struck seven.

'I'll have to go,' Shirley said. 'Dad won't get any supper at all at this rate.'

'I'll come with you,' Owen said. 'I can give you a hand with things, like.'

They turned and walked away, and Jo looked at Phyl.

'I'm worried about our Alice. She's going to be so upset about going away and having to leave Robbie behind. I'll have to go and see her.'

'We'd better go home after work tomorrow,' Phyl agreed. 'We can't let her go off to the country and not say goodbye. Perhaps we'll be able to persuade her to see sense about Robbie, too.'

'Oh, Phyl,' Jo said with a break in her voice, 'it's really coming, isn't it? This war. It's going to change everything. Nothing's ever going to be the same again.'

Phyl bit her lip. She thought of the evening when the same realisation had dawned on her, when she had known that war would come and might take away the man she loved – the man whom, until that moment, she hadn't even realised she loved, and whom she now seemed to have lost.

Oh Mike, she thought. Mike. What happened to us? What went wrong?

'No,' she said dully, 'I don't think anything is ever going to be the same again.'

Chapter Twenty-Four

A lice was almost frantic.

'I won't go without Robbie, I won't! I'd never sleep a wink at night, wondering what was happening to him.' This was something she'd heard her mother say when they were talking about Eric being called up. 'He'll be miserable without me, and I'll be miserable without him.'

Carrie and Bill were at their wits' end. They had tried coaxing and persuading, they'd tried simply telling her she had no choice. Bill had repeated his assertion that Robbie had important war work to do at home, and that the country cats would probably attack him. Nothing made any difference.

'I won't go without him. I won't.'

Jo and Phyl, coming home the next evening, added their persuasions. 'There'll be plenty of other cats out in the country,' Phyl said, earning a look of scorn from Alice. 'What I mean is, I know none of them will be like Robbie, but they'll be missing their people, too – the men who have to go off and be soldiers, and that. And there'll be lots of kittens needing someone to love them. Robbie'll be best off here, waiting for you to come back.'

'Willy Crewe says we won't come back for years and years,' Alice said tearfully. 'Robbie could be dead by then.'

'Alice!' her mother said sharply. 'Don't you dare say such things. And Willy Crewe's a wicked boy, putting ideas into your head. I don't know about this evacuation, I don't really,' she said to Jo. 'What with children like that Willy Crewe going, and us not knowing who'll be looking after her . . . I honestly wonder whether it wouldn't be best just to keep her at home.'

'You know what they say, Mum.' The posters were everywhere, showing mothers with their children under a tree, with an ugly picture of Hitler skulking on the other side. 'She'll be safer out in the country.'

'I know. That's what your Dad says. All the same . . .' They glanced towards the hearthrug, where Alice was cuddling Robertson fiercely, determined not to let go of him for a minute. 'I don't know how we're going to get her to go without him. She's going to break her heart, you know.'

Phyl and Jo went back to Auntie Holt's feeling subdued. Their own troubles had begun to look rather small. Even Phyl's misery, and Jo's anxiety over Nick, seemed to pale beside Alice's determination and her mother's worry. Bill was adamant that Alice must go to the country, but no one would let her take her cat along, too. It seemed impossible to find a solution.

'She feels it just as much as we feel about our blokes,' Jo said with a sigh. 'I know she can be really pig-headed, but I couldn't help feeling for her tonight. That cat's her whole life.'

'Well, they've only got a couple of days to sort it out,' Phyl observed. 'The children are going on Friday. They've done all their rehearsals and everything. The kiddies have all got to go to their own schools first thing Friday morning, with their gas masks and their sandwiches and a luggage label tied to them with their names on. They've made special bus routes to take them to the railway stations, and they know what station they're going to. They've even found a way to get hundreds of them across the road at once without any accidents, if they've got to walk part of the way.'

'It must take hours, something like that,' Jo said, still thinking about Alice. 'I mean, if they go two by two, there must be a queue about a mile long.'

'That's just it. They don't make 'em cross two by two. They get a policeman at each end of the line and when they need to cross, they just walk out into the road and stop the traffic, and all the kids cross at once. Then they just carry on in a line, same as before.'

'Fancy.' Jo spoke absently, not really interested. The sight of her little sister's face had struck her to the heart. She could imagine just how Alice was feeling – Jo herself had had a guinea pig years ago, and although it hadn't been half as interesting as Robbie, she'd still been heartbroken when it had died. I wish we could do something to help, she thought, but she knew there was nothing. Alice was going to have to say goodbye to her beloved cat.

'There must be thousands of kiddies going through this,' she said. 'Leaving cats and dogs behind. And their mums and dads and all their families. I reckon it's that that's upsetting Alice, just as much as leaving Robbie, only she doesn't realise it.'

'It's going to be awful,' Phyl agreed soberly. 'I mean, some of them are going to finish up in places that don't want them at all or aren't used to children. How are they going to get on? And even if they go to a nice place, they're still going to miss their mums. I can't imagine what it would have been like to leave my mum and go off to some strange place when I was Alice's age.'

'You know what?' Jo said. 'I almost wish we didn't have to go to Maggie's wedding on Saturday. I ought to be at home, with our Mum. I feel as if I'm, well, abandoning her.'

'We'll come back again on Sunday,' Phyl said. 'She wouldn't want you to miss the wedding – specially this one, being a Pearly wedding and all. We'll come on Sunday and spend all day at home.'

It was late when they arrived back at Elmbury Street, and Auntie Holt had gone to bed. As usual, however, she had left a plate of sandwiches and a fruit cake out for the girls to have for their supper, and there was a teapot and a caddy of tea ready for them to make a drink.

'We've been really lucky, finding this place,' Phyl said, putting the kettle on. 'Let's hope your Alice ends up somewhere as good, Jo. And I wouldn't mind betting that if they've got a cat or two about the place she'll settle down all right. She's only little. She won't fret for long.'

'I hope you're right,' Jo said. 'I hope you're right.'

The Corner House did its best to keep things normal. Every morning the Nippies reported for work as usual, were inspected just the same as always, and sallied out into the restaurant with bright, cheery smiles to welcome their customers. The Seaters attended to the queues that always formed outside as lunchtime drew near, making sure that everyone had a place to sit, and the Sallies at their counters served chocolates and flowers with never a hint that anything might be wrong. For the customers, ranging from young men joining the Forces to mothers preparing to part from their children, the Corner House was like a sanctuary.

'We all have worries and anxieties,' Mr Carter told them as he outlined the menus and arrangements for the day, 'but we must never allow them to affect our relationship with our customers. We must always remember that they come here for relaxation as much as for food. The Lyons motto has always been "Happy to Help You" and that must be as true now as it ever has been.'

'It's easy for him to talk,' Irene Bond grumbled, sighing with exasperation as she found a ladder in one of her stockings. 'He's never had a day's worry in his life, you can see that just by looking at him – smug so-and-so.'

'That's not fair,' Jo protested. 'Mr Carter's had a lot of worry. He's got an invalid wife for a start. Just because he manages to keep a smile on his face and be pleasant—'

'Well, he's a man, isn't he?' Irene said bitterly. 'They always get things their own way, don't they?'

Jo stared at her and gave up. Irene was being even more unreasonable these days. She was all right with the customers, smiling and speaking nicely to them, but behind the scenes she was like a bear with a sore head. She hardly spoke to the other girls, and there was a real atmosphere between her and Phyl.

'What's it all about?' Jo asked Phyl later. 'Have you had words?'

Phyl shrugged. 'I bit her head off for saying nasty things about Maggie, but that was weeks ago. I don't know what's got into her and quite honestly I don't care. If she never speaks to me again, it'll be too soon.'

Maggie was eaten up with anxiety over the wedding. So far, Tommy's leave still seemed to be safe but, with all the talk buzzing about, who could tell? There were rumours that the Army would be recalled at any moment. It was too late to bring the wedding forward. They could only keep their fingers crossed and hope for the best.

'I'll die if we can't get married, after all this,' she moaned at tea-break time. 'And all the bridesmaids' frocks and every-thing ... Etty looks a real picture in hers. We've got a photographer and all. It can't go wrong now, it can't.'

'It won't,' Shirley said. 'They won't start the war in the next two days. It'll be all right, Maggie. By Sunday you'll be Mrs Maggie Wheeler, with a ring on your finger.'

'Mrs *Tommy* Wheeler,' Maggie corrected her. 'You only say the wife's name if she's a widow ...' Her voice trailed away and she got up suddenly. 'Sorry, I got to go and spend a penny—'

The other girls looked at each other.

'Poor Maggie,' Jo said soberly. 'Even if she does get married, she's going to have to say goodbye almost at once. I reckon it's true, you know, about the Forces' leave being stopped. All those people in Downing Street aren't there for the fun of it. And look at the way they're getting the kiddies out of London. I reckon they're going to do it pretty soon.'

The children were due to go next day. Jo had wanted to go home again once more to see Alice, but everything seemed to be topsy-turvy, with buses and trains crowded with Service-men and people making last-minute visits to friends and relatives, or even going to the country of their own free will. It took her and Phyl twice as long to get back to Elmbury Street, and by the time they arrived they were too exhausted to think of travelling out to Woolwich. They sank into their chairs and gratefully drank the tea Mrs Holt made them, and Jo laid her head back on the chair.

'I really would have liked to see our Ally again. But it'll be hours before we get there, and we'd never get back again tonight. And I'm just worn out. It's been busier than ever today.'

'I know. Everyone's coming to London – it's as if they think there won't be a London to come to by this time next week.' Phyl shuddered. 'Is it really going to be that bad, Jo? What's going to happen, do you think?'

Jo's eyes were closed. She shook her head wearily, but before she could reply, they heard the doorbell ring. Mrs Holt answered it and they heard a murmur of voices. A moment later their landlady came into the room, looking frightened. At Phyl's sudden movement, Jo opened her eyes and saw an orange envelope in Mrs Holt's hand.

'What is it? Who's sending us a telegram?'

'It's for you, Jo. You'd better open it, quick. The boy's waiting for a reply.'

Jo glanced out of the window and saw the telegraph boy outside, straddling his red pushbike, his hands in his pockets. She took the envelope and ripped it open and gave a little cry.

'What is it?' Phyl reached across as if to snatch it away. 'Jo, what's the matter?'

'It's Alice,' Jo said with a strangled sob. 'It's our Alice. She's taken Robbie, and she's run away. They don't know where to find her!'

All tiredness was forgotten as they battled their way home on crowded trains and buses. All they could think about was Alice, only ten years old, having run away from home with her big ginger cat.

'Where's she going to go?' Jo asked over and over again. 'What will she *do*? She's only little . . . Oh, Phyl if anything happens to her—'

'I know.' Phyl was every bit as anxious. The two families had grown up as one, cousins more like brothers and sisters, and they would be as one in their fears for the little girl. 'But I'm sure they'll find her, Jo. She can't have gone far. By the time we get home she'll be back with Robbie and eating a big bowl of bread and milk, ready for bed and wondering what all the fuss is about.'

'I hope so.' Jo didn't sound convinced. 'She must have been more upset than we realised. I mean, we all knew she was kicking up a fuss about going and leaving Robbie behind, but nobody ever thought she'd go this far. We thought she'd give in . . . We ought to have known better. She's always been an obstinate kid.' She stared out of the window for a moment, willing the bus to go faster. 'And there's another thing, Phyl. Rob's a big cat. If she tried to carry him, he'll get away from her and then what? *He'll* get lost, and Alice will be even more upset. Mum'll never be able to send her away not knowing where he is.'

'I don't reckon your mum will want to send her off anyway,' Phyl said, 'not after this.'

They arrived at last at the bus stop and hurried along the road to their own corner. Even before they got there, they could tell that Alice hadn't yet been found. All the neighbours were out, either walking up and down the street peering into any likely – and a good many unlikely – places, or standing in little knots talking and glancing anxiously around. It was beginning to get dark, and the gaslamps were coming on.

Carrie came out of the house as Jo and Phyl turned the corner and ran across to them, holding out her arms.

'Oh, Jo! Jo!'

'Oh, *Mum,*' Jo said, folding her mother in her arms. Carrie's eyes were red and swollen, her face blotched. 'Mum, don't cry. We'll find her, I know we'll find her.'

'I don't even know when she went,' Carrie sobbed. 'She was here after dinner, playing on the hearthrug with that blessed cat, and when I finished washing up and cleaning out the oven, she'd gone. She never even said goodbye. She just vanished, and Robbie with her.'

'She can't have gone far, not carrying him,' Jo said. 'You know he didn't like being carried. Even Alice couldn't take him far.'

'She must have taken him in my shopping bag. I can't find

it anywhere. He never minded going in that, not since he was a kitten and she used to cart him about in it. They could be miles away, Jo, miles away.'

'He wouldn't want to stay in it long. She'd either have to let him out or stop somewhere. And if she'd let him out he'd have come straight home. You know what, Mum? I reckon she'll be back any minute, soon as she sees it's getting dark. You know she doesn't like the dark.'

'Oh, my poor little Alice,' Carrie cried, her tears breaking out again. 'She'll be so frightened all by herself in the dark!'

Jo bit her lip, annoyed with herself for saying the wrong thing. 'She won't be by herself, Mum, she's got Robbie. Look, why don't we go in and have a cup of tea? Phyl and me are parched. We've been on the bus for hours, there's so many people around. Someone'll come and tell us the minute they find Alice.'

'I don't know as I can face tea,' Carrie began, but Jo folded her arm into the crook of her mother's elbow and drew her towards the house.

'You'll want it when I've made it. Proper Lyons tea it'll be, strong and sweet, just the way you like it. Where's Dad, and our Freddy and Eric?'

'Out looking,' Carrie sniffed. 'So's everyone else. They said I ought to stop here in case she comes back. It wouldn't do for her to find the house empty.' Her eyes filled with tears again. 'I've never let her come home to an empty house, Jo, I never let *any* of you come home to an empty house. Oh, what d'you think's happened to her?'

'Nothing.' Jo opened the front door and pushed her mother inside. 'Now, you sit down in your armchair while I put the kettle on. You're coming in, too, aren't you, Phyl?'

'I'd better pop in and see Mum first. Or – I suppose she's out looking, too, is she, Auntie Carrie?'

Carrie nodded. 'She wanted to stop with me, but I wouldn't let her. I wouldn't let anyone stop. The more out looking the better, that's what I said, and we knew you'd be home soon. Oh, Jo – Jo—' She curled herself up in the chair, and the two girls went out into the scullery.

364

'She's in a terrible way, Jo,' Phyl whispered as Jo filled the kettle. 'I wonder if we ought to get the doctor.'

'She's not ill – just upset. What could the doctor do?'

'I don't know – give her something to calm her down, or something. She'll make herself ill if she goes on like this. Suppose they don't find Alice? Your mum's going to be frantic if she's not home by dark.'

'Of course they'll find her! She can't have gone far, Phyl, not with that ruddy great cat. He weighs a ton. I can hardly lift him myself.'

She made the tea and they took it into the next room. Carrie was sitting crumpled in the chair, looking no bigger than a pile of ironing. She looked up drearily as the girls came in.

'There you are, Mum. A nice hot cup of tea. That'll put a bit of heart into you.'

'There's only one thing'll put heart into me, and that's seeing our Alice again.' Carrie looked hopelessly at the cup and Jo lifted it to her lips.

'Come on, Mum. Take a sip. You need it after all the crying you've been doing.'

'Well, wouldn't you cry?' Carrie demanded. 'She's only ten – she's my baby still. It was bad enough knowing I'd got to send her off to strangers in the country tomorrow, without— Oh!' Her hand flew to her mouth, almost knocking the cup from Jo's hand. 'Tomorrow! They're supposed to be at school at half past eight in the morning, with their sandwiches and everything, ready to go. Look at that – over in the corner. Her little suitcase and her gas mask, and her label already written out with her name and address, ready to tie round her neck . . . What am I going to do if she's not found by then?'

'Well, she won't be able to go, will she?' Jo said reasonably, and then at the look on her mother's face added hastily, 'Don't talk so daft, Mum, of course she'll be found by then. She'll have come back of her own accord. Now drink some of this tea. Phyl and me are having a cup, aren't we, Phyl? But we can't drink ours till you've had yours, see?'

Hardly noticing what she was doing, Carrie took a sip, and

then another. A touch of colour came back into her cheeks and she sipped again. She drained the cup and then looked at them ruefully.

'I do feel a bit better for it, Jo. And I know I've got to pull myself together. Now you drink yours – I don't know what I'm thinking of, letting you come all this way and then not even putting the kettle on for you.'

'You're thinking about our Alice, and nobody expects you to do anything different.' Jo drank gratefully. The journey had been long, hot and tiring and she had been feeling as dry as a bone. 'Phyl, I forgot to top up the pot, would you—?'

'Done it already.' Phyl took the cups and refilled them. 'After we've had this, I'm going to go out and help look. Jo can stay here with you.'

'I'd rather she went, too—' Carrie began, but both girls shook their heads firmly.

'You need someone with you, and Jo's the best one to stay. There.' Phyl set down her empty cup. 'Now I'm off.' She turned her head suddenly as they heard a sound at the front door. 'Who's that?'

Carrie was out of her chair. 'It's her! It's our Alice! They've found her – oh, thank God, thank *God* . . .' But the words died in her throat as the door opened and Bill Mason came in, his face grave. In his arms was a big, ginger cat.

'It's Robbie! Oh, you've found them. Oh, *Bill*.' She stopped and stared at him, her hand once again at her mouth. 'But – but where's Alice?' She reached out and took the cat, holding him to her and staring into his face as if he could speak and tell her what she wanted to hear. 'Where is she? *Where's my Alice?* '

'I don't know, love.' Bill Mason's voice was tired and hoarse. He laid his hand on his wife's arm and drew her close, and they stood there, the two of them, with Robbie held between their bodies. 'We found him coming down the street by hisself. He was crying his heart out, he was that tired, and he just let me pick him up as if he couldn't walk another step. But Alice wasn't with him. Our Alice wasn't nowhere to be seen.'

Chapter Twenty-Five

By eight o'clock next morning, the children of the street were already on their way to school to begin their evacuation. Jo and Phyl stood at the corner, watching as they went, a long parade of boys and girls, each bundled up in a mac or winter coat, carrying small cardboard suitcases or holdalls, brown luggage labels tied to their lapels, their gas masks slung across their shoulders. Their mothers went with them, some in tears, others with stiff faces. The few children who were not going stood by and jeered to hide their own feelings.

'Runnin' away! Cowards! Runnin' away from 'Itler!'

The children took no notice, although some of the boys squared their shoulders and clenched their fists. They passed Jo and Phyl, and disappeared up the street. In a few moments they would gather in the school playground and board the buses to go to the railway station and set off on their great adventure.

'Did your mum get any sleep?' Phyl asked, looking at her cousin's tired face. 'You don't look as if you did.'

Jo shrugged. 'I dropped off a bit. I didn't go to bed – just stopped in the chair all night. Mum wouldn't go to bed without someone being downstairs in case she came back. Dad and the boys were out almost all night, just roaming the streets. There wasn't much they could do really, but they couldn't settle at home. They're down the police station now, reporting it.'

'I can't understand it,' Phyl said. 'Once she'd lost Robbie, you'd think she'd come home. What was the point in stopping out then?'

'She might have been frightened to come home. She must have thought she'd get into trouble.'

'Frightened?' Phyl scoffed. 'Your Alice? She's never been frightened of anything – except the dark.'

'Yes. The dark – Phyl, you'd think she'd come home just because of that, wouldn't you? She'd never go out in the dark by herself! The stories that Willy Crewe told her, she used to be frightened to go outside to the lavvy at night by herself sometimes. Why didn't she come home when it got dark? What's *happened* to her, Phyl?'

'Nothing's happened.' Phyl caught the rising note of panic in her cousin's voice and gripped her arm. '*Nothing's happened*, Jo. She'll be back, you'll see – large as life and twice as natural. Nothing could happen to Alice.'

Jo sighed and wished she could believe it. Unhappily, said, 'We ought to let them know at work, Phyl. I can't go in today. I can't leave Mum.'

'I know. And I can't either. I'll go up to the phone box and telephone them.' She hesitated. 'There's Maggie's wedding, too—'

'The wedding! But that's *tomorrow* – she'll be back by then, surely!' Jo stared, horrified. 'Phyl, you don't think – Phyl, if anything's happened to our Alice—'

'No. No, I don't think anything's happened. I've already said so. Of course we'll be at the wedding. Look, you go back to Auntie Carrie, she'll be wondering where you are. I'll go and phone . . .' She turned and hurried up the street, praying that her words would be proved true, knowing that they could not be so, knowing that something had happened to prevent the little girl from coming home and dreading what it might be.

Alice had been out all yesterday, all last night. Something must have happened . . .

All the girls had seen the processions of children on their way

368

to work that morning.

'They were all in the playground down our school,' Shirley said as they got ready for their shift. 'Lined up like little soldiers. They looked so small in their macs and holding their suitcases. Crying their eyes out, some of them were, and clinging to their mums, it broke my heart to see them.'

'It's awful,' Etty said. 'Kiddies didn't ought to be took away from their mums.' Her face was pale and the others guessed she was thinking of her own bleak, motherless childhood. Maggie, however, sympathetic though she was, couldn't help her mind turning to her own worries.

'I just hope they don't cancel my Tom's leave. I'll die if we can't get married tomorrow.'

'I'm surprised they haven't cancelled it already,' Irene said. 'I thought all troops were on standby.'

'They are.' With war looming, it seemed petty not to talk to Irene, spiteful though she could be. 'Tom told me he's on a minute's notice to be recalled. We're just hoping it'll be the minute after we say "I do", and not the minute before!'

Shirley glanced around the dressing room, frowning. 'Where are Jo and Phyl? They're not usually late.'

'Buses all over the place with this evacuation business,' Maggie said. 'They've all been brought into service to get the kids to the railway stations, and they're on special routes and everything. I was lucky to get in meself.'

The manager, Mr Carter, came into the dressing room at that moment, his torch in his hand, but for once he didn't seem interested in hemlines. He came over to Maggie and the others, frowning.

'I've just had a message from Josephine and Phyllis. They were called home unexpectedly last night, it seems. The little sister's missing – I'm not sure whose sister, but they've both gone home. They're cousins, aren't they?'

'Yes,' Maggie said, staring at him in alarm. 'But they're more like sisters themselves – their mums are twins and they live next door to each other. It must be Jo's sister, little Alice. Didn't Jo tell us she was kicking up about having to leave her cat behind?'

'That's right,' Shirley agreed. 'She must have run off with him. Oh, how awful! How long's she been missing, Mr Carter?'

'The message doesn't say, but if they were called home last night and she's still gone this morning . . .' He shook his head. 'Well, we must get a couple of key Nippies in to cover for them till they come back. Poor girls – what a worry.' He went off to organise two of the experienced Nippies, part of the team who could go to any Corner House at a moment's notice to deal with such emergencies, to come and take over Jo's and Phyl's stations. The other girls looked at each other in dismay.

'That's terrible,' Maggie said. 'Poor Jo. And what must her mum and dad be feeling? They must be worried sick.'

'What I don't understand,' Shirley said, 'is where a kiddie like Alice could go, with a great big cat as well. I mean, she'd have to carry him, he wouldn't follow her like a dog. She couldn't get far like that.'

'I don't suppose she did,' Etty observed. 'I bet she lost him early on and now she's looking for him. Poor little kid, she must be terrified.'

The others looked at her. They'd been thinking of the way the grown-ups would be feeling, their fears and anxieties, but Etty, who had never had anyone to worry about her, had thought of the little girl, lost and alone, frightened about herself and her cat.

'What d'you think she'll be doing?' Shirley asked.

Etty shrugged. 'Well, if she got very far and then he ran off, she'll probably have tried to follow him and then not known where she was. If she'd gone the right way, she'd have got back home, or somewhere she knew – but it doesn't look as if she did that.'

'She must have gone the wrong way, then,' Shirley said, and Etty nodded. 'She could be anywhere.'

It was time to go through the tunnel to begin setting out their tables. They hurried through in silence, each one thinking of Alice and her family. As they came into the brightly lit Corner House, Maggie turned to the others, her face sad.

'I know this is going to sound ever so selfish,' she said quietly, 'but you know what else it means, don't you? If Alice isn't found, Jo and Phyl won't be coming to my wedding tomorrow.'

The day wore on without any news. Everyone in the street was out looking for Alice, and now the police were searching as well. It was all made more difficult by the huge numbers of children trying to leave London that day. The bus and railway stations were crowded with school parties, some lined up dutifully and waiting with varying degrees of patience to be told where to go, others milling about totally out of control, fighting, shouting, swarming over the platforms at the peril of their own lives and the lives of those who tried to restrain them. Teachers and railway staff were hot and perspiring, hoarse from shouting, wondering desperately if this nightmare would ever end. Police, trying to keep order and attend to other traffic as well, were beginning to think that London would be a safer and better place to be once the evacuation was complete.

The search for one small girl amongst all this mayhem and confusion was like looking for a needle in a haystack.

'They're not going to find her,' Carrie said hopelessly as Jo tried to persuade her to eat a bit of dinner. 'Something awful's happened to her, I know it has. Oh, Jo, my poor little Alice.'

'They'll find her, Mum,' Jo said, trying to ignore the terrible fear gnawing at her own inside. 'They'll be bringing her home through that door any minute now.'

Carrie shook her head. 'She'd have been here by now if she'd been all right.' She looked across at Robbie, still fast asleep on a cushion in Bill's chair, where he was never normally allowed to sit. 'Look at him, he's worn out. He must have walked miles. How far did they get before he got away? And why did he leave her?'

'He's a cat, Mum. A dog might have stayed with her, but

cats aren't like that. If he got out of that bag, he'd have been frightened, he'd have just wanted to run and find his way home. And Alice couldn't have carried him far, you know how heavy he is.'

'Well, why's he so tired then?' Carrie demanded. 'He *must* have come a long way.'

'Perhaps he ran off in the wrong direction first. And he wouldn't know the shortest way back. He must have tried lots of ways.' Wondering about Robbie's route home wasn't really helping Jo, but at least it kept Carrie's mind occupied. 'Think how pleased Alice is going to be to find him here,' she said. 'When she comes through the door and sees him waiting for her, her face is going to just light up. I bet that's why she hasn't come home – she's looking for him.'

Carrie wiped her eyes. She seemed to have an inexhaustible supply of tears, like a deep well somewhere inside her. She looked up at Jo, her face white and drained, all crumpled up like a paper bag. 'I don't think they're ever going to find her,' she said, her voice little more than a thin, hopeless thread of sound. 'I think she's just got lost for ever, and we're never going to see her again. Oh, Jo – Jo!'

'Don't, Mum!' Jo cried, terrified. 'Don't say things like that. Little girls like Alice don't just disappear. Look, even if she is lost, she's got a tongue in her head, she knows where she lives. She'll be back, bright as ninepence, you wait and see. We won't lose our Alice that easy.'

But Carrie had lost hope and wouldn't be comforted. She folded her arms and laid her head on them and wept, and nothing that Jo could say or do made any difference. Her tears were not those of panic and hysteria, as they had been yesterday – they were steady and relentless, like rain that had been falling for hours and showed no sign of stopping. It was as if she meant to cry for the rest of her life.

Phyl came in from next door. She'd gone home only to sleep, and then up the street to the telephone box to let them know she and Jo wouldn't be at work. She glanced at Jo and sat down beside her aunt, holding the shaking hands in hers and stroking them gently. 'Don't cry, Auntie Carrie,' she said over and over again. 'Don't cry.' But Carrie couldn't stop. Softly, steadily, without pause, she wept, and there was nothing they could do but hold her and try to comfort her with their presence.

'What did Mr Carter say?' Jo asked in a low voice.

'I didn't speak to him. I spoke to that girl Annie on the switchboard and asked her to get a message through. I expect he'll be all right about it, though. He's not a bad chap.'

'I wish we could have spoken to Maggie as well,' Jo said wistfully. 'It's her wedding tomorrow and we're not going to be there. It would've been nice to wish her all the best.'

The front door opened and Carrie started up, her eyes wide with sudden hope. Jo and Phyl looked up, too, as Bill Mason came in. He looked worn out, his face drawn and haggard, his eyes rimmed with red from not sleeping all night. He looked at them and gave a brief shake of his head, and they sank back, the flicker of hope extinguished.

'We've bin everywhere I can think of, Carrie, love. We've bin to places I never *would've* thought of. I don't know what else we can do.'

'Could they put out an appeal on the wireless, d'you think?' Jo asked, suddenly eager as the idea occurred to her. 'You know, like they do sometimes – an SOS. Only usually it's for someone who hasn't been heard of for years whose mother's dangerously ill, that sort of—'

'Don't talk like that, Jo!' Carrie exclaimed. 'Alice hasn't been missing for years – that's a horrible idea!'

'I didn't mean that. I only meant—' Jo looked at her father. 'Couldn't they, Dad?'

'I don't know. I'll ask the policeman. It might help.' He sat down in his chair, lifting Robbie on to his lap. 'If only he could talk. Where is she, old chap?' he asked the cat, fondling its ears. 'Where did she take you, eh?'

Jo got up and went out to the scullery. 'I'll make you a cup of tea, Dad. You look all in. And there's a bit of dinner keeping hot in the oven for you – I'll get it.'

She brought him a plate of cottage pie and a big cup of tea, and he sat at the table and ate it without interest. As he forked the meat and potato into his mouth, he stared in front of him, his eyes hollow and vague as if he were looking at something quite different. He didn't seem to have anything else to say. Indeed, Jo thought, there didn't seem to be anything else *to* say.

They sat there, the four of them and Robbie, aching for the missing part of the family to be back where she should be, while outside in the streets the search went on.

Charlie and Mike had arranged to take Tommy out for a last drink as a free man. Getting leave was a problem with the situation so tense, but they'd each managed to wangle a few hours' pass, and Tommy's leave of one week for getting married was still in order. They met at their favourite pub early that evening and Mike went to the bar.

'How're you feeling?' Charlie asked. 'Nervous?'

'What d'you think?' Tommy said. 'There's hundreds in that family, and what with half of 'em being dressed up in them Pearly outfits, it's going to be a proper circus. Still, so long as me and Mags get spliced, it's okay by me. I don't reckon I'm going to be around long enough for a second chance.'

'Steady on,' Charlie said, 'you're not thinking of getting bumped off, are you?'

Tommy grinned and shook his head. 'Me? Not on your nelly! I'm indestructible, I am. No, I just meant I reckon we're going to be off on our travels pretty soon and there won't be no marriage leave for a while then. I'm not taking the risk of leaving my Mag a free woman while I'm overseas punching Jerry's nose for him.'

Mike came back with two beers in glass mugs and set them down on the table, then went back for the third. He sat himself down opposite Tommy and raised his glass. 'Cheers, mate. All the best.'

Charlie nodded and did the same. 'All the best.' They drank and set their glasses back on the table, wiping the froth from their lips. 'Seriously, mate, you don't reckon Maggie'd do the dirty on you if you weren't married, do you?'

'It's not her I'm worried about. It's all them other blokes coming into that Corner House, flashing their uniforms and all. She's only human.'

'Go on, she's the salt of the earth, Maggie is. She wouldn't let you down.'

'I want to make sure we're married, all the same,' Tommy said, and drank again. 'You two don't know what it's like, being in love.'

The other two hooted, but Mike's laughter seemed forced and he stopped quite soon and stared into his glass. Tommy glanced at him.

'You going to make it up with young Phyl at the wedding tomorrow?'

'Make what up? We never had no row.'

'Whatever it was you did have, then,' Tommy said, exasperated. 'Are you going to be friends again? That's what I'm asking.'

Mike looked at his glass again. 'I dunno. It's up to her, isn't it?'

'I wouldn't say so, mate. I'd say it's up to both of you. From what I know, and from what my Maggie tells me, neither of you knows what's the matter and it's time you got together and found out.'

'Why? What's it matter to you?'

'We're your mates, that's why!' Tommy cried. 'And if you want it straight, we're all fed up to the back teeth of seeing the pair of you mooning about like someone what's lost a bob and found a tanner. It's obvious you're both missing each other, so why not use a bit of sense and get together again? It's all a stupid misunderstanding and a couple of words would probably put the whole thing right.'

'It's a couple of words Phyl could say, then,' Mike said obstinately. 'Like why she never come to meet me at the bandstand that day, and never sent a word to say why.'

'Maybe she never got the message,' Tommy said. 'Have you ever thought of that?'

'Course I thought of it. I asked that girl the next week if

375

she'd ever told Phyl, and she said yes. She got the message all right.'

'What girl?' Charlie asked.

'That other Nippy. The flashy-looking one. Eileen, or something. I gave her the message that Saturday, when I couldn't sit at Phyl's table, and she said she'd deliver it right away, and I went in the next week to see why Phyl never turned up, and this Eileen said she'd definitely told her. So there you are.' Mike looked at them defiantly. 'It's Phyl what started all this, not me, and it's up to her if she wants to put it right.'

Tommy sighed. 'Well, I dunno. I still reckon there's more to it than that. I reckon you ought to have it out with her. It'd clear the air if nothing else. At least you'd know why she never turned up.'

'I don't know as I want to know,' Mike said. 'Maybe it's best forgotten and swept under the bridge.'

Tommy drained his glass. He set the mug back on the table and leaned forward. He glowered into Mike's face.

'Now, look here, mate. You're coming to my wedding tomorrow, you're going to be my best man, and you're going to look *happy* about it, see? And Phyl's going to be there too, and you're going to be a bit pleasant to each other. There's going to be no rows, and no "not speaking". This is my Maggie's day and I'm not having it spoilt, all right? You're going to be friends. I don't care what happens afterwards, you can ruddy murder each other if you want, but while you're at my wedding, you're going to be *friends*.'

Mike said nothing for a moment. Then he looked up and grinned.

'Okay, mate. If that's the way you want it. Matter of fact,' he added ruefully, 'I really wouldn't mind getting back with Phyl again. She's a smasher, and I've really missed her these past few weeks.'

Tommy sat back, a satisfied smile on his face.

'That's it, then. That's all right. And you know what?' He winked at Charlie. 'I reckon by the end of the day tomorrow, we'll have another engagement on our hands, and another wedding to look forward to!'

'I'll have to let Maggie know we won't be there,' Phyl said miserably.

Jo nodded. Her mother had finally gone upstairs to lie down and try to get a bit of sleep and the two girls were sitting exhausted in their chairs, sharing yet another pot of tea. The day had been a long and frustrating one. Neither of them had been out of the house, though they longed desperately to be part of the search, because Carrie had been in such a state they were afraid to leave her. At last, worn out by her crying, she'd almost fallen asleep and Jo had persuaded her to go to bed, but she and Phyl were twitching with pent-up energy, matched with the peculiar weariness that comes from a sleepless night.

'You'd better go and ring up again before she goes off shift. I wish we didn't have to tell her why – it's bound to upset her, you know how she is about kiddies, and her sister's about the same age, isn't she?'

'Ginnie's not being evacuated, though,' Phyl said. 'Her mum don't want her to go. Anyway, she's being bridesmaid – it would've been cruel to send her off with all the rest today.'

Jo nodded again. The news on the wireless had been all about the evacuation, how children all over London and in some of the other big cities, like Portsmouth, had been crowding on to buses and trains to make for the countryside. Once there, they were all to be sent to 'billets' – homes which had a spare room or sometimes no more than a spare bed, and who had been told, not asked, to take them in. There they would stay until it was safe for them to come back home.

'I suppose they're all just about there now,' she said drearily. 'Going to their new homes. I hope they get looked after proper.'

'They've all got postcards to send home,' Phyl said. 'Their mums and dads won't know till tomorrow morning where they are even. I can't imagine what it'd be like, sending a kiddie of six or seven years old off to strangers and not even know where they're going.'

'Our Alice won't be sending a postcard,' Jo said, and they fell silent again.

After a bit, Phyl stirred herself and said she'd go up to the phone. She walked up the street, conscious that all the neighbours were eyeing her curiously. Several stopped her to ask if Alice had been found yet, although the whole street would have known the minute she was back, and by the time Phyl reached the red telephone box she felt as though she'd been through a mangle.

She got through to Mr Carter and he listened to what she had to say and then told her to hang on while he fetched Maggie herself. 'She's just coming off shift. It's best if you have a word with her, Phyllis.'

He really was a kind man, she thought, like all the managers at Lyons – strict but kind, and always fair. She waited for Maggie to come to the phone, ignoring the small queue of people forming outside the telephone box. With everything so tense at present, everyone wanted to make phone calls to friends and relatives, but Phyl was determined to speak to Maggie before she put down the receiver.

'Hullo? Hullo, is that Phyl?'

Maggie was almost shouting. We hardly need a phone, Phyl thought. She's only got to go outside the door and I'd be able to hear her anyway. 'Yes, it's me. I just wanted to tell you—'

'Has she been found?' Maggie's voice was sharp with anxiety. 'Mr Carter didn't seem to know—'

'No, she hasn't. Look, I'm ever so sorry, Mag, but it don't look as if me and Jo are going to be there tomorrow. We can't leave her mum and dad and everyone while all this is going on. I didn't want you to think we'd forgotten.'

'Forgotten! I wouldn't have thought that. Oh, Phyl. Poor Jo. And her mum and dad, they must be going round the bend. I wish I could come and help.'

'You can't,' Phyl said. 'We've got all the neighbours out looking as it is, and the police and all. I don't know where else there is to look. Jo's dad's getting on to the wireless to ask them to put out a special SOS. Someone might have seen her.' Phyl's voice shook. 'Maggie, if anything's happened to her—'

'It won't have,' Maggie said. 'She'll turn up. And – if she does – you'll come to my wedding, won't you? If she does come back in time.'

'If Alice comes back, we'll come to your wedding,' Phyl promised. 'We might even bring her along with us!'

'Bring the whole blooming family,' Maggie said. 'The more the merrier, specially if your Alice is one of 'em!'

A second night went by without much sleep. The BBC put out the SOS after the nine o'clock news. Bill went down to the police station shortly afterwards, but they told him nobody had telephoned the number given. There was still no sign of Alice, and nobody could think of anywhere else she might be.

'They've searched empty houses and garden sheds and railway arches, the lot,' Bill reported, returning to the anxious family. 'The copper said we might as well all go to bed. It won't do no good for us to get ill on top of everything else.'

'I can't go to bed,' Carrie said. She had slept for a couple of hours that afternoon and then come down again, heavy-eyed, with a thumping headache. 'You go up, Bill, I'll stay down here. I won't have her coming back to a dark house, and no one to let her in.'

Nobody really thought that Alice would return in the middle of the night but, then, nobody had thought she would run off in the first place. Bill, almost too tired to speak, nodded and went off upstairs. 'I won't get undressed,' he said. 'I'll just lay down on top of the bed. You be sure and give me a shout the minute anything happens, now.'

Carrie settled herself in her armchair and Jo took her father's chair opposite. Just as Carrie couldn't leave Alice to come home to a darkened house, neither could Jo leave her mother alone. The boys went to bed and Phyl went back next door. A heavy silence settled over the house. They all closed their eyes and dozed fitfully, but nobody was really asleep.

On the other side of London, Maggie and her family had also gone to bed late. The preparations for the wedding were almost complete. The wedding cake had arrived from Lyons, and there were several hampers of pastries, sausage rolls and assorted small cakes. There were a few cases of beer in one corner of the living-room and Maggie's ivory dress with its encrustation of pearls hung from the picture-rail. The other Pearly outfits – Ivy's skirt and jacket, the men's suits and waistcoats – were upstairs in the front bedroom, every tiny button firmly sewn in place. They were richly patterned, some with hearts or bells, others with huge, full-blown roses in silver or mother-of-pearl on a maroon or deep blue background. The women's hats with their huge feathery plumes lay carefully placed on Jim's bed, while Jim heroically slept on the floor.

Etty was staying, too, sharing Maggie's bed. They lay for a long time, talking in whispers. Ginnie was asleep in the same room and Ivy had already called out twice to tell them to be quiet and go to sleep. They were both too excited to take any notice, however, and now they had Jo's anxiety to think about as well.

'It must be awful,' Maggie said. 'That poor mother . . .'

'And poor little Alice, wandering the streets,' Etty agreed. 'Wherever can she be, Maggie? I mean, you'd think she'd have gone to a policeman or someone and asked for help, wouldn't you – especially after she'd lost the cat?'

'Maybe she just went on looking for him.' But it didn't make sense. At some point, surely, Alice would have given up and tried to get home. They lay silent for a while, not wanting to think about what might have happened to her.

'Well, there's nothing we can do about it,' Etty said at last. 'What we've got to think about is tomorrow. Just think, Maggie, this time tomorrow night you'll be a married woman, and you and Tommy—' She stopped, feeling her face blush even in the dark.

'Never you mind what me and Tommy'll be doing,' said

Maggie, who knew only too well. 'What you and the rest'll be doing is having a right old party. The whole street'll be coming, you know, and Mrs Watkins is going to get her joanna brought outside. She's a smashing player, knows all the best tunes. Let's hope it don't rain!'

'If I have to tell you girls again, I'll be in there with a rolling-pin!' Ivy's voice came through the wall. 'Stop that nattering and go to sleep. We've got a wedding to go to tomorrow, just in case you've forgotten!'

Maggie smothered a laugh. 'Forgotten! As if I could have forgotten. Come on, then, Etty – let's do as we're told and get a bit of shut-eye. This time tomorrow, there's only one person entitled to tell me what to do, and that'll be my husband, and you can bet *he* won't be telling me to go to sleep!'

Chapter Twenty-Six

By next morning, however, it seemed doubtful that there would be a wedding at all.

'It's looking bad,' Sam Pratt said as the family grabbed whatever breakfast they could. Ivy had been up since six, sorting out all the last-minute jobs, and there was hardly a plate or a cup in the house that she would allow to be used – the rest were set out in the front room, ready for the reception. There were also boxes full of glasses lent by the pub to be put out, and the cases of beer to be unpacked, as well as the wedding cake and the presents to be arranged on the sideboard in all their glory.

'What's looking bad?' Maggie was in a panic about her hair. She'd lain awkwardly on it during the night and it was going all ways. Etty had damped it down and sprinkled it heavily with Amami setting lotion, and was winding it into curlers. 'What are you on about, Dad?'

'This Hitler malarkey. I heard the news before you lot come rampaging down the apples and pears. They've issued him with an ultimatum. If he don't agree to pull out of Poland, that's it. We'll be going over there to bash his head in. And *that* means—' he looked at Maggie '—there won't be no leave for His Majesty's daft and barmy.'

'Army,' Maggie told Etty automatically, and then took in what her father was saying. 'Dad! You don't think they'd stop my Tom coming out to get married!'

'They can do anything if it suits them,' he replied grimly.

'They'll want all troops standing by, won't they? We could be at war this time tomorrow.'

Maggie stared at him and then turned her head towards her dress, hanging from the picture-rail. The curler Etty had been winding in fell out and rolled on to the floor. Maggie's eyes filled with tears. 'Dad, they couldn't—'

'Well, maybe they won't, love,' he said hastily. 'I reckon we'd have heard by now if they were. Anyway, there's nothing we can do except get into our duds and carry on. No point in not being ready when your Tom arrives at the left in the lurch.'

'You don't have to call it that,' Maggie said. '"Church" would be good enough this once. Haven't you finished with my hair yet, Etty?'

'I'll finish the minute you stop bobbing about and keep still,' Etty said. 'There's only two more to go, and for goodness' sake don't go pulling 'em out before the lotion's dry or it'll look worse than ever.'

'It's going to look awful anyway. I don't know what it is about hair – it looked smashing last week when it didn't matter and today I look as if I've been pulled through a hedge backwards. And I feel fat. I'm never going to be able to get all them buttons done up. Not that it matters if my Tom's not going to be able to come after all. Oh, *Et* . . .' Her eyes filled with tears again and she sniffed loudly.

Someone knocked on the front door and everyone jumped. 'If that's a telegraph boy—' Maggie began, her voice trembling.

'It's not a telegraph boy. It's your flowers.' Ivy went to the door and came back with a huge bouquet. 'Florrie up the shop's been up since six doing this for you. Ain't it lovely?'

'Oh, Mum!' The bouquet hung like an enormous teardrop from Ivy's arms. It was composed of roses the colour of clotted cream, with ivy leaves trailing amongst them and a cloud of white dots of gypsophila misted like a bridal veil across their dewy faces. Maggie reached out and took it, staring in admiration. Gently, she touched the blooms and then lowered her face to sniff their fragrance. 'Mum, it's beautiful.'

'It's your gran's wedding present,' Ivy said, nodding towards the old woman in her corner. 'She went up herself, specially, and told Florrie just what she wanted. She said it had to be like her own wedding bouquet and this was it.'

'Gran?' Maggie turned towards the squat, black figure with the umbrella standing close at hand. Ada Pratt had put her teeth in early, in honour of the occasion, and as she and Maggie stared at each other, she opened her mouth in her unaccustomed smile. Maggie choked and flung herself at her grandmother. 'Oh, Gran, *Gran* – oh, thanks, they've lovely. I never *seen* such a lovely bouquet. It's beautiful, just *beautiful*.'

Ada Pratt mumbled something in her cracked old voice, and then spoke again, more loudly. 'That's all right, girl. Got to give you a proper send-off.' She looked a little sadly at the huge bunch of flowers. 'My Bert brought me a bunch just like that from the Market, the day we was wed. Well, I hope you has better luck than we did, that's all. Give your old gran a kiss, then.'

Maggie did so, feeling subdued. Her grandparents hadn't had much of a marriage. Bert Pratt had been killed in the Boer War, leaving his young wife to bring up her family alone. What was it Mum had told her? Ninety shirts a week she'd washed, by hand, and all with collars to starch and iron, and even that had only been just enough to keep the wolf from the door . . . I hope that doesn't happen to me, Maggie thought with a sudden cold feeling in her heart. I hope this lovely bouquet's going to bring me good luck, not bad.

There was no time to brood, however. The house was buzzing with people all wanting to wash at the kitchen sink at the same time, neighbours calling in, telegrams arriving. With each one, Maggie's heart lurched, expecting it to be from Tommy telling her he couldn't come after all, and it didn't help that her father, quite without realising it, had begun to hum an old music-hall song that went, 'There was I, waiting at the church . . . waiting at the church . . . waiting at the church . . .' She wanted to scream at him.

'Come upstairs and help me with my hair,' she said to Etty. 'It must be dry by now.'

'It'd be better to leave it in till you get your frock on. Then we won't mess it up, see.'

'Well, when can I put my frock on?'

'About two o'clock,' Etty said, considering. 'The wedding's at three, so that gives us time to get it looking nice and do your hair and put a bit of lipstick on. Did you get that new pot of vanishing cream?'

'Yes, and if Dad sings that bit about "then I found he'd left me in the lurch" once more, I'll rub it all over him and hope it works!' Maggie threatened. 'Oh, Et, I feel awful. I feel sick. I never expected it to be like this.'

'It'll all be over by teatime,' Etty said comfortingly. 'You're getting married, Mag! You're bound to feel a bit nervous.'

'Nervous?' she moaned. 'I feel as if I'm going to jump off a huge cliff!'

'It's time you had a cup of tea and a bit of toast,' her mother said, coming in from the front room where she had been spreading tables with white sheets. 'You never had no breakfast, that's your trouble. Sit yourself down by your gran for a few minutes and stop looking as if you're going to your execution.'

Maggie flurried for a few minutes and then did as she was told. In fact, there wasn't much more for her to do. Ivy had everything under control and all Maggie needed do was get herself ready. She sat down beside the old woman who had been a part of her life ever since she was born, and looked into the wrinkled face.

'Did you feel like this when you were married, Gran?'

'Course I did. Everyone does. It wouldn't be a wedding without a few nerves. Mind you, we didn't have no Pearly costumes to wear, because that was only just starting. Young Henry was just getting Pearlies going when me and your grandad got spliced. All that's happened since.' She looked at the pearl-covered dress and at Ivy's skirt and jacket hanging beside it. 'It's summat to be proud of, that is. All come about from one young nipper who wanted to help other people, even though he didn't have nothing himself. Not a brass farthing when we first knowed him. But he had some grub in his belly and a shed and a pile of sacks to sleep on, and a lot of mates what he made, and he thought he was rich. And so he was.'

'Yes,' Maggie said softly, 'he was. I'm glad you knew him, Gran. I'm glad your mum and dad helped him.'

'You couldn't do nothing else for Henry Croft,' Ada Pratt said. 'You couldn't look at his cheeky face and *not* help him – specially when what he wanted you to do most was help others. A little saint, that's what he was, a little saint.'

'Help others . . .' Maggie said slowly, and then, her face alight, 'That's it! That's what we'll do. We'll get the Pearlies to look for young Alice. If anyone can find her, they will!'

The word spread quickly. There was nothing like a child in distress to bring the Pearly kings and queens of London out in force. Before the hour was out, every Pearly in the boroughs of London knew about the plight of little Alice Mason, and was out looking for her. They even put on their costumes so that everyone would recognise them and know something was up. In full regalia, they scoured the streets, asking if anyone had seen a small lost girl, and there were so few children left in London now that it seemed certain, as Maggie had said, that they would find her.

'I'll let Jo know right away,' she said. 'There could still be time for her and Phyl to come to the wedding.'

Jo and Phyl, however, had lost all hope of getting to Maggie's wedding. The journey there took so long that they'd have to leave within an hour to make it, and even that didn't allow for getting themselves ready. When Jo went up to her bedroom – the one she shared with Alice when she was at home – she saw her new frock hanging on the back of the door, and knew that she wouldn't wear it. Not today, anyway – perhaps not ever.

It'll always remind me of the day our Alice got lost, she thought, searching in her drawer for fresh hankies. There seemed to be no end to the amount her mother needed to dry her tears. Carrie was being brave – she'd pulled herself together and was getting dinner ready even now, saying that Bill and the boys would need a good meal inside them – but she couldn't stop the tears that rolled endlessly down her cheeks. Jo took out her last half-dozen and went downstairs again.

How she'd missed hearing the doorbell ring, she didn't know, but it must have done because a telegram had arrived while she was upstairs, and Carrie was staring at it in terror while her sister May and Phyl tried to persuade her to open it.

'I can't,' she whispered, her hand shaking as she held the little brown envelope. 'I can't. I'm frightened . . .'

'You've got to know,' May urged her. 'It might just as easily be good news . . . Let me do it, Carrie, love. Let me open it for you.'

Jo, staring at them from the doorway, thought she had never seen the twin sisters look less alike. Carrie was white and drawn, her eyes red and swollen, her hair uncombed and straggly. She seemed to have lost weight overnight. May, no less anxious, was flushed and almost vibrating with energy. Unable to wait a second longer, she took the envelope and tore it open while the rest of them watched.

The colour drained from her face. She looked at her sister with wide, almost black eyes.

'Oh, Carrie,' she said in a trembling voice. 'Oh, *Carrie* . . .'

It was touch and go whether Mike and Charlie would be able to attend the wedding either.

'All leave's been cancelled,' their officer told them. 'You know that.'

'It's only for a couple of hours, sir,' Charlie pleaded. 'It's a mate of ours. We've been mates since we were at infants' school. We'll be back straight after – we won't even stop on for the party.'

The officer scratched his neck. Charlie and Mike had been good recruits, getting through their basic training without too many scrapes, and he had hopes that they'd get promotion themselves before too long. Although the tensions this weekend were at breaking-point and men were being recalled from full leave, so far they hadn't been stopped from actually going out of the gates. These two could be at their wedding and back in less than three hours, quicker if need be.

'Write down the church where this wedding's taking place, and the address of the bride if that's where the reception's being held,' he said. 'And don't be surprised if the MPs come to hoick you out before it's all over. And if you're not back here on the dot of seven this evening, you're for the high jump, understand?'

'We'll be here,' Charlie said joyfully. 'Thanks, sir.'

Mike was less overjoyed. Although he wanted to go and back up his mate Tommy, a part of him was still reluctant to face Phyl. Yet another part wanted to see her again, and the two – or was it three? – parts warred within him, creating a turmoil of feelings he couldn't begin to sort out. He'd more or less decided to ignore all these peculiar feelings and just go along with whatever happened. If we can't go, we can't go, he told himself, and if we can, we can, and if I see Phyl, well, then, I'll *see* her – and just wait and see what happens.

'It's lucky we don't have to change into our best suits,' Charlie said as they hurried back to their hut to get ready. 'Uniform'll take you anywhere! We'll have the girls all over us.'

Mike looked at him in surprise. It wasn't like Charlie to talk about 'having girls all over him' but this wedding seemed to be bringing out a different side to the shy young man. 'I'm not sure you're safe to go,' he said. 'Don't forget it's jankers if we're not back by seven.'

Charlie grinned. 'That's the beauty of it,' he said. 'They'll be all over us, but we've got a good excuse to get away from them. I reckon we're going to enjoy this wedding, Mike.'

Mike grinned. Maybe Charlie hadn't changed so much after all. 'You always were one for knowing where the escape route was,' he said. 'Come on, mate, get a shine on those boots and let's get cracking!'

They met Tommy outside the church. He was pacing up and down the pavement, looking smart in his uniform but nervous. He breathed a sigh of relief when he saw them.

'Thank God you've made it, chums. Have you got the ring?' He looked at it in the palm of Mike's hand and nodded distractedly. 'You know Phyl and Jo aren't coming, don't you?'

Mike stared at him. 'Not coming? Why not?'

'Jo's little sister's got lost. Ran off with the cat, from what I can understand. Wouldn't leave him behind when she got evacuated, and now the cat's come home and there's no sign of whatsername—'

'Alice,' Mike said. 'But—'

'—and the whole family's out looking for her, and Maggie's got all the Pearlies out as well, and as far as I can make out,' Tommy said, taking his cap off and running his fingers frantically through his hair, 'we'll be lucky if enough people turn up to be bloody *witnesses* to the wedding!'

'But what do they think's happened to her?' Mike asked. He had been to Phyl's home and met all the family, including Jo's parents and brothers and little Alice. He'd even met Robbie. 'I mean, how long's she been missing?'

'Since Thursday, I think. They were supposed to be evacuated on Friday.' Tommy glanced at his watch. 'Crikey, look at the time – we'd better get inside or Maggie'll be coming round the corner in her uncle's van and I'm not supposed to see her till she walks up the aisle. It's bad luck . . .' He tugged at their arms. 'Come *on*, for God's sake.'

'It's all right, mate, she won't be here on time, they never are. Bride's privilege.' They followed him into the little church all the same and the vicar came forward to meet them. He was a tall, thin, cadaverous-looking man with a long, mournful face and a voice that Mike thought would be better doing funeral services than weddings. However, he seemed to understand that this was meant to be a joyful occasion and led them to the front pews. Charlie went in first, then Mike and lastly Tommy.

'What did you say about the Pearlies?' Mike whispered as they sat there.

'Maggie's got 'em all out looking for her,' Tommy

389

whispered back. 'All over London. Didn't you see any on your way?'

'Yes, we did, as a matter of fact,' Charlie said. 'Don't you remember, Mike? There was a whole bunch of 'em on a corner – one of 'em was up shouting the odds on a soapbox. I never heard what he was on about but I suppose he was telling everyone about Alice.'

'That's right,' Tommy said. 'They're all at it. If anyone can find her, they can.'

'I hope they do,' Mike said. 'She's a sweet kid.' He thought sadly about little Alice, wandering alone and lost in some unfamiliar part of London. Poor Mrs Mason must be frantic, he thought, and Jo, too, and Phyl . . . He had a sudden urge to see Phyl, to hold her in his arms and comfort her, to help her . . .

Oh, Phyl, he thought with a surge of misery, Phyl, what went wrong? Why didn't you come that day?

The church was filling up. People were filling the pews behind them and on the other side of the church. The three young men glanced about them and recognised a few faces. Tommy's family were behind him, his dad leaning forward to poke him in the back and mutter a few words of encouragement, his mum in a flowery hat, her face thick with powder, wanting a kiss. Cousins, uncles, aunts and friends were cramming in behind, some of them trying to pass messages to him. It sounded as if the whole church was whispering.

Those on the other side were just as bad. The Pratts, led by George and Gerry escorting their grandmother, and Evie following on with her husband and Billy, filled the first two pews, leaving room for Jim who would be bringing his mother, and Sam who would be giving his daughter away. Behind them was a swelling crowd of family and friends and neighbours, many of them in Pearly costume. The church glittered.

'The Pearlies'll be out looking for Alice again straight after,' someone came over to tell Mike and Tommy. 'But they couldn't miss seeing our Mag getting spliced.' He looked at his watch. 'She should be here any mo.'

'Oh, God, she's *coming*,' Tommy moaned, as if this were the last thing he wanted to hear. 'You sure you got that ring, Mike?'

'I showed it to you outside the church. I'm not going to have lost it between the door and here, am I?'

'Just check, will you? It won't hurt. Just to settle me mind.'

Mike fished the ring out of his pocket again and held it out. Tommy took it and examined it, as if suspecting it to be a bogus, but as he held it there was a slight flurry at the church door and the organ began to play 'Here Comes The Bride . . .'

'All fat and wide,' Mike heard Charlie mutter, and he nudged him sharply in the ribs. What had got into the bloke today? Quiet as a mouse when you'd appreciate a joke and yet today, when he ought to be on his best behaviour . . .

Maggie was coming up the aisle on Sam Pratt's arm. The congregation stood and Tommy and Mike turned to look at her as she approached. Mike heard Tommy give a slow, almost whistling intake of breath, and he almost felt like it himself.

Maggie looked gorgeous. Plump she might be, but today her plumpness looked exactly right in the magnificent, pearl-encrusted ivory dress. She seemed to glimmer with every step, a soft, opalescent fairy queen, her glowing face framed by a cloud of golden hair and the bouquet her grandmother had given her held loosely before her.

Sam was almost as impressive. His black jacket was patterned with pearls, his waistcoat stiff with them, all sewn into an intricate pattern of hearts and flowers. He carried his cap beneath his arm, and his face was red with pride, heat and – possibly – last night's beer. He delivered his daughter to the altar steps and stood beside her while she lifted her face to smile at Tommy Wheeler.

The vicar began the service. 'Dearly beloved, we are gathered together before God to witness the joining of this man and this woman in marriage . . .' His voice, so mournful when he'd brought in the young men, had suddenly taken on a new timbre, a resonance that gave the words their full

391

meaning. His eyes, dark and sunken in deep hollows, began to glow and he looked at Maggie and Tom as if he knew them both and loved them. You would have thought, Jo remarked to Phyl afterwards, that it was the first wedding he had ever conducted.

The two girls had slipped into the church almost immediately behind Maggie and her father, unnoticed by the rest of the congregation. They found a pew at the very back and watched as Maggie and Sam walked up the aisle, followed by Etty in her bridesmaid's dress and Queenie and Ginnie as Pearly princesses. And as Tommy turned to greet his bride, his face a sudden radiance of love and delight, they dropped quietly to their knees and gave thanks.

Neither would ever forget the torment of the past twenty-four hours. The anguish of knowing that Alice was lost, the agony of waiting, the pain of watching and sharing in Carrie's and Bill's distress. The dreadful, gnawing despair.

It was too soon, they'd told themselves, to give up hope, yet what hope could there be? How could a child just disappear, a child quite sensible enough to ask for help and be able to give her name and address. Once Robbie had been lost, there was no reason for Alice to stay away from home, and every reason for her to come back. She would have known she'd be welcomed with open arms, she would have known her mother would be upset. There had been no reason *not* to come home – and yet she hadn't done so.

Now they knew why. The telegram that May had opened for her sister had brought the news that Alice had been caught up in the evacuation of another school, two miles away. Less well rehearsed than Alice's own school, the children had been unruly and uncontrolled, the teachers harassed and worried as they tried to create order. Half the children didn't have their labels on, others had forgotten – or already lost – their gas masks, many were crying, some were fighting, others intent on getting all the enjoyment they could out of this unexpected adventure. It was little wonder that Alice, lost and confused, had been caught up in the throng and dragged along, willy-nilly, to the railway station where she had been shoved aboard a train and taken away to a village hall somewhere in Wiltshire.

It was a Pearly who had made the discovery. Not by shouting on street corners or searching empty houses or garden sheds, but simply by reading the postcard sent home by her own child, who had found herself sharing a bedroom with a girl she'd never seen before, who did nothing but cry and ask for someone called Robbie. The child, who could squeeze more information on to a postcard than most of her classmates could spread in big, loopy writing over a large sheet of paper, said she thought Alice was a spy and she was going to tell the village policeman about her just as soon as she was let out of the house.

'It's that lost kiddie,' the Pearly mother said to her husband. 'It must be.'

Within half an hour the police had been contacted, the telephone calls made and Carrie, her face washed and her best hat on, together with her husband and sister, had left for the railway station. And Jo and Phyl were free to come to the wedding.

The vicar had reached the part of the service where Tommy was to put the ring on Maggie's finger. The congregation was hushed, watching and waiting. There was a short pause.

Mike felt in his pocket. He took out his hand and felt in another. He glanced a little wildly at Tommy and tried a third, and then the last. Two in his jacket, two in his trousers. His face began to burn.

Oh, God, Phyl thought, staring at him, unaware of the love in her face, the fool's gone and lost it.

Tommy glanced sideways. 'Come on,' he muttered, 'get on with it.'

'I can't,' Mike hissed. 'I haven't got it.'

'What do you mean, you haven't got it? Course you've got it. I saw it in your hand.'

'Well, I haven't got it now.' Mike glanced at the vicar, whose expression had reverted to deep melancholy. 'Don't you know what I did with it?'

393

'Why the hell should I know what you did with it?' Tommy caught the vicar's eye and blushed scarlet. 'Oh, God, I'm sorry – I mean, I'm sorry, sir – but the bloo—I mean the silly idiot's gone and lost the – the ring. What the – what on earth are we going to do now?'

'Are you sure you've looked everywhere?' the vicar murmured. Behind them, they could hear the beginnings of stifled, hysterical giggles.

'Well, where else could I look?' Mike went through his pockets again. 'I tell you, it's not here.'

There was a movement beside them and Charlie leaned across and touched Mike's arm. He turned, bent his head and listened. Then his face cleared and he turned back to Tommy.

'*You've* got it, you blithering – I mean – look, it's in *your* pocket. You were looking at it when Maggie came in, remember?' He watched as Tommy dubiously put his hand into his own pocket and, with a look of utter disbelief – as if Mike had performed the most amazing conjuring trick – drew out the ring. He handed it to Mike, who glanced at the vicar and then handed it back. Tommy, with one final murderous glance, took Maggie's hand in his and slid the ring on to her finger, hampered somewhat by her silent, shaking laughter, and the vicar, with a deep sigh and a voice that seemed to prophesy doom for all concerned, pronounced them man and wife.

'Gawd,' Maggie whispered in her husband's ear, 'I thought we were going to have to borrow one.'

'I tell you what,' he muttered back, 'I'm going to *kill* that Mike when I get him outside. I'll never have *him* as my best man again!'

'Tell us what happened.' Maggie, looking like a queen in her satin gown, caught Phyl's arm. 'I never thought you'd be here and then as we were walking out of the church, what should we see but your two ugly mugs? What's happened about young Alice? Did she come back?'

Phyl shook her head and quickly recounted the story. 'And

394

Jo's mum and dad and my mum have all gone off to fetch her back. Oh, Maggie, you should have seen Auntie Carrie's face! I thought she was going to burst with happiness. And since they were going off straight away, and there didn't seem much point in the whole lot of us going, Jo and me got ready quick as we could and come straight over. Congratulations, Mags,' she said, giving Maggie a kiss on the cheek. 'I hope you and Tom'll be really happy.'

'We will – for about an hour,' Maggie said wryly. 'All the boys have got to go back to camp the minute the cake's been cut. There's been a recall. Me and Tom are going to have half an hour to ourselves. And that's all the married life we're going to get for the time being.'

'I know. I heard.' Phyl's face was sober. 'I – suppose that means Mike, too?'

'Well, he ain't got no special dispensation that I've heard about,' Maggie said. She gave Phyl a considering look. 'Know what I'd do if I were you? I'd go straight over there and make it up with him. He's been looking at you ever since we got home. He's starving for you, Phyl, and if I'm not mistaken you're the same way about him. Go on, now—' She gave her friend a push. 'Go and give him a smile and see what happens.'

Phyl glanced across the Pratts' front room. It was true that Mike had been looking her way. She's known it all the time they'd been in the same room, only a few yards apart but separated by the chattering, laughing throng of wedding guests. She hesitated, seeing Tommy muttering in Mike's ear, and then realised they were both looking in her direction. Before she could look away, she saw Tommy give Mike a push in her direction, and as he began to move she found her own feet carrying her towards him, and knew that this was what she'd been wanting all along.

It seemed to take an age to get across the room. People moved between them, carrying plates laden with sausage rolls and sandwiches. Someone called out for speeches and was shouted down. Someone else wanted three cheers, and Phyl had to wait until the hubbub died away. But eventually she found herself in the middle of the room and there, as if by a miracle, stood Mike.

He seemed taller than she remembered, and more serious. His eyes were dark and grave. She looked up and met them steadily, and then felt the heat of tears in her own, and the trembling of her lips.

'Oh, Mike—'

'Phyl,' he said, and took her in his arms. '*Phyl* . . .'

Jo and Nick were standing on the fringe of the crowd, close to the front door. The party was already spilling out on to the pavement. Later, it would take over the whole street and there would be dancing to Mrs Watkins's piano, but until the cake was cut and the happy couple seen off on their honeymoon – half an hour in Maggie's bedroom – the reception remained tied to the Pratts' household.

'It was a lovely wedding,' Jo said. 'I'm glad we could make it. I'm so relieved about our Alice, I can't tell you.'

'What'll happen?' Nick asked. 'Will she go off to wherever her own friends have been evacuated?'

Jo shrugged. 'Don't know. I suppose so – that's if Mum can bear to part with her again. I wouldn't be surprised if Alice stays at home after all this.'

'So she'll get her own way,' he said with a grin. 'She'll stay with the cat.'

'That blessed cat!' Jo said. 'Yes, I suppose she will. But our Alice usually does manage to get her own way in the end.'

They stood quietly for a few minutes and then Nick said, 'I'm glad you came, Jo. I was feeling really lonely there in the church till I saw you two slip in. It made me think, you know, seeing Maggie and Tom standing up there to get married. It made me think about you and how much I love you.'

'Did it, Nick?' she asked softly.

'Yes,' he said. He lifted her hand and looked at the engagement ring he had placed there only a few months before. 'It made me wonder why we weren't getting married ourselves.'

Jo looked at him. 'But we were going to wait – save up—'

'What for?' he asked. 'There's going to be a war, Jo. It could start tomorrow. What's the point of waiting? What's the point of saving up?' He caught her other hand and held both tightly in his own. 'Let's do it! Let's go and see the vicar tomorrow and ask your dad, and get it fixed for as soon as possible. I don't want to wait any longer, Jo.'

'But you're not in the Services—'

'I will be soon,' he said quietly. 'Jo, there's nothing certain any more. Anything could happen once this ultimatum they've given that man goes over time. We can't take risks. If we want to get married, now's the time to do it. Please, Jo.' He looked into her eyes and added very quietly, very intensely, 'Please.'

Jo met his eyes.

'All right, Nick,' she whispered, and tightened her own grip on his fingers. 'All right. Let's get married, the first minute we possibly can.'

'But what happened?' Phyl asked. 'Why did you just drop me like that?'

'Drop you?' No one had taken a scrap of notice as they met and kissed in the middle of the room. People just washed around them, as if they were a rock in the tide. 'I never dropped you. It was you dropped me, Phyl. Why didn't you come and meet me at the bandstand that day?'

'The bandstand?' She stared at him. 'What are you on about? What bandstand?'

'*You* know. In Hyde Park. That Sunday, when my mum was ill and I could only get out for a couple of hours. I waited ages, Phyl, and you never came. And you never sent a message to say why. And what with that and what that other girl told me about you and Richard Godwin—'

'Me and Richard Godwin?' To her annoyance, Phyl felt her face colour. 'But I haven't been out with Richard Godwin for ages.'

'No, that's what she said, but you still never turned up at the bandstand. And the next time I came to the Corner

House, you weren't there and this other girl was, and she told me—'

'Hang on,' Phyl interrupted. 'What other girl's this? Who are you talking about?'

'That other Nippy. She's a friend of yours. I couldn't get on your table that Saturday and I asked her to give you a message about the bandstand and she said she would. But you never came, and—'

'What other Nippy?' Phyl asked, a dangerous, angry feeling creeping over her.

'Well, you ought to know. Smart-looking girl, dark hair, green eyes. Eileen or something. She definitely told me—'

'We haven't got a Nippy called Eileen,' Phyl broke in again. 'It's *Irene* you're talking about. Irene Bond. And she's no friend of mine.' She stared into Mike's eyes. 'She never gave me no message. She never said a flipping word. She was just trying to make trouble between us, that's what, and she blooming well did it, too.'

'You mean she never told you?' Mike's face darkened. 'And I've been blaming you all this time? I'll kill her!'

'No,' Phyl said. 'I'll do any killing that's going round here. As a matter of fact, she's been a bit quiet lately, I've got a feeling she bit off a bit more than she can chew . . . Anyway, it doesn't matter. We're together again now and that's all that matters.' She looked at him with sudden anxiety. 'It is, isn't it, Mike? You do still want me? You haven't – you haven't got anyone else?'

'Anyone else?' he muttered, and gathered her into his arms again. 'Phyl, I haven't thought of anyone but you since it happened. I've been going out of my mind . . .' He looked impatiently around the crowded room. 'Can't we get out of here? Oh, God, I've got to go back to camp . . . Phyl, we haven't got much time. I can't even propose to you properly, not in this scrum. But – tell me you love me, will you? Tell me you'll wait for me?'

'Oh, Mike,' she said shakily, 'of course I'll wait for you. And of course I love you. I think I always did . . .'

*

Shirley and Owen were by the cake, looking at the three iced tiers, the pattern of roses, the two little figures standing arm in arm on the top.

'I wish it could be us, *cariad*,' Owen said wistfully.

'I know. So do I.' Shirley touched the little figures with the tip of her finger. 'Lyons do well by their staff, don't they? It can't be us, though, can it? Not for a long time yet.'

'No.' They had discussed this at length and finally decided, sadly, that they couldn't get married until after the war was over. With Owen's father chronically ill, and Shirley's mother now in Wales, neither could leave home. They held hands instead and resigned themselves to the wait. 'It'll be over by Christmas, anyway,' he added with an effort at optimism. 'We'll have a proper white wedding then. Snow and all.'

Sam Pratt was banging a beer mug with a spoon to attract everyone's attention. The hubbub slowly lessened and when he could finally make himself heard, he began his speech.

'I won't keep you long because our Maggie and her Tom haven't got much time. This is going to be the quickest honeymoon in history. But we've found a smashing little place for them to stay, got a honeymoon suite and all. So all I want to do now is ask you all to raise your glasses in a holy ghost to the happy couple. Young Maggie's bin a pretty good bricks and mortar to me these past twenty years and now she's young Tom's trouble and strife, and I wish 'em both well. To Maggie and Tom!'

They all lifted their glasses high in the air and shouted, 'To Maggie and Tom!' Mike went round quickly to fill up glasses, and Sam shouted out again.

'Now, then, there ain't going to be no more Brighton beaches. They got a lot to do in the next half-hour—' he was interrupted by ribald laughter '—and if you don't mind, I'd like 'em to get on with it. Young Tom's got to get back to camp and if I remember rightly from me own days in the daft and barmy, there's a hell of a lot of buttons on them uniforms . . . So make way there, and let 'em get up the apples and pears while the rest of us gets on with the hale and hearty. Ivy! When are you going to cut this here cake?'

'I'm going to do it now,' his wife cried, brandishing a huge knife. 'Evie! Etty! Come and get these plates and start passing round. We'll cut the bottom tier now—'

'Save the next one for the first christening, eh?' someone shouted, and she looked round in mock disapproval as another cheer went up.

'Well, there's no need for that, you dirty-minded lot! I'll have you know our Maggie's a good girl.'

'I'll have you know she's a married woman!' someone else called out, and they all laughed again.

Phyl and Mike slipped their arms around each other's waists. Jo and Nick moved closer and Phyl took one look at her face and knew exactly what her cousin had to tell her. Across the room, Jim was standing close to Etty as she passed round plates of cake, and Shirley was just beside them, her hand held tightly in Owen's.

We're all here, she thought, all except Irene. And angry though she was with the sixth Nippy, she still couldn't help feeling a little bit sorry for her. Irene had been bitter and spiteful and she'd tried to spoil things for Phyl, but what good had it done her? While all the rest were happy together, she was at home alone; while all the rest were loved, she had no one.

It serves her right, Phyl thought, but all the same she's a human being and she's miserable. It's a shame.

Chapter Twenty-Seven

The wedding was over.

Up in Maggie's bedroom, she and Tom stood and looked at each other, their exhilaration dropping into despair. They moved into each other's arms and held each other close, without passion. Maggie rested her head on Tommy's shoulder.

'Oh, Tom . . .'

'I know.' He stroked her hair, gently rubbed her back. 'I know.'

'I can't bear it. We've only been married a couple of hours and you've got to go away. And I don't know when I'll see you again.' She shook her head, the tears sparkling on her lashes. 'It's not fair.'

'At least we're married, girl. At least they let me out for that. Blokes whose weddings are fixed for next week or the week after—' he shrugged '—well, they don't know when they'll get home again. Their girls might stay single for years.'

'Years! Oh, don't. It's never going to last years, Tom, never.' She looked up at him. 'It isn't, is it?'

'No. Course it isn't.' But he knew, and she knew, that he was only saying it to cheer her up. He didn't know how long this new war would last. Nobody did.

'Oh, well,' she said with an attempt at a smile, 'we'd better do what we come up here for, hadn't we? Have our honeymoon.'

Tommy looked at her and said, with some surprise, 'I

dunno, Maggie. I don't sort of feel like it somehow. I mean, I love you just as much – more than ever – and I want to make love to you – but not just now. It seems sort of rushed, what with everyone downstairs knowing about it and all . . . I'm sorry, Mag.'

'It's all right,' she said. 'To tell you the truth, I feel the same way myself. Tell you what – let's just get undressed and lay together for a bit. Help me out of this frock—' she began to struggle with the buttons '—and get your things off, and we'll just lay on the bed and cuddle each other.' She laughed, a little shakily. 'We've never done that, you know. We've never had all our clothes off before and been in a proper room, on a proper bed. It's always been in the park.'

'I know. It's what I've looked forward to most – being in a real bed with you.' He began to undo the buttons and slipped the mass of encrusted fabric from her shoulders. 'You looked lovely in this dress,' he murmured, kissing her breasts as they sprang from the tight bodice. 'But d'you know what? I reckon you look even better without it!'

Maggie laughed and began to undo his own buttons. They didn't take so long, and within a few minutes both were quite naked. They stood and looked at each other.

'This might be going to have to last a long time, Tommy,' Maggie said tremulously. 'I want to know I'm going to recognise you again next time I see you.'

Tommy reached out and drew a line down her body, from neck to thigh, with one finger. Then, as she began to shiver, he drew her down on to the bed. He enfolded her quivering body in his arms and held her closely, then he began to kiss her, small, feathery kisses that covered her face and neck and breasts. And as he did so his passion increased until he looked down into her face at last and said in a husky voice, 'I reckon I've changed me mind, Mag. I reckon I want to love you after all.'

'Oh, *Tom*,' she said, and pulled him so hard against her that he slid inside almost without realising it. 'Oh Tom, yes, *please*.'

★

It was almost midnight when Phyl and Jo returned to Auntie Holt's. They knew they would never get back to their own homes that night, and their first thought as they crept indoors was to see if there had been any message from their parents. The only way a message could have come through this quickly was by telegram, but no little brown envelope awaited them and, after a cup of Ovaltine and a sandwich from the plate their landlady had left for them, they padded softly up the stairs and slid wearily into bed.

'That was a smashing wedding,' Phyl said sleepily. 'And what a party! There must have been at least three streets in that conga, and I thought that old woman in the Pearly costume would have a heart attack, doing Knees Up Mother Brown. And if we did the Lambeth Walk once I reckon we did it a dozen times.'

'What a day it's been,' Jo said. 'What a *few* days. Oh, Phyl, I'm so thankful about our Alice.'

'I know. So'm I. Fancy her getting evacuated after all! It's funny, when you think about it, isn't it? I mean, not laughing funny but sort of funny-peculiar. I bet she'll be glad to get back home, anyway, and glad to see that blessed cat again. It's a good job he managed to find his way back.'

Jo didn't answer. Phyl glanced across at the other bed and saw a darkened, unmoving hump against the window. Her cousin was fast asleep.

'I heard on the wireless that Mr Chamberlain's going to speak to the nation at a quarter past eleven,' Auntie Holt said as the girls stumbled downstairs next morning. 'You know what that means, don't you?'

'It means we'll be at war,' Jo said.

'It might not,' Phyl said, her hand in the cornflakes packet. 'There's still time. They gave out that ultimatum, didn't they? Hitler's got till eleven to promise to get out of Poland. He might still—'

'He won't,' Jo said. 'You know he won't.'

But there was still a chance and after breakfast, restless and unable just to sit and wait, the girls went out and caught a bus

403

into London. They went to Trafalgar Square and found it crowded with people, not happy, interested, excited people feeding the pigeons and admiring the great lions and the fountains and Nelson on top of his column, but anxious people, with worried faces and frightened eyes, wandering as aimlessly as they were themselves.

As if it had been arranged, they came across the other girls – Shirley with Owen, Etty with Jim and even Maggie, looking tired and sad. Nick came up and took Jo's arm silently, and Phyl wished sadly that she could see Mike's face in the crowd. But he would be back at camp, preparing to go to war.

The thought was like a blade of ice in her heart.

'Where's everyone going?' she asked, seeing a general movement towards one corner of the square.

'They're going down to Westminster to see Big Ben strike eleven,' Jo answered. They followed, driven by an inexplicable desire to be somewhere significant when this most significant moment arrived. Eleven o'clock on the third day of September – the moment which could either plunge the world into catastrophe or turn the course of history in an entirely different direction. The fear was black in everyone's hearts, but until the declaration was made there had still to be a tiny flicker of hope.

'It doesn't have to happen,' Phyl said, trying to cling to that hope. 'He could still give in . . .'

Maggie found her hand and gripped it tightly. They looked at each other with understanding, the two whose men were already committed, who might within days be fighting for the freedom of their country. Without speaking, they followed the others down the broad sweep of Whitehall, past the Cenotaph where the Armistice Service was held every 11 November, down to the imposing buildings of Westminster on the banks of the uncaring Thames, to stand below the looming tower of the famous clock that held the bell Big Ben, which would strike the hour of destiny.

'It's five to,' Jo breathed. 'I wonder what's going on over there.'

Nobody knew quite where 'over there' was. The 'ultimatum', which had been no more than a word, an idea, became at that moment a real piece of paper, an agreement that someone had drawn up and put into complicated legal language and sent – or taken – to Hitler, for him to look at and read and sign. Or not sign, according to his mood. What had that mood been when he woke that morning?

He became, suddenly, a man rather than a concept of evil and dread. A man who went to bed at night and got up in the morning, who wore pyjamas and went to the lavatory and washed his face and hands. An ordinary, commonplace little man, with a plain face and straight hair and a small black moustache. How could such a man wield such power? How could such a man threaten the safety of an entire continent?

The hands of Big Ben moved slowly closer to the hour. The crowd below stood waiting, watching. You could sense them holding their breath.

The last minute came. The hands stood exactly on the eleven and the twelve. If Hitler hadn't signed by now . . .

Over their heads, the famous Westminster chimes rang out and then, deeper, more sonorous, and slower than ever before, it seemed, the measured and throbbing notes of the hour.

The crowd let out its breath on a long, collective sigh.

'But we don't *know*,' Phyl whispered in panic. 'We don't know what he's done . . .'

'Let's get home, quick. Let's get somewhere where we can hear the wireless.'

They turned and ran back up Whitehall, back to Trafalgar Square, and as one into the Charing Cross Corner House. Someone there would have a wireless. They bypassed the queue that always stretched out of the door and on to the pavement and slipped inside. They stood by the wall, waiting.

Someone had brought in a wireless and set it up in the restaurant. The tables were crowded with people, and others stood around the walls. Phyl and Maggie stood hand in hand, with Shirley and Owen beside them and Jo and Nick close behind. It was fourteen minutes past eleven.

The clock of Big Ben sounded again, chiming the quarter, and as the notes died away they heard the voice of the Prime Minister, Mr Neville Chamberlain. The man who had come back from Munich only eleven months ago, brandishing a piece of paper and declaring that it was 'peace in our time'. The man who sounded now as sombre and sad as he had sounded confident then.

'Berlin has been warned,' he said, 'that if Germany does not stop all aggressive action against Poland and begin its withdrawal by eleven a.m. today, Britain and Germany would be at war.' He paused and the Corner House was silent, waiting. 'I have to tell you,' he said, and his listeners knew then what he had to tell them, 'that no such undertaking has been received and that consequently this country is at war with Germany.'

There was a cold, horrified silence. Someone switched off the wireless. Everyone looked at everyone else and somebody began to cry.

'Oh, God,' Maggie said. 'Oh, Tom . . .'

Outside in the street, like the eerie call of a banshee, the wail of an air-raid siren rose as if from the earth itself. The war had, it seemed, begun at once.

After that, there didn't seem to be anything else to do but go home.

Jo and Phyl walked down their street, not knowing if their parents would be at home yet or if they were still in Wiltshire where Alice had finally ended up, yet knowing that this was where they wanted to be. They came round the corner and found the neighbours all out in the street, talking together, their faces grave yet oddly excited.

'It's awful, isn't it?,' someone said as they passed. 'When that siren went off, I nearly died. We couldn't get to the shelter fast enough. But, there, it turned out to be a false alarm.'

Perhaps not entirely false, Jo thought. There had been no air raid, but it was a fitting start to a war that was expected to be mostly air raids. She came to her own front door and knocked. I ought to have a key, she thought. It's just daft that I haven't got a key, just because I'm not twenty-one yet . . .

I hope Mum and Dad are home, she thought. I want to see them. I want to be with them. Please God, let them be home.

The front door opened. Jo looked down and saw her sister Alice, standing there with Robertson the cat held closely in her arms.

'Oh, Ally,' she said, sweeping them up against her. 'Oh, Ally . . . Ally . . .'

☐ **Goodbye Sweetheart** £6.99
LILIAN HARRY
1-8579-7812-9

☐ **The Girls They Left Behind**
£6.99
LILIAN HARRY
0-7528-0333-6

☐ **Keep Smiling Through** £6.99
LILIAN HARRY
0-7528-3442-8

☐ **Moonlight & Lovesongs** £6.99
LILIAN HARRY
0-7528-1564-4

☐ **Love & Laughter** £6.99
LILIAN HARRY
0-7528-2605-0

☐ **Wives & Sweethearts** £6.99
LILIAN HARRY
0-7528-3396-0

☐ **Corner House Girls** £6.99
LILIAN HARRY
0-7528-4296-X

☐ **Kiss the Girls Goodbye** £6.99
LILIAN HARRY
0-7528-4448-2

☐ **PS I Love You** £6.99
LILIAN HARRY
0-7528-4820-8

☐ **A Girl Called Thursday**
£6.99
LILIAN HARRY
0-7528-4950-6

☐ **Tuppence to Spend** £6.99
LILIAN HARRY
0-7528-4264-1

☐ **A Promise to Keep** £6.99
LILIAN HARRY
0-7528-5889-0

☐ **Under the Apple Tree** £6.99
LILIAN HARRY
0-7528-5929-3

☐ **Dance Little Lady** £6.99
LILIAN HARRY
0-7528-6420-3

☐ **A Farthing Will Do** £6.99
LILIAN HARRY
0-7528-6492-0

☐ **Three Little Ships** £6.99
LILIAN HARRY
0-7528-7707-0

All Orion/Phoenix titles are available at your local bookshop or from the following address:

Mail Order Department
Littlehampton Book Services
FREEPOST BR535
Worthing, West Sussex, BN13 3BR
telephone 01903 828503, *facsimile* 01903 828802
e-mail MailOrders@lbsltd.co.uk
(Please ensure that you include full postal address details)

Payment can be made either by credit/debit card (Visa, Mastercard, Access and Switch accepted) or by sending a £ Sterling cheque or postal order made payable to *Littlehampton Book Services*.
DO NOT SEND CASH OR CURRENCY.

Please add the following to cover postage and packing

UK and BFPO:
£1.50 for the first book, and 50p for each additional book to a maximum of £3.50

Overseas and Eire:
£2.50 for the first book plus £1.00 for the second book and 50p for each additional book ordered

---

BLOCK CAPITALS PLEASE

name of cardholder ....

address of cardholder ....

....

....

....

postcode ....

delivery address
(if different from cardholder)

....

....

....

postcode ....

☐ I enclose my remittance for £............................

☐ please debit my Mastercard/Visa/Access/Switch (delete as appropriate)

card number ☐☐☐☐☐☐☐☐☐☐☐☐☐☐☐☐☐☐

expiry date ☐☐☐☐   Switch issue no. ☐☐

signature ....

prices and availability are subject to change without notice